RUDE BUAY

VOLUMES 1-3

Original Stories

By

#1 International

Bestselling Author

John A. Andrews

The RUDE BUAY Series®

Published in the U.S.A. by

Books That Will Enhance Your Life™

Cover Design: John A. Andrews

Cover Graphic Designer: ALI

Cover Photo: Anthony Johnson, Adrian Carr.

Edited by: Pernell Marsh/ALI

ISBN:**9798342061407**

The RUDE BUAY Series®

"Ask not what your country can do for you - ask what you can do for your country."

- John F. Kennedy

RUDE BUAY

The Unstoppable

aka Rude Boy ... The Unstoppable by

International Bestselling Author

John A. Andrews

Over 80 Titles in Print.

A MULTIPLE AWARD-WINNING SHORT FILM

TABLE OF CONTENTS

1

A CUPBOARD DOOR SLAMS SHUT… BLAM!
"What's taking you so long to pack your bag, boy? Randy, you will be late for school again, the second day in a row." That parental voice came screaming from the kitchen and echoing upstairs through Randy's untidy room. Randy urgently forces his tattered notebooks inside his one-strap, still-hanging book bag.
"Mom, I got it; will you stop screaming at me?"

"You, too Rude Buay! Don't make me come up there!" Footsteps heard coming up the stairs alert Randy, as he comes running down the stairs, passing his mom, who misses her swing at him. His Afro-pick comb falls out of his unzipped bag at the bottom of the stairs; he turns back to pick it up.
"That's what your rudeness would do for you." Shoeless but neatly dressed. He grabs a mango and a banana from the kitchen counter, throws them in a plastic bag, and darts through the door.

Several kids, neatly dressed, wearing designer sneakers, and carrying laden book bags, speed up to keep pace with him. "Rude Buay, what's the rush we are all going to the same class." He keeps on running. Suddenly, they catch up with him going up the steep hill. The pack leader, Mike, tugs Rude Buay's book bag away, retrieves the afro pick, and combs his hair aggressively. Rude Buay retaliates due to the comb made from bicycle spokes bends.

Frustrated, Mike punches Rude Buay hard in the stomach. Rude Buay, now holding his stomach, falls over in the gutter. The brawl escalates as it continues. Mike lands a few more punches in Rude Buay's stomach, leaving him breathless. The other kids kick Rude Buay's bags into the street.

Suddenly, with a burst of energy, Rude Buay athletically catches up with Mike and the other kids. He fights back, throwing wild punches. Mike counterattacks. Rude Buay retaliates. Mike grabs him and engages in a wrestling bout. The struggle intensifies. Mike reaches for Rude Buay's jugular. The loud exhaust of a truck "backfiring" could be heard in the distance. None of the kids seem to pay any attention to the oncoming traffic. They are focused on the two-kid brawl, which has now transcended onto the street. Mike's supporters are cheering him on. The gasping Young Rude Buay removes Mike's hand from around his neck and darts after his now no-strap disheveled book bag and lunch sack. Mike loses his footing on the banana in the plastic sack and falls onto the street. The approaching truck, unable to stop, runs Mike over before coming to a complete stop. The kids on the sidelines all yell.

"You pushed him! We saw you, Randy! You killed Mike!

The truck driver JUMPS out, shaken up and flustered. The front tire left its mark on Mike's khaki shirt as he lay trapped under the bus's chassis. The truck's conductors jump out, staring at the "whose fault is it" catastrophe. They assist the driver in removing Mike's body from underneath the truck's chassis. He discovers that Mike doesn't have a pulse and tries CPR. Mike responds negatively to resuscitation. Meanwhile, Rude Buay, drenched in tears, shakes like a leaf on the nearby rocky embankment.

ONE YEAR LATER:

All lights are out except the one in Rude Buay's room. He lies on his back, studying from a grease-stained book by candlelight. The Officer walks by and notices. With a vindictive look, he opens the door, and in thick patois dialect, he confronts Randy. "That is murder, you know, me na know way dem ah talk bout when dem say it's only manslaughter. You wicked mon! Him ah me sister's son, her only begotten. Bend over!" He retrieves a twisted switch and whips Randy across his backside several times. Randy cries out, "I did not push your nephew. He slipped! " Another prisoner across the way witnesses and yells at the Officer,

"Leave the boy alone, mon! The law is whether you live on a hill or inside a tenement yard."
The Officer discontinues his brutal attack on Randy, puts out the light, confiscates the book, and extinguishes the candle.
Randy staggers to get up off the floor and onto the bed. He's bruised so severely that blood trickles down the backside and forearms.

SIX YEARS LATER:

Randy's older brother Clifford, on his way home, was confronted by several drug dealers outside the perimeter of their tenement yard. He tried eluding the Uzi-wielding quartet, but they had him cornered. The pack leader yells, "This is our turf. You are hurting our revenue."
Clifford arguably replied, "I and I live here! I sell what and where I want."
Gunshots like popcorn ring out from their weapons as they cut Clifford down, leaving him blood-drenched on the sidewalk.
Several tenement dwellers rush to the scene as the supped-up green, yellow, and black Mustang speeds away.
A woman wearing an oil-stained apron and carrying a large kitchen fork yells out. "Miss Bascombe, it's Clifford! They shot up Clifford bad, mon." Randy and his mom abort dinner at the table and rush to the scene. She pushes through the gathered crowd

towards her son Clifford. Trying to comfort him, she's now immersed in his blood. His limp hands and body indicate his lifelessness.

Randy, bathed in tears, looks on.

A Jamaican police Land Rover pulls up. Two officers jump out and proceed with their investigation. Several tenement dwellers retreat because of the police presence. The senior officer in his 50s asks, "Are there any witnesses?" as the junior officer releases Miss Bascombe's tight grasp on Clifford. Simultaneously, he notices the kitchen fork in a woman's hand. The woman pointing up the street with the fork yells in deep patois, "Mustang, the color of the flag! You all better find them…"

The officer interrupts.

"Miss, my name is Officer Lent. What is your name?"

Now holding her fork with her hand on her hip, the woman responds.

"Maude! Maude Davis."

Maude Davis, what you hold in your hand is considered a deadly weapon."

She continues,

"Worry bout me, Officer Lent, and let the murderers go free; instead of fighting crime, you are fighting me. Shoo, fire ah go burn you." And she moseys inside the tenement yard, leaving Randy and his mother to complete the police report.

ONE MONTH LATER:

Before daybreak, a taxi pulls up outside the tenement yard and waits. The only illuminated dwellings belong to Miss Bascombe and Maude Davis. Suddenly, the light at the Bascombe's dwelling goes out. Miss Bascombe locks her door and follows Randy in tow as he knocks on Maude's door with a suitcase and a carry-on bag in hand. Maude comes to the door and embraces him.

"Take care of yourself, Rude Buay. I will look after your mother for you."

Randy replies gratefully,

"Thanks, Godmother, I'll miss you."

The car horn honks. He continues,

"The cab is waiting."

He departs and enters the cab accompanied by his mom.

Later, he stands amongst travelers at Michael Manley International Airport and embraces his mom in tears. Then, swiftly, Randy heads towards the American Airlines departure lounge, waving goodbye.

2

ARRIVING IN NEW YORK, Randy Bascombe acquired a parking attendant job while figuring out exactly what he wanted to do with his life. He was determined to put the imprisoned past behind him. Deep in his psyche, he knew that he wanted to fight crime. However, becoming a police officer would be a mediocre accomplishment. Plus, he tragically witnessed firsthand the ineptness of that entity when his brother was shot and killed by drug dealers. That Jamaican tragedy stood out like a sore thumb.

He worked hard during the week, and on weekends, he frequented the library.

Before 1960, Americans did not use drugs as acceptable behavior. Neither did Randy Bascombe, who was born after that era. He saw it as a severe offense. Additionally, losing his brother in a drug-related incident contributed to his abstinence.

Randy gravitated to materials on drug enforcement. He was very much taken aback when he read the stats that DEA Special Agents grew from 1,470 in 1973 to 2,135 in 1975, two years later.

Retrospectively, his present, once quiet neighborhood, where he played street basketball, was now saturated with drug dealers, buyers, pimps, and prostitutes.

This growing Law Enforcement entity became increasingly attractive to him. Consequently, he not only studied what the U.S. was doing to fight the war on drugs but became so immersed in the subject that he decided to attend college.

He earned a bachelor's degree there, majoring in Criminal Justice and Police Science. Randy came clean on his background check, among other requirements. Coincidentally, the Jamaican authorities had recently cleared him from manslaughter charges as a kid. Judge Hastings had revisited the case and found him innocent of the charges.

Randy Bascombe felt like a new man when he received the phone call that he was hired as a Drug Enforcement

Agent. Bascombe left New York for Virginia, where he underwent basic training. Upon completing this process, he looked at several major cities where he would like to work. Miami and New York were his top choices, but to give the other cities an equal chance, he included their names in a hat, closed his eyes, and drew one. He picked Miami, Florida. To him, this was a perfect choice for two reasons:

(1) Miami was close to Jamaica, and it would only take a few hours to hop on a plane and visit his Mom and Maude Davis.
(2) His graduating class wanted to work for Special Agent Bob White. Why? White was not only highly skilled, but he was also an intuitive, motivated, and profoundly committed agent.

So, Bascombe was interviewed and joined the DEA in Miami. Sadly, though, after only being under Bob White's tutelage for two months, White was executed during a friendly fire incident. Jose Mendez's assistant was appointed to "fill his shoes."

3

MRS. BLACK, a middle-aged history teacher, collects her students' last test papers. She places the stack on her desk and reminds the students to return to their seats immediately after the lunch break. The school bell rings.

Ray, a skinny teenager, shows his disgust with her request. He darts out of the classroom and rushes through the crowded schoolyard. Chattering kids mingle. In the distance, Ray breaks across the street to the local grocery store.

Moments later, dozens of kids assemble in the L-shaped cafeteria, enjoying lunch. A variety of food odors fill the air. On the outside, Ray appears. He is more significant than life, demonstrative by a hard wine interlude. Many kids follow suit in the revelry, which expands and intensifies as it progresses inside the cafeteria.

Teenagers enjoying their lunch would instead not participate in the carousing. But they indulge in a food-tossing attack on the boisterous intruders. Fighting back, their partying turns into a display of their food-tossing skills.

Two security guards abandon catching up on the sports scores in the Jamaican Gleaner and rush to the scene. After their intense wielding of the batons, the kids are subdued. Many leave the scene, while the sane ones stay behind and clean up the food residue. A few yards away, Ray and many of his partying buddies huddle. Their voices are inaudible. A vicious chain reaction and skin-scratching dilemma begins. Rashes break out on their face and hands. Uncontrollably, they start falling onto the school grounds. Some kids tough it out.

Teachers, students, and increased school security personnel rush in an attempt to investigate and comfort the ailing kids. The persistent ones are now gasping for air, eventually falling to the ground—the fallen attack the sympathetic cries of their classmates, other students, and school personnel alike. Mrs. Black emerges on the scene terrified.

Ray lies in a fetal position, biting hard into the unpaved school grounds. His classmates and teacher hovered, puzzled; they couldn't believe what had transpired since the bell rang. The following bell rings, some students trek back to the classroom; others remain to bathe in grief.

The sound of sirens can be heard in the distance. The increase in decibels indicates their closeness. Suddenly, ambulances pull up. The schoolyard is now a spectacle of flashing cries and flashing lights. Medics rush out, wheeling stretchers. The debilitated teens are placed on them and rushed inside ambulances, one at a time.

Jamaican Police vehicles emerge onto the scene. Officers jump out and investigate. They carefully collect food residue off the ground and deposit it into trash bags.

Meanwhile, inside the principal's office, terrified teachers congregate. They rummage through the backpacks of ailing kids. Contents are emptied onto the principal's desk. Tiny, neat packets in aluminum foil and textbooks fall from a midnight blue backpack onto the desk bearing the name Ray C. The two overworked security guards overseeing the search unwrap one of the packages. Inside, one of the guards discovers a white powdery substance. He refolds it and places it, along with the other unopened ones, inside a brown envelope. He seals it airtight. The on-looking teachers wail hysterically as a result of the findings.

Two officers wearing transparent gloves enter and confiscate the envelope. Then, they rush to their cruiser and drive away speedily.

In the meantime, medics steer gurneys with bodies wrapped in white sheets to the morgue at the general hospital. Dozens of tagged bodies (reading Cyanide Overdose) are transported inside this small rectangular-shaped facility. Ray Collins' body makes its way in, followed by his breathless mother, bawling and engulfed in tears. Wearing a soiled dress, an apron tied around her waist and a multi-colored head tie blowing in the wind, she carries her shoes. Other parents, in search of their kids, embrace one another in tears. The busy medics sense their grief.

5

THOUSANDS OF MILES AWAY in Bogota, Columbia, livestock graze noisily behind a warehouse. From the hills above, clouds of dust rise from between the trees. The dust follows in tow of a moving object. That yellow hummer speeding through the bushes finally reveals itself as it emerges and comes to a bumpy, screeching halt.

Immediately, three women jump out:

First, beautiful dark-skinned Agnes Richards. She is in her late 20s, wearing unkempt braids, and carrying two black duffel bags. Second is Asian trophy woman Denise Gomez. She is in her late 20s. Denise holds a duffel bag over her shoulder and a semi-automatic rifle in the other. The considerable diamond stone on her ring, kissing her wedding band, glitters in the sun as she kisses her wedding band. She's all business. Following Denise is a tall, aggressive, WWE type, Shelly Hall. A Caucasian in her early 30s. She sports a ponytail hairstyle and totes two larger duffel bags in one hand. On the other, a semi-automatic rifle. She proceeds in tow of her two traveling partners.

Denise gives them a wink and leads the way to the shack. The livestock disperses as she moves up to the steel door. Denise enters a code. The door unlocks. She pulls it open. The three women enter in haste and quickly load up duffel bags with packages containing about five kilos each, labeled DRAGON X. They load up their Hummer and drive away, leaving a trail of dust behind.

Outside the general hospital, the sounds of sirens fill the air in Jamaica. Ambulances eventually show their presence. Now idle, with lights still flashing, the paramedic's wheel gurneys out toward several excessively vomiting kids. One paramedic, sporting an elongated dreadlocks hairstyle, wheels a teen foaming extensively through the nose inside the ER.

Upon entering, the paramedic glances at the kid and announces:

"This one stopped breathing!"

He checks for a pulse, but there is none. He quickly administers CPR. He pauses. Then echoes:

"Nothing! We lost her."

Sirens were heard in the distance as emerging ambulances raced to the scene. Police vehicles joined the emergency response units.

Mourners crowd the ER entrance. Their cries increase in decibels, sandwiched by deep patois, transcending into an inaudible lamentation—so much so that they compete with the ambulance siren.

Jamaican police rushed from an occupied gurney after an occupied gurney, using a pen and clipboard to collect data.

Meanwhile, a twin-engine plane taxis in Colombia as the yellow Hummer races towards it. The aircraft speeds up and takes off to the sky, dusting the vehicle. In the interim, in a downtown Bogota hotel, Axel James sits on a couch smoking a long marijuana spliff. He is of Colombian descent and in his mid-forties. Axel displays a dragon tattoo below his right ear lobe, has a missing index finger, and has expensive gold rings on the four fingers of his right hand. Ricardo Herrera, also of Colombian descent and in his mid-thirties, robust in demeanor, sits across from Axel James and cogitates. Behind his right earlobe, Ricardo sports the same signature as Axel.

In walks Ian Baynes, an African American in his late thirties. He is dressed in a pilot's uniform and has rimmed glasses. The handle of his glasses almost kisses his dragon tattoo. Ian faces Axel but dares not look him in the eye. Instead, he looks away and addresses him.

"Boss, we've got problems."

"That's why I hired you," responds Axel James authoritatively.

"I know, but you don't understand. Boss, the X product has become very lethal in Jamaica.

That last shipment was probably too concentrated. Kids are dying off like flies."

Axel stares him down in disbelief.

"That is what's causing the…"

Ricardo interrupts,

"How about a recall?"

"A thousand kilos…? Too expensive…No deal. That was only one bad apple,"
claims Axel James.
Let's find another turf,"
Ricardo urges.
"Right! How about Port Antonio,"
commands Axel.
"That will never work,"
responds Ian.
"Why not?"
remarks Axel James.
"Those Ministers of Parliament will be getting all up in our business. We might check in there but never check out."
Ian cautions.
"That's bull…! We'll buy them out,"
says Axel James.
"How?" Ian questions.
Axel James replies,
"Set up roadblocks and dominate.
That's virgin territory…"
Ricardo interjects,
"Boss and the girls?"
To which Axel responds,
"Too many…questions. If they fail, we'll ship the product to the stomachs of Colombian kids. All they have to do is take a monitored dump, and we…cash in. Let's move it!"

Axel James retires from the meeting. He gets up from the table with his semiautomatic in hand and exits. Ricardo and Ian follow closely behind him.

They escape the view of hotel guests and jump inside a red pickup truck. Ricardo is armed in the back, Axel is in the front passenger seat, and Ian takes the wheel. Axel's gun glitters, casting its shadow on Ian. The pickup drives off.

The powdered, brown-yellow hummer arrives outside the warehouse in Bogota. Agnes, Shelly, and Denise disembark. Armed with semiautomatic rifles, they aggressively surround the timber warehouse. Carefully, they scan their surroundings. Denise moves towards the door.

Un-expectantly, the red pickup truck arrives from the opposite direction. Ricardo jumps out from the back, waving his automatic weapon. Ian Baynes exits from the driver's seat and follows suit. Axel James exits like a madman. He releases the safety on his semiautomatic.

Shelly reacts.

"It's late, Axel; where…is the good blow?"

Axel James advances towards them. The women readily perfect their deadly aim. Denise shoots at the truck's left front tire. Instead, the bullet hits and disunites the left fender reverberantly. The next round connects, deflating the tire.

"Calm down, sisters. Let me explain," remarks Axel James.

Agnes responds,
"No time for your explanation. Our clients are waiting. The last shipment was laced with cyanide. People are dying, Axel."
Ricardo creates a decoy. Denise refocuses.
"That's not the way we do business. Clients wait until the goods are delivered. X label was a glitch,"
states Ricardo.
'We paid in advance!"
Says Shelly as she aims at Ricardo's head.
Axel James interjects,
"We are trying to bring a fresh shipment into Port Antonio. One is already on its way; give it time."
Denise eyeballs him while she caresses the trigger on her rifle.
"No one informed me about the crap you sent us. Now, picking up in Port Antonio would create a nightmare. Too many sniffing MP'S."
Denise states.
"That's right. You've.."
says Agnes.
"Time is our money, Axel."
Denise reminds him.
Looking at Denise, he responds.
"Your husband's aware of the delay. His business in Miami is hurting... Meet us in Montego Bay tomorrow morning. We'll be covering all of our tracks."
Axel, Ian, and Ricardo board the red pickup truck and drive off.

The three women withdraw their arms, jump inside the Hummer, and depart unhappily.

5

AT THE DRUG ENFORCEMENT AGENCY in Miami, Special Agent Jose Mendez, in his late forties, lights up a cigar. He then hands over a set of keys to agent Randy Bascombe and departs. Bascombe, nicknamed RUDE BUAY, colloquially" Rude Boy," is of Jamaican descent and in his early forties. He's adorned with a scorpion tattooed to his bald head, with fangs upstaging his forehead and tail extending towards his right earlobe. Bascombe familiarizes himself with the surroundings. He removes a portrait of Jamaica from a box, hangs it on the wall, and stares at it retrospectively. Next, he retrieves a portrait of his older brother. Reminisced by the picture, he fumbles. The portrait falls. He catches it before it hits the ground. He takes in a second look.

The office phone rings. He lays the portrait securely on top of his desk before answering.

The voice on the phone states, "Requesting DEA presence at the corner of Main and Broadway." Bascombe picks his brother's portrait off his desk and hangs it securely on the wall. He throws on his jacket over his strapped two semiautomatics and heads out, hitting the streets.

Bascombe pulls up on Broadway and waits. A red Monte Carlo is parked on Main. A rugged-looking Hispanic Man in his mid-thirties emerges from the high-rise office building on Broadway. He's carrying an attaché. Bascombe gets out of his car in a calculated pursuit. The Man gets inside the hot rod. Bascome, on foot, is catching up to him. The Man attempts to stick the key into the ignition. Bascombe sticks his left hand through the driver's window, grabbing the keys. Bascombe fails to hold the keys, but the suspect rolls up the electronic window, putting Bascombe's hand in a vice.

The car takes off. Bascombe tries to keep pace with the speeding vehicle. The Man looks at Bascombe's trapped hand and laughs hysterically. The Monte Carlo turns a corner, throwing Bascombe's body onto the hood. His hand is still fastened. He manages to viciously shoot at the suspect through the windshield, using his other hand, at the suspect. An oncoming tractor-trailer honks as it closes in on the Monte-Carlo, now zigzagging over the yellow line. Before the trailer could clip Bascombe, the Man shoots at Bascombe's trapped hand and blows out the driver's side window. Bascombe is thrown free onto the sidewalk. The car slams into a telephone pole.

The man crawls out on the passenger side, bloodied and shaken up, yet he escapes on foot. The trailer proceeds, regardless.

Bascombe incurs several lacerations to his face and head, along with minor bruises over some parts of his body. In pain, he gets up, puts two fingers in his mouth, and whistles to stop an oncoming taxi cab. His whistle is inaudible. The cab passes him by. Moments later, an ambulance arrives and whisks him away.
Meanwhile, Shelly, Agnes, and Denise embark on their Jamaican quest. They board a taxi cab and occupy the rear seat. The driver adjusts his rearview mirror, attempting to eavesdrop.
Shelly declares,
"We're going to MO BAY airport. Could you get us there in fifteen?"
Driver nods, yes.
The taxi turns in the opposite direction. Shelly notices.
"Where…are you going?"
She asks.
"Shortcut,"
Replies, the cab driver.
"I don't like shortcuts!"
Shelly echoes.
The driver makes another turn and swings into a driveway. The three women are frustrated as they feel cornered.
Immediately, the taxi stops. Abandoned vehicles create a spectacle. Axel James emerges from behind an abandoned car. He has a black bag and a gun in one hand.
"Do not get out of the car,"

He commands.

In dismay, Shelly looks at the cab driver and then at Axel.

"Where is our merchandise? Con Man!"

Shelly asks demandingly.

Axel inches towards the cab. The cab driver, fearing a shootout, exits the cab.

Axel is distracted. Shelly swings the front passenger door open, walloping Axel and knocking the gun entirely out of his hand.

The three women jump out with switchblades in a confrontation before Axel can retrieve his gun. Axel is trapped. Sensing a bloody end to his boss, Ian Baynes comes to his aid.

Pointing his gun at the three women. Ian exclaims, "Not so fast ladies."

Shelly tosses her knife at Axel James. He dodges. The knife misses him and lodges in the board behind him. Axel grabs the knife by its handle and flings it back at Shelly. She ducks. As a result, the knife sails through the taxi's rear window and lodges in the seat. Shelly comes at Axel with a left uppercut. He ducks. She returns with a left uppercut. Again, he ducks out of it. This time, he grabs her hand and twists it behind her back.

Following up, he whacks her hard in the face. Shelly staggers and falls to the ground.

Witnessing the manhandling of Shelly pisses off Denise. Frustrated, she yells,

"Where's our product, Axel?"
Axel James points to the black bag on the ground. Agnes picks the bag up and opens it. Satisfied, she throws it inside the taxi. Finally, Shelly gets up and crawls in on the other side of the cab.
Ricardo, taking no chances, keeps his gun pointed at Denise. Ian Baynes, sensing water under the bridge, returns to the car. Axel signals "let's go" to Ricardo. The taxi driver observes from a distance. Axel, while departing, looks over at him authoritatively.
"Take those bitches to the airport!" He commands.
The driver nervously walks over to his taxi. He gets in. Agnes and Denise get in. The cab drives off.
Axel, Ricardo, and Ian witness their peaceful departure, enter their car, and take off in the opposite direction.
The taxi travels speedily through the potholed streets of Montego Bay. Shelly wipes her face and stares at her blood-stained hands.
"I have to piss. Driver, can you pull over?"
He complies.
"Now get out of the car,"
Shelly commands.
He tries to grab the car keys.
Shelly opens her switchblade and stabs him once. He manages to open the door and exit the cab. She gets out in pursuit. Shelly stabs him several times. He crouches, falls to the ground, kicks around, and stops breathing. Shelly gathers some leaves and cleans the blade. She

looks at it. Noticing blood residue, she cleans it thoroughly with her red bandana, after which she takes the wheel.

6

LATER, AGNES, SHELLY, AND DENISE, dressed to the nines, all emerge from the ladies' room at Montego Bay Airport. Their sensualistic physique grabs attention as their oversized "rack" giggles. Shelly holds on carefully to that black bag recovered from Axel.

A luscious hottie, exquisitely outfitted, Jamaican style, joins them as they meander through customs all toting duffel bags. A Caucasian businessman, traveling in the opposite direction, is distracted by the estrogenic aura. He smashes into a pillar, sending his carry-ons flying. Embarrassingly he recovers but finds himself blanketed by the crowd he attracted.

Hours later, the American Airlines 747 touched down in Miami, Florida. The aircraft comes to a complete stop, but its doors remain closed.

A U.S. Marshall steps out of the cockpit and forms a huddle with two flight attendants. Sage Ross, in her late twenties, is as sophisticated as they come. Her Ivy League status shows through in her communication skills. Sean Williams, in his late thirties, listens attentively. The Marshall glances at Agnes, who grabs his attention in many different ways.

He compartmentalizes his thoughts and then refocuses.

"She fits the description…conveyed to us by Jamaican police,"

states the U.S. Marshall.

"What do we do?"

asks Sage.

Meanwhile, Denise seductively applies hot red lipstick. A passenger across the aisle devours a pack of multi-colored M&Ms.

"Keep the passengers in their seats. Bring in the DEA."

Sage picks up the microphone. She announces with an air of sophistication:

"Thanks for flying American Airlines flight 1934. When the aircraft comes to a stop, we ask that you please remain in your seats for further instructions."

Sage enters the cockpit as the aircraft comes to a stop. Passengers panic, in a state of restlessness, mainly those four women in question. The Hottie, sitting behind Denise, reaches inside her pocketbook and pulls out an object. She quickly removes the rubberized casing, revealing a "Dillinger." She shoots at the Marshall. The bullet misses him and hits a passing male flight attendant, who falls on top of several passengers. She shoots again.

The agile Marshall moves, and the round grazes his shoulder, ricochets, and penetrates the plane's skin. Marshall returns fire and shoots her in the face.

Passengers are screaming, some of them swearing. Denise, Agnes, and Shelly rummage nervously through their carry-on luggage under the seat. They cleverly remove a package each. Unnoticed by everyone else, they place their luggage under their seats, behind other luggage. The Marshal, surveying, steps over the dead body in the aisle and then returns to the cockpit area. Now more concerned than ever, two pilots remain seated at the controls. Sage dials.

The Marshall, somewhat annoyed with himself, exclaims,

"She's dead."

He fetches the phone and dials in front of the cockpit.

A pen phone rings on DEA Bascombe's desk. No one is there. In the office, the wall displays portraits of Jamaica. Agent Bascombe's nameplate stands out amongst the folders on his desk. The phone continues to ring.

Inside the green room, Bascombe fetches a cup of coffee and leaves the green room with a cup of coffee in hand. He accidentally spills some of the drinks on his suit and tie. Yet, he pays no attention to the spillage. He's got a more urgent task - getting to the phone. He grabs the pen phone that's been ringing unremittingly.

"Hello, this is agent Randy Bascombe!"

He listens in speaker mode as he handwrites on the pen phone.

"Okay. No one gets off that plane!"

He dials on the device.

Agent Desmond Scott, a Caucasian, good-looking stud in his mid-thirties, aborts the name search on the computer. He picks up the call.

"Scott, this is agent Bascombe. Meet me outside with the black Tahoe, ready to go."

Scott dashes out.

Bascombe dials again.

Heidi Hudson, Caucasian, in her late twenties, aborts applying her makeup and picks up

"Agent Hudson, we need you on this..."

She jumps up and checks her gun. Satisfied, she darts out. Bascombe inspects his tie. He goes to his locker. He opens it. Inside the locker, there's a sports coat that matches his pants. He removes his jacket and tie, hangs them in the locker, puts on the sports coat, and takes off as a man possessed. He turns the doorknob to Mendez's office. The door is locked. Bascombe dashes out towards the lobby. There, he bumps into Mendez, knocking the box of Kentucky Fried Chicken to the ground. Bascombe regains his balance. Mendez picks up the box of KFC.

"Yet another wild goose chase?"

He asks.

"This is huge. Dade County Airport."

Responds Randy Bascombe.

"Aren't you supposed to check with me first?"
Asks Mendez.
Bascombe, glancing at the KFC box in Jose Mendez's hand, replies,
"Sorry..."
Mendez, focusing on Bascombe, asks:
"Who's the informant?"
Bascombe reflects and then replies,
"American Airlines. The flight originated in Jamaica."
Heidi Hudson barges in. She stares inquisitively at Bascombe and Special Agent Mendez. She readily arranges her hair into a ponytail.
"Are we going to the Caribbean?" she asks smilingly.
Bascombe is focused. He addresses Mendez.
"Chief... "
Mendez interrupts him.
"I know. I'll be sending you some needed backup."
Outside, the Black Tahoe emerges from the parking structure and stops abruptly. Desmond Scott is at the wheel.
Bascombe jumps in the front passenger seat. Agent Hudson scurries in the rear seat and reaches for the seat belt.
"So where are we heading?"
Asks Agent Hudson.
The Tahoe takes off. Agent Hudson accidentally loses her balance.
Bascombe, with a delayed response.
"Dade County Airport!"

"Who's involved?"

She asks.

Bascombe was overwhelmed with her questions.

"Step on it, Scott. One woman, there could be more."

Meanwhile, inside the aircraft. Shelly tries to switch another passenger's bag with hers.

Seth, a flaming guy, catches her in the act.

"Did you move my bag?"

He yells.

"I'm sorry, it looked like mine,"

Shelly remarks.

"Don't be sorry. Can't you read? It says SETH!"

"Bitch, I said I'm sorry."

Replies Shelly.

She sits back down, clutching onto her carry-on.

Seth, not trusting her, gets up and examines his bag. Opening it, he discovers two pieces of silicone stuffed with small zip-locked packages. Staring at Shelly's reduced "rack."

Seth erupts,

"Help! This bitch is trying to frame me. You've got the wrong man..."

He removes both objects from his bag and holds them in his hand. Treating them as a personal object, he draws an audience.

"This is a "D" cup."

Seth removes the packages from the silicone.

Meanwhile, the Tahoe pulls up outside the aircraft. Agents, armed and ready to shoot rush towards the aircraft. Back inside, Shelly removes herself from that seat and sits in an empty seat a few rows back. The Marshall, returning from the cockpit with a log, intercedes.

Seth, still obsessed with the fake breasts, gently lays them on Shelly's empty seat.

Now on board, Agents huddle with Sage and the Marshall, reviewing the passenger's log. The Marshall points to the three women and Shelly's fake breasts on the seat. Hudson eyes the pieces of silicone, perturbed.

Bascombe commands: "My name is agent Randy Bascombe - Miami Drug Enforcement Agency. Shelly Hall, Denise Gomez, and Agnes Richards, you are under arrest for alleged drug possession. Come to the front of the aircraft with your hands on your head immediately."

The women reluctantly cooperate. Bascombe, place them in handcuffs. The other agents swarm the aircraft, collecting their carry-on.

Outside the abandoned aircraft, more Police vehicles converge, including a Coroner's vehicle. The three handcuffed women are pushed inside of a police utility vehicle. It drives outside Dade County Prison. The women are escorted inside the prison and booked by Miami police officers.

7

IN KINGSTON, JAMAICA, festive music is playing. Pedestrians crowd the busy streets in a dancing mood. Busy vendors display merchandise, enticing tourists to shop. One tourist walks up to a vendor and window shop. Every style of hat under the sun is stocked. The tourist cleverly slips him a U.S. Twenty dollar bill. The vendor takes it in his left hand and sticks it to his right, asking for more. The tourist opens his wallet and hands him another twenty. The vendor discretely hands him a brown bag. The tourist surveys his surroundings and secures it inside his pocket. He proceeds up the street. A Teen enjoys fresh cotton candy as he helps a blind man cross the street. Voluptuous women parade the streets, creating a "turn-on" for the men to enjoy the view.

A Taxi pulls up. Two Hotties with oversized tanks (breast) jump inside. The cab takes off.

Making a B-line, the Teen dashes out of its way to avoid getting run over by the taxi. Meanwhile, the indulging cabby looks at the rearview mirror of the cab. Suddenly, he asks the passengers,

"Where do you, two bumptious women... "

The taller of the two respond."
"University of the West Indies, West Kingston. Hurry!" The Cabby "steps on it" while he scans the radio station. He finds the right music to compliment the vibe and personalizes "Sweet Jamaica" in a sweet baritone voice.
The song ends, and another starts. He searches for the right key to this ballad and gets it.
"This is our stop!" announces the Hottie.
The Taxi pulls up to the curb and stops outside a booth with a variety of merchandise on display. Two women of less voluptuousness step out of the booth and trade places with the two Hotties. The cab takes off.
Moments later, teenagers flock to the booth in droves, like flies to molasses. They are eager to purchase the white powdery substance in a transparent wrap. The teen, previously helping the blind man across the street, shows up breathless, pays for his packet, and smilingly opens it.
One of the Hotties gets into a taxi. Later, the taxi pulls up next to a closed grocery store. The Hottie jumps out and slides a large envelope underneath the door. She returns to the waiting cab, which takes off speedily.
An approaching police cruiser with flashing lights pursues the taxi. The taxi pulls over and stops curbside. Without hesitating, the Hottie jumps out and shoots at two approaching officers. One is hit, he falls to the ground. The other officer shoots back, striking the Hottie. She collapses and falls to the ground. She

dies instantly. The Officer attends to his partner, who is still breathing. Sirens in the distance accompany a blanket of pedestrians, now converged onto the bloody scene.

8

A TEACHER RUSHES through the school gate and boards the waiting airport bus with a folder in hand. After entering, she closes the door securely. Two women disguised as tour guides emerge from the back of the bus. The Teacher hands over the folder to them. They quickly scan through the folder and conduct a careful headcount. They present the folder to the Bus Driver. His dragon tattoo behind his right ear lobe is very revealing. He conceals the folder.

The Women reach into their aprons and pull out several fist-sized aluminum foil packets resembling those recovered from Ray's backpack. These packets are quickly distributed to each kid, along with a bottle of bottled water and a sheet of instructions. The anxious kids review the instruction pamphlets and then consume the packets, aided by water. The bus pulls into a small airport hangar. A twin-engine jet with propellers turning in slow motion - waits. The kids are transferred to that waiting aircraft.

Back in Miami, at the DEA Headquarters, Bascombe paces while Mendez sits at the desk smoking a cigar. Bascombe, perturbed, throws the newspaper onto the desk. He composes himself, facing Mendez squarely, and addresses him.

“I would like to put in my request for an early vacation.”

Jose Mendez asks:

“Family...?”

It is as if he is not up to speed on the current fiasco in Jamaica.

Bascombe, feeling as if his intelligence has been insulted, remarks,

“No one seems to be doing anything about all these kids dying off like flies in Jamaica,” Mendez reassures.

“I am sure their government is handling that situation.”

Bascombe, not giving up:

“Their MPs could be in on this whole fiasco.”

Mendez responds,

“They’ve already imprisoned the Drug Lords. That’s progress!”

Bascombe reflects.

”My mom always used to say,

“There’s more in the Marta besides the pestle”

Mendez, understanding the cliché, comments,

“Do you think there’s more to it? I think you should let the government do their job. They are ...” Suddenly, the four eyes in that room are glued to the TV set as a news reporter interrupts the scheduled program.

“Late-breaking news as we continue to follow this fiasco in Jamaica. The death toll continues to rise as three teenagers died today as a result of using cyanide-laced cocaine. One drug dealer, a woman, was also shot and killed by Jamaican police. As a result of this shootout, one officer has been hospitalized. The death toll equals ninety."

Mendez, to it all, responds.

"Everyone seems to be using the word "F" way too much - FIASCO."

In disbelief (concerning his boss's attitude), Bascombe goes to the window. Reflecting, he looks outside. Bascombe retreats. Before further addressing Mendez, he points to his brother's portrait on the wall.

"My only sibling. Lost him in a drug-related incident."

Mendez, nods, indicating that all that is old news. Then he remarks,

"My condolences..."

Bascombe has endured enough.

"I refuse to let more of my relatives go through this fiasco. If not now? When? Some innocent person's kid is going to be next. That is my final "F" word." Bascombe throws the keys on the desk at Mendez and walks out of the office.

Mendez gets up from his seat at Bascombe's desk and takes in a close-up view of the portrait for the first time. Moments later, Mendez moseys up behind Bascombe in the Green Room. Bascombe, adding cream to his coffee, sees him peripherally. Mendez apologetically returns the keys to agent Bascombe. Scott and Hudson surprise them by barging in during the reconciliation.

Mendez bids farewell to Agent Desmond Scott and Agent Heidi Hudson. The three agents board a Miami Police SUV with their luggage in tow.

9

THE 747 AIRPLANE touches down at Michael Manley Airport in Jamaica. Agents Bascombe, Scott, and Hudson scramble through the crowded Jamaican airport terminal.

Outside the terminal, the agents hustle toward the blue unmarked police vehicle, waiting. A Distinguished Gentleman, dressed in white attire, steps out. He hands Bascombe the keys and a folded piece of paper. Bascombe reads the address: The Villa, 23 Pine Grove, St. Andrew, Jamaica.

Before getting inside, Bascombe asks.

"Is this thing GPS equipped?"

The Gentleman replies,

"Rude Buay, it has recently been installed in our entire fleet. On the other hand, I must tell you that the Jamaican government is not very happy with your involvement."

Bascombe replies.

"I understand. Dual citizenship has its advantages. Doesn't it?"

The Gentleman continues.

"How about your team?"

Heidi Hudson interjects.

"Where agent Bascombe goes, we go!"

"A dual name does have its disadvantage, agent Bascombe. I'm sorry, RUDE BUAY. Anyway, your brother will appreciate this homecoming."

The Gentleman admonishes.

Rude Buay looks towards heaven.

Heidi Hudson admires the gentleman. He then makes the sign of the cross and smilingly gives Rude Buay a thumbs up. The Agents jump inside the vehicle. The Distinguished Gentleman departs and moseys inside the terminal as their car takes off. It's a great distance from the airport to the Villa. Agent Bascombe takes control of the vehicle along the winding roads of Kingston en route to Mandeville. A beautiful, Victorian-designed house with an earthen extended driveway nestles on the hill above homes of lesser value.

Rude Buay stops the car. With Hudson covering him, they move in, weapons drawn. Scott waits outside the vehicle, armed and ready.

Rude Buay and Hudson arrive closer to the house. They scrutinize their surroundings. Feeling satisfied, Rude Buay inches closer to the front door. He kicks the door in and charges inside with Agent Hudson in tow. Now inside, both agents proceed intensely but with immense caution. Their entrance has them staring into a sunken living room with a giant screen TV, a black leather couch, and a huge glass center table. The neatly folded maps get their attention momentarily on the table, but they remain focused.

Commandingly, Rude Bauy cautions. "US drug enforcement agents! Come out nice and slow with your hands on your head."

There is no response. A black Cat emerges. Rude Buay releases the safety on his gun. The cat meows. Hudson, now standing over the center table, looks closer at the contents. She notices three separate sets of maps of the Jamaican city of Port Antonio. Next to the maps lay syringes on a tray, straws, a crack pipe, two cigarette lighters, and cocaine residue, validating the habits of the dwellers. Rude Buay's attention is drawn to several pieces of luggage in a corner. However, he proceeds into the room where the cat exited. Agent Hudson enters the other room while covering Rude Buay from the corner of her eyes.

Rude Buay rummages through the room. He cautiously checks a closet as he slowly pulls the door open. It's empty. He throws off the bed mattress and box spring. He checks under the bed; nothing's underneath it. On the nightstand, he notices a replica of "The Tempest," a beautiful yacht. Rude Buay admires it.

Hudson's voice penetrates the room.

"Rude Buay! You've got to see this." Rude Buay, with a gun, still drawn, vacates that room and joins her.

In the second bedroom, Agent Hudson stands in front of a giant-sized closet with its door ajar. She proceeds to rid it of its contents. Packets labeled Dragon X, attaché, guns, stacks of Jewish bankrolls in various currencies, grenades, and survival kits put things in perspective. Rude Buay and Hudson, more committed than ever to the manhunt, continue rummaging through the house.

In a Jamaican prison, a rat runs across the entrance to cell number fifteen and disappears. Axel James, dressed in prison garb, stares at the disappearing creature.

In the meantime, outside the prison, a Black sedan rolls up. Ricardo and Ian Baynes, dressed in prison security uniforms, step out and hasten through a massive iron gate.

An on-duty Security Guard sitting in the booth acknowledges them with a nod of the head. They proceed into the interior of the prison. Back at the booth, a new Guard replaces the on-duty guard.

Inside the prison, Axel's men hustle as if they are heading to break up a brawl. A guard getting some snacks from the snack machine is alerted. He draws his gun while curious inmates eavesdrop.

"Follow us, the alarm malfunctioned. There's a fight outside cells ten through fifteen," warns Ian Baynes.

The Guard remarks, "Trouble zone since fourteen went to the pit. Let's move it!"

They're now right in front of cell #15.

Ian Baynes grabs the prison guard around his neck. The Guard spins around, facing Ian Baynes and

Ricardo as his weapon falls to the ground. Two guns with silencers attached are pointing at him.
"Your clothes…and open fifteen!"
Commands Ian Baynes.
The Guard is bewildered until Ian Baynes quickly points the gun in his face. The Guard nervously disrobes, removes several keys from his belt, and unlocks the cell door.
Ian Baynes caps the Guard in the head and tosses his clothes to Ricardo, who hands them to Axel. Axel emerges from his cell, clothed in a prison guard's uniform.
Ian Baynes and Ricardo drag the semi-nude guard inside cell # 15 and shut the door. They exit the prison interior, accompanied by Axel James. The on-duty guard approaches the three of them questioningly.
"What is going on…with you three?"
"Going to get a smoke. We soon come back, you hear?"
Baynes answers in patois and hands the Guard a bag of weed. The three Drug Lords exit through the prison gates.
Outside the prison, Axel, Ian, and Ricardo enter the black sedan and drive away, laughing hilariously.

10

BACK AT THE VILLA, A Jamaican Police Officer, armed like a SWAT member, ambulates outside the police cruiser. The Black sedan drives up, carrying the three Drug Lords. Axel barges out, followed by Ian and Ricardo. They immediately open silent fire on the police officer. His exchange is too late. Hit by several rounds, he falls to the ground while his ammunition soars. Axel pumps bullets into all four tires of his vehicle as well as the parked DEA Agent's car. Their black Sedan rolls up in the driveway. They are still oblivious of the search going on inside by the DEA. Inside, Rude Buay and Hudson are now joined by Agent Scott, who recently aborted his surveillance duty on the exterior of the Villa. He rejoins his colleagues with a thumbs up and assists in the seizure assembly inside the living room.

A ray of light reflects, shining into the living room, from the sedan's headlights.

The agents, sensing pending trouble, disperse respectively.

Scott leans up behind the front door. Rude Buay goes through the back door while Hudson hides behind the door to the first bedroom. Now out of the car, Axel

James reacts to the moving shadow behind the first bedroom door.

Axel James hints at Ian and Ricardo.

"We've got more company. PIGS! (Police) " Rude Buay not only notices Axel but also hears his voice and adjusts to the perfect aim. He would instead take out Axel, but as soon as he gets the ideal aim on him, Axel darts in through the front door.

Already engaged, the bullet from Rude Buay's gun flies towards the sedan and blows out its front windscreen. Ian Baynes and Ricardo, hiding on the ground behind the back of the car, return gunfire, which misses Rude Buay, who dodges on time.

Behind the front door, Agent Scott and Axel James, end up in each other's space.

Scott tries to get a close-quarter shot off, but Axel "gets a drop," and the two engage in hand-to-hand combat. Axel outdoes Scott by a long shot.

Hudson emerges from behind the door and into the corridor. At the same time, Ricardo shotguns through the front door. While witnessing a duel between Axel and Agent Scott, Hudson takes aim at Axel James' head. She shoots at Axel, and simultaneously, Scott punches Axel in the right eye; Axel rolls over. The bullet penetrates the wall.

Bullets go flying everywhere from Ricardo's gun like popcorn.

Before Agent Hudson can retaliate, a bullet from Ricardo's gun grazes her face. She's all shaken up. Axel regains his presence of mind and lands a punch into Scott's stomach. Scott catches his breath.

Axel stumbles around with blurry vision. On the outside of the Villa, Rude Buay engages in a shootout with Ian Baynes. Both men miss their target. Finally, Ian reacts to being hit. He goes down. Rude Buay, satisfied, dashes to the inside through the front door.

Ricardo peripherally sees Rude Buay entering the house and dashes towards the back door.

Ricardo, whispers to Axel,

"Let's get out of here, Boss."

Axel manages to recoup. They sprint to their car on the outside.

Ian Baynes crawls in the back seat, with blood trickling down his neck.

Ricardo takes the wheel.

Axel scoots in on the other side. With no front windshield, the black car takes off in reverse, down the long, extended driveway. Rude Buay, seeing the car disappear, rushes back outside in frustration.

The black cat saunters across the driveway. Rude Buay aims at the animal but changes his mind. Heavy pouring rain presents a hazard for Axel James, Ian Baynes, and Ricardo Herrera. They are soaking wet, and the car swerves off the road. The sedan pulls over to the side of the road.

They exit. An approaching vehicle casts its light in their direction. The oncoming Mini-Van gets closer. The three men run out into the middle of the street.

Their guns are drawn on the driver. The Mini Van comes to a screeching halt, running off the road and into the gutter.

The Driver is a Rastafarian. Before he could get a word out, Axel James shouted at him,

"Get out!"

The Driver complies and starts running for his life. Before he could escape, Axel pumped several bullets into his body.

The driver falls over the embankment. Axel follows him and confiscates his wallet. They speedily transfer their cargo from the sedan to the Minivan, using it as their getaway vehicle. The Minivan pulls up outside the dock. A sailor from "The Tempest" waves in acknowledgment. Axel James, Ian Baynes, and Ricardo step out and hurry on aboard the waiting yacht with huge duffel bags.

The sailor lifts the yacht's anchor while another releases the line and leaps back onto the sailing yacht.

At the Villa, sunrise casts its rays as the three DEA agents vacate the premises.

They look at their sedan with its deflated tires.

Scott, the first one to speak, says:

"They could have already fled to Cuba."

Heidi Hudson responds,

"With all that rain last night, driving without a front windscreen is impossible." Rude Buay, after radioing for help, reminds them, "I wouldn't put it past them. For all you know, they could have driven in reverse."

"Reverse? In the rain? On these winding roads? Asks Agent Hudson.
"Yep! If the desire is strong enough, the facts carry no weight," replies Rude Buay as they wait beside the abandoned sedan.

11

TWO JAMAICAN POLICE Officers show up in an SUV and a Land Rover. They jump out apologetically. The officer driving the jeep hands over his keys to Rude Buay.

"You can use this," he instructs. Rude Buay, looking at the jalopy, certainly does not resonate with it.

"Get us a helicopter, Officer," Rude Buay responds.

"That's not my call, Mr. Bascombe." Rude Buay stares at him more intensely. "Time is running out," remarks Rude Buay as he attempts to take the SUV wheel.

"Hold on, this is a Government Utility Vehicle. I am the only one allowed to drive this GUV," says the other officer.

Rude Buay ignores him. The two other agents jump in. The officer retaliates. Rude Buay takes the wheel, anyway, leaving both officers behind. The retaliated officer, yelling in Patois, echoes,

"Don't you realize the roads have changed! Motorists are skilled at driving in reverse. You need I and I to..."

Rude Buay, realizing that he needs some help navigating, makes a roundabout turn. The officer hops in.

The GUV drives away, followed by the Land Rover.

Later, a helicopter carrying Rude Buay, Scott, and Hudson circles over the countryside. They spot an abandoned sedan on the roadside in Montego Bay. Moving in closer, they discover the body of the carjacked Rastafarian in the gutter. Scott remarks, "Yep. These guys could have already fled the country."
"What if they're still here?" responds Rude Buay.
Hudson interjects.
"I doubt it,"
Rude Buay, unconvinced, says,
"Navigating seems to be their cup of tea." Using a pair of binoculars, Hudson notices as a tow truck backs up to the Mini Van and engages in a tow. The name on the tow truck reads Black River Towing.
Later, the copter returns to the small Jamaican airstrip. Rude Buay and Scott step out. The accompanying officer directs Rude Buay and his agents to a parked sedan.
During this interim, cries from mourners are heard in the city of Mandeville as more dead bodies are wheeled into a makeshift morgue. The stench is unbearable from the regular, overcrowded facility next door.
Outside the hospital, hundreds of mourners congregate, waiting in tears to identify the body of their child.
"Could this have been prevented?" one mourner asks another.

"Yes, kids ought to learn not to play with matches," the intercepting Peace Keeping Officer responds. The agents pull up outside Black River Towing.

Inside Rude Buay's car, his Pen Phone rings. He reviews the caller's ID. By the customary look on his face, his fellow agents suspect that it's their boss on the other end. So, they eavesdrop. "Hello. Agent Mendez," Rude Buay responds. "Bascombe, we've been monitoring the Jamaican situation. Axel James and his allies have fled the country. Possibly to Cuba:" Jose Mendez remarks. "Apparent, how? Is Castro signed on?" asks Rude Buay.

"What goes on in Cuba stays in Cuba. My hands are tied. I'm having all three of you brought back to Miami tomorrow:" Mendez insists.

Rude Buay says to Hudson and Scott, "Search has been called off," and to Mendez, "We'll see you then."

12

IN A DOWNTOWN, ritzy, Miami hotel: Carlos, of Asian descent, in his mid-thirties, removes his bloodstained clothes and discards them in a black trash bag. Semi-clothed, he rummages through a bag, scanning through logs and other prison-related documents. He goes to a suitcase, where he retrieves a toupee, and carefully affixes it to his mask. He then removes four Warden Uniforms from a suitcase and puts them on.

The name on his lapel reads Warden Richard Culligan. Carlos takes a detailed look at himself in the full-length mirror. Again, he studies Warden Culligan's picture, scotch-taped to the wall next to the mirror. He uses some paper tissue and creates padding for his biceps. He is satisfied with his new look. Carlos picks up a laden black duffel bag and departs.

A sedan pulls up outside Florida State Prison. Carlos steps out. He passes a prison guard, filing away paperwork in the booth.

"Wide-eyed and bushy-tailed?" Carlos greets him, signing in.

"Hi Boss! Warden Culligan," replies the Guard.

"Anything to report, Miles?" Carlos asks.

The Guard responds,
"Everything's dandy, except my replacement is usually here fifteen minutes early, and he's..."
Carlos interrupts.
"I'll look into that for you."
Carlos proceeds towards Warden Culligan's office. He unlocks the door and enters. Shedding three layers of prison uniform, Carlos deposits them, one per paper sack.
Outside Culligan's office, Bruce, the guard on patrol, ambulates. He removes a pack of cigarettes from his pocket—it's his last one—and lights up. Carlos steps out of the office, noticing Bruce's name tag.
Carlos greets, "Hey Bruce, you got a cigarette?"
"Sorry, I've just smoked my last,"
Bruce responds.
"What you smoke, Salem?"
asks Carlos.
Bruce nods yes.
"You want to pick up a pack of Salem Lights?" asks Carlos.
"Yes, Mr. Culligan," Replies Bruce.
He hands Bruce the money. Bruce departs.
Carlos makes his move, stopping in front of cell numbers one, twelve, and thirty. Agnes Richards resides in cell # 1.
Carlos unlocks Agnes' cell and deposits a paper shopping bag inside. He then hands Shelly a cell phone and a handwritten page of instructions and departs.

Denise Gomez resides in cell # 12. Carlos unlocks Denise's cell and deposits a paper shopping bag. He then hands her a cell phone along with a handwritten page of instructions and departs.
In cell # 30 resides Shelly Hall.
Carlos unlocks her cell and deposits a paper shopping bag. He hands Shelly a cell phone along with a handwritten page of instructions. He leaves, is noticed by other inmates, and exits hurriedly. Most seem not to care. However, the Prison Guard at the booth is somewhat confused by all this unusual business.
"Warden Culligan, it's your off night. You're ..." he asks inquiringly.
Carlos steps up closer to the booth and interrupts:
"Inside here, your off night is always on. After your third month, you'll see what I mean."
The Prison Guard removes the sign-in sheet from the clipboard and sticks it in a brown manila envelope, sealing it with his saliva and then with scotch tape.
Sensing the Prison Guards' strategic move to log a genuine report, Carlos sees the clock inside the booth. The clock shows seven minutes to midnight. Carlos pushes the door open.
"So, you're covering for him?" Carlos asks and pulls out a semi-automatic from the duffel bag with a silencer attached. He aims it at the guard. Surprised, the guard remarks,
"You don't want to do that! I'll keep everything confidential. I swear..."

Carlos pumps several bullets into the Prison Guard's body. He falls outside of the booth, to the ground, to his death. Carlos PICKS up the handheld radio and radios. Three guards sitting in separate towers tune in. Carlos announces:

"The next shift will be coming in five minutes early."

The Guards respond,

"Good deal!"

Carlos picks up his cellular phone and speedily dials.

Shelly, dressed in prison guard's attire, holding Automatic with a silencer attached and emerging from within prison compounds, answers.

"We are coming out!"

Shelly is oblivious and steps on a line in the pavement. Immediately, the prison grounds floodlights come on all over the compound. The three women, attired in the Warden's uniform, disperse. They rush towards an individual, separate tower. Now situated, they proceed to trade places with the three on-duty guards. The guards, before completing their descent, are shot simultaneously. They fall precipitously to their death. The women race to the prison exterior, dash towards the sedan, and enter like greased lightning. Carlos drives away.

Back at the State Prison, Bruce returns with the cigarettes but notices three empty cells and Warden Culligan's empty office. He's dumbfounded and confused.

Shelly, Agnes, and Denise rid themselves of the Warden's garb inside the car, revealing their true identity.
Suddenly, the reflection of red and blue flashing lights streams inside the sedan. Sirens accompany the kaleidoscopic illumination.
Shelly, Agnes, and Denise reach for their gun simultaneously, in readiness.
The Miami police cruiser aggressively tails the sedan. The Sedan reduces its speed and moves to the road's right shoulder. The Police cruiser stops closely behind. The Officer barges out, proceeds towards the driver's side of the sedan, and draws his gun. Inside, the women, with guns still drawn, are poised, ready to shoot.
The officer cautiously proceeds, trying to look through the rear-tinted windscreen. Instantly, three sets of bullets storm through the rear windscreen, laying the Officer flat onto the street. The women return guns to their original position. Broken glass everywhere creates discomfort. The sedan speeds away and merges with the flow of traffic.
Moments later, it drives into an underground parking lot where the limo waits.
Shelly, Agnes, and Denise exit. Still armed, they survey before getting inside the limo. The limousine door closes. It speeds off merges into the flow of traffic, and subsequently arrives at the dock. Carlos, Shelly,

Denise, and Agnes join Alberto aboard his yacht, "Gomez."
Inside the other yacht, "Tempest," the phone rings.
Axel, on deck, picks up.
"Axel let's go to plan B," commands Alberto.
Axel reaches for and reviews the city of Port Antonio.
He glances at his watch and responds.
"Okay, Boss! All the lights are green. Port Antonio by midnight."

13

THE "TEMPEST" SAILS BY Port Antonio's Peninsula. Axel James, Ian Baynes, and Ricardo plunge into the water, dressed in wet suits. Each carries a bag strapped to their back. The ship continues sailing towards Port Antonio, where it docks. A customs official boards the vessel. He inspects thoroughly. The captain of the Tempest over-accommodates. Content the customs official returns to his booth.

In the wooded area of Port Antonio, shrubbery provides privacy as Axel James, Ian Baynes, and Ricardo remove their water suits, dry off, and get into street clothes retrieved from waterproof bags. They remove and open their duffel bags. Retrieving their weapons, they rush through the bushes.

They hit the streets of Port Antonio. A minivan designed to seat twelve passengers pulls up at the bus stop. They jump in. The door closes, and it drives off. The van, almost full to the max, with seats aligned with theatre style and minimal legroom between them, takes on the treacherous hillsides.

After finding a seat, Ian Baynes takes out a wad of mixed currency and pays the conductor upfront. The locals, noticing the U.S. currency, eye him enviously.

One man even sticks his hand out. Ian ignores the beggar's plea.

The Van stops. Axel James, Ian Baynes, and Ricardo exit and board another van.

This Van is filled mainly with Rastafarians wearing massive dreadlocks. The driver's dreadlocks are wrapped up in a knitted tam, black, yellow, and green.

Axel James studies the passengers, but mainly, two high school kids with untied shoestrings grab his attention.

Ian eyes the driver, an Afro-Asian.

"Central Port Antonio?" "We just passed it!" replies the driver.

"Really?" asks Ian.

"Yes, mon!"

Assures the driver.

The Van stops. They get off.

Ian and Ricardo travel back on foot towards Avis and rent a white van. Axel and Ricardo await Ian's arrival.

Ian pulls up in a white van. Axel and Ricardo jump aboard, duffel bags in hand.

Inside the Van, Axel unzips a duffel bag and admires his gun extensively. Finally, he utters, "When do we return this vehicle?"

Ian, turning up the music, responds, "All we have to do is call them at Avis if we need an extension. My brethren rule that joint, and besides…"

Axel James interrupts Ian,

"Where's your weapon?"

"My bag's behind the back seat. Where's base camp?"
He answers.
Ricardo interjects,
"Hope Bay! Close enough."
Ian replies very sarcastically,
"Is that close to Agent Banks?"
Ricardo eyes Axel questioningly.
Ian continues,
"Don't worry. We'll find Banks. First, we'll take out the government,"
Axel comments.
"Banks? He's a small fry. If we could get the MP on our side...They wouldn't have a problem giving us the 411 on a former MP."

14

A SMALL DIMLY LIT HOUSE overlooks the city of Port Antonio. Lights from ships in the harbor create a picturesque subterranean backdrop. Maps, radios, headsets, binoculars, microcassette players, and miscellaneous gadgets contribute to the ambiance. With salt and pepper hair, Walter Banks, an African American in his late fifties, sweats. He is fiddling disparately with his spy tech gadgets. An intermittent sound from his Pen Phone gets his attention. Banks retrieves it from his desk and listens in. The sound comes in and out, muffled; finally, he loses it.

On top of a mountain in Columbia, camouflaged between some trees, nestles a tiny shack built from wood and painted in green grass color. Chelo, a Colombian dressed in a straw hat, ruffled clothing, and shoe-less, runs out of the shack. He tiptoes and adjusts the dismantled wire antenna on the roof. Like a champion, he hurries back inside.

The computer screen reveals a parked airplane in Bogota with a substantial vacant cargo area. Scanning further, he notices several crates loaded with sacks of Dragon X Cocaine destined for Port Antonio, Jamaica. He's possessed, like a kid in a candy store. The way he

handles the mouse device says he is hungry for this information. His screen reveals and captures an airport bus registered in Bogota. Twelve teens take time inside the bus to review instructions and small packets.
Sitting in his living room in Port Antonio, Jamaica, Walter Banks is enjoying the live feed. Suddenly, the computer screen goes blank. Banks desperately adjusts the picture via TiVo. He tunes in and replays. Over the blank computer screen, he hears Chelo's voice.
"Come in, Banks!"
"Go ahead, Chelo."
Banks replies.
Chelo exclaims:
"A huge shipment of contaminated Cocaine is being prepared. Destination: Port Antonio - Jamaica. The Dragon Drug Cartel has got it all lined up."
Banks, sharing Chelo's hunger for the info, review the entire video. Jumping up from behind his desk, he echoes,
"Bastards! Never!"
Banks goes to the window, pen phone in hand, to take in the harbor view. Nothing is visibly unusual, so he returns to his desk. Using the pen phone, he writes on a slip of paper. He sticks the paper in an envelope and seals it with his saliva. Then he grabs his keys, along with the envelope and his Pen Phone. He dashes outside to his car, turns it on, and drives away.
An hour later, he arrives at Kingston's Ministry of Tourism and Culture Office.

A red-eyed Jamaican security guard patrols the premises. Banks turns off the headlights. He travels on foot, eludes the guard, and slips an envelope under the door before exiting.

15

THE FOLLOWING MORNING, inside the Ministerial Building across the street, a meeting is in session. Five men dressed in suits sit facing each other around a huge mahogany table.

Dalton Castello, the deputy Prime Minister, who is African American in his late forties, presides.

Michael Young, Caucasian, is in his early forties. Vince La Borde, a bald African American, is in his mid-fifties. Bazil Taylor, an African American, is also in his mid-fifties. William Russell was an African American with salt and peppered hair.

This quintet of think tanks waits anxiously, ready to write.

Dalton Castello addresses:

"The Prime Minister has asked me to preside over this meeting."

He searches through a stack of documents and continues.

"As you know, he will return from CARICOM next week. The Jamaican economy is..."

The door opens. A drop-dead gorgeous, sophisticated Mildred Simms, the desire of any man's heart, in her late twenties, enters.

Five pairs of eyes pierced her soul questioningly. Mildred, though slightly embarrassed for interrupting, radiates, "Excuse me!."

She hands the envelope to Dalton Castello and exits hurriedly. Castello opens the envelope and reads its contents.

"Gentlemen, it seems as if a Drug Cartel, "The Dragons," is about to infiltrate our country with a shipment of over $25M worth of "cyanide-laced" cocaine. Our shores will now need to be guarded twenty-four-seven. Starting with Mo Bay. He EYES the clock on the wall and continues reading.

"They're known for taking out governments; they did so in Grenada a few years ago. Watch your backs. Let's reconvene tomorrow."

Unnerved, they shut their folders and exit speedily.

Outside, a Mini Van stops abruptly. Axel, Ian, and Ricardo jump out, armed with automatic weapons.

The men are masked, with their tattoos covered up. A Minister of Parliament standing outside acknowledges Axel and walks briskly ahead them. As soon as they catch the MP, he hands Axel a piece of paper. It's a blueprint. Axel, "crash studies" document. They enter RAMBO STYLE. Two guards are jovially conversing inside the lobby. The guards, called to action, attempt to un-holster their uncompetitive weapons. The unwarranted visitors quickly tie up the guards and throw them inside a closet. They meet the government ministers coming down escorted by a Police Officer.

Before he could draw his gun, Axel shoots him in the chest. The government officials were scared and tried reversing upstairs.

Axel commands:

"All we need is your cooperation. Your choice, resistance, or termination? Extinction?" Dalton Castello stares at Axel James with surprise.

Axel continues:

"Just do as you're told. Place your hands on top of your heads." The five Ministers comply.

Axel, commandingly, directs: "You are boarding the minivan across the street. Come on, move it!"

They are now on the outside, unnoticed. Ian Baynes opens the door to Mini Van.

Dalton Castello, Vince La Borde, Basil Taylor, Michael Young, and William Russell are forced inside. The Mini Van speeds away.

16

COMMISSION RICHARD BAPTISTE, a tall, slim, kingly man in his forties, sits inside the commissioner's office. Sitting across from him is the governor-general Dr. Bradford Wiley, intellectually sound and in his sixties.

"We have no choice but to bring in Rude Buay," suggests the commission. Bradford Wiley agitatedly responds.

"Might as well sell our souls to the Devil."

"People like Rude Buay get hired to find the Devil. Plus, he has a vendetta - his brother. Make it happen no matter what the cost,"

Advises the Commissioner.

The governor reminisces:

"We're still in a deficit from the last time, commissioner. Why should we have to pay for him? He's the son of our soil. JFK said, "Ask not what your country can do for you - ask what you can do for your country."

Richard Baptiste explodes,

"This is Jamaica in crisis! The death toll has reached 150."

Bradford Wiley, shaken up and prayerfully composed, responds:

"Calm down, Richard. Ask, and it shall be given you; seek, and ye shall find; knock, and it shall be opened unto you:

Matthew 7:7"

The Commissioner picks up his phone and dials.

At DEA Headquarters in Miami, the stone-faced Jose Mendez walks into the ringing of his office phone. He picks it up after the first ring,

"Jose Mendez!"

The Commissioner responds,

"Mr. Mendez, this is Richard Baptiste, the police commissioner in Jamaica. As you know, we've inherited Axel James and his allies from the U.S., as well as a colossal epidemic; our kids are dying by the minute. We don't want to run our government using interns. Plus, we're still recovering from the effects of that devastating hurricane. We need to broker a deal for Rude Buay's services. Mendez replies,

"He's already headed back to Miami. Let me be clear...Rude Buay is the United States Drug Enforcement Agent, not a mercenary." Baptiste reminds him.

"You didn't have a problem taking a fee when his services were required prior..." Mendez, matter-of-factly.

"Twenty percent increase and wire my handling fee to the same account. Happy hunting, Commissioner."

The Governor-General and The Commissioner shake hands and depart, accomplished.

17

A TAXI PULLS UP OUTSIDE the Michael Manley Airport departure terminal. Rude Buay steps out, followed by Agent Hudson and Agent Scott. Rude Buay's cell phone rings. He answers.

"Bascombe, you've just been hired to put out Axel James' trash in Jamaica. It's a sizable raise from your last trip off of the reservation," commands Jose Mendez.

Rude Buay responds,

"According to Benjamin Disraeli: 'Nothing can resist the human that will stake even its existence on its stated purpose."

Mendez, instructional replies,

"The Commissioner has already arranged for you and the team to meet him tomorrow in Montego Bay."

"There could be a conflict in the schedule as Mr. Banks is also expecting to meet with me tomorrow in Port Antonio,"

Instructs, Rude Buay.

Jose Mendez responds sarcastically,

"What could a former MP do for you? That old racehorse is tired."

Rude Buay, disagreeing remarks.

"The greatest tragedy in America is not the destruction of our natural resources, though that tragedy is great. The truly great tragedy is the destruction of our human resources by our failure to fully utilize our abilities, which means that most men and women go to their graves with their music still in them.' So said Oliver Wendell Holmes."

Hours later, the plane touches down at Montego Bay Airport. Rude Buay, Agent Scott, and Hudson deplane. Jamaican police patrol the grounds, armed with automatic weapons, forming an impediment.

Mildred Simms is sandwiched like a rose between two sharp thorns, the commissioner to her left, Banks to her right.

Rude Buay emerges, followed by the agents. The commissioner greets.

"Welcome. Meet Mildred Simms, the eyes, and Banks, the ears, of Jamaica."

Rude Buay replies,

"Meet my partners, Agent Scott and Agent Hudson; if it moves, he can drive it. If it's there, she can find it."

Glancing at Banks, he remarks.

"Mr. Banks, thanks for readjusting your..."

The Commissioner intercepts, "Welcome Agent Scott and Agent Hudson." Banks announces.

"Jamaica? One Love!"

They walk over toward a waiting black Hummer.

Mildred Simms states,

"In less than an hour, you'll be briefed on the current situation involving Axel James."

Banks, suggestively,

"Tonight, we'll be partying Jamaican Style at the Beach Resort in Montego Bay. Sam's Taxi Tours will pick you up.'

Hudson, echoes,

"I love this place!"

Rude Buay replies,

"I'm here to work, Mr. Banks."

To which Banks responds,

"You have to assimilate into your environment, no?" Hudson wastes no time, securing the seat belt around her. Rude Buay and Scott throw the luggage inside the Hummer; they climb in as the Hummer departs. In the meantime, at an Airfield in Port Antonio, a small aircraft touches down. Passengers of multiple Colombian descent rushed from the helicopter and onto a waiting bus. The bus drives away.

Additionally, on top of an Ocho Rios hillside, Jamaican police comb through the bamboo trees with dogs in search of Axel, Ian, and Ricardo Hererra. In a Mandeville park, a posted sign reads: PARK CLOSED UNTIL FURTHER NOTICE.

Outside a Vegetable Market in Kingston, Produce is offloaded from trucks. Desperate shoppers bid for a supply in quantity, fearing scarcity. At a tenement yard in Kingston, where Rude Buay once lived, a couple stacks up on a food supply of corned fish, starch, canned foods, rice, peas, flour, sugar, and cooking oil.

Over the airwaves, the breaking news continues. One announcer throws himself into it. He reports: "Power 106 FM. Radio Jamaica is on the go. Gas prices continue to soar. While several vehicles wait in line at the pumps. The Jamaican Coast Guard cutter aggressively patrols the shores. Helicopters fly at low altitudes to find Members of the Dragon Drug Cartel. Meanwhile, the death toll continues to climb as several adults have also lost their lives as a result of using contaminated drugs. Sources close to the Prime Minister's Office claim that American DEA agents are expected to be briefed shortly regarding this fiasco, as five Government officials are still missing." On several drug trafficking streets in Port Antonio, MPs oversee the setup of roadblocks. In particular, those leading towards the airfield. Several locals wait in line with parked vehicles as individuals displaying Dragon tattoos exchange sacks of cocaine for cash.

18

OUTSIDE THE CROWDED Port Antonio Hospital E.R., many patients wait on gurneys. Despite her stunningly eye-catching medical garb, 25-year-old Attending Physician Dr. Tamara Ross draws applause—mainly from the male gender. She is focused as she enthusiastically watches over the growing life-and-death drama of the unfortunate children.

In Kingston, outside the police barracks, the streets are lined with early morning vendors, flanged by carnival demonstrators. The Jamaican and U.S. flags wave in the breeze. In his 50s, Steve is shirtless and establishes the tune on his steel pan.

Steve, in a rugged falsetto, sings:

"Don't stop the carnival. Down with the criminals. We want Steel band, Calypso, and Mardi Gras." The black Hummer pulls up, sandwiched by Jamaican police on motorbikes. Rude Buay, Agent Scott, and Hudson step out and enter through the police barracks. Jamaican policemen gait excessively. Seated behind a long desk are the Governor-General Dr. Bradford Wiley, Deputy Police Commissioner Winston Davis, and the honorable Pete Bacchus. Seated in front of the desk are

Prison Warden Ralph Bullock, Mildred Simms, and five distinguished officers of the Jamaica police force. Rude Buay, Scott, and Hudson walk in, occupying the front-row seats. Police Commissioner Richard Baptiste emerges from the back room and sits next to the Governor-General. They shake hands. Jamaican police officers close the door. The Commissioner stands and addresses:

"Good morning. I want to introduce Dr. Bradford Wiley, the Governor General of Jamaica."

Applause! The Commissioner sits.

Dr. Bradford Wiley removes an index card from his breast pocket, puts on his reading glasses, and, after glancing at the card, addresses the working group.

"Rude Buay, Agent Scott, and Agent Hudson, welcome to Jamaica." He continues,

"Our collaborative efforts in finding the missing and ensuring that justice is served will certainly protect the lives of our future generation: THE KIDS."

The gathering applauds.

Dr. Wiley removes his reading glasses, puts them inside the case, and sits down. The projector light comes on. Police Commissioner Richard Baptiste stands. He points to the screen, which shows a picture of exhibit #1: Axel James.

Baptiste continues,

"Axel James, mid-30s, Colombian decent, scarred, and stone-faced. Axel is a fugitive, murderer, drug lord, sailor, and con artist."

Next, a picture of exhibit #2: Ian Baynes Baptiste, continuing:

"Ian Baynes, mid-30s, African American."

Followed by a picture of exhibit #3: Ricardo Herrera. Baptiste states,

"Ricardo Herrera, early 40s, descent. Both are known Axel James associates and have extensive rap sheets throughout the Islands and several Southern States. They are also known as the notorious Dragon Drug Cartel gang members." Next, a picture of exhibit #4: Dalton Castello.

There is silence. You can hear a pin drop.

The Commissioner echoes,

"Dalton Castello, Minister of National Security (Police, Prisons and Seaports)! The Public Service and Airport Development. Missing!"

A picture of exhibit #5, Michael Young, follows.

Baptiste echoes,

"Michael Young, Minister of Tourism and Culture. Missing!"

A picture of exhibit #6, Vince La Borde, follows.

Baptiste continues.

"Vince La Borde, Minister of Telecommunications, Science Technology and Industry. Social Development, the Family, Gender and Ecclesiastical Affairs. Missing!"

A picture of exhibit #7, Bazil Taylor, appears.

Baptiste continues.

"Bazil Taylor, Minister of Transport, Works and

Housing. Missing."
This is followed by a picture of exhibit #8: William Russell
He continues,
"William Russell, Minister of State in the Ministry of Education, Youth and Sports. Missing!
The projector light goes off.
The Commissioner engages the podium. All eyes are focused on him as he expounds:
"Those ministers of government were kidnapped at the Economic debate… The carnival celebrations are still on hold for security reasons. Agents, your assistance in this crisis is invaluable."
He shakes hands with the Minister of Health and Environment, Honorable Esther Graves. Then, he exits briskly on the heels of the Governor-General.
Rude Buay stares with displeasure at prison Warden Ralph Bullock, a man of East Indian descent. His name tags glitter in the dimly lit room of aggravated government officials.
Mildred Simms moseys out from the briefing room and connects with Rude Buay. "Rude Buay, the Governor-General wants to see you in his office."
Rude Buay leaves Bullock an eye full of "it's all good."
Inside the Conference Room, the Governor-General and Commissioner sit face to face.
Mildred Simms enters, followed by Rude Buay.
Wiley greets them and remarks,

"Rude Buay, whatever you need. The Commissioner and his team are here for you."
Rude Buay, without batting an eye, replies,
"I need maps containing every street, track, river, stream, gutter, sewage line, mountain, hill, and valley, blueprints of buildings, homes, huts, outhouses, and every dog house and "pig pen" in Port Antonio. Plus, I need Helicopters, speedboats, and fast automobiles."
He pauses and continues: "If a hammer hits a nail on its head there after today, I want to know who did it and where." The Commissioner responds,
"Why our police barracks?"
"Because you never know who is rolling in the mud."
The Commissioner eyes Wiley and Mildred and then focuses on Rude Buay.
"And how soon do you need these?"
Rude Buay responds,
"Tomorrow by sunset." Mildred Simms looks at the Governor-General.
Baptiste eyes Rude Buay with concern.
Wiley ponders before responding.
"Rude Buay, we don't have enough manpower. We can access one extra helicopter, which we borrow from Haiti only on Sundays…Two Coast Guard cutters, and they've been working around the clock since...We have one Hummer; the next shipment has been delayed..."
Rude Buay leans across and says to Scott,
"Get on the phone. We have a few favors to call in. Ask Banks to show up half an hour earlier."

Scott, questioningly,
"Am I in this meeting?"
Rude Buay responds sarcastically,
"Only if you speak Patois."
Rude Buay shakes hands with Baptiste and Wiley. Mildred Simms escorts him to the door. She waves goodbye.
Mildred returns to the room. The Commissioner walks over to Mildred and addresses her in Patois.
"Keep a close eye on Mr. Rude Buay and his partners. Don't lose them out of your sight. This isn't his show. He's our... "
Mildred senses his trend of thought and trails Rude Buay.

19

SAM'S TAXI TOUR bus arrives at the dock in Negril. Rude Buay, Agent Scott, and Hudson step out dressed to the nines.

A short Jamaican Police patrolling, carrying semiautomatics, approaches the agents. Five additional officers observe.

The officer confronts the agents.

"May I take a look at your IDs?" he asks.

Like clockwork, the three DEA agents flash their badges. Police continue,

"I'm sorry, but you're not allowed." Rude Buay replies,

"Looks like you boys didn't get the memo."

The Police replies,

"What "memo" would that be, Mr. American tourist?"

Rude Buay lashes out at him after that comment. "The "memo" that this "tourist" is here to save your country from the bad guys."

The other five policemen advance. Six weapons are now pointed at Rude Buay, but before they know it, Rude Buay, Scott, and Hudson have swiftly disarmed and subdued two of them. The remaining Police train their weapons on the two Agents. Five additional police officers draw closer towards the agents with guns cocked.

There's radio transmission. The Policemen listen in.

Mildred's voice echoes,

"Send Rude Buay and Scott and Hudson in. Over."

Rude Buay and Scott release their captives and promptly escort them inside. An Elderly man yells from the crowd in Patois. "Yardy Buay, come home to roost with Yankee gal!" Rude Buay ignores the welcome. A Police Officer escorts them inside Negril Beach Hotel.

Mildred is sitting alone at a table.

Rude Buay rambles in her direction, with agents Scott and Hudson tailing him. Banks is at the bar drinking a beer. Rude Buay pulls up a stool next to Banks:

"Pardon my tardiness. What can I say about some of these locals?"

Remarks, Rude Buay.

"They see you as a sophisticated American who has a vendetta against them. But it's all good. Now, how can I help you?"

States, Banks,

Rude Buay takes a beer and responds. "Your commissioner wants me on this case, but their resources are limited."

Banks is very diplomatic. He ponders, then states,

"I still have some Cuban ties."

Mildred gets up from her seat at the table and walks over to the bar.

"Mr. Rude Buay. Your agents are waiting for Sir," States Mildred.

"Let's talk later, Mr. Banks,"

Says Rude Buay, excusing himself.

Rude Buay joins the others at the table.

Mildred, observing him closely, states,

"Welcome to NEGRIL Resort."

Maître D steps up, seats them, and leaves. Agent Scott scans the room discreetly. The dance floor is crowded, and booze is everywhere. The DJ plays a slow song.

Rude Buay and Mildred exchange glances.

Hudson, jealously, clues in.

Mildred continues,

"Would you like to dance, Rude Buay?"

Mildred Simms gets up and leads Rude Buay to the dance floor.

Scott notices a hot woman sitting alone at another table. She winks at him and touches her neck on the jugular vein. Scott clues in, that's how the women in that clique introduce themselves. Scott strolls in her direction. Her added smile says to Scott, "we belong." Scott leads her to the dance floor. Hudson is left alone at the table.

Hudson scouts, looking for someone she could lead to the dance floor. She notices Scott as he departs with the woman.

Shelly, Agnes, and Denise, all wearing bandanas, arrive at the dock. They huddle with Jamaican police officers, who point them in the direction of the resort.

Inside, Rude Buay and Mildred pass by the bar en route to a busy dance floor. Banks, full of man talk, cautions,

"Easy now, Rude Buay!"

Rude Buay smiles.

Banks resumes,

"Enjoy the music "Reggae Style." The bartender serves Banks another beer, and a Local joins Banks with "cheers."

Banks ask the Local:

"Are you participating in the festivities?"

The Local responds.

"Not this year, Banks."

Banks follows up.

"Burnt out?"

The Local replies,

"Drug lords are seeking refuge here. On top of that, cops get shot down like flies, and five government officials... Who wants to venture out and get shot?"

Banks looks at his beer and takes a calculated sip.

Banks encapsulates,

"It used to be Jamaica "One Love" until..."

Rude Buay and Mildred Simms return to the table. Banks' eyes are fixed on them, wishing it was him in pursuit of the Jamaican beauty, Mildred.

Banks turns to leave.

"So, tomorrow, we'll continue our manhunt?"

States, Rude Buay.

Banks returns to the bar.

Mildred addresses Rude Buay.
"Yep. You find Axel first, or I will."
The Waiter brings another round of drinks. Mildred removes the cherry from her drink and dangles it before Rude Buay's face. Finally, she puts it inside her mouth and chews the life out of it. Rude Buay feels like Mildred has thrown a ninety-mile-an-hour curveball.
Adjusting, he asks,
"How much does Banks know?"
Mildred, responds.
"His grey hair speaks for itself, Mr. Rude Buay."
Rude Buay remarks.
"You've called me that name twice tonight. Are we going to keep this on a business level?" To which she responds,
"All I can say is, 'what is to will be' Sir."
Rude Buay excuses himself from the table and moves into Banks' space. Mildred pursues. Hudson remains at the table, writing in her journal. She sees the three familiar women. Before she could respond in self-defense, they invaded her space offensively. Shelly whacks Hudson in the head with her automatic weapon. Hudson falls to the ground and struggles to get up. Shelly whacks her again. This time, she falls to the ground hard. Denise grabs her, blindfolds her, and escorts her through the back entrance.
BANG, BANG, BANG. GUNSHOTS.
People run for cover. Beer bottles from aroused locals are hurled in the direction of the bar, accompanied by

gunshots from the three women. Rude Buay and Scott, struck by beer bottles, hit the floor. Getting up, they give chase, trying to get an aim in through the dense crowd.

Agnes sticks a rag inside Agent Hudson's mouth, seals it with duct tape, and quickly binds her with rope. There's a massive crowd of people trying to get out. Agent Scott exits through the side doors.

Mildred Simms follows close behind. Banks notices an unclaimed lady's purse on Mildred's table. Next to it lies a napkin, drawn on it in red ink, a dragon. He yells, "Miss Simms, you forgot something." Mildred turns around and goes back to retrieve it. She notices the Dragon tattoo drawn on the napkin. Mildred reflects. She had seen the same signature worn by agent Scott earlier at the table.

Outside the resort, the three women rush Hudson aboard a speed boat. Rude Buay pursues on foot. He runs into two Jamaican police officers. Rude Buay pushes his way through, slightly brushing against one of the officers who loses his balance. Several Officers respond in retaliation.

Mildred rushes out and sedates Rude Buay. Meanwhile, the boat speeds off. Leaving Rude Buay along with white water waves at the vacant dock.

Agent Scott returns—Rude Buay notices. Not pleased about his absence during a manhunt of this magnitude, he addresses Scott.

"You missed it, huh? Did she French kiss you on the brain?" Agent Scott claims,

"Too many double-crossers."

Rude Buay responds,

"Welcome to the real WAR, Manhunt in the Caribbean"

20

INSIDE THE NEGRIL HOTEL, Rude Buay sits at a desk conducting a computer database search of names—his Pen Phone rings. The caller ID reveals Mendez's number.

Rude Buay takes the call.

"This is no good. Bascombe, what did you find out on Hudson?" remarks Mendez.

Rude Buay responds,

"Nothing so far."

Mendez replies,

"Rude Buay, it's clear that you failed to cover her." Rude Buay, getting straight to the point, responds. "Hold on! Are you accusing me of... Chief, this had to have been a..." Mendez questions,

"By whom?"

Rude Buay replies,

"I'm still gathering info. Possibly the three female fugitives."

Mendez responds,

"Are you trying to say that they escaped prison in less than twenty-four hours and are already raining on your parade?" Rude Buay states,

"They showed up in Jamaica. How did they know where to find her?"
Says Mendez,
"No idea! Bascombe, you've left me with only one choice... I'm going to have to bring you back to The U.S."
Rude Buay responds,
"Never! Why? So that the drug Lords feel that they've won? We're flirting with the possibility of having Hudson's body returned to us in a body bag. Never! I will never concede!"
Mendez continues to break him down. "You begged to have her and agent Scott join you. We don't want to have their bodies returned to us in caskets."
Rude Buay states,
"I need time...as well as resources. Plus, there are too many probabilities." Mendez reminds him.
"We don't have much of it."
Rude Buay, cogitates, then responds.
"48 hours?"
Mendez replies,
"When and if you get into my seat, you can run things your way, but until then, in this department, what I say goes. This case is going to be... reassigned. Rude Buay, you begged for this assignment. Plus, her son calls you Uncle Rude Buay. You're not even..."
Rude Buay senses not only the racist overtone but, for the first time, his boss called him by his local name.

Could his boss be in on this also? He ponders before responding. "Too many cooks spoil the broth."
Jose Mendez persisting,
"That's all you have: 47 hours 59.30 minutes."
Rude Buay retorts.
"I'll take you up on that mandate, but from here on in, I am going to run things my way. My playbook! This is my soil!"

21

INSIDE THE HOTEL ROOM, Rude Buay engages in pushups—his hotel phone rings. The thought occurs. Could this be his boss? He grabs it.

"Rude Buay, this is Alberto. I can tell you that you are not a good swimmer. Anyway, getting down to business, I have your partner. In exchange for her, I want you out of the Caribbean for good. For Good! In 24 hours, I'll have a jet waiting to fly you back to Miami. My peeps will contact you."

"How much?"

Asks Rude Buay.

Alberto responds,

"I don't need the cash. I want you out of Jamaica."

Rude Buay replies:

"This is the land of my birth. I will not give up this right to... I will fight in the hills, in the valleys, on the seas, in the air, underground. If I go down, I will go down fighting!"

Alberto responds.

"A very poor rendition of Winston Churchill..."

Rude Buay hangs up the phone and research documents on his computer. The name Alberto Gomez surfaces. He double-clicks on the profile. An error message comes up: INFORMATION NOT AVAILABLE. He inputs the name for a second time. The same result. Rude Buay picks up the phone and dials.

On Walter Banks' wall, there's a portrait of Banks and Chelo. The red phone, sitting on his desk, keeps ringing. Nobody's there. Rude Buay dials a different number.

"You've reached 876-322-7171. Leave a message after the beep."

He does not leave a message. On the beach, Banks lies on the sand. He's cuddled beside a hot babe, sharing a beach towel. Waves wash up against their feet.

Rude Buay dials in desperation. At the office of Tourism and Culture, Mildred Simms picks up the phone.

"This is Mildred Simms!"

"Mildred, this is Rude Buay. An assignment has been thrown at me. What do you know about...Alberto Gomez?"

Waiting for her response, he gets ready to write on a notepad.

Like magic, Mildred responds:

"Nothing. I've never heard of him. Banks should have more of the inside scoop on him."

Rude Buay asks,

"Where's he?"

Mildred licks her lips before responding.

"It's a sunny day. Try the beach. He likes playing Casanova. It's the Island in him,"

Rude Buay asks.

"Which beach?"

Mildred asks.

"It's 96 degrees in the shade, and the water stays warm all night."

Rude Buay informs her.

"I've got a big fish to deep fry. If you hear from Banks, tell him to call me ASAP."

Mildred replies,

"It's apparent that you will have a fish frying party before this whole thing washes out. Huh?

Rude Buay responds,

"Thanks. I need a 20 on Scott."

Mildred replies,

"To my knowledge, he's with that woman from the party. They both display similar tattoos."

Rude Buay cautions:

"No one gets my whereabouts except Mr. Banks.

Rude Buay hangs up.

Rude Buay's phone rings. He picks up.

"This is Bascombe".

Banks, the voice comes in…

"Rude Buay..."

Rude Buay answers enthusiastically:

"Walter Banks! The man of the hour. Banks, I know you're a beach bum, but I have something that might

interest you. How would you like to team up with me?"
Banks asks,
"Why?"
Rude Buay responds:
"I've got a big fish to fry. The agency is trying to hold me responsible...for the kidnapping of Heidi Hudson. All I have to go on is a name... Alberto Gomez." Banks asks with concern:
"How do I come in?"
Rude Buay answers:
"I need a guy who knows them inside out. I understand you've spent several years working underground in Bogota and an MP for the Jamaican government."
Banks replies,
"I let sleeping dogs lie."
Rude Buay states,
"I'll protect you exclusively."
Banks asks,
"What about your guys?"
Rude Buay replies.
"You know how shafted these guys are. I need someone who can deliver. Someone with a destiny and a passion and purpose to fulfill it.
Banks replies,
"I believe in priorities…"
Rude Buay interrupts:
"God, family, job..."

Banks interrupts,
"Country! You don't identify with us."
After a beat, Banks continues:
"It was Kennedy who said: Ask not what your country can do for you - ask what you can do for your country."
Rude Buay informs,
"So said your commissioner."
Rude Buay reflects, then continues,
"Except that he forgot that A man without vision shall perish."
Walter Banks has had enough. He responds.
"Rude Buay, I've been there and done that. You don't need your third-party tactics. How much?"
Rude Buay responds,
"Half a mil..."
Banks inquires,
"Who picks up the tab?"
Rude Buay assures,
"The PEPI account."
Says Banks,
"I'm in!"
Banks hangs up the phone and immediately surveys the coastline using his binoculars. He reaches into his pocket, retrieves his Pen Phone dials, and makes contact.
"Come in, Chelo."
Chelo responds,
"Come in, Banks."
Banks replies:

"Go ahead, Chelo. What you got?"
Chelo is always excited when he discovers a plot:
A blue ship operated by the dragon cartel dubbed *Tempest* dropped off a shipment last night in Mo Bay. It could be heading your way, pronto.
Banks responds,
"Thanks. I've got it on the radar as we speak. By the way, I need everything on Don Alberto Gomez."
Chelo is not sure.
"I don't know...Maybe..."
Walter Banks demands,
"Everything!"
Banks hangs up and dials Rude Buay.
"Rude Buay, this is Banks. A blue ship named "Tempest" has stepped onto our radar. Destination: Negril. Mildred will meet you onboard *Hairoun* at the Negril's Dock. The coast guard ship will be tailing you."
Rude Buay exuberantly,
"Good. Very good."
Rude Buay gets up from his chair, STRAPS a gun to his left leg, and summons agent Desmond Scott.

22

NEGRIL OVERLOOKS A VAST body of blue water with various ships nesting on it. White sand beaches, hilltop houses, and trees provide a paradisiacal backdrop. The sounds of horns and engines from boats on the go drown out the sound of waves washing up against the shoreline. The water reflects the rays from the sun.

Rude Buay scans the harbor through binoculars. He zooms in for clarity. He spots the "Tempest." But notices that its country of origin is missing.

Rude Buay adjusts the focus and notices cargo transferring from yacht to yacht.

Mildred's hair blows in the wind. She looks through her binoculars to catch that view... Rude Buay says to Scott.

"Do you see what I see?"

Scott responds.

"No. Not really."

Rude Buay indicates, "Straight ahead to the left."

Agent Scott fires up the engine and heads in that direction.

Their ship, *Hairoun,* picks up speed, heading toward the suspected ship. It drops anchor. Rude Buay and

Mildred climb aboard the Tempest. With weapons drawn, they proceed to amble closer.

There's a shadow. Rude Bauy yells with an aimed weapon.

"Freeze! DEA."

The sailor hastily releases the anchor chain and dives into the water. Three men wearing masks emerge on deck with guns drawn.

Rude Buay continues.

"Drop your weapons! Now!"

Ian Baynes emerges from the ship's hull, wearing an expensive blue business suit and dark sunglasses. His gun is drawn.

Ian yells.

"You're trespassing! Private property."

Ian is distracted by two Jamaican and one Cuban coast guard, who are cutting water and heading in that direction. Three

Jamaican Coast Guard officers and one Cuban aim towards the Tempest with a drawn semi-automatic. It's now a standoff. The Jamaican coast guard officers concentrate their objective on the masked men. Meanwhile, a Haitian Helicopter circles overhead. Rude Buay commands.

"Drop your weapons!"

They hesitate.

Rude Buay shoots. The bullet hits the "made over" Ian Baynes in the chest. He falls overboard.

Scott remarks,

"Maybe he'll listen next time."

Coast guard officers dive into the water and fish out Ian, who is still alive. They drag him aboard the Coast Guard boat. Blood is pumping out of the bullet hole in his chest.

Jamaican Police deal with him. Some place cuffs on the other three men: Michael Cox, Sebastian Perez, and Nigel Davis. With Banks in tow, rude Buay and Scott proceed into the ship's hull. Mildred guards the deck. They cautiously enter.

Rude Buay stops abruptly, listens, and then moves a few steps with ears cocked. He hears a squeaky sound. He draws up behind the door and opens it. The way looks clear, so he beckons Scott in his direction.

Scott ambles up close to him. Banks follows in tow. There's another door. They try to open it, but it's locked. The sign on it says: ENGINE ROOM DOOR MUST BE KEPT CLOSED.

Rude Buay glances back at Scott. Moves to the other side of the door and begins to grasp the handle. He checks his gun, grabs the doorknob, swings it open, and charges in with Agent Scott and Banks on his tail. They scan the room hastily.

Rude Buay notices some canvas draped like a tablecloth. He grabs it in disgust, throwing it on the floor. There's a lid. Rude Buay lifts it off.

INSIDE: Stacks of twenty-dollar bills in Jamaican currency, binoculars, hammocks, blankets, survival

kits, grenades, and a vast gun collection. Another lid gets Rude Buay's attention.
Inside: Dalton Castello's body, bound with ropes, wounds to the head; he's still breathing. So, they carry him to the deck to be transported to the hospital.

23

THE AMBULANCE PULLS UP in front of the E.R. entrance at Port Antonio Hospital. Medics wheel out a gurney with Castello on it. Simultaneously, a Taxi pulls up to the gate. Out steps Tamara Ross. She's dressed in blue scrubs, a stethoscope hanging from her neck. She hustles through the entrance to the E.R. and assists in treating Mr. Castello.

A pot of coffee is brewing in the kitchen at Banks' house. Steelpan music is playing in the background. Rude Buay is admiring the view of the Port from the window. Banks return with a massive roll of blueprints.

Rude Buay, looking out the window, exclaims,

"Great View!"

Banks replies,

"Like a basin decorated with toy boats."

Rude Buay returns to the dining room table, now cluttered with blueprints. Rude Buay follows up on his comment.

"Yep! Do you sail, Banks?"

Banks, enjoying the conversation:

"I love yachts."

Rude Buay feeds his ego.

"You must have captured some great pictures from this location."
Banks responds,
"Oh yes, but most of my pictures come from Bogota'."
Rude Buay asks,
"Great place?"
Banks, replies,
"I spent five years there, working undercover for the U.N."
"What was it like?"
Asks Rude Buay with concern.
Banks replies,
"Scary. One moment, you're alive knowing that the next moment, you could be eaten by vultures flying overhead."
Banks shows him a stack of pictures. One shows a man wearing a dragon tattoo—Rude Buay clues in.
Banks continues.
"The night they caught Chelo taking pictures of their operation, they captured him and decided to hang him."
Rude Bauy likes what he hears, and he thinks it's invaluable to build such a bridge with his new sidekick, so he asks.
"Really?"
Banks reminisces:
"I rode into their camp strapped to the truck's chassis driven by the guy commissioned to hang Chelo. When the truck stopped, I untied myself and waited

underneath. The Driver stepped out; I grabbed him by his feet, took him down, crawled out, grabbed his rifle, wasted him, put his clothes on, drove Chelo to the gallows site, and shot the men waiting for "the Kill." Chelo and I have been buddies ever since."

Rude Buay wants more,

"How did you learn about their plan?"

Banks, full of wisdom, scratches his head, and responds,

"When your ear's to the ground, you learn many things, my friend."

Rude Buay, feeling as if he had just received some things to consider, responds, "Tell me about Alberto Gomez."

Walter Banks is opening up.

"Man's like a sealed case. He's not your average Czar."

Rude Buay inquires,

"Who funds him?"

Banks responds,

"Your agency hasn't...?"

Banks phone rings. He answers. It is Chelo.

Chelo's voice is like music to his ears. He buoys up.

"Banks, what I know you already know..."

Rude Buay eavesdrops.

Banks replies,

"Thanks!"

Walter Banks realizes that there is nothing new about Alberto. So, he continues informing Rude Buay. "They claim that he has billions in Swiss accounts, yet nothing has turned up in his name. He posted record profits in the last two years. He controls most of the traffic up and down the coast. Axle James' former boss, he's married to Denise Gomez, whom you busted last year."

Rude Buay reminisces.

"No wonder she's broken out of prison so easily."

Walter Banks ponders, then continues questioning.

"Where does he reside?"

Banks replies,

"Every agent who has met with him in person is already dead or on his waiting list. His home address is never published. No landline telephone. His ships are not registered. He owes the IRS over $2.8 Million in back taxes. They can't bring him down. The man's untouchable."

Rude Buay asks:

"How do we get him?"

"Contact his wife Denise; hold her as ransom. We could start there,"

Banks says.

Rude Buay lets that sink in, and questions.

"Could she be our doorway to Heidi Hudson?"

Banks answers,

"They work independently at times, but they could have teamed up on a kidnapping of this magnitude."

Rude Buay's cup is full.

"Where there's a will, there's a way."

Banks states sarcastically,

"I thought that your Mom practiced..."

Rude Buay, endowed with limited knowledge of the craft, replies,

"She never taught me those tricks. She said it would make me mentally lazy. Neither did she leave a catalog in her WILL."

Banks, continuing unraveling like a runaway train, declares. "When the Philistines wanted to take out Samson, they went through Delilah."

Rude Buay ponders that gesture, then picks up the pen phone and dials immediately afterward. He receives a busy tone. Meanwhile, Banks phone rings in the other room. Banks leaves to get it. Rude Buay redials.

Rude Buay reaches Mildred.

"Mildred, I am having a challenge getting through to the commissioner. He's not..."

Mildred replies,

"It's 2:00 a.m. Rude Buay, I'll get him for you."

24

THE PHONE RINGS inside the Commissioner's bedroom. Commissioner Richard Baptiste and his wife, Christine, are asleep in bed. He snores like a freight train. She rolls over, pokes him in the ribs, then grabs the phone. Mildred echoes.

"Richard! Richard!" Christine responds.

"He's..."

Christine jealously looks at the clock and continues.

"Mildred, he's fast asleep after a steamy night. I'll tell him that you called. Is there a message?"

Mildred responds,

"Police business."

Christine is about to hang up.

Richard rolls over and tugs the receiver from her.

She removes the handcuffs from the bedhead, opens the nightstand's drawer, deposits them, and meanders towards the bathroom - semi-clothed.

Richard is occupied with the phone call.

"Hello?"

Mildred responds,

"Commissioner, I have Rude Buay on a 3-way call."

Looking at the clock, the Commissioner senses serious business by this 2:00 a.m. call.

Rude Buay informs,
"Commissioner, Rude Buay here. I didn't mean to wake you."
The Commissioner, still half asleep,
"Rude Buay, didn't you get them?..."
Rude Buay informs,
"If we, meaning U.S. Government personnel and equipment, were to guard the shores tomorrow, would you have enough manpower to piggyback our effort?"
Commissioner responds,
"That's a somewhat hypothetical question."
The Commissioner composes himself and continues.
"Why do we need to guard the shores?"
Rude Buay, wishing the Commissioner gets his concept, replies,
"It's a possible escape route that Axel James and his men could use. If he rejoins Alberto, we could have more trouble on our hands. Agent Hudson could be history."
To which the aggravated Commissioner responds,
"Do you have any idea as to how much it's going to cost the government of Jamaica to conduct such a feat? On top of that, our police force is already working overtime."
Rude Buay goes for the jugular:
"Let me put it like this...for a few extra dollars, you can either help save your country from the tyranny of the Axel James' of the world or become pawns under the weight of their oppressive cartels?"

Commissioner Baptiste responds,
"We're already over budget for you, Mr. Rude Buay. That Cuban helicopter drinks up a lot of fuel."
Christine returns all dolled up and crawls in bed.
The Commissioner continues,
"Plus, that's not the way we do things here."
"This is your baby. You couldn't pay me if you wanted to," Replies Rude Buay.
Baptiste looks over at Christine and says.
"I'll have a word in at sunrise," and he hangs up the phone, chased.

25

RUDE BUAY LOOKS across at Banks, who is head-bopping frequently. Rude Buay picks up his phone and dials.

At the DEA office in Miami, Mendez walks out towards the door, attaché in hand. His phone rings. He returns to his desk and picks up. Looking at the caller ID, he sees Agent Bascombe's number displayed.

"This better be good," he says under his breath.

Picking up the call, Rude Buay addresses him.

"Mendez! Bascombe here."

Mendez is expecting great news:

"Lay it on, Rude Buay!"

Rude Buay responds.

"What are the chances of rescinding the offer?"

Mendez asks:

"Which offer?"

Rude Buay reflects and feels like he's now in a vice. He wants to save his country, but trust is waning in these critical moments. His existing team of U.S. agents is down to the rather untrustworthy Desmond Scott. His sidekick, Banks, wakes up and pours two cups of coffee. He hands one to Rude Buay. Rude Buay responds to Mendez's question.

"The one that you've made with the Commissioner."
Mendez looks at his Rolex. Admiring it states:
"Why? What's the hurry, Rude Buay?"
Rude Buay responds,
"Everyone seems to be in on this, including the man who brokered the deal with you,"
Mendez replies.
"Are you saying that you don't trust your countrymen? Is the doctor in on this also?"
Rude Buay would rather not discuss his love interest.
"You know as well as I do in a war like this... no one can be trusted. Not even..."
That went over Mendez's head, focused on his attaché loaded with cash.
Mendez asks,
"Yeah, but how can you help me help you."
Rude Bauy advises:
"Let's take out the Commissioner. Run this operation as we see fit. We can bring in the tanks and the whole infantry. Then it becomes our war and not theirs."
Mendez, liking where this conversation is going, says,
"You're thinking on your feet. Go on."
Rude Buay follows up:
"Pressure these guys to come out of hiding."
Mendez asks:
"What's the payoff?"
Rude Buay is deep in thought. Mendez senses this. He makes his chess move and continues.
"Yes, Rude Buay, the payoff? We're in it...to win it."

Mendez aborts that call and dials. He talks into the phone.

"Commissioner, this is Jose Mendez. I must let you know that I will need a substantial increase or pull my agents out within twenty-four hours..."

Baptiste responds.

"Wait a minute..."

Mendez reminds him of this fact:

"Rude Buay works for us. I repeat ... Twenty-four hours!"

He hangs up.

It's sunrise outside the Commissioner's home, but Richard Baptiste's not happy. He dials Rude Buay.

"Mr. Rude Buay!"

He answers,

"Rude Buay here."

Baptiste, knowing that he can't win this without Rude Buay, replies,

"I'm here for you."

Rude Buay, feeling some local support, says.

"Good deal, Commissioner. If Axel James tries to leave tomorrow, he must get through reinforced surveillance." Christine strides in – make-up and hair in place. The commissioner notices her enhanced sensuality. Baptiste hangs up the call and chases Christine around the room.

26

BANKS, REFRESHED BY THAT CUP of coffee, paces back and forth in the kitchen. The sunlight beams through the glass window. Horns resonate from ships leaving and entering the harbor. Banks discontinues his ambulation and joins Rude Buay at the table, uttering.

"You remember the guy you shot in the chest during the arrest, search, and seizure in Negril?" "Yes. What about him?"

"Sources close to the Axel team claim that he was the driver involved in the kidnapping of those government officials. He changed his identity after fleeing from Jamaica with Axel. His real name is Ian Baynes." Banks informs Rude Buay.

"Information left out at the briefing; don't you think."

"Don't think it was done purposefully. Late Breaking News, that's all."

Rude Buay reflects on growing up as a kid, always late for school. He says to Banks,

"Get me the number for a taxi."

"Where to?"

Banks asks.

Rude Buay, in an exasperated huff,

"Port Antonio Hospital." Rude Buay's Pen Phone rings. He picks up. It's Agent Scott who asks:
"Any leads?"
Rude Buay, looking for possible reform in his fellow agent, advises,
"Meet me at the Hospital. I need someone I can trust!" Banks says.
"Call Sam's Taxi!"
Rude Buay dials.
"Will be here in five minutes," says Rude Buay as he departs.
Rude Buay sees a display of Rastafarian hats with wigs attached inside an illuminated Vendor's Booth. He purchases one. The Vendor puts the hat in a shopping bag. A taxi pulls up. He gets in with the bag in hand.
The Taxi runs into a roadblock. Several vehicles are held at bay. Boisterous and angry locals protest in a thick Patois dialect. Drug dealers conduct business amongst barricades as if it is highly legal to do what they do. One man, no doubt, fed up with the disregard for the upkeeping of the law, holds up a sign: I AM RUNNING FOR MP.
Rude Buay, sensing trouble, retrieves the hat and puts it on his head. He sticks his finger in his throat and pukes up outside through the window. That outside door gets plastered… Then he lays flat, face down on the rear seat. An MP approaches the taxi and asks the driver, "Where are you heading to?"
He responds in Patois,

"Port Antonio Hospital. Sick patient. The man is sick bad and could be poisoned."

Covering his nostrils, the MP signals a policeman to let the cab proceed.

The taxi takes off speedily.

Later, the taxi pulls up outside Port Antonio Hospital. Rude Buay removes the hat. Before exiting, he hands the Driver a U.S. $100.00 Bill. The Driver smiles. Rude Buay exits and enters the hospital. Baynes is wheeled out of E.R. to a room nearby, accompanied by Tamara. Rude Buay notices her but remains unaffected. Always professional, she is focused on her patients. Agent Scott, just arriving, observes from close by.

Rude Buay moves into Dr. Tamara Ross' space.

"Hello, Doctor."

She glances up and quickly returns towards the E.R.

Rude Buay, continuing,

"When he wakes up, I need a word with him."

Tamara, very curt,

"When he awakes, Rude Buay."

Agent Scott is bewildered. Did they introduce themselves?

Tamara continues:

"In my professional opinion, he might not wake up, period. The bullet to his chest came out through his rib cage, barely missing his aorta. It's also possible that he could have suffered considerable memory loss due to a decrease in the blood supply flowing to his brain."

"Memory loss. Sounds like someone else I know," asserts Rude Buay.

Scott eyes Rude Buay, surprised.

Tamara continues her work. Meanwhile, in the hospital room, Ian Baynes holds his breath and assumes the dead fetal position. Scott, oblivious, draws closer inside the huddle with Dr. Ross and Rude Buay.

"So, you don't think there's any chance..."

He asks.

A nurse walks out and echoes.

"TAMARA, TAMARA, the patient just died."

"Sorry."

Tamara says to the agents and departs. Rude Buay steals a backside view of the doctor. He goes in one direction while Scott meanders in the opposite direction.

27

LATER, RUDE BUAY, driving through the streets of Kingston in a Hummer, reaches the glove compartment for his pen phone and calls Mildred. "Miss Simms, this is Rude Buay. Ian Baynes died while we were at the hospital."

"Did you get any info from him?" she asks.

"Not a thing. I know he worked with Axel back in Jamaica. He shot at me during the shootout at the Villa. Also, he was shot during the sting in MO Bay."

He pauses, then continues.

"Plus, my source claims that he could have been in the van when the government officials were kidnapped."

"Who's your source?"

"Why didn't you guys provide us with that information?"

"If you did not receive it through the... commissioner's office, it could be a setup in an attempt to create a decoy."

"If I'm going to continue on this manhunt, I need an entire profile on Baynes. Who he knew, who knew him, where he spent time together, everything!" Rude Buay states bluntly.

"I'll see what I can do. It's up to the commissioner."

"Is he...?" asks Rude Buay.

Mildred responds:

"You're walking a thin line, Rude Buay." An African American man wearing scrubs and a mask prowls inside the hospital. He is carrying a doctor's bag. He opens Ian Bayne's room door, deposits the bag, and disappears.

Ian Baynes turns in bed and looks around the room. He retrieves his iPhone from under the mattress. Then he pulls out the top drawer. Baynes slips on a doctor's uniform and a stethoscope around his neck. He throws his iPhone into the doctor's bag. He picks up a syringe and dispenser off the night table and injects himself in the arm with morphine. He disposes the utensils in the trash and sneaks out of the hospital. A Taxicab pulls up. Ian gets in. The Taxi drives off. Meanwhile, Agent Scott and Rude Buay are reviewing maps. Rude Buay looks preoccupied but tries to mask it.

Scott asks.

"What's going on?"

"Those three Crooks arrested during the Cold hit on the Tempest. I'll bet they've got the info we need to wrap up this manhunt."

Agent Scott responds.

"I don't think you'll get it out of them."

"Why not?"

"Fear. Fear that they and their family are getting killed and fed to vultures."

"What if I offered them protection and the chance to live."
"They know that there's nowhere for them to hide."
Rude Buay measures Scott and states:
"I'll have to do this solo."
"Why?"
"I've got a hunch, my friend,"
Scott asks, feeling like he and Rude Buay are now full cohorts.
"What's that?"
"Strike while the iron's hot. Find a Stool pigeon."
Rude Buay turns to leave.
Scott gets his attention:
"I thought we were in this together."
"Time will either promote or expose..."
Responds Rude Buay as he picks up his gun and exits.

28

AFTER ENTERING THE KINGSTON Police Barracks, Rude Buay hands over a document to the Desk Police. He reviews it, gets on the phone, and announces,
"Bring out Michael Cox!"
Rude Buay comes to an office with a small desk, a computer, filing cabinets, and chairs. Cox is seated on a chair in the middle of the office.
Rude Buay surrounds him, the Police look on.
Rude Buay proceeds.
"Michael, my name's Rude Buay. I'm going to ask you a couple of questions. I ask that you be truthful in your answers."
Michael rubs his nose, unsure what Rude Buay wants.
Rude Buay continues,
"Your name's Michael Cox. Born in Bogota' Colombia?"
"I don't speak English."
"Como se llama?"
"Sorry, I don't understand."
Rude Buay, in disbelief, removes his gun, pointing it towards Michael's head.
"Yesterday, when you were arrested on the *Tempest* in Negril, what were you doing on that yacht?"

"Kill me, and I will not tell you anything!"
responds Michael Cox.
Rude Buay looks over at the desk police.
Bring in Sebastian Perez.
The police remove Michael from the room and return with Sebastian speedily.
Rude Buay wasting no time -
"Sebastian, what's your affiliation with Michael Cox?"
Sebastian replies,
"Who is that?"
Rude Buay punches him hard in the face. He bleeds.
Sebastian whimpers,
"He's my boss."
"How long has this boss-employee relationship been in force?"
"I don't remember."
"Answer the question. How long?" demands Rude Buay.
"As long as I could remember!"
"And how long ago was that?"
Sebastian nervously responds,
"I don't remember."
Rude Buay gives his last words a digestive interlude.
"What were you doing on the *Tempest* on the day of your arrest?"
Sebastian is tight-lipped.
"I..."
Rude Buay punches him again.
Rude Buay restates,

"What were you doing on the *Tempest* on the day of your arrest?"

"Sorry, I see nada, hear nada."

Rude Buay says to the desk police,

"Bring in Nigel Davis."

The Police escort Sebastian out of the room and reenter with Nigel.

Rude Buay shows Nigel a picture of Ian Baynes and asks Nigel,

"Do you know this man?"

"No. It's my first time seeing him."

"Do you know who Ian Baynes is?"

"I've never heard of him."

"What's your affiliation with Ricardo?"

Nigel responds,

"I don't know him."

Rude Buay is pissed. He grabs Nigel by the collar and throws him up against the wall.

Nigel continues,

"Sorry."

Rude Buay punches him mercilessly. Nigel spits out blood.

"He's my boss."

"For how long?"

"I forgot."

Rude Buay's cup of avoidance is filling up.

"How long...?"

"Sorry, I don't remember."

"You've seen some gallows before?"

"Yes."

Responds Nigel,

"Could you see yourself hanging from one?" Rude Buay gaits.

"How long since you've been an employee of this...?"

"Long time!"

Replies Nigel,

"And how long ago was that?"

"Since..."

"Since when?"

Nigel deliberates.

"Since he bought the yacht."

"Which yacht?" Rude Buay pressurizes.

"I'm not a snitch."

Rude Buay, sensing a victory, moves in closer to Nigel-

"Which yacht...?"

"The blue one."

Responds Nigel.

"Was it the "Tempest"?"

Nigel, showing signs of fatigue, says,

"I'm fatigued."

Rude Buay not giving in -

"Was it the...Tempest?"

Nigel responds,

"He had two yachts. Yes."

The Police handed a passport to Rude Buay. He reviews it.

Rude Buay asks, "Nigel, is this your passport?" Nigel gives it a good look.

"I think so." Rude Buay discloses.

"This Colombian passport was recovered at your home. It has not been stamped by Jamaican immigration. How and where did you enter the country?"

Nigel hesitates.

Rude Buay punches him hard in the already bloodied right eye. Nigel's vision becomes blurred.

"We flew by airplane at Runaway Bay and then took a bus."

Nigel pisses on himself. Urine trickles down his trousers.

"You never got this from me, okay."

"Who else was on the flight?"

"I don't remember."

"Think, recall!"

Nigel ruminates and then comes clean.

"Rebecca Herrera."

Rude Buay inquires,

"Ricardo's wife?"

"Yes, sir," retorts Nigel.

"Where did she get off the bus?"

Nigel reluctantly answers,

"Ocho Rios."

Rude Bauy meanders away from Nigel. He mulls over and then asks pointedly.

"What else was on the plane?"

"Fifty kilos,"
Replies Nigel.
Rude Buay returns the passport to the Police and exits like a man on a mission.

29

THE BLACK HUMMER pulls up in Ocho Rios. Rude Buay arms himself, strolls out, and hastens outside to a large wooden house. With the use of his gun, he blows out the lock and kicks the door in.

Ricardo, dressed in pajamas, emerges from the bedroom with a gun. He shoots at Rude Buay. The bullet misses him. Rude Buay gets a few shots off at Ricardo, who jumps through a window in an escape. Rude Buay takes off on foot in pursuit.

The Foot RACE continues through a dark alley. Coming around a bend, Ricardo cuts through the bushes.

Rude Buay approaches the bend; there's no Ricardo insight. So, Rude Buay proceeds with caution.

Ricardo sees Rude Buay go by and shoots desperately at him. Rude Buay dodges the bullet and lies face down, then rolls over on his back, shooting randomly through the bushes. A bullet hits a wall close to Ricardo. The sound deafens him. He grabs his ears with both hands. His gun falls to the floor. Ricardo recollects himself. Scrambling for his gun, he locates it, picks it up, off-balanced, and discharges several rounds at the now-standing Rude Buay. He misses his target.

Rude Buay returns fire, hitting Ricardo in the chest and uprooting several plants. Rude Buay gets a close-up look at Ricardo's blood-saturated corpse. He returns to Ricardo's house, opens his closet, and rummages. He discovers and confiscates twenty kilos of coke. Rude Buay texts Scott via pen phone, notifying him of Ricardo's massacre.

A Taxi pulls up outside a mansion overlooking Montego Bay Airport. Ian Baynes ambles out. He proceeds inside the mansion.

Axel opens the door and embraces Ian.

Ian hands over the bag. Axel opens it, removes items, and lays them on the table. The living room is packed with Dragon X cocaine.

"Are you ready for battle?"

Asks Axel.

"I've got enough morphine in me."

Observing the cargo, Ian replies,

"Where's Ricardo?"

"At his house. We'll sail tomorrow," Responds Axel.

At Banks' partially lit house in Port Antonio, a man dressed up as a black man steps out of a car. He surveys. Then, he moves closer to the house. He removes a gun from under his coat and gets a perfect aim at Banks, who reads blueprints at his desk. Maps and highlighters clutter the table where he sits. Banks' phone rings. He moves away from his desk and picks

up the phone on the wall. Vehicles drive by. They cast beams of light onto the house.
The Man crouches and lies on the stomach.
Banks returns to his desk.
The Man gets up and recaptures his aim.
He discharges several rounds through the window. Banks ducks too late and gets shot in his left arm. All he sees of the intruder is his disappearing shadow. The man rushes back to his car and disappears. Banks rolls over onto his uninjured side in pain. Later, Ian Baynes and Axel James meet with Banks' failed assassin. He's still masked, however. Axel hands over an attaché. He opens it and counts the money. Nods. Departs.
Rude Buay's driving back to the hotel. His cell phone beeps. He tunes in and reads this congratulatory text message from agent Scott.
"Glad you got him before I did. Cause I had a bullet in my gun for him." D.S.
Rude Buay savors the moment and scans the radio for a great music station. He catches the fading of The Harder They Come by Jimmy Cliff. The RADIO ANNOUNCER breaks in:
"The weather outlook for Port Antonio calls for clear skies, brisk winds of 10-25 knots, with a high of 86 degrees and a visibility of 30 miles. The high tide is at noon. News just coming into our newsroom: Jeff Cyrus, aka "Walter Banks", a former Minister of Parliament and broadcaster here at WE FM, was shot at his home in Port Antonio earlier this morning. Banks

was rushed to Port Antonio Hospital. He remains in critical condition."

Rude Buay calls Banks from his cell phone and gets a busy signal. He turns the steering wheel to the left and U-Turns, burning rubber. The Hummer merges with the flow of the early morning traffic. It later arrives outside Port Antonio Hospital. Rude Buay hurries inside.

He sees a sign reading: NO VISITORS ALLOWED. Rude Buay ignores the sign and approaches Banks' bedside. Banks' eyes are closed, tubes attached to his arm.

Tamara enters.

Their eyes meet.

She eyes the sign.

Rude Buay forces a smile.

He leaves.

She smiles.

30

AT BANKS' HOUSE, Jamaican police are busily collecting evidence. Blood is splattered everywhere. Rude Buay approaches and engages a plainclothes Officer. The Officer points to a shattered glass window.
"How did they get inside?" asks Rude Buay.
"Any leads?"
"No one claimed responsibility,"
Answers the Jamaican Police.
"If anything turns up, give me a call,"
Says Rude Buay, who gives the officer a business card and heads back to his Hummer.
"Where are you, partner? You heard the news?"
Rude Buay answers his Pen Phone.
Scott asks.
"Yes, looking for answers,"
Rude Buay responds as he contemplates.
"I'll be trying my luck tonight at the dock. Feel like catching a few Jacks?"
Agent Scott responds.
"I'm in the area. I'll meet you there."
Rude Buay arrives outside Agent Scott's hotel room. He knocks on the door; no one answers. He breaks in using the screwdriver part of his Pen Phone. Rude Buay rummages through the room and discovers an

attaché. He opens it. There's an African American Man's mask underneath and stacks of Jamaican dollars. Rude Buay takes possession of the attaché. Soon after, Rude Buay leisurely leaned up against an iron rail at the Negril Dock, viewing the coastline through binoculars. A Taxicab pulls up. Agent Scott gets out and steps into Rude Buay's space. Scott extends a hand. Rude Buay accepts. They shake as good buddies do. Scott observantly asks,
"No fishing gear?"
Rude Buay answers, "The bait shop has plenty available."
Scott, sensing an intensity in his voice, asks.
"Any new information on our manhunt?"
"Very little since Banks' accident,"
Replies Rude Buay.
Scott, sarcastically,
"Yep. He helped us out a lot."
A small ship sails by in the distance. Rude Buay reaches for binoculars and surveys.
Rude Buay remarks,
"Somebody is trying to double-cross us, Scott,"
Scott responds.
"Really?"
"Yep,"
replies Rude Buay.
"But why? We're here to clean up the mess."
"You think it could be Mildred?"
Rude Buay asks.

"I thought she was on our team,"
remarks agent Scott.
"Everyone seems to be until... "
Scott interrupts.
"They say you can never trust a woman."
Rude Buay ruminates.
"Not even Delilah."
Rude Buay resumes.
"You wouldn't sell out... would you?" Scott, without hesitating, responds. "You've known me since the first day of training. I wouldn't sell out on you or the administration." Rude Buay punches him hard in the face. Scott loses his balance.
"Well, you just did, partner,"
reminds Rude Buay.
Agent Scott struggles to get up and does. He successfully lands a punch into Rude Buay's' stomach.
Scott replies,
"You have no proof, Rude Buay."
Rude Buay gasped for air. Coughs and spits out blood.
Scott comes at Rude Buay with a left hook and misses.
"Proof? You've been gone for most of the time. Since that shootout at the Villa, your time card has missed much ink. Your tattoo is the signature of the Dragon Drug Cartel. I've got more." Rude Buay punches him in the face.
Scott retaliates.
"You are not my boss. He's..."
"The Cartel?"

Asks Rude Buay. Rude Buay hits him hard with a right uppercut. Then a left jab. Scott falls to the wooded dock thunderously. The attaché now lays flat on the pier.
Agent Scott looks at the case suspiciously, then at Rude Buay. Rude Buay kicks attaché into Agent Scott's space.
"Open it, Scott!"
Commands Rude Buay. Scott hesitates. Rude Buay reaches for his gun and resumes.
"That's all they paid you to be a rat?"
Rude Buay throws a left uppercut at Scott and misses. With a resentful look to that name, Scott comes at Rude Buay swinging the attaché. Rude Buay ducks, and the attaché tumbles to the ground behind him. On impact, it opens up, displaying the mask and stacks of Jamaican currency. Scott gets that final look at the contents as Rude Buay shoots him in the chest.
Scott falls to the ground and kicks several times to his death. Rude Buay picks up the attaché, closes it, and heads towards his Hummer.
On his way there, a car approaches, creating a roadblock. Ian Baynes jumps out.
"Put the attaché' down nice and slow and drop your weapon, Rude Buay."
"How convenient. I could not have planned this," states Rude Buay.
Ian releases the safety on his gun.
"You've overstayed your welcome, Agent Bascombe.
"Says who?"

"Alberto,"
Replies Ian.
Rude Buay hesitates. Ian shoots at him. Rude Buay ducks to the ground. Lying flat on his back, he fires and shoots Ian in the groin. Ian, in pain, tries to get up. Another car pulls up. Axel jumps out from that vehicle and corners Rude Buay.
"Drop your gun and hand over the attaché! Who's paying you to be a pain in my ass, Rude Buay? The U.S. Government? I know that the government of Jamaica cannot afford to,"
States Axel.
"Why? Because you put the brakes on their economy for your benefit and continue to kill innocent kids with contaminated Cocaine?"
Axel releases the safety on the gun. Rude Buay proceeds to comply.
Ian, regaining his composure, demands,
"Your gun, Rude Buay."
Rude Buay drops the attaché and spits out blood onto it. He aims the gun at Axel's head. His gun's jammed. Axel James whacks Rude Buay in the face with his rifle. Rude Buay falls over, then staggeringly gets up. Axel James, not trusting him, asks,
"Who's picking up the tab?"
Rude Buay refuses to enlighten. Axel hits him again. This time, he falls over, thundering to the ground. He remains there. Axel removes a rag from his back pocket and sticks it inside Rude Buay's' mouth. He removes

Rude Buay's shirt and ties his hand behind his back with it.

Axel picks up the attaché' and Rude Buay's gun. He opens the rear door and throws them inside the car. He returns with some rope, which he uses to tie up Rude Buay. First, he ties the rope in his mouth, like a bit in a horse's mouth, and then he ties his hands and feet. He drags Rude Buay to the back of the car and throws him in the trunk. He closes it and gets ready to drive off.

Ian heads to his car. Axel yells out,

"Join me for the Kill!"

Ian accelerates towards his car and opens the rear door. A white car speedily approaches a few blocks away, pending a head-on collision with roadblocks. The car stops. Banks gets out with his bandaged left arm and removes the roadblock. He gets back in and drives away. Further up the street, he encounters the same scenario. This time, he drives through, clearing the obstacle. The car spins around with him this time, and he almost loses control of it. He continues driving, avoiding all traffic signs. Pedestrians dash out of the car's way.

Ian finally locates his bag of weed and then retrieves a Uzi from the rear seat of his car and jumps in the front passenger seat.

Walter Banks's car pulls up at the dock.

Walter Banks jumps out. He's just able to get a few rounds off at Axel's disappearing car. He gets back inside his vehicle and engages in a chase, unable to match the speed of Axel's automobile.

31

A HUMMER PULLS UP outside the Kingston Police Barracks. Mildred jumps out and scurries inside the building. A Jamaican Police Officer pushes his coffee aside and hands Mildred an envelope marked fingerprints report. Mildred enthusiastically breaks the seal and examines the contents.
She says, "Thanks!" and leaves in a hurry.
The informed officer, with his eyes stuck on her, yells.
"Aren't you going to need some backup?" "Thanks, but I've got it under control from here on in." She darts outside.
Mildred meets the Commissioner coming in, and she hands him the folder. He opens it and reviews the fingerprint report. He cautions.
"You know as well as I know now that we can't trust Agent Scott."
"I assure you I'll get to the bottom of it."
She promises.
Richard Baptiste, appreciative of her commitment, declares,
"My job is on the line, Miss Simms! " Mildred picks up the folder and exits.

Mildred jumps inside the black Hummer and drives away.

Banks, previously noticing Rude Buay's car at the dock, maintains a suspicion that Rude Buay is inside that getaway car and continues in pursuit. He reaches into his breast pocket and pulls out his Pen Phone. He radios.

"Rude Buay, come in. This is Banks."

There's no answer.

He continues,

"Rude Buay, where the hell are you? We've discovered the Snitch."

Still no answer.

Banks aborts that call and dials Mildred's number. Inside the hummer, Mildred picks up. She knows it's Banks.

"Mr. Banks, give me the good news!"

"News? The bad, the good or the ugly? The bad: Agent Scott's body rests at the dock. The Ugly: My car is in shambles after going through two separate roadblocks. The good thing is that I am still looking for him after having a shootout with Axel and Ian. Rude Bauy's vehicle was there, but he wasn't there. I have a strong hunch that they took him captive."

Mildred asks. "Or where else can he be?" Banks replies.

"With the doctor."

Mildred is peeved.

"That's impossible." She declares.

Banks, mockingly,
"I'll bet you..."
Mildred responds.
"Did you call him on his pen phone?"
Banks states,
"No response."
"Let me call you back if you hear from him before I do. Please ask him to call me,"
demands Mildred.
Mildred aborts the call and dials again. She is more peeved. She gets no answer and goes on a tirade.
"Rude Buay, you need to pick it up...You're a ... a disgrace to this country...the U.S. Government, the Deceiving Evil Administration. If this manhunt goes sour, your ass will rot in a Jamaican prison. Pick up or else...You flake."
Mildred stops outside a coffee shop. She gets out and goes inside.

MOMENTS LATER: Mildred sits at a table sipping coffee. Her Contractor walks in. He's dressed in a Jamaican police uniform. She motions him to a seat at her table. Mildred surveys and waits for privacy, then hands him an attaché. He opens it. It's loaded with stacks of E.C. Bills. He closes it. Mildred eyes her Contractor as he leaves and commands.
"Finish her!"
Her Contractor takes off with it in a hurry. At the Port Antonio Hospital, A tall Jamaican police officer

parades the corridor. Dr. Tamara Ross, dressed in blue scrubs, delivers a chart to the Nurse.

"Give this medication to Mr. Castello in an hour. No visitors are allowed,"

The doctor admonishes.

The Nurse asks.

"That Baynes guy didn't wind up at the Morgue, huh? Could this be Voodoo?"

Tamara informs her that:

"The Jamaican police are conducting their independent investigation."

She smiles deceitfully as Dr. Ross exits.

Crickets creak as Tamara sits on the grass beside the old breadfruit tree. Burning candles form a periphery around her. She holds up pictures of Mr. Castello towards the heavens. With her eyes closed, she meditates.

The Contractor, disguised as a Jamaican Police Officer, arrives. He surveys the area. There's no sign of Tamara, so he departs.

Back at the hospital, the Nurse is on the phone with Axel. She informs him.

"The doctor has just left for the Botanical Gardens."

Axel is ruffled. He can't stand the thought of the doctor escaping. He yells at the Nurse.

"Find her and finish her!"

32

WITH NO SPACE TO MOVE around in the car's trunk, Rude Buay uncomfortably tosses and turns, trying to break himself free from the ropes.

Tamara instantly receives an epiphany of her purpose in Rude Buay's life. She expediently blows out the candles and gets into her black BMW, speeding away. An Unmarked sedan pulls up. The contractor steps out. He surveys for the second time. He returns to his car and drives away. A White van appears. The Nurse exits, gun in hand. She notices the candle's residue. Upset, she KICKS them over, returns to the white van, and makes a swift U-Turn.

Tamara glances in her rearview mirror as she senses being tailed. She is, so she speeds up.

The Sedan with the contractor tailgates ferociously. She nervously speeds up as panic sets in deeper and deeper.

The white Van turns a corner. It proceeds illegally in the opposite direction at high speed, focusing on a head-on collision. The Sedan is still in pursuit of the Tamara. Her BMW veers left speedily. The Van crashes head-on with the sedan, killing the Contractor and Nurse instantly.

INSIDE AN UNNAMED SHIP, in a black armchair wrapped in a white sheet, sits Agent Hudson. She has many bruises and concussions to her face and head. Her feet are tied together, her hands tied behind her back, and duct tape fastened over her mouth.

She tries desperately to PRY herself loose. Finally, she breaks loose the rope around her legs and takes baby-like steps as she drags the chair she's attached closer to the door. Shelly enters from the deck and notices that Hudson has moved somewhat. She slaps Hudson in the face. Denise and Agnes run down into the hull of the ship. Shelly slaps her again, grabs her by her hair, and tugs viciously. Hudson's head rocks back and forth, complementing the movements of Shelly's hand. Shelly warns her:

"Don't even think about it, Bitch. If this happens again, we'll pluck out your ten fingernails, one every morning until..., and then we'll work on your toenails. We'll call it the *Mani-Pedi-vicious-extract*. You hear me?"

Agnes re-ties Hudson's feet tighter. She winches. Agnes pulls the rope tighter, thus adjusting her stance. She looks Hudson dead in the eye and declares boisterously:

"Do you have any idea what it's like living in jail? Bitch! "

Then she slaps Hudson twice in the face and continues.

"FYI, it stinks like hell, just like your feet."

They drag the armchair with Hudson on it back to its original location. This time, Shelly ties Agent Hudson's hair around a pole.

Denise stands to her left, Agnes to her right, and Shelly, facing her, asks,

"Who is paying to keep Rude Buay in Jamaica?"

Hudson, surprised to be asked this question, says. "I don't know what you're talking about."

Denise disagrees.

"She's lying!"

Agnes insinuates.

"You've worked with him for six years. You know how he squeezes his toothpaste." Shelly, trying to break her down:

Tell us. You know he sleeps around."

Hudson responds,

"I'm not seeing..."

Shelly inquisitively asks.

"Where does he live in Miami?"

"I'm afraid that I don't have the answer to your question," replies Hudson.

A lassoed rope dangles from the ship's mast outside on the deck.

Denise reflectively calls Hudson's attention to the rope.

"How would you like to be hung from the mast of this ship tonight?"

Hudson shudders.

A Blonde Woman walks in and hands over a stack of pictures to Shelly.
Shelly browses through the unique collection, asking,
"Who feeds information to Rude Buay from Colombia?"
To this question, she answers,
"I don't know."
Agnes, not believing her, asks,
"What do you know?"
Shelly, agitated by Hudson's avoidance of supplying information, goes into her deep past…
"Bitch, who did your dad pay to take out my MAN in Bogotá?"
"I don't know what you're talking about."
Denise insinuates,
"You got this job based on nepotism, didn't you?"
"Let my dad rest in peace. I've paid my dues."
Shelly shows Hudson a Polaroid.
"Who's this standing next to you?"
Asks Shelly.
"Ross! Dr. Tamara Ross."
Shelly removes a picture of Hudson, Hudson's daughter, Hudson's dad, and Rude Buay from the stack. She shows it to Hudson inquisitively.
"How old is she?"
Hudson refuses to answer.
Agnes fetches the tray with a pair of pliers and lint on it and lays it on the table in front of Hudson. Looking at Hudson's daughter, Agnes says,

"We can use her as a Mule. Her granddad will tell us."
Agnes gets ready to extract Hudson's nail on her right index finger.
Alberto walks in. Shakes his head.
Agnes changes her mind and slaps her instead.
The three women untie her hair from the pole. They remove Hudson from the chair, bind her from head to foot with a rope, and attach weights to her legs.
Shelly hands Alberto a piece of paper with Dr. Ross's name.
Alberto reminisces,
"We financed her education at the medical school in Grenada. The best in her class."
Then he looks at the clock, reaches for his cell phone, and dials. He's oblivious that Rude Buay is inaccessible. Rude Buay's Pen Phone rings in the car trunk. He frantically tries prying himself loose. His Phone rings several times, then stops.

33

MILDRED SIMMS GLIDES IN. Her office phone rings. She answers on the first ring. It's The Commissioner.
"Mildred Simms."
She senses something different in his voice.
"Oh, hi Mr. Baptiste."
He reports,
"The curfew's lifted. Tomorrow the carnival celebrations will begin under strict supervision." She jumps up out of her chair. The phone's still off the hook. She is euphoric -
"Yes! Yes! Yes!"
(singing and dancing)
"It's carnival time again."
The streets of Kingston are teeming with trucks, carrying steel bands and masqueraders. Buses and minivans drop off passengers and make U-Turns to accommodate those waiting to be brought into the city. The sound of steel pan music and calypso fills the atmosphere. People dance and wind up under the heat of the blazing sun. Standing on top of a truck, Steve plays music from his steel pan as a man possessed. Calypsonians and Reggae artists are singing their hearts out. It's masquerading galore! People dance to the calypso beat. The procession continues for several blocks. Music and more music fills the air.

ALBERTO DIALS FROM HIS CAR. Salvador, in his mid-forties, of descent, picks up the phone in faded blue jeans, a muscle shirt, ostrich boots, and a red bandanna.
Alberto commands,
"Hold the shipments for seventy-two and a half hours."
Salvador enlightens,
"Boss, too much traffic. Can't get through."
Alberto recommends,
"Instruct the truck drivers to postpone their pick up until after we dock."
Salvador whimpers,
"This causes mucho problema. The police, the police...You know?"
Alberto disapproves,
"What do I pay you for?"
Salvador butters up,
"You know I got your back, boss...I fix it."
"Maricon! That's what you said when you used
"Cyanide" to cut it."
Alberto chides before hanging up.

A CADILLAC DRIVES UP and stops in Compton, Los Angeles. Several customers rush out into the street, like passengers fighting for a yellow cab on a rainy day in New York City. One bargain hunter gets in and slams the door shut. The Cady takes off. That Buyer drooling says,
"Can I get a kilo, Holmes?"
The Dealer ponders,
"Only half a kilo, dawg. It's going to cost you the same price as a regular kilo. You know that, right?" "When is the rain going to fall?" asks the Buyer.

“Who knows? El Nino could be seriously delayed.” "If it doesn't soon, this place could become an inferno. Thanks!” He shouts and gives the cash to the Dealer. The Dealer hands over his last bag to the Buyer. The Cady stops, the Buyer opens the car door and exits in a hurry. The Cady continues on its way.

SEVERAL WOMEN DRESSED IN SCRUBS, masks, and surgical gloves, holding onto bed pans, wait in line in front of the restrooms at a Jamaican hotel. Teenagers join a line in front of the restrooms. The women serve them a pill and a glass of water. One by one, teens are escorted into stalls by an attendant carrying a bedpan. Individual flushes follow minutes after each teen’s exit. Women exit later carrying a covered bedpan.

Outside the hotel, the tired kids re-board the bus, accompanied by two tour guides and a Hispanic woman carrying an attaché.

The Bus departs.

34

INSIDE THE CAR TRUNK, Rude Buay, with his ear to the ground, is still lying on his back. He battles against time as he vigorously rubs the ropes that bind his hands against the metal hinge. Strands of frayed rope increase with the continued rubbing. Beads of sweat ran down his face and into his mouth. Tirelessly, Rude Buay keeps trying. Finally, the rope severs. He rolls over from his back and onto his right side. Rude Buay reaches into his jacket pocket and pulls out his Pen Phone gadget. He proceeds to scan the trunk with it. A diagnostic Light flashes from the gadget. He then uses his hands to grope in that direction. The agent tugs on the wire harness and peels away the sealed black electrical taping. He sees so many of the wires; now he's confused. The car gains altitude, going up a steep hill.

Rude Buay clicks on the pen section on the pen phone, and the screwdriver portion comes out. He utilizes it, stripping away the blue and red wires on that harness. Now, he's more confused as he tries to decide which wires to unite. He closes his eyes and then opens them. The Car comes to a stop on top of the steep hill. Axel dials Alberto's number, envisioning a "Three Man

Execution" of his kidnapper. Rude Buay unites two wires. The car trunk pops open. He JUMPS out and scuttles down the mound.

Upon noticing the shadows of the split-second movement of the car trunk, Axel James opens the car door. He and Ian Baynes release the safety on their guns and rush cautiously towards the back of the car. They look inside the trunk and over the embankments on either side, but there's no sign of Rude Buay. They get back inside the vehicle, peeved, and speed away.

Laying beneath the thick shrubbery over the mound, Rude Buay radios from his Pen Phone.

"Banks come in."

He dials from that phone in a hurry. There's no response.

Rude Buay sees a donkey tied to a stake. He unties the animal and gets on for a ride. The donkey begins to gallop and kicks him off. He gets back on; again, it gallops and kicks him off. He grabs the donkey by its right ear, twisting it, and forces a rope into its mouth, creating a bit. Now controlled, he briskly rides it to a distant shack.

He notices a wrecked Land Rover parked in the yard at the shack. Rude Buay jumps off the donkey's back and DASHES inside the jalopy. He hotwires it with his gadget. It cranks up. The noise attracts several barking dogs embarking on the property in investigative pursuit. Rude Buay hit the road inside the vehicle.

35

INSIDE THE UNNAMED SHIP, Alberto waits, staring at an unopened bottle of champagne on a table. Axle and Ian arrive empty-handed.
Alberto demandingly inquires –
"Where is our MAN?"
Axel James apologetically retorts,
"Boss, we've lost him."
Alberto advocates,
"The girls would not have..."
Axel challenges,
That guy is very slippery...
Ian Baynes interrupts,
That guy is unstoppable…
Alberto vetoing their incompetence - Shoots Ian Baynes in the head.
"The girls don't think so, pieces of...

INSIDE THE REARVIEW MIRROR, Rude Buay sees a black Hummer approaching. He stops the Land Rover abruptly on the side of the road and jumps out. Rude Buay quickly removes his jacket and waves it at the oncoming vehicle. The Black Hummer comes to a SCREECHING halt. He retrieves a gun from under his trousers foot and pulls the gun on the female driver.

Surprisingly, it's Shelly Hall. The rear doors open. Out jump Agnes and Denise, with guns drawn. Shelly peers into his soul seductively. He feels the penetration but compartmentalizes in exchange for an aim at Shelly's head.
Rude Buay commands,
"Give up Hudson. End this ordeal!" Agnes, previously preoccupied with the white Mini Van parked several yards away, inches up closer toward Rude Buay in protest.
"Not a chance, Rude Buay!"
"Stop this drug trade. You are destroying..."
Shelly proposing,
"We need your little Mildred Simms and Banks."
"Why?" Asks Rude Buay.
Shelly declares,
"They are impeding traffic."
"They're the property of the Jamaican government." Retorts Rude Buay.
"Help! Help!"
A Voice echoes from the vicinity of the white Mini Van. Rude Buay's attention is drawn peripherally to the abandoned Mini Van. The three women's guns remain focused on Rude Buay.
Shelly goes to the rear of her vehicle and fetches a five-gallon container. She opens it and immediately creates a broad wet gasoline trail leading towards the abandoned vehicle. On purpose, she pours some on Rude Buay's lower trousers and his shoes.

The cry for help coming from the abandoned vehicle intensifies. Denise releases safety on her gun. Rude Bauy aims at Denise but gazes at the wet trail on which he stands.

Agnes moves into Rude Buay's space and whacks him behind the head with her gun. He falls to the ground. Before he could reciprocate, Denise whacks him with her weapon. Rude Buay gets up and staggers. His weapon is now wet after touching the ground. With one continuous kick, he sends their rifles sailing into mid-air. Their weapons fall back to the ground. Unfortunately, their guns are now wet with gasoline. All four of them scuffle for the wet weapons. The scene turns into an impasse; everyone knows the deadly effects triggered by a little spark.

Inside the Mini Van, Bazil Taylor, one of the tied-up government officials, struggles to free himself. He finally slips his right hand out of the noose.

Meanwhile, Rude Buay inches closer to the abandoned vehicle. He slips due to the incline and gasoline-drenched surface. He regains his balance and knocks the pursuing Shelly to the ground. She gets back up. It turns into a fistfight, with Rude Buay gaining the upper hand.

Bazil Taylor is now out of the abandoned vehicle and crawling towards them on all fours. His feet are still tied to his right hand. Denise unties the malnourished Taylor and throws the rope to Agnes. Shelly is still engaged in hand-to-hand combat with Rude Buay.

Agnes catches the rope and twists it into a lasso. She throws it towards Rude Buay's neck and lassos him. She DRAGS him towards the hummer. Despite his fighting tactics, they manage to subdue him and throw him inside the SUV. Denise grabs the three rifles and puts two in the Hummer. Shelly grabs one from her, dries it off with her red bandana, and jumps out. She gets ready to waste Taylor.

A white car pulls up and makes a swift U-turn. Every second counts, and she realizes that they have Alberto's Man, Rude Buay. So, she aborts shooting Taylor and boards the Hummer.

Inside the white car is the bandaged left-arm man, Walter Banks. His eyes connect with the disappearing hummer driven by Agnes. Taylor steps into view. Banks is breathing gasoline and the mud on his shoes, which is saturated with it. Banks yells out,

"Mr. Taylor! Mr. Taylor! Mr. Taylor! You are alive! Those idiots."

Banks puts Mr. Taylor in the rear seat of his car. Before leaving the scene, he rummages through the abandoned vehicle and discovers the other three ministers of government all tied up yet still alive. He unties William Russell, Vince Laborde, and Michael Young and puts them in his car. He drives away from the scene with a mixture of joy and sadness.

ALBERTO SITS ON THE SHIP'S DECK, across from Axel. Axel focuses on his boss's gun pointing towards

him. Alberto removes safety and perfects his aim. Two men, PEDRO and RAPHAEL, dressed in expensive business suits, white gloves, and sunglasses, observe.
Agnes, Denise, and Shelly emerge, dragging Rude Buay. Alberto takes away his deadly aim,
Alberto signals Pedro and Raphael. They lift Rude Buay into a semi-upright stance. Rude Buay regains his presence of mind and realizes he's now faced with ALBERTO.
Their eyes lock. Axel, Shelly, Denise, Agnes, Pedro, and Raphael are the captive audience.
Alberto interrogates,
"Rude Buay. You've been a thorn in my side. You didn't keep your promise. OUT means I want you OUT."
Rude Buay inquires,
"Where's Hudson."
Alberto retorts,
"Her funeral? You wouldn't attend, Rude Buay."
Rude Buay recaps,
"You've killed innocent people, including kids." Alberto does not bat an eye.
Rude Buay continues,
"You are a menace to the Caribbean and all that it stands for."
Alberto reduces the effect -
"You killed that teenager when you were a kid. Sin is sin. Right? How's the doctor? Are you aware, Rude Buay, that I've funded her education?" Rude Buay is

surprised; he does not want to believe what he just heard.

Alberto continues,

"Whenever you think pleasant thoughts of her, you should always think of me."

He gets up, circles, and punches Rude Buay hard. Rude Buay falls over. He shakes it off and gets back up. Alberto hits him again. This time, he stays down. Pedro grabs and drags him down the steps into the ship's hull.

There's no one in the hull except for tiny droplets of blood scattered on the hardwood floor. Rude Buay stares at the bloodstains. Before he could bathe in his pain and sorrow, Pedro and Raphael quickly strap him into the same black armchair previously occupied by Agent Heidi Hudson. Axel and Alberto enter.

Alberto's cold as ice. Stands erect.

Alberto commands,

"If he moves, kill him."

He smilingly says,

"Goodbye Rude Buay! "

Pedro looks at Raphael in agreement. Nods, yes. Axel and Alberto head off in a hurry.

36

AXEL JAMES GIVES Alberto a tour of the city of Port Antonio. He looks across at his boss, sitting in the passenger seat.

"Boss, Shelly, and Agnes are anxious to join Denise if she wants to traffic again,"

Alberto responds,

"Every agency is looking for them by now."

Alberto looks at his watch.

"When does our intestinal shipment arrive?"

Axel informs,

"The LA and Miami shipments have already cleared customs. No word yet on our next local shipment."

Alberto instructs - "I need an update." Alberto's phone rings.

While sitting in her car outside Michael Manley Airport, Denise Gomez bites her fingernails. She's not happy.

"Hello,"

Replies Alberto.

Denise reports,

"Pappy! Those three kids got sick and are held in custody at Michael Manley airport,"

"Conyo!"

Yells Alberto.

Continuing, he questions,

"Where are you?"

"Waiting in my car outside the airport."

She replies.

Eavesdropping Axel James discloses,

"Salvador blew it!"

Alberto dials again.

Inside a tent filled with empty seats in Bogota, Columbia. Salvador answers his cell phone.

"Hello!"

"Salvador! I'll kill you and your whole... family,"

Threatens Alberto.

"Que pasa senor?"

"You're selling me out."

"No, senor!"

"The kids got busted, Sal."

"I no tell nobody."

"How much are they carrying?" Inquires Alberto.

"Two kilos, senor."

"Overweight! Only one... kilo! "

Alberto frustratingly hangs up the phone, screaming out -

"Maricon! Maricon! Maricon!"

A few blocks away at the hospital, Dr. Tamara Ross, accompanied by her medical team of two Nurses, cuts through Junior Carlos' stomach wall. They remove several tiny packets of cocaine and lay them on a tray. The Commissioner stares at the tray and then at the patient. He's concerned. Junior Carlos begins to slip in and out of a coma.

One of the nurses checks the intravenous equipment attached to his forearm. It is secured. Tamara checks his pulse—once, twice, three times. All eyes are focused on the heart monitor. The heartbeat is irregular and continues to worsen. Finally, he stops breathing.

Tamara looks at the tray and exclaims,

"Tough kid!"

Commissioner Richard Baptiste shakes his head and walks out of the room.

37

BANKS AND MILDRED pull up outside the hotel. Mildred is driving an SUV, and Banks is in his banged-up wreck. Several vehicles are double-parked, blocking the narrow street. They jump out and ZIGZAG their way through the cars in a mad rush toward the hotel lobby.

Patrons mingle, some with drinks in hand. The music reverberates from the room nearby. Banks and Mildred push through the crowd. They open a door leading to the stairway. The intoxicated patrons react to their intrusion. A woman staring at them pulls out her cell phone and makes a call. Then she rejoins the party.

Mildred knocks on Rude Buay's door. There's no response. She fires and blows out the lock. Banks kicks in the door.

An open, half-empty suitcase is on the bed. There's no sign of Rude Buay. Banks looks in the bathroom while Mildred looks under the bed. He's not there. On the dresser is a framed portrait of Clifford, Rude Buay's brother, nestled alongside pictures of two ships - "The Tempest" and "Gomez." Banks clues in. They exit and rush through the exit door leading downstairs. Shelly,

Agnes, and Denise drive up. They enter the hotel in haste.

Denise, Agnes, and Shelly shoved the already distressed patrons out of the way. Armed to the maximum, they got onto the elevator. The elevator door closed. Simultaneously, the exit door opened. Mildred and Banks exited and rushed outside.

They race to their vehicles and depart.

Patrons have gradually vanished, anticipating a showdown. Denise, Shelly, and Agnes get off the elevator, survey, and anger turns into fury. They rush outside. Banks and Mildred are nowhere in sight. They jump into their SUV and travel in the same direction. Banks and Mildred arrive at the dock. They survey. Banks notice the ship "Ambassador" with a fresh coat of paint. They climb aboard with guns drawn. Raphael is alerted. He reaches for his Automatic weapon. Just before he can get one-off, Mildred blasts him, and he soars overboard.

Denise, Shelly, and Agnes' SUV arrive at the dock. They see Raphael fall overboard. They enter the ship with their weapons drawn.

Inside the hull of the ship, Pedro responds to the sound of gunfire, leaves Rude Buay unguarded, and goes to the ship's deck.

Pedro encounters Mildred and Banks. He shoots at them and misses. Now on deck, the three women are inching closer on Banks and Mildred's tail. In the hull, Rude Buay tries hard to pry himself loose. On deck,

Denise, Agnes, and Shelly are now shooting furiously at Banks and Mildred. Banks returns fire, and Shelly gets hit and goes down.

Banks turns around and shoots at Pedro, but he misses. Denise shoots at Mildred, who goes to the floor, rolls over, and shoots back at Denise. The bullet grazes her right leg.

After falling to the ground, Denise shoots back at Mildred and misses. Mildred gets up in an attempt to get a shot off at Denise.

Denise shoots at her again. Mildred ducks, returns to the floor and lies flat on her stomach. She fires and shoots Denise in the leg. Denise accidentally falls overboard.

Rude Buay finally slips his leg out of that noose with his tied hands.

Banks, at the duel with Pedro, eludes him. Pedro shoots back at Banks and then at the emerging Mildred in a flash. He misses.

Banks and Mildred reposition themselves, aiming at Pedro, who positions himself before the entrance to the ship's hull. Losing that aim, Pedro searches for the perfect one.

Rude Buay cuts his way out of the ropes. He picks up the armchair with both hands and heads towards the steps leading to the deck.

Pedro focuses on Mildred, who continues to rain bullets in his direction. Rude Buay, now nearby, hits Pedro in his back with the chair. Pedro falls backward

into the hull of the ship. His gun falls out of his hand in the process. Rude Buay stands over him with the hoisted armchair. "Where's Hudson?" Rude Buay inquires. Pedro looks at him and doesn't reply. Rude Buay strikes him again with the chair.
"Where's she?"
Once again, he does not reply.
Rude Buay hits him again with the chair.
Pedro rolls over; this time, he grabs Rude Buay's two feet, attempting to bring him down. Rude Buay stumbles. In the process, he picks up Pedro's gun and shoots him in the chest, killing him. Rude Buay notices a door to a closed room in the hull. He turns the doorknob, swinging the door ajar. Inside, he discovers dozens of guns, stockpiled, a massive assortment of bullets, along with stacks of grenades in a corner. Additionally, there are two shelves with stacks of cash in various currencies. He grabs two of the guns and checks them to see if they're loaded with bullets. They are. He hurries to the deck, with guns in hand.
Banks and Agnes exchange gunfire. Mildred reloads. Shelly gets back up, staggering.
Rude Buay EMERGES. Both guns were drawn, demanding -
"Drop the gun, Agnes. You're under arrest."
"Says who?"
She responds.
Rude Buay aims at her head.

"Where's Heidi Hudson?"

"I'm not your Bitch's keeper."

"Lead me to her and you'll go free."

"I'm not for sale Rude Buay."

She reaches for the pulley attached to a rope overhead and SWINGS it in Rude Buay's direction. He ducks. She jumps overboard. Rude Buay dives into the water after her.

Shelly staggeringly regains her presence of mind and challenges Mildred into a fistfight.

Mildred drops her gun and takes her on.

Shelly shows her the "snake". Mildred shows her the "eagle". Banks observes as they go at it "karate style." One kick from Mildred finally lands Shelly overboard. Meanwhile, Denise does not resurface. Rude Buay swims viciously in pursuit of Agnes. He sees her. Agnes somersaults and eludes him.

Shelly dives under and goes after Rude Buay.

Agnes emerges and grabs at Rude Buay's legs.

He senses her move and punches her in the face. Her head rocks backward; she goes under.

Rude Buay comes up for air and spits out a mouthful of water.

Shelly pursues him. He grabs her by the head and pushes her under. She kicks hard, gasping for air. Agnes resurfaces and grabs hold of Rude Buay around his neck. He fights her off, thereby releasing his hold on Agnes, who, at this point, is drinking water like a fish. Shelly resurfaces, fatigued. He PUSHES her under; after she takes in many gulps of water, he releases her.

Jose Mendez, smoking a Cuban cigar, observes from the dock. His eyes lock with Rude Buay's. "Rude Buay, we've got bigger fish to fry. Who's left on board?" Mendez asks.

None of the women resurfaces. Rude Buay considers them drowned. So, he climbs up out of the water. He notices Mildred carrying two guns. He grabs one of the guns and points towards the ship. Mendez tips his cigar, releasing some ash.

Mendez commands,

"That wouldn't be a good move, Rude Buay." Rude Buay is preoccupied.

"Still no word on AGENT HUDSON, huh? Rude Buay ignores him and SHOOTS viciously into the ship. You are blowing it up into pieces."

Mendez looks at Rude Buay with concern and continues.

"Hudson's not on that ship. Is she?"

Rude Buay does not respond. Instead, he looks around and realizes that he has a choice of who he rides with, Banks or Mildred. He gives both of them a thumbs up. He chooses to ride with Banks in his banged-up car. They take off, leaving Mendez at the dock, with Mildred proceeding in tow.

Rude Buay begins rubbing his nose. "Thanks. Is your car leaking fuel? And how did you find me?"

Banks responds,

"I'll answer the second first."

"Banks, what if someone cut your...fuel line?"

Rude Bauy gets ready to open the car door. In the rearview mirror, Banks notices Mildred taking a detour.

"Relax, Rude Buay. You are safe. The water dried from your feet, but mine are still wet."

"Fill me in. Enough of the parables. *When the student is ready, the teacher appears."*

Banks reciprocates,

"Well, your footprints were at the scene. And if they finished you off, they had to be heading back to sea, and this was the nearest port of escape. Plus, Mildred and I, trying to find you, had to break into your hotel room. We saw your brother's photo on both cartel-owned ships."

"Really... and Mr. Taylor?"

Retorts Rude Buay.

"I took all four of them to the hospital. They were treated and discharged."

Inquires Rude Buay.

Banks fills him in:

"Russel, La Borde, and Young were also in the back of this getaway vehicle."

"Nice work...horse. I mean Bloodhound. Great instincts! Dinner is on me. But first, I need to stop at the Haddon Hotel."

Banks pulls up outside the hotel. Rude Buay receives a text message on his waterproof cell phone.

TEXT READS: I received a tip. Alberto is at Sunset Shores. M.S.
Rude Buay says to Banks.
"Wait here. See who shows up. I'll be at Sunset Shores Hotel!"
Rude Buay gets out of the car and catches a Taxi.

38

THE SOUND OF THE WAVES creates a musical ambiance for the oceanic backdrop at the Sunset Shores Hotel. Alberto and Axel, sitting in a suite, are joined by Carlos, dressed in an expensive suit and dark sunglasses, along with a Blonde Woman. They sit around a table, drinking. Axel takes out a pack of 555 cigarettes from his pocket. He opens it, withdraws five from the box, and lays them on the table. Carlos strips the tobacco out of the five cigarettes, creating a heap.

Axel takes some cocaine from off a plate on the table and sprinkles the base onto the tobacco, creating half and half. He then feeds the cocaine-laced tobacco back into the empty cylinders of paper until the cigarettes are three-quarters packed. He twists the unfiltered end, creating a closed valve.

Carlos lights a match and holds it under the cigarette to heat it. The cigarette is toasted gradually, as the oil from the base shows through the white paper. Carlos lights the cigarette and passes it first to Alberto. He takes a toke and passes it to Axel, who takes a toke and passes it to the Blonde, who takes a toke and burns her finger while she passes it to Carlos, who takes a toke.

Feeling the buzz, Carlos looks up at Alberto and asks, "Don Alberto, when do we sail?" Alberto doesn't respond.
Carlos inquires:
"Manana?"
Alberto finally pays him some attention and asks,
"Did you tie her down properly?"
Carlos is high as a kite:
"Si don Alberto."
The Blonde Woman intercepts:
"I didn't see him put holes in the ship."
Alberto winks at Axel. Axel pulls out his gun and shoots Carlos in the face. The place becomes a bloody mess.
"Let's get out of here!"
Commands Alberto Gomez. "Where, too?" Asks Axel.
"Hudson knows too...much,"
Responds Alberto.
Alberto's phone rings. He answers,
"Hello!"
It's Shelly and Agnes.
"Alberto, the Ambassador has been destroyed. Rude Buay has once again escaped. He was last seen at the dock with Banks and Mildred. Your wife Denise is missing. She could be feared dead." "Where are you?"
"Heading to Sunset Shores,"
Responds Shelly.
Alberto hangs up. He is unhappy.

39

A TAXI DRIVES UP at Sunset Shores Hotel. Alberto, Axel, and Blonde Woman get in. The taxi drives to the Port Antonio dock. Alberto JUMPS out of the cab. He's FURIOUS.

Axel and the Blonde Woman exit the cab staring at the remains and simultaneously at their boss. Alberto sees a Catamaran speedboat docked on the other side. He heads in its direction. Axel and the Blonde Woman follow in Alberto's tracks.

With guns drawn, Alberto, Axel, and the Blonde Woman climb aboard. Three people: Tommy,

Margaret and their teenage daughter Niki sit around a table enjoying a lobster dinner.

Alberto, Axel, and Blonde Woman move in. Before the family could take flight, bullets started raining on them.

Bullets hit Tommy and Margaret, who soar overboard from the impact. Niki runs for cover. Axel follows Niki. Alberto reminds Axel - "Spare her, she's a hot commodity!"

Axel refrains from shooting her but maintains his aim. Axel heads into the cabin and cranks up the engine. The Blonde Woman, playing team, runs ashore, loosens the rope that ties the ship to the dock, and makes her way back on deck—the Ship sails. The

Blonde Woman seeks out the teary-eyed Niki. Axel releases his aim at her and throws her a Snicker bar. Niki, scared but deprived of her dinner, takes a bite. The Woman reaches into her pocketbook, retrieves a hairbrush, and gently styles Niki's hair into a ponytail. Niki dries her tears. The Woman grabs some rope, attaches it to Niki's hair, and ties it to the mast.
Alberto is busy scanning the shores through a pair of binoculars.
Catamaran KICKS up white water.

SHELLY, DRIPPING WET at a phone booth, dials in a hurry.
"I need a taxi at Hope Bay Terrace."
Momentarily, a taxi drives up. Shelly pulls the driver out of the cab, places him under a chokehold, and pops his neck. The Cabbie falls to the ground to his death. Agnes emerges behind the tree and takes the wheel while Shelly accesses the front passenger seat. The Taxi drives away. Shelly calls on Cabbie's cellular phone, which she found inside the taxi.
Alberto's cell phone rings. He picks it up.
Agnes responds.
"We're heading to the Sunset Shores Hotel. Is our man there?" "He's waiting for you. Hurry," Replies Alberto.

WALTER BANKS ENCOUNTERS PROBLEMS as he tries to get a signal on his laptop outside The Haddon Hotel. Finally, he does, as he picks up a video of Shelly and Agnes getting inside the taxi. He discovers that it is not in real time. He catches up to speed and overhears their phone conversation.

Banks gets Rude Buay on the phone.

"Rude Buay, Shelly, and Agnes just left the beach. They are heading to the Sunset Shores Hotel."

Rude Buay replies,

"Cover the Sunset Shores Hotel. I'm heading there, too."

Banks arrives and waits in his car. A taxi pulls up. Shelly gets out and enters the hotel. Agnes continues the ride.

Banks picks up his phone and dials Rude Buay.

"Rude Buay, Agnes dropped Shelly off in a taxi." "Did you get the tags?

"Yep. The license tag is H 29562. She's driving that thing like a darn maniac."

Rude Buay responds,

"Keep an eye on Shelly. Do not let her leave the hotel."

Rude Buay's car accelerates through the crowded night street. The Cab in question leaves, heading in the opposite direction.

Rude Buay's SUV immediately makes a swift U-turn in pursuit. Shooting at the taxi, he deflates the rear tires. The cab slows up. Rude Buay hit it again, shooting Agnes in the neck.

The car collides into the wall, bursting into flames.

Rude Buay departs.

His Pen Phone rings.

Banks, on the other end, discloses, "Rude Buay, Shelly just walked into the hotel. She's alone."

"Great! Hold on."

Rude Buay reviews a text message he received earlier from an informant. Carlos Chavez, a guest at Sunset Shores Hotel, is on that list.

"Banks, I need the profile on... Carlos Chavez." Banks goes to work and pulls the info from his laptop's database.

Banks discloses,

"A Former DEA worked alongside two of your superiors, Bob White and Jose Mendez. He moonlighted as a prison guard, busted for cocaine possession in 2002, a master in disguise. He has a Miami address. Do you need it?"

"No. Awesome! Call the commissioner and ask him to send in backup."

Rude Buay responds as he pulls into the Hotel's parking lot.

In the hotel room, Shelly, almost unclothed with bruises on her body, rolls out of bed. She glances at her lover in bed, lying on his stomach. She strides to the bathroom. Before getting out of the car, Rude Buay radios Banks.

"Banks, I want you to stay put. I'll call you if I need you."

"What's up with that? Are you a loner?"

"DEA business!"

Rude Buay meets his informant in the lobby. He gives him a wad of cash and hands Rude Buay a slip of paper with room # 122 on it.

Rude Buay moseys up to the door. He is disregarding the hanging no-disturb sign. He aims at the lock with a silencer attached to his gun and fires, blowing out the lock.

He kicks in the door.

On impact, Shelly darts out of bed and grabs a gun from on top of the dresser, along with her lover's bulletproof vest. The man turns over in bed. A close-up reveals him. It is Special Agent Jose Mendez. Rude Buay is oblivious. He scuttles out of bed, turns off the lights, and seeks refuge in the vacant suite. Shelly hides behind the dresser. She pulls her blouse over the vest.

Rude Buay enters gun in hand. Shelly accidentally bumps into the dresser.

Rude Buay fires; a bullet penetrates the dresser and grazes against Shelly's gun-holding hand. She loses control of it. The gun hits the floor. She's off-balanced and tries to regain her presence of mind while lying on the floor. She succeeds and retrieves the weapon. Getting up, she shoots at Rude Buay. He returns fire. The bullet misses her as she hits the floor behind the dresser.

Meanwhile, bullets from another room come flying at Rude Buay. He turns in wonderment. Shelly shoots again. Rude Buay dodges and fires back at Shelly as he gets up. The bullet strikes Shelly in the chest, knocking her to the ground.

Rude Buay stares at her in admiration but shoots her again in the chest. She kicks a few times. Rude Buay thinks that he has taken her out with that last shot. Rude Buay hears the front door to the adjacent room open. He rushes through the front door to the hotel room.

He locates a light switch, turns on the light, and peeps inside the adjoining room. It is empty. Peripherally, he notices a shadow. He turns and sees a man's shadow going around the corner. Rude Buay pursues the shadow, still ignorant of the performer's identity. You can HEAR a pin drop as Rude Buay carefully grazes the wall.

Suddenly, he hears the sound of a gun reloading. It sounds just like his. Rude Buay checks his gun and proceeds with caution.

Mendez is now moving closer towards Rude Buay, in the same proportion as Rude Buay is moving towards him. If it weren't for the 90-degree wall between them, they would be shaking each other's hand. Rude Buay gets off a random shot. So does Mendez. The shadows of their outstretched hands on the wall alert them to the tiny distance between them.

Rude Buay hugs the wall with the gun in his right hand and fires. The Bullet misses Mendez's ducking head. Mendez purposefully goes flat on his stomach, gun in

hand as he aims, waiting for Rude Buay to turn the corner.
Coming up the stairs, Walter Banks darts through the exit door with a gun. He sees the perpetrator's backside. The man is lying flat on his stomach with his gun pointed in the opposite direction. The Exit door closes after Banks's entry. Rude Buay is alerted. Banks yells out,
"Rude Buay! Hold your fire. I've got him cornered!"
Responding to both sounds, Mendez rolls over on his back and shoots at Banks. The shot misses him. Rude Buay appears around the bend and yells,
"Banks don't shoot! He is mine!" Mendez is still facing Banks with his back turned to Rude Buay. Rude Buay, still uncertain of the man's identity, commands:
"Turn around you... prick!"
Mendez, sensing that two guns are now pointing at him, turns slowly. He is now facing Rude Buay, who criticizes,
"Suit? Lies! Deception! Duplicity! Sabotage!"
"We're on the same team, Rude Buay."
"We are?"
Asks Rude Buay.
"We've always been, Agent."
"Really? Where's Agent Hudson?"
"You should be answering that question, Rude Buay... You turned her over to Alberto. She stood in your way." Mendez responds.
"Which way?" inquires Rude Buay.

"Your promotion. You brought her to the Caribbean so that you could orchestrate her kidnapping," responds Jose Mendez.

Banks eyes Rude Buay and then Mendez. Not trusting anyone, he's aiming at both men. Is this what I came out of retirement for? He reasons.

Mendez continues,

"How much did Alberto pay you, and how much more did you agree to pay Carlos Chavez?"

"Nice try. You know what, Boss? You stand in the way of my promotion. So, I'm going to have to cap you. Then I'll find Alberto and cap him. Then..."

"Do you think that Alberto is going to fall into your trap? You'll never catch him. He's invincible,"

Interrupts Mendez.

Rude Buay aims at Mendez's head, motioning him to get down on his knees. He does. "If you kill me, the parasites that devour my body will tell me. You'll never catch Alberto."

Rude Buay retorts,

"The record states that You've killed off several officials in the 1990s and gave Alberto Gomez control of the most vicious cartel. Etched his name and signature. Claiming that it will be so hot. All five oceans wouldn't be able to cool it."

Rude Buay continues,

"Off the record, I'm about to release that DAM, Jose. Drop your weapon!"

Mendez shoots at Rude Buay and misses. Rude Buay fires, shooting Mendez in the head. Mendez kicks and stops breathing. Rude Buay confiscates his gun. Looking at it, he declares,
"In every arena, there's a need for great teams. Men and women would become champions if they committed to playing team." Rude Buay and Banks make a B-line inside Shelly's hotel room.
They rummage through the room. Rude Buay discovers an attaché with the initials JM. He pries it open and throws everything out on the bed. He delves into the contents while Banks observes.
List of recovered items:

1. A shotgun
2. A pair of binoculars.
3. A miniature camera.

Pictures of:

1. Rude Buay and Tamara cuddled up on the beach.
2. Rude Buay struggles with Shelly in the water at the dock.

Rude Buay notices Axel's name on the back of one of Mendez's business cards, along with phone number 876-3620800 Ext. 27.
He hands it to Banks.
Banks respond instantly,

"This Hotel!"

They throw the evidence back inside the attaché. Toting it along, they leave in a hurry.

Rude Buay and Banks approach room # 27. A no-disturb sign hangs from the doorknob. Rude Buay blows out the lock with a bullet. He enters, followed by Banks in tow. They react to the pungent stench. Lying on the ground, soaked in blood, is Carlos Chavez. There's a gunshot wound to the head. Rude Buay rolls him over and discovers the dragon tattoo behind his right ear. A flashing infrared light directs Rude Buay to a cell phone inside Carlos's breast pocket.

Rude Buay removes the phone. Their attention is then drawn to the four-chair dining table. On it lies the residue from a free-basing session. Banks collect the residue.

Rude Buay toys with Carlos' cell phone. First, with the camera wallet. Several thumbnails exist. Rude Buay searches through the pics:

Pic # 1: A close-up of Warden Culligan's corpse.

Pic # 2: The Ambassador.

Pic # 3: Warden Ralph Bullock's house.

Pic # 4: A close-up of Warden Ralph Bullock.

Pic # 5: Agent Hudson bound with ropes in a dinghy.

Rude Buay goes to a full screen on the thumbnails. Next, he accesses the phone book. Two phone numbers for Alberto Gomez pop up. Rude Buay dials the first one. There's no answer, so he tries the second number.

"Hello, this must be good news!"

Answers Alberto.

The sound of a boat's engine and waves splashing against a huge object are heard in the background.

Rude Buay quickly hangs up. He exits, departing with Walter Banks.

An SUV pulls into the driveway, followed by Jamaican police. Mildred steps out, almost colliding with Rude Buay and Banks.

Mildred articulates,

"The hotel called saying that you were on the premises. Where's Axel? Is he finished?"

"We're about to find out,"

Replies Banks.

Several Jamaican police cruisers with flashing lights have blocked the driveway's entrance, making it a hazardous exit.

Mildred jumps inside Banks' jalopy, which is fully loaded with wiring and gadgetry. Jamaican police officers, who had already entered the building on foot, returned and responded to tooting horns. They clear the entrance of parked police cruisers. Rude Buay manages to turn his car around speedily. They drive away at top speed to the dock.

The two cars pull up, parking precariously. They jump out and proceed hurriedly on foot. A Native administers serious elbow grease as he polishes a blue and white 400 SuperSport speedboat.

Rude Buay demands,

"DEA, we need to use your boat."

The Native looks at him like he's crazy.
Mildred supplicates,
"Come on! We'll return it."
The Native, checking out Mildred's physique, articulates:
"Not even my wife gets behind this wheel..."
Rude Buay pulls out his gun on the native, exclaiming,
"This is a rescue mission. We don't have time to explain. Don't make me have to force you to..."
The Native jumps ship.
Rude Buay, Mildred, and Banks jump in. Banks grabs the wheel. The boat takes off careening between other ships at the dock.
Native yells,
"You return it one scratch...mon, you'll be...dead meat!" In afterthought, he continues,
"It's almost on empty!"
Rude Buay asks,
"What did he say?"
Holding on tightly to the rail, Mildred answers,
"Something like...don't bring it back on empty. His patois is awful."

40

THE 400 SUPERSPORT picks up speed as it travels through the waters of Jamaica's north coast. A Jamaican police helicopter follows overhead. Inside this speedster, Rude Buay and Mildred scan the coast with binoculars. Rude Buay answers to the ringing of his Pen Phone.

It's The Commissioner.

"Rude Buay, we've given you all we have available."

Rude Buay looks up in the distance, acknowledging the helicopter.

"The man found dead at the dock was identified as sailor Tommy Clarke and his wife Margaret, owner of the missing Catamaran. Autopsy results indicate that they could have been killed less than thirty hours ago," Informs The Commissioner.

Rude Buay rejoins Banks, who's enjoying the machinery.

"They could have already made their escape to Colombia. They have got a considerable head start on us. How fast can this thing go?"

Walter Banks looks at the gauge meters, showing signs of uneasiness.

"What's the fuel capacity on this...?"

"It says two hundred and fifty gallons," Indicates Rude Buay, after which the fuel gauge grabs his attention.
"It's on empty. So is the reserve tank."
He continues,
"Where can we refill?"
Mildred walks in, binoculars in hand, comments,
" Are we really on empty?"
"We're eight miles from land," Indicates Walter Banks.
A ship heading in the opposite direction passes nearby, leaving a water trail and causing a colossal undercurrent. The SuperSport gets caught up in that current, creating maneuvering problems for Banks. Rude Buay and Mildred grab onto the rail to avoid losing balance. Mildred informs,
"Making this stop is going to cause us to lose those bastards. I want Axel's head served up on a... platter."
Rude Buay responds,
Would that make them the property of the government?"
"They could refuse to release them to us,"
Banks cautions.
"How much faster can this thing go?"
Banks asks, with Cuba now close in view.
Rude Buay replies,
"The faster we go. The more fuel this rocket consumes.
Inside the Jamaica Helicopter overhead, the pilot adjusts his binoculars, stating:

"We've spotted the Catamaran off the coast of Cuba."
"There's not enough time for us to refill in port," States Rude Buay.
Banks radios,
"400 SuperSport heading south, five miles off the Island Cuba, requesting assistance! Running low on fuel. I repeat: We're running low on fuel."
Radio static intercepts.
Suddenly, the engine stops, and the boat begins to drift. In Port Antonio, a Pickup truck pulls up at the wharf. The Jamaica Helicopter circles overhead. Two natives hurriedly secure the laden gas container inside the helicopter's lowered net. The Helicopter takes off with assistance.
The Helicopter attempts to lower the container onto the 400 SuperSport. Rude Buay tries to grab it. High tide creates treacherous waves, causing the ship to drift from underneath the descending net.
Copter flies right, making another attempt. Another wave rocks the ship further right, making that drop-off more difficult.
Meanwhile, the Catamaran picks up considerable speed heading north. Axel helms the ship while Alberto and the Blonde Woman engage in a freebasing session on deck. Niki observes. Two Automatic weapons resting in the men's arms extend onto the table. Looking through his binoculars, Alberto spots a dinghy adrift in the distance. His curiosity increases as he zooms in for clarity.

"That could be Hudson!"
He remarks.
The dinghy's passenger continues waving a portion of a sheet to the distant, rapidly approaching Catamaran. The 400 Super Sport continues to drift briskly further as the waves rise higher and higher. The Copter comes in for its third attempt. Before the container was deposited on board the 400 SuperSport, the Co-Pilot noticed the catamaran traveling at runaway speed up ahead. The Pilot unites the net with the 400 SuperSport. Rude Buay fetches the container and immediately starts the refueling process.
The Helicopter's Co-Pilot reaches for his pair of binoculars. He sees the Catamaran in the lens and the dinghy sailing away, with someone in it waving a large piece of fabric.
He reports:
"We've spotted the missing Catamaran cutting water towards Cuba. Someone in a dinghy is ahead of it, waving for help."
Rude Buay FIRES up the engine and takes over the wheel.
Mildred joins Rude Buay in the helm seat. She is armed with her 350 magnums.
Walter Banks surveys the coast from the cockpit, binoculars in one hand and gun in the other. The SuperSport begins CUTTING water at an increasing speed.

The Catamaran continues sailing at a step-up speed. The Helicopter up above progresses with increased velocity.
Axel draws Alberto's attention to the dinghy still drifting at sea. A woman's image is now visible. The Blonde Woman onboard the catamaran grabs a pair of binoculars and zooms in. Realizing that it's Heidi
She exclaims,
"That bitch is still alive?"
The sound of the approaching helicopter changes the mood as three binoculars are tossed aside in exchange for automatic weapons. Alberto, Axel, and the Blonde are now in a shootout with (a) the helicopter pilots and (b) firing simultaneously at the dinghy. Niki tries desperately to untie herself from the mast. The Blonde Woman notices her planned getaway and aims at Niki, yelling:
"Don't you dare!"
Niki retreats. The Catamaran's engine is turned off. The tide favors it, pulling away from the 400 SuperSport trapped in its rapids.
The Dinghy continues to drift. Gunshots begin to rain down onto the Catamaran from the Helicopter overhead. The exchange of firepower continues. Axel and Alberto retreated with several rounds. However, none of these bullets contact the helicopter. Moving at full speed, the 400 Super Sports are gaining momentum on the Catamaran.

The Catamaran is now at a comfortable shooting distance from the SuperSport. Rude Buay, Mildred, and Banks proceed with the onslaught. Several bullets ricochet onto the Catamaran.

A Bullet from Mildred's gun hits the Blonde woman explosively. She hits the deck hard. Her breath dissipates from her body.

Axel and Alberto return fire onto the 400 SuperSport, missing everything but the water. The Dinghy with the lone, tired, sunburnt Agent, Hudson, is now in close view.

Alberto shoots at her. The Dinghy rides the vast wave, causing him to miss but putting a gaping hole into its left side.

Water begins to seep through, filling up the dinghy. Hudson is discombobulated.

A helicopter swoops down, lowering its net for Agent Hudson. She reaches the net like it was the last straw amidst the continued shooting between the DEA agents and the two drug lords. She is unsuccessful. Axel gets back to helming the Catamaran speedily.

He desperately tries to create some distance between it and the SuperSport.

Rude Buay returns to the helm seat.

The 400 SuperSport picks up speed in pursuit. The swift movement of the water, enhanced by the water current caused by both ships, washes away the dinghy as soon as Hudson successfully grabs onto the net. The Helicopter briskly departs from the area with Agent

Hudson holding onto the net. Alberto shoots excessively at the rescued Agent Hudson. He misses his target as he competes with the wind's trajectory. Rude Buay continues to shoot at Axel and Alberto from the helm seat. Banks moves to the bow in an attempt to secure his stance. He is off-balanced but shoots desperately at Alberto, stationed in the Catamaran's cockpit.

Several bullets from Alberto's gun intended for Banks strike the 400 SuperSport, damaging it. Banks retaliates with several rounds. Bullets severely penetrate the Catamaran. One of the bullets brushes against Alberto's leg. He's off-balanced. More bullets rain, hitting the Catamaran's mast and grazing near Niki.

"No. Please! No!" Screams Niki.

Niki's screams aren't heard. Rude Buay, Mildred, and Banks are oblivious that she is aboard. They continue to shoot aggressively at Alberto and Axel.

A colossal wave pushes the Catamaran out of focus.

Bullets from the 400 SuperSport miss that ship. Alberto returns fire. A Bullet from his gun hits Banks in his left upper arm. He goes down. Mildred runs to his aid. He's still breathing but aching severely.

Rude Buay evens the score, blowing out several portholes. A series of waves rock the punctured Catamaran and Pushes it closer to a "run ashore" collision on the Island of Cuba. Axel emerges with Niki as his human shield. A huge wave hits the Catamaran. Niki screaming hysterically,

"Don't kill me! You son of a bitch!"
Mildred eyes Rude Buay as he aims for Axel's head. The boat's movement makes it challenging to maintain the focus of the bullet's trajectory.
Axel points his Automatic weapon towards Niki's head. Her screaming intensifies.
Rude Buay emerges closer on deck. He eyes Mildred assuredly. He shoots. Instead, a bullet from Axel's gun hits Rude Buay in his chest. He falls onto the deck.
Mildred keeps dodging Axel's bullets. Rude Buay, with blood on his vest, rolls over onto his stomach and gets a good aim at Axel. Discharges.
The bullet HITS Axel right between his eyes. He falls backward thunderously onto the deck. Niki falls forward into the deep.
A mountain-like wave beckons. It hits the Catamaran viciously. Alberto, dressed in a wet suit, jumps overboard into the wave, unnoticed by everyone on the other ship. The Catamaran sails speedily towards an unavoidable collapse onto the island of Cuba. Mildred dives into the deep and clutches Niki around her neck. Rude Buay throws out the life rope. Mildred catches it. Rude Buay reels them in.
Another mountainous wave hits the Catamaran, it slams into Cuba at full speed, bursting into flames, debris, spikes, and fragments of lumber.

THE HOSPITAL LOBBY IS CROWDED with Jamaican police officers. Banks is pushed around in a wheelchair with his left arm in a sling. The Police commissioner, Mildred, and Rude Buay admire compassionately. Rude Buay walks up to Banks and hands over an attaché. Banks opens it. He smiles upon seeing the stacks of crisp C notes. He closes the attaché, gives Rude Buay a thumbs up, and departs. Agent Hudson walks out of the discharge room, accompanied by Tamara. Rude Buay greets Agent Hudson smilingly.
They turn to leave.
Richard Baptiste steps into their space and utters -
"Thanks, Rude Buay."
"My pleasure,"
Says Rude Buay.
Tamara rushes past the commissioner and right into Rude Buay's space. Their eyes become locked momentarily. Mildred moves closer to Rude Buay, scrutinizing her.
"Rude Buay, you forgot something."
says Tamara.
"My vest!"
Tamara flies into his arms. Mildred eyes them enviously.

BOOK 2

RUDE BUAY THE UNTOUCHABLE

"I firmly believe that any man's finest hour, the greatest fulfillment of all that he holds dear, is the moment when he has worked his heart out in a good cause and lies exhausted on the field of battle - victorious."

- VINCE LOMBARDI

TABLE OF CONTENTS

1

A DENSE MIXTURE of blackened and gray clouds opens up to sparse streaks of lightning, followed by severe and intense intermittent thunderstorms. Torrent rain showers burst out of those sporadic illuminated clouds as a follow-up to the rumbling fiery interlude. Meanwhile, trees sway noisily, splitting into halves at their trunks, sending splinters of timber flying in the distance. Additionally, the downed power lines and the uprooting of multiple plants indicate that whatever is about to happen in Port Antonio, Jamaica, mid-Friday afternoon is more than just a severe rainstorm.

It could equal or top the destruction of Port Royal back in 1692.

"Could this be Déjà Vu or what some may call voodoo? These inclement weather conditions are not felt elsewhere, not even in another parish on the Island. Weather conditions have not been this severe since Mount St. Helens blew its top, sending trees downstream, or since the destruction of Port Royal in 1692."

One enthusiastic yet subdued radio announcer with a sophisticated British twang candidly remarks: Patrons at a Port Antonio restaurant not only hear and watch the news but feel the earth tremble continually and intermittently for several minutes while the sea roars like a hungry lion, adding to Mother Nature's audio effects.

Meanwhile, high-magnitude waves boisterously crash against protruding rocks and the battered shoreline at sea.

Small crafts sway as they are tossed back and forth by the wind. Some crafts, under duress, even sever the ropes that tie them to the small wooden dock. Huge waves form in succession. Sand, gravel, and the deposits of the last waves are removed from the shore and then viciously REDEPOSITED on the debris-saturated beach.

Nervously and securely docking his boat, a frazzled American Sailor senses futility as the dock that held his forty-foot Casper collapses. The raging storms eventually and hastily send his small vessel and others alike into the now tsunami-like waves of the ocean. While watching his boat tossed away in the current, the Sailor, like the enthusiastic famous crocodile catcher from Australia, fights the treacherous waves as he swims back to shore in an investigative pursuit of the human carcass that just washed ashore. The sailor rushes to the beach as the waves draw. With his hand covering his nostrils, he runs over to the mostly decomposed body in investigative pursuit. The body is motionless. The sailor gets a close-up of the man's corpse. In the corpse's left hand tightly clenched, he bears the leg portion of a multicolored wet suit. The Sailor is drenched and remains startled by the dramatic unfolding toxic scene.

In the subsequent moments, the rain recedes as a long extended rainbow decorates the flustered, angry, still overcast cloudy sky.

The Sailor embraces the opportunity to call 911 using his rubber-cased, protected cell phone, which he has retrieved from his seat pocket.

He enthusiastically yells into the device, drowning out the sound of the waves. His voice echoes in the distance.

"...My boat, Casper, is gone! All the boats have been pulled out to the ocean. A man, a dead man! I swear so dead he filthy rots. The corpse sports a dragon tattoo behind his almost decomposed right ear lobe. He looks multi-ethnic-mixed, could be of Hispanic descent, in his mid-forties. He has a missing index finger and expensive gold rings on the four fingers of his right hand. In his tightly clenched left fist is a wet- suit. His grasp on it is so tight not even the rough seas had a chance to dislodge this object from his lifeless hands. What an ... eclipse!"

MOMENTS LATER, FLASHING LIGHTS accompany the coroners' vehicle, with Jamaican Police vehicles in tow. It races to the scene. The medics quickly place the "washed ashore human body" in a body bag and haul it away aboard coroner's transport.

2

In the interim, retrospectively, over a thousand miles away, it is a beautiful sunny day in St. Georges, Grenada. The local TV weatherman takes his reporting to another level by boasting the clarity of the sky and the warm water beaches in and around the capital city. This much smaller Island to the south is nestled between St. Vincent and the Grenadines, a group of 32 Islands neighboring Trinidad and Tobago, two Islands in the Greater Antilles.

In the meantime, the brisk wind and the heat extract the spicy aroma from various produce, particularly those transported to the market by late vendors in pickup trucks.

The savory, spicy fragrances saturate the air. Ships, arriving and departing, toot their horns as they signal their mix with the sailing traffic.

Several people congregate A few blocks away, including a priest and other dignitaries. ALBERTO GOMEZ, drug Czar and leader of the Dragon Drug Cartel emerges. The man who was once assumed dead after a most recent high seas shoot out with DEA agent Rude Buay, back in Jamaica.

Alberto is in his mid-to-late 30s and dressed in an expensive business suit and dark glasses. He is of descent. The Drug Czar is poised with a pair of scissors in hand.

"Ladies and gentlemen, today we celebrate a new landmark in the history of the Caribbean. This library stands as a cornerstone for the men and women...of tomorrow. What good is a man if he ducks ... his education? Worthless! Your children's future has never looked brighter."

He cuts the ribbon to the sound of a standing ovation and applause, accompanied by a brief interlude of steel band music.

The librarian, a Caucasian woman in her early 50s, wearing spectacles and proudly displaying her name tag: VERONICA TOWNSVILLE, saunters across and shakes Alberto's hand.

DAVID LEE, an Entrepreneur and Asian Drug Czar wearing an expensive suit and dark sunglasses, ambles through the crowd.

David hands Alberto a slip of paper. Alberto reads the handwritten note and accompanies David back to his car.

They embark.

The car driven by Lee takes off SPEEDILY.

3

The car pulls up just a few blocks away at the Grenada Medical School. Alberto Gomez steps out of the car. The car continues. With a clipboard and pen in hand, Alberto urges the students charismatically,

"Sign up for educational funding! The future of your country rests in your hands, not in your government."

It's not long before he attracts an enormous crowd. Amongst the gathering, several enthusiasts eagerly sign up in response to his plea.

In the crowd, AMANDA KINGSLEY stands out. Amanda is African American and in her late 30s. She softens her stern demeanor as she looks out at the growing line of candidates, all waiting to benefit from her boss' financial aid program. Alberto makes eye contact with her. She evolves and, with sophistication, handles the dense crowd. After satisfying the many would-be students, Alberto and Amanda depart on foot.

Smiles from that upcoming medical fraternity sweeten the two organizers' goodbye. Alberto and Amanda board a waiting taxi. A black limousine pulls up moments after the cab drives off.

AGENT RANDY BASCOMBE nicknamed RUDE BUAY - aka "Rude Boy," is of Jamaican descent. He exits the car from the rear seat on the driver's side. He's in his early forties, adorned with a scorpion tattooed on his bald head, with its fangs upstaging his forehead and a tail extending towards his right earlobe. Dressed in street clothes, he steps out.

The agent is oblivious that Alberto Gomez and his team have left the building, so he waits for Alberto's exit from the medical compound. Alberto is a no-show. To Rude Buay, from how things look on the outside, everything indicates it's a typical day at any school. Even so, he enters the compound just in case Alberto lingers. A Guard meets and greets him.

"Are you looking for someone?"

The guard asks.

"Where is your restroom?"

Rude Buay inquires.

The guard accommodates nonchalantly.

Rude Buay visits the facility, noticing nothing rather unusual. He departs and reboards the waiting limousine. The limousine waits. Rude Buay dials DEA headquarters in Miami.

MICHAEL ORTIZ, in his early 50s, replacing the snuffed out Jose Mendez Rude Buay's former boss, picks up the phone.

"This is Rude Buay,"

"How are things in Grenada?"

"Nothing to report on Alberto's whereabouts just yet, except he is like a cat with nine lives."
Rude Buay responds.
"Well, we need you back in Miami… seeing that the dead man has not shown up yet,"
Ortiz says sarcastically.
Feeling like the last statement is seasoned salt in his wound,
"Why? What is going on in Miami?"
Rude Buay asks double questioningly,
"We can always use good DEA in Miami. One who can afford to let sleeping dogs lie."
Rude Buay ponders and ends the call. The Limo makes a hard U-turn and later arrives outside the airport.
Rude Buay hurries inside the terminal, boarding a plane bound for Miami.

4

One day later. Outside the dock in Montego Bay, a taxi pulls up with two women seated on the rear seat. Alberto saunters from one parked taxi to one with the occupants. He boards on the front passenger seat. On the rear seat, seated, is his wife, DENISE GOMEZ, and SHELLY HALL. Denise is an Asian trophy woman in her late twenties. Her engagement ring, touching her wedding band, is to be significantly desired by any woman. The blinding rock speaks for itself. Denise's new hairstyle also gives her a much more sophisticated, younger look. Alberto is happy to see her alive, and vice versa. On the other hand, SHELLY HALL is Caucasian, tall, aggressive, and a WWE type. Looking for a fight, Shelly is in her 30s, wearing a red bandana that coordinates with the healing bruises on her face. Both women are armed with semiautomatics. Night falls. The taxi pulls up outside the Blue Lagoon Hotel. Alberto and Denise exit the cab and enter the hotel. Shelly continues the ride to MO BAY airport. Alberto's newly acquired outfits are lying on the bed in the hotel room. Among them are nicely tailored suits and a wetsuit. He goes to the bathroom, discards the upper portion of another wetsuit in the trash, and passionately reacquaints himself with Denise.

Alberto's cell phone rings. He answers it. "Don Señor Alberto, the shipment is ready to be picked up, pronto,"

The voice of SALVADOR, his counterpart, assures. Sal is better known as a Colombian in his late 30s and stationed in Bogota. He is overseeing the day-to-day operations of cutting and shipping cocaine to Miami, The Caribbean, and Asia. His inaccurate cutting was responsible for the glitch in the lethal.

Dragon X, which caused the death of many Jamaican kids a few months prior.

Salvador hangs up the cellular phone and drives off in his white pickup truck.

"Gracias,"

Alberto says.

He speedily dials another number,

Shelly Hall, rushing out of the shower with a towel wrapped around her, picks up the phone from her hotel room.

"I need you on the plane heading to Miami in the morning. I need a clean job, no flaws."

Alberto demands.

"I'm on it!"

Shelly responds.

5

Later that evening, a private airplane touched down at Dade County Airport in Miami and parked at a hangar. Shelly deplanes, under disguise, and dressed to the nines. Shelly's demeanor says she is anxious to team up and be back in Miami with the cartel. A RASTAFARIAN, wearing a green, yellow, and black team, the colors of Jamaica, with his dreadlocks hairstyle almost touching his butt, greets Shelly enthusiastically—the Rastafarian hands over a set of keys and an envelope.

Shelly opens the envelope. She pulls out the white sheet of paper with instructions written on it. She reads them and departs the airport terminal en route to the parking lot. Shelly presses the remote, and a black-on-black Jaguar answers like an obedient child. She hurries to it, gets in, and drives away. This automobile is quite her style.

ON THE FOLLOWING MORNING, after many failed attempts, the sun shines some tiny rays of sunlight on the Dade County Prison. This enormous structure, nestled in the suburban area of Miami, Florida, is a landmark to many. It is public knowledge that the walls are over twenty-five feet below the ground as they are above the ground. They boast a diameter of over three feet in thickness. Built over a hundred years ago, no one has ever escaped those walls. This prison has housed many non-celebs as well as celebrities.

A midnight blue van pulls out from the facility's underground parking area. It exits the compound and merges with the steady flow of morning traffic, carrying three guards and the driver: RAYMOND PEREZ, of Cuban descent. Raymond is armed to the max.

In the rear: TONY CLINTON, Caucasian, and DARRELL WEEKS of African American descent. Both men are also armed to the hilt.

Darrell Weeks looks across at his co-worker, who has a gun pointed at the prisoner en route to Miami's maximum-security prison. Their man is JOHNNY, alias "Too Bad."

Johnny is a Jamaican of African American descent who was recently captured in Jamaica and extradited to America by the U.S. Government. It was claimed that Johnny was one of the most notorious Drug Lords to ever operate on the Island of Jamaica outside of ALBERTO GOMEZ leader of the Dragon Drug Cartel. Johnny ruled Tivoli Gardens. Looking across at Clinton, Johnny remains stone-faced while shackled with hands and feet.

The Miami Prison Official blue vehicle approaches the Miami Bay Bridge as traffic diminishes. A black Jaguar tailing it for more than half a mile speeds up from behind and passes the moving van, slicing its way directly in front of it to avoid a head-on collision with a tractor-trailer. The two guards in the back of the prison transport are discombobulated as they grab onto the vehicle's seat for support.

Johnny is shaken up. Even so, he remains poised and stoned-faced.

"That is a sick ...! Where the heck did she get her driving instructions?"

Raymond, the driver, mutters.

"She must have bought it in South Beach."

Responds Darrell Weeks.

The correction officers share a jovial laugh in regard to the South Beach allusion.

"BTW, did any of you watch that repo show about South Beach?

Clinton states in gest.

There is silence as no one seems to get what he is talking about.

He answers his question by saying,

"It's sick."

Moments later, along the mid-point portion of the bridge, the Jaguar comes to a complete stop. Before the van could complete its unavoidable rear-end collision with the Jaguar, the driver of this chic, luxurious vehicle, Shelly Hall, opens the door. Shelly jumps out of the car and over the bridge, plunging into a frigid body of water.

The airbag in the prison vehicle malfunctions. The no-seatbelt-wearing Perez sails through the front windscreen and out onto the bridge's roadway, head first. Perez's weapons and most of his warden accessories disperse as he crashes hard onto the metal and concrete pavement. He tries to get up but is unable to make it solo. So, he falls unconscious back to the ground.

Flustered and in a state of panic, Tony Clinton jumps out to assist Perez.

Johnny seizes the opportunity, and he head-butts Darrell Weeks with full force. That severe blow and impact caused Weeks' head to crash hard against the longitudinal interior of the van. Knocked out, he collapses onto the floor.

Johnny, still chained, hands and legs, sits on top of Weeks, now in the fetal position. Johnny seizes the opportunity, searches through the Warden's pockets, and retrieves the keys he uses to free himself.

Prowling, Johnny darts outside and finishes off Raymond Perez and Tony Clinton, one round of bullets per officer.

Johnny speedily returns to the van and discharges one round of bullets inside Weeks' mouth, finishing him off.

Before making his escape, Johnny pulls out a plastic bag of weed from inside his underwear. It is a large Ziploc bag.

He empties the contents on the driver's seat. One whiff of that deposit is enough to get one high and sustain it for hours.

Johnny secures his gun inside the bag, seals the bag, and slides the package inside his waist. He plunges into the frigid water of Miami Bay. Traffic is at an all-time standstill as the bridge is only now accessible by foot traffic.

The early arrivers seem to want to dive in after Johnny, but they dare to carry out such a feat from so high an altitude and pursue any armed criminal.

When rescue teams finally press their way through, they plunge into the deep with bloodhound dogs. News reporters converge on the scene. The rescue teams come up empty, as neither Shelly nor Johnny are recovered from the Bay.

HOURS LATER, AND MILES AWAY from the scene, a 75-foot-long submarine made of fiberglass and wood surfaces picks up Shelly and Johnny Too Bad.

6

Back in Jamaica, a Caucasian woman named BEVERLY HASTINGS, adorned with a lengthy dreadlocks hairstyle, almost touching her butt, is bottle feeding her toddler. Beverly is in her mid-thirties, and at a younger age, it looked like she could have been a runway model if she wanted to. She aborts feeding her five-month-old son, Andrew. This kid has just finished sucking on the residue in that eight-ounce bottle.

Before she could adequately burp Andrew, her three-year-old daughter Leticia, once seen sucking the residue from her bottle, falls off the high chair and onto the floor below.

Beverly puts the toddler in his crib and rushes to her daughter Leticia's aid. Three other kids, two boys, and one girl, all under the age of five, rush out of the bedroom to the scene.

Beverly picks up Leticia, who is now limp and in a daze. Leticia's vital signs are almost nil, save only for a little visual movement in her upper torso. Beverly tries comforting the little girl in her arms. Finally, Leticia collapses with the climax of one last breath while lying in her mother's arms. Beverly is not only flustered but mortified. She desperately tries CPR. That doesn't revive her three-year-old Leticia.

Beverly screams out, as do the other kids, except for baby Andrew, who lies innocently in his crib playing with his hanging toys. Beverly calls 911 and then huddles with three of her kids. They are all sobbing, engulfed in tears.

Moments later, the Medics arrive.

Inquiring Neighbors also show up. The Medics enter the house and return with Leticia on a Gurney. Leticia was rushed away aboard the Medical vehicle earlier.

THE FOLLOWING MORNING, two middle-aged women from Child Protective Services arrive at Beverly's door. Jamaican Police officially escort them in a squad car. One of the women carrying a clipboard knocks on the door. Beverly answers. The police officers introduce themselves as Officers Bailey and Carter.

Bailey addresses her,

"Miss Hastings, my name is Officer Bailey with the Jamaica Police Department, and this is Officer Carter. Based on autopsy results, it was determined that your daughter, Leticia, died as a result of a drug overdose. We have been authorized to assist in the removal of four kids, Andrew, Michael, Max, and Sherunda Hastings, from your custody, pending an investigation."

The officers round up the kids and carry them through the door.
Beverly sheds tears as she witnesses her kids escorted inside the Child Protective Services vehicle. The officers return to the house. Bailey once again addresses,
"Miss Hastings, I am afraid we will have to take you to the station for further questioning."
They escort Beverly outside. The two Jamaican police officers shove Beverly into the rear seat of the squad car, and the vehicle departs.
Beverly returns to the house a few days later, but the kids don't. Maintaining her innocence, Beverly, in her mind's eye, knew that she was framed and couldn't understand why and by whom. Even so, she is determined to solve this gruesome mystery. Beverly sits on the side of the bed, smoking a Hookah. It poses an enormous challenge for Beverly to recall everything relating to her five orphaned kids, mainly in those moments before the mishap. So, she decided to retrace her steps calculatingly.

In her mind, she relived the entire meal preparation process for little Leticia. It started with washing and sterilizing the feeding bottle and putting the eight-ounce milk bottle in Leticia's hand. Beverly's intuition led her to the milk can container, where she scooped the milk to make Leticia's meal. Upon opening the can, she recalled sensing nothing abnormal. Yet, she could not leave the milk can alone for some reason. She read up on the contents, prepared instructions, and even where they were packaged.

Beverly frustratingly turns the can upside down, emptying all the powdered milk onto the kitchen table. To her surprise, a plastic Ziploc bag is on the top of the milk pile. The size of the bag averaged at least one eight of a kilo of a white substance. While removing it, the powdered contents continuously seep out and onto the heap. Using her pinky finger, Beverly takes a taste test. The sordid look on her face indicates that there wasn't all milk inside the milk container. Saddened, her scream alerts the neighbors.

Some neighbors abandon their chores in an investigative pursuit. Some of them show up barefooted.

One woman, in particular, wears her bathrobe and house slippers. Another woman arrives with one-half of her hair styled and the other half still in rollers.

In tears, Miss Hastings immediately called 911. Minutes later, her house is now not only filled with visitors but the same two police officers who orchestrated her arrest. They showed up. The officers, trying to mask their apology, confiscate the contaminated combination of milk and cocaine. They put the can inside the squad car's trunk and drive off.

7

A light blue sedan pulls up outside the Miami Drug Enforcement office. The car builds the agent's radio transits before the driver, Agent Rude Buay, can slam the door shut.

The voice states, "Requesting DEA presence at Milky Way Warehouse, at the corner of Providence and Dixie Highway. Rude Buay gets back inside his car. He is making a swift U-Turn, and his sedan merges, tires squealing, with the intercepting traffic.

Rude Buay speedily pulls up in front of the warehouse. He jumps out armed but with caution. He notices a man's body, bloodied, lying in the gutter. The man's face, though bloodied, looks familiar.

Rude Buay goes to his car and retrieves a pair of gloves. He rolls the man over for a close-up look. Rude Buay shakes his head. He knows him. Rude Buay releases him.

The victim's badge falls out of his jacket pocket along with a Polaroid picture.

Rude Buay confiscates the two pieces of evidence along with the victim's wallet. He puts them in a plastic bag and lodges it inside the car trunk. Rude Buay notices the agent's car across the street. He investigates the agent's car for additional evidence. Moments later, Paramedics arrive and remove the body from the scene. Medics place the body inside a body bag. Miami Police Officers intervene and yellow tape of the area. Before the dispatch call, Agent Rude Buay was dispatched to the scene. The victim, undercover agent MARK JONES, showed up outside the Milky Way Warehouse and purchased two kilos of cocaine from Shelly Hall.

After the deal was made, FRANKIE O'NEAL, in his early 40s, pulled up in a black limousine to fetch her and Johnny. One Arm Frankie- as he is nicknamed decked out in a suit and tie, wearing an artificial left arm with a stub and a clip at the end of it is all business. Shelly and Johnny board the black limo while the undercover agent approaches his vehicle. Johnny, seated in the limo's front seat, rolls the window down and blows the man's brains out with the stolen warden's gun.

Shelly, getting inside the rear of the limo, asked,

"Why did you shoot him?"

Johnny responded,

"Just another PIG who deserved to die. Every pig ought to be dead; they get in the way of business." Johnny retrieved the narcotics from the undercover agent and threw them back inside on the rear seat of the limo.

Frankie drives away, taking the back roads and side streets to the Manor atop the hill.

Back at DEA headquarters, agent Rude Buay tries to glean more detailed information about the Polaroid photo recovered at the crime scene. So, he searches the web for all the elite homes in Dade County. He comes up empty. Flustered, he goes to the office next door. No one is there except for a box of Crispy cream doughnuts. He indulges.

Rude Buay's new partner, MILES TATE, a Caucasian in his early 30s, whose youthful demeanor says I am a rookie. He walks in with a soda in hand. On the other hand, he carries a copy of the chronicle Rude Buay … The Unstoppable, along with a yellow highlighter.

Tate, looking at Rude Buay, states,

"I thought you didn't like chocolate,"

Rude Buay replies,

"It looked so good, I couldn't resist."

Rude Buay continues,

"On the first day of work, you often study people's preferences. Plus, only overzealous students read with a dual-colored - high-lighter."

Tate responds,

"I was in the Greenroom and noticed that only chocolate donuts were left in the box. So, I assumed you…"

Rude Buay, looking at the book in Tate's hand for a second time, remarks,

"Reading, killing time, or studying?"

Tate replies,
"Digesting and assimilating." "Have you ever seen this house before, Miles?' Rude Buay asks, pointing to the Polaroid.
Tate responds,
"Never. No sir."
"Who owns this …?" Rude Buay questions,
"Your guess is as good as mine and as well as Mark Jones'." Tate replies.
"Look it up and see what you find."
Rude Buay finishes the doughnut. He picks up the Polaroid and exits from the Green Room.
Tate yells,
"Do you need me for backup?"
Rude Buay responds,
"I got this. Call me if you find something." Rude Buay hits the streets in his sedan. The car tires burn rubber upon take off.

8

Rude Buay pulls up in his sedan outside a REMAX real estate office and barges inside.
A tall, peerless woman who looks straight out of Desire Magazine and is wearing a nametag that reads ROCHELLE HUNTER answers the buzzer. She takes on a sophisticated business-like persona.
Rude Buay saunters into her office. She acts like Real Estate Person of the Week adept, although unraveled by Rude
Buay's presence,
"I'm Rochelle Hunter. Who do I have the pleasure of finding their dream home today?"
Rochelle states while directing Rude Buay to a seat.
"I'm Randy Bascombe."
"What brings you to REMAX, Mr. Bascombe?"
She asks,
Rude Buay responds,
"I'm very intrigued by your properties. I am looking for something very chic."
Rochelle responds,
"What's your interest? Mr. Bascombe, what can we help you move into within the next ninety days?" Rude

Buay is captivated by her beauty. Even so, he tries to conceal that desire.

Rude Buay replies,

"I'm looking for something Colonial with much privacy, maybe. I want to be able to entertain my friends, well, … there."

Rochelle replies,

"We're out of those colonials, but there's a lovely Victorian on the market right now. It's an entertainer's dream and is privately tucked away in one of the chicest locations in Dade County. This impressive 3-acre new estate will have you staying for a long time. There is a private and gated entrance, sprawling lawns for volleyball and basketball, an adjacent tennis court, organic gardens, an artist retreat, and a detached guest house. Mr. Bascombe, the ground floor plan offers five bedroom suites, great natural light, his study, her study, and a craft room. A professional theater, billiards room, an extensive wine cellar, a full-size gym, and much more. Fit for a King!" Rude Buay removes the Polaroid from his jacket, walks over to her desk, sits on its edge, and lays them out before Rochelle. She browses through. Rude Buay says,

"I'd like one just like that or similar." Rochelle reflects on that particular sale as she scans through the database.

Rochelle states,

"Six months ago. Three million dollars! That's a rare one."

Rude Buay asks,
"Who's the proud owner?"
Rochelle responds,
"That's strictly confidential, Mr. Bascombe."
"Really?" Rude Buay inquires.
Rochelle informs,
"We are not under obligation to give out confidential information to potential buyers."
Rude Buay remarks,
"Could you have the owners give me a tour, just in case they ever decide to sell?"
Rochelle replies,
"Not on this one! We could have one like that built for you. It will take years…"
Rude Buay insists, still sitting on the edge of her desk.
Have you ever been...?
Rochelle questions,
"Why did you ask?"
Rude Buay pulls out his gun, pointing it towards her head. She's trembling.
Rude Buay continues, "I need a name and the address."
Rochelle retrieves the data from her Rolodex.
Alberto Gomez. 712 Palm Grove.
Bang! Bang! Bang!
Bullet shells were scattered throughout the office. Several rounds of bullets through the glass window strike Rochelle.

Meanwhile, Rude Buay ducks for cover. Lying on the ground, he fires a few rounds at the perpetrator. The villain, Frankie, is unhurt, as nothing connects owing to his agility.

Frankie speeds away from the scene inside the black limousine, his gun occupying the front passenger seat. Rude Buay gets up, dusts himself off, darts outside, boards his sedan, and follows aggressively in the pursuit of One Arm Frankie.

The fast-driving One Arm Frankie eludes Rude Buay as his limo disappears.

Agent Rude Buay radios DEA Headquarters for backup while he continues pursuing Frankie O'Neal, the culprit.

9

On top of a hill, Rude Buay's vision is suckered into the much sought-after Colonial Manor.

Its grandeur is a majestic sight to behold. He is poised for this dream come true and the grand tour—except that now it's officially DEA business. Finally, the most desired house is less than a half mile away. His adrenaline rush is at an all-time high. Rude Buay reaches inside his breast pocket and retrieves the blood-stained Polaroid. He very quickly discerns that it's a perfect match. He radios DEA Headquarters for backup.

Miles Tate responds.

"I am coming up the hill. After you left, I went to work and found the information about the house you were looking for. Alberto Gomez owns it. It is one of a kind. Very rare…"

"Enough! Tate. Just meet me there ASAP."

Says Rude Buay,

Tate speeds up. His sedan swerves as it careens through the narrow uphill streets. The Manor is now in sight. Realizing that it's his first day on the job, Tate is up for the task ahead.

MOMENTS LATER, RUDE BUAY steps out of his car. Tate pulls up behind him and follows suit. Rude Buay is confronted with multiple gate entries inside the Manor. He presses the buzzer outside the monumental Iron Gate to the manor while Tate covers.

There's no response.

Unfortunately, he tries again, to no avail. Rude Buay relocates. He detects a switch box behind the Iron Gate. He squeezes his hand between the gate and the wall and PRIES opens the box. The device is harnessed with multiple colored wires and an excess of black, blue, and red wires.

Rude Buay is puzzled by the sophisticated wiring of the switch box. However, he is occupied with bridging the buzzer with his device, which takes precedence. At the same time, Tate keeps any possible retaliation at bay. Immediately, two Guards march out from the house toward the gate trigger, happy. Tate is alert and ready. While they train their weapons, Tate counterattacks.

Tate CAPS both of them before they could accomplish their objective. With the two guards dead, Rude Buay focuses more on bridging the connection to the intercom. Yet, he remains unaccomplished.

The Black Limo PULLS up from the opposite direction, with full-beamed illuminated headlights. Johnny Too Bad and his partner Frankie O'Neal are out of the limo RUSHES.

They immediately discharge multiple rounds at Tate and Rude Buay.
The agents retaliate, trying to MATCH Frankie's onslaught and Johnny's firepower. A smaller adjacent gate opens as if by its own accord. Johnny and Frankie swiftly make their way through that gate while dodging the bullets from the agents' onslaught as if they were the size of an NBA basketball. The gate closes abruptly behind them. Rude Buay notices the infrared light on the surveillance camera up ahead. He aims and SHOOTS at the camera, dismantling it with the camera now out of commission. Johnny and Frankie's shooting intensifies as they REFUSE to let up. In the meantime, Tate hides and shoots from behind the left wall pillar supporting the massive Iron Gate. Rude Buay does the SAME from behind the right pillar.

Rude Buay, in an effort to limit the Drug Lord's possible getaway tactics, SHOOTS up the black limo, deflating all four of its tires with his rounds of fire. Tate single-handedly manages to keep Johnny and Frankie at bay during a fierce, fiery, DEBRIS-FLYING exchange caused by a sequence of RAINING bullets. Bullets sailing through and over the iron gates from all the parties involved. Yet nothing connects.
Suddenly, Frankie realizes that his guns are out of bullets.
Rude Buay clues in and aims for Frankie's head.

Frankie turns to flee.

Rude Buay aims for his head and SHOOTS. Frankie somersaults. The bullet ricochets and catches Frankie in the left leg.

Frankie falls to the ground and gets back up, limping and tossing rocks at the agents. Johnny hurriedly reaches under his coat and, with his right hand, BRINGS out a semi-automatic. Now two-gun-equipped, he does a 360-degree turn while he UNLOADS on Tate and Rude Buay.

The gun in Johnny's left hand goes CLICK, CLICK. He THROWS it to the ground and BRINGS out another with his left hand from under the left side of his coat, he continues to shoot with the one in his right hand. Tate DARTS through flying bullets during the swift exchange of this gunfire interim. He SPRINTS towards the limo and opens the rear door. Johnny sees the move made by Tate, but he concentrates on TAKING OUT Rude Buay, who is still attacking with a vengeance. The wall pillar begins to sag as the Iron Gate moves a few inches horizontally, leaving a wider gap.

Rude Buay senses the pending collapse of the Iron Gate but RELOADS and continues shooting at Frankie and Johnny.

The Limo is penetrated with multiple bullet holes. Tate searches inside and discovers a collection of Uzis, grenades, and other weaponry, in addition to several milk cans. Tate exchanges his semi-automatic for two Uzis and EXITS like Rambo in full force. Tate

DISCHARGES from both Uzis. Still, he's no match for Johnny's experience and firing power, although unscathed by Johnny's onslaught. Johnny yells out,
"Catch me if you can, Rude Buay!"

Rude Buay emerges from behind the twisted pillar and glimpses at Frankie's and Johnny Too Bad's backside. He aims for Johnny Too Bad. However, they immediately disappear inside the interior of the Manor. The two agents with enough room barely
SQUEEZE their way through the partially opened gate. They enter the grounds very cautiously in pursuit.

The agents enter the gigantic living room through the front door. The ceiling is almost twelve feet high, and a gigantic fireplace with ash residue greets them. The Living room is decorated with oriental rugs and other chic furniture. A large glass screen door leads to the pool area. There seems to be no current activity on the part of the dwellers except for the incongruent display of bloodstains.

They move through each room in a "take-down" style, looking for a trace of consistency. They wind up in the dining room, which is next door to a bathroom.

They search inside the bathroom, but no one's there. The table in the dining room catches their attention, so they return to it.

Entering the dining room, they careen by the vast dining table, with twelve disheveled arranged chairs and a bar secluded in the far corner. On the table: two huge partially fresh mounds of cocaine with two straws and two razor blades reside refilled cigarettes, a pile of laced cigarette extracts, a crack pipe, syringes, and several Polaroid shots with groups of Asian kids. Next to those pictures are opened milk cans. The agents sweep the house room by room but still come up empty-handed, as the dwellers have left the premises without any apparent exit trail. The agents, puzzled by their exit strategy, rummage through the Manor a second time to collect evidence and hope for a blunder on the part of the Drug Lords so they can roast them.

IN THE MEANTIME, Alberto, Shelly, and Johnny Too Bad vacate the premises using a trap door leading underground beneath the building's foundation. The trio boards a black limo. Frankie is in the driver's seat. A trail of blood leads to the driver's door. Frankie, who had stopped the bleeding at the house, is unaware that he is bleeding again as blood continues to trickle down his trousers' leg.

The limo departs and arrives at a small dock. There are 75-foot submarine surfaces and docks. Alberto, Shelly, and Johnny Too Bad exit the limo and board the ship. Meanwhile, Frankie oversees as the Sailor unloads several kilos and laden milk cans onto the waiting limo. Frankie O'Neal gets back inside the limousine. The limo drives off. The Sailor re-boards. Moments later, the submarine submerges and departs. Frankie, in pain, drives to the Milky Way. He gets out of the limo. He unlocks the back door to the building and unloads the milk cans into the warehouse. Blood droplets still accompany his every move. He is hurt but skillfully masks the pain. He returns to the limo and retrieves a milk can from the front seat. He opens it and takes out the Ziploc bag of cocaine from underneath the powdered milk. Now powdered milk is all over the front seat. In a sense of urgency, he opens the bag of coke, creates a few lines on the dashboard, and snorts them up as if to ease the pain. In added desperation, he places some on the wound and whimpers as the substance unites with his flesh. Anyway, he feels like there has been some relief to his pain. Even so, he is high, in a daze, and now unable to drive. So, he parks the car curbside.

10

At the same time, DEA agents arrive, swarming the exterior of the Manor. They yellow-tape the crime scene and depart.

Meanwhile, deep in the Manor's interior, Rude Buay hears a sound from the pool area. So, he conducts another sweep of the premises, with Tate covering him. Exiting through the rear door towards the pool, they encounter a caged PARROT, which is too quiet for its good.

Rude Buay, entertaining the bird, asks,

"You want a banana?"

The articulate Parrot yells,

"Thieves! Thieves! Thieves!"

Rude Buay convincingly,

"No, we're not."

The Parrot, not believing a word he says, argues,

"Liars! Liars! Liars!"

Rude Buay questions,

"Undercover?"

The Parrot argues,

"Same thing! What's with the gun? Who'd you shoot, Osama? Bang, Bang, Bang, Bang!"

Rude Buay probes,
"Self-defense, that's all. Where's Alberto, Johnny, and the rest of the gang? Where did they go?
TATE is enjoying the exchange.
The Parrot responds,
"That's confidential!"
Rude Buay urges,
"Come on, stud, I'll give you a peanut." Parrot dances.
After the imaginary curtain, the parrot unveils,
"Sailing. Sail away."
Rude Buay feeds it another peanut and asks,
"How do they do that?"
Rude Buay inquires.
The Parrot responds,
"Trap door opens up! Ship sails!"
Rude Buay removes the cage and its occupant. Suddenly, the alarm for the building goes off. The sound of a siren fills the air. Even so, Tate leads the way, holding onto the bag of confiscated evidence. Rude Buay exits the house with the caged bird.
The Miami Police arrive in response to the alarm. Police cruisers swarm the grounds. Tate flashes his DEA badge.
"Miles Tate. DEA business."
Rude Buay in confrontation,
"Where the hell you were when we needed you, Tate?"
One of the Officers responds,
"Better late than never."

Rude Buay and Tate jump into their respective vehicles. Rude Buay carries the caged bird. The vocal Miami Police Officer eyeing the caged parrot warns.

Officer continues,

"That's stolen property, Agent Rude Buay."

Rude Buay argues,

"He's a witness."

The Parrot addresses,

"Where's the subpoena? I no see nada nor hear nada. The vocal Miami police officer, somewhat amused, reaches for the bird. Could the parrot have witnessed a getaway, knows the escape route in the house, or possess a human-like vivid imagination? These thoughts lingered in Rude Buay's mind.

Anyway, he reluctantly hands over the bird to the Miami Police Officer.

Rude Buay, feeling a hunch, says,

"You can hold onto the bird but cover the exterior, or your A… is mine."

The Officer doesn't seem to get it.

Rude Buay continues,

"I have some unfinished business to complete on the inside. We will call you if I need you."

Rude Buay returns to the house's interior with Miles Tate.

Inside the Manor, Rude Buay eyes every square foot of the floor, looking for anything resembling a rug and carpet crack. From room to room, he surveys. Inside the master bathroom they previously visited, they come up upon a rectangular crease in the rug. The rectangular outline in the carpet indicates that a door, the size of a trap door, is concealed. The agents tug on the rug. A door opens up in the floor of the bathroom floor. Engaging the descending steps, with their guns cocked, the two agents wind up inside the partially lit tunnel.

Agents Rude Buay and Miles Tate descend inside the tunnel and discover several luxurious, expensive automobiles. In an investigative pursuit, they notice cars are parked on one end. The other end leads through a thoroughfare with a fork. The two agents walk the entire length of the small tunnel, which opens into a small dock.

11

Rude Buay notices the fresh tire marks in the mud beside the dock.

Additionally, bloodstains create a trail at the scene. Rude Buay "rolls up his sleeves" and calculates the measurement of the vehicle's chassis based on the impressions of the tire marks most dominant and resident in the mud. Based on his calculations, he estimates that this vehicle had to be at least 120 inches or more in length.

Staring across the blue-watered horizon, he adds another piece to the getaway puzzle.

"So, this is where they made their escape."

Rude Buay declares,

Miles Tate responds,

"Sure, looks like it!"

Rude Buay nods yes.

Miles Tate inquires,

"So, what's next?"

Rude Buay thinks long and hard as if he is not entirely up to it. Then, looking at Tate with direct eye contact, he responds,

"The Caribbean! If it's going to be up to me."

Miles Tate responds,
"Lies, corruption, deceit, and sabotage. Some trip, huh?"
Rude Buay, looking across the horizon, responds,
"You've got to be in it to win it. Before the Caribbean, though, I need to pick up some milk."
Miles Tate questions,
"Really? Milk?"
Rude Buay answers,
"Yep! Milk!"
The agents drive through Miami and pass several supermarkets in SEPARATE DEA CARS. Tate doesn't get Rude Buay's epiphany, so he radios Rude Buay.
"You forgot to get the milk?"
Tate asks,
"No, I didn't. Stay on my tail, and don't shoot unless I say so."
Rude Buay advises,
Moments later, the duo pulls up at the Milky Way. The Black limousine driven by Frankie pulls away from the curb. Rude Buay recognizes Frankie and vice versa. Rude Buay is in pursuit, followed by Tate.
The race proceeds through the streets of Miami.
Frankie tries to make a getaway before the entrance to the Interstate 95 Freeway. Rude Bauy is following him closely, so he changes his mind and opts for the highway's ramp. The two agents pursue him resolutely.
Rude Buay radios Tate.

"Get ready, and I'd rather have him alive than dead."
Tate questions,
"What's his value?"
Rude Buay informs his rookie,
"He didn't lose that one arm for nothing. I am sure."
Rude Buay tunes to his favorite reggae station. The DJ is playing his favorite. The vibe soothes. Rude Buay instructs Tate via other radio, "Call Headquarters and request a search and seizure at the Milky Way Warehouse, will you?" The Limousine merges with traffic as it enters the HOV lane. The two agents' vehicles follow suit.
They are now keeping pace with the limo. That dancehall music is still playing as if it's an extended version. Frankie, sensing being tailgated, exits the HOV lane illegally and merges to the right, thus causing a multi-vehicle collision while making his getaway. Rude Buay skillfully avoids the mayhem while Tate is boxed in because of the related accident. Rude Buay continues in pursuit of Frankie. The chase escalates through city streets, where the maneuvering of this 120-inch stretch limo is now problematic at such a high speed, posing a problem for other motorists.
On-lookers see a fatality brewing as pedestrians and motorists use their cell phones to videotape the happenings. Catching Frankie alive would appease Rude Buay, but in his mind, not at the expense of the lives of other motorists.

Suddenly, bullets from the limousine begin to rain in the direction of Rude Buay's sedan. Rude Buay aims for the right rear tire and connects.

The limo, swerving from side to side, careens slams into a retaining wall, lands on its roof, and bursts into flames.

Rude Buay gets out of his vehicle in an attempt to observe the demolition. Meanwhile, Tate pulls up, gets out of his sedan, stares at the flames, and then back at Rude Buay. Tate asks,

"I thought we wanted him alive."

Rude Buay replies,

"In life, you go after what you want, but nothing is wrong with accepting what you get. The
the thrill lies in the effort."

Tate looks at Rude Buay while assimilating that thought. He begins buying into Rude Buay's positive mental attitude. Rude Buay asks,

"Are you still up for the Caribbean?"

Tate smiles and responds,

"I wouldn't renege on the Caribbean for anything in the world."

They board their vehicles and depart for DEA headquarters. Agent Tate is excited about going to the Caribbean.

12

Rude Buay is in his office typing an email. He later submitted it to Michael Ortiz.

Walking out of the parking garage, Ortiz retrieves the email via his cell phone. He senses the importance, knowing that sending him an email is not Rude Buay's style.

Ortiz mulls over the contents as he knocks on Rude Buay's office door. Rude Buay answers the door. Ortiz barges in and looks squarely at Rude Buay in the face. Immediately, two junior agents enter through the still-open office door. Both agents are laden with part of the seizure recovered from their Milky Way drug bust. One of the agent's remarks while focusing on one of the milk containers:

"That place has recently turned into a narcotics depot. I don't think any place in Asia, Colombia, Canada, Mexico, or even the Caribbean has been this busy lately when it comes to narcotics trafficking. We just lost Agent Jones; he was a good man. It will be necessary to put Milky Way under surveillance 24/7." Ortiz responds, paying attention to the email and then to Rude Buay.

"Rude Buay, you've been there before. The U.S. greatly favored them by extraditing Johnny Too Bad from Jamaica. That should have helped. It's about time the locals fight their own narcotics war."

Rude Buay responds,

"So said your predecessor, the deceitful agent, Jose Mendez. This is our war. If we lose this one, we could be in for one of the most tragic recalls this world has ever encountered – Milk.

The prison authorities did the locals a disfavor by setting Johnny free.

With a menace of that caliber on the loose, who knows what will happen next? Who knows what his next target will be?

Our freedom gets eroded every day. Mainly because we fail to be all we can be.

To know something is wrong and not do anything about it is worse than not knowing that thing is incorrect."

Agent Rude Buay looks over at the junior agents and continues.

"Let me set the record straight. If you feel so sentimental about Milky Way, maybe you should step out of your comfort zone by honing your skills so you can protect your love interest."

They both make their exit feeling agitated regarding Rude Buay's sentimentalism statement.

Ortiz saving face,

"Rude Buay, give me until tomorrow to come to a decision. You understand that we are short-staffed. Who knows when agent Heidi Hudson will be well enough to return to active duty?"

Rude Buay reminds,

"Boss, the clock has been ticking since that submarine sailed from the Miami dock. Let me remind you: The most notorious Drug Lord since Alberto Gomez is on the loose. Not only that, but he has also linked up with Alberto, and his name is Johnny Too Bad.

Who knows what the two politicians could be concocting?

I will be packed and ready to go in the morning.

This is my country, and they are my people. If not Me? Who?"

If not Now?

When?"

13

It's late evening in Shanghai, China. Femme Fatales Denise Gomez, Shelly Hall, and Amanda Kinsley appear outside the Shanghai Karate School. The women are all dressed in karate gear, accessorized by luggage, including duffle bags. They survey and wait. Suddenly, David Lee gets off the elevator. The women are alerted as he turns the corner inside the lobby. They unzip the duffel bags and remove their semiautomatic weapons. The dark alley behind them adds to the grittiness and pre-nightfall.

David steps onto the sidewalk and is confronted with three women and three weapons pointing directly at him as they sucker him inside a portion of the dark alley.

David single-handedly disarms all three women in high-flying Kung Fu style, leaving them defenseless.

Even so, they remain verbally confrontational.

"This is not right, David…!"

Denise yells,

"Don't blame me, blame Sal. He cuts and packages…"

David responds.

"What does Sal have to do with this? This is a tough economy. Recession is eating away at our profit margin. Thankfully, we've got milk; that's our only conduit. Your packaging is horrendous that's why we...."

Denise explains.

"Do you know what could happen if milk gets recalled?" Shelly interjects. "Kids will starve."

David Lee replies.

"So would we!"

Denise responds.

"How many containers were in your last shipment?"

Denise asks.

"One thousand cans..."

David responds,

"One Thousand Cans?"

Denise, Shelly, and Amanda questioningly interrupt.

"That's what I said. One Thousand Kilos,"

David restates.

"We will have to use a different vendor for our containers, bags, and cans. That's not our style. It is all about quality. That is our entire existence."

David continues.

"Too late. Too ... LATE! No wonder you flunked out of high school, you bozo. What else have you fallen short on? Those Ziploc bags are defective."

States Shelly Hall,

Denise reminds David.

"My husband pays you well. Not for a botch job."
"This is my living. Yes, I flunked High School. If there is no me, you don't eat. Plus, wear that expensive jewelry."
Shelly attempts to retrieve her gun from the ground.
David senses her move.
David remarks,
"You touch that gun, and I will break your jawbone."
Denise looks across at Amanda—the Boss Woman
Amanda clues in. Amanda shows David the snake.
He responds with the crane.
They engage in hand-to-hand combat, Kung Fu style, with Amanda gaining the upper hand. When it is all over, David lies on the sidewalk, not only exhausted but badly hurt, "licking his wounds and embarrassed."
His lady, CHU LING, an Asian model in her late 20s, pulls up in her fully loaded BMW. She steps out, glides across, and onto the sidewalk, peering inside the dark alley.
As a result of the humiliation and the pain endured by her man, Chu's take-out order of Chinese food falls out of her hands and onto the paved sidewalk in decorativeness.
Denise, ignoring Chu's presence, responds sarcastically as they leave the scene,
"Take that! Get your act together or next time, or you will experience a threesome."

14

The following morning, Michael Ortiz walks inside Rude Buay's office and notices he's all packed with Tate's luggage aligned next to his. Tate walks in, and in acknowledgment of his superiors, he smiles, accompanied by a slight nod of the head.
Ortiz addresses:
"Your return to Miami is very much anticipated, gentlemen. Who knows where the next tunnel will be constructed? Our city needs you now more than ever."
Rude Buay and Ortiz shake hands. Rude Buay and Agent Tate leave in a sedan. Tate takes the wheel.
On the drive to the airport, Rude Buay catches up on making some phone calls.
He dials.
Inside the gadget-filled living room, WALTER BANKS, an African American man in his fifties with salt and pepper hair, is on the phone. On the other cell phone, in Bogota, Colombia, is a barefooted CHELO, in his mid-30s and of descent. Chelo secures a newly constructed ladder to a tree overlooking the village and, mainly, its long stretch of dusty unpaved roadway.

"What is next for him and Johnny? Nobody knows. I am sure if matters get worse, Rude Buay will respond."
Walter Banks states,
"Did he ever pay you from that last…?"
Chelo asks,
Banks interrupts,
"Hold on, Chelo. We talked about the devil, and here he is. I have to grab this call. Let's talk later."
Banks abort that call with Chelo and facilitate Rude Buay's.
"Man after my own heart, Mr. Rude Buay! Chelo and I were talking about you. When are you going to visit the homeland? So, we could enjoy roast breadfruit with Ting, ackee, and salt fish."
"Don't tempt me with that finger-licking food, Banks. You know how this black man loves to feed his stomach? I will be there on the first flight from Miami in the morning. Why don't you, Mildred, and the Commissioner meet my partner Tate and me for a midday debriefing at the hole in the wall?"
"I don't foresee a problem with Mildred attending; you know how that woman feels about you. On the other hand, the General Election talks are heating up. I'm unsure about the Commissioner, but one never knows if he can meet with you on such short notice."
The sedan pulls up at the airport parking lot. Rude Buay is still on the phone.
"Banks, 9:00 a.m., see you then."

Banks calls MILDRED SIMMS, a Caribbean beauty in her late twenties. She is a drop-dead gorgeous, sophisticated African American beauty every man's heart desires. Mildred is filing her nails at the office. She picks up on the second ring.

"Mr. Banks ah whey yo, ah deal with?" She answers in deep patois.

Banks took aback as he had never heard Mildred drop some patois before.

"Rude Buay will be in tomorrow. He wants to meet at noon at the hole in the wall. Are you available...?"

"Is that doctor going to be there?"

Inquires Mildred, "It's a debrief..."

Banks responds.

"Okay, will you come to get me?"

Mildred suggests.

"Will do!" Says Banks.

RICHARD BAPTISTE, the commissioner, sits across from the Governor-General Bradford Wiley. The two men are casting light on the Beverly Hastings situation. Wiley suggests that Beverly be reunited with her four kids. Based on the fact that she was oblivious, the milk was contaminated with cocaine.

On the other hand, Baptiste feels that the situation should not be rushed. Additionally, he argues that Beverly should be retested for any possibility she was under the influence at the time of Leticia's death or has recently been a narcotics user. Baptiste's office phone rings. He gets it.

"Mr. Commissioner, it's Walter Banks!"
Baptiste accommodates.
"I know you are a busy man. Mr. Rude Buay will be coming in tomorrow. He will arrive at 9:00 a.m. If you are available, Rude Buay would like to meet at noon to catch up on old times and the current crisis."
"Oh Really? Do you mean that he did this on his own accord? What a changed man! Tell him I will oblige. By the way, do you know if that scorpion he had on his head is a temporary fixture or a permanent one?"
Baptiste inquires,
"You may want to ask him about that yourself. I am sure he will fill you in. See you at the hole in the wall, Commissioner."
Banks replies.
The Commissioner returns to his discussion with the Governor-General.
While Walter Banks aborts the call and continues to enjoy the sunset view of the harbor.

15

The shadows lengthen as the sun sinks beyond the horizon in Montego Bay, Jamaica. Late workers enjoy the light traffic flow as they leave their jobs for their respective domiciles. A few vagrants hang out on the corner streets. Some are getting high while others are just chilling, listening to music via earphones on their iPhones. A cargo van displaying U.S. diplomat license tags pulls up and parks on the outside next to the Ministry of Tourism building. Inside under the wheel is Shelly Hall, Denise

is upfront in the passenger seat, while Amanda is in the rear seat with her gun in hand.

A security guard notices the vehicle but fails to investigate, taking those diplomat plates for granted. In his mind, it could be nothing more than a UN diplomat conducting official business. Workers continue to file out of the Ministerial compound, some pedestrians and motorists, and carpoolers. Mildred Simms steps out of the building and travels towards her car. That stud of a security guard steps out of the booth and walks over to her. He sneakily indulges in walking her to her car. She gets inside. He closes the door behind her. The car takes off.

Mildred drives out of the parking lot. Suddenly, her car is sandwiched between three other cars, one in front and two behind.

The diplomat-wearing tag van now has several cars behind Mildred's car tailing it.

Approaching a small street, Shelly Hall notices the right indicator light blinking on Mildred's car up above. Mildred pulls up next to a hair salon. She parks the car and gets out of her car. She is heading towards the salon.

The van speeds up and stops parallel to Mildred's car. Mildred is sandwiched. Denise and Amanda jump out while Shelly completes the van's parking. Denise immediately stalls Mildred as she steps out.

Amanda, with a gun in one hand, wraps a huge bath towel continuously around Mildred's head. Tying a knot where the fabric ends.

Mildred's scream is almost muffled under the towel.

They drag her to and inside of the van.

The van takes off as they finish binding her with ropes. They remove the towel and duct tape over Mildred's mouth.

Simultaneously, Johnny is positioned in a cube truck a few hundred feet from the Commissioners' home in MO Bay. Johnny Too Bad waits.

Secluded in a chic suburban neighborhood, not only very little evening traffic but the chirping noise of crickets accompanies Johnny's' linger.

The Commissioner's car pulls up. Richard Baptiste is always a sharp dresser. He is fitted with a nice shirt and tie. He looks suave and debonair. I'm happy to be home after a long day at the office. His car stops, waiting for a lounging cat to clear its stroll across the street. Baptiste prepares to pull into the driveway. Johnny takes off in the cube truck and intentionally rear-ends the Commissioner's car. The Commissioner gets out peeved, as he evaluates the damage done to this car.

Johnny steps out as if to console the Commissioner and possibly exchange some vehicular documental information. Instead, Johnny displays his gun. He puts Commissioner Baptiste under a chokehold, sticks a rag deep in his mouth, escorts him to the rear of the truck, opens it, and shoves him inside. Johnny duct-tapes the Commissioner's mouth, closes the door, returns to the driver's seat, and takes off. Now underway, Johnny radios Alberto.

"Mission accomplished, Boss!"

Albert responds,

"Let's meet up in Port Antonio close to the MPs blockade. Stay put once you get there. I will drive to meet you."

Johnny responds in patois,

"Scene, Rasta! I love those Ministers of Parliament to … rarted."

16

A taxi pulls up and waits outside Walter Banks' Port Antonio home. Under the wheel sits
Drug Czar and leader of the Dragon Drug Cartel, Alberto Gomez. Meanwhile, inside Walter Banks' house, the house phone rings. Banks answers it on the second ring.
On the other end is Chelo, his understudy. He's sitting on his living room floor in Bogota, Colombia, toying with his espionage gadgets. He picks up a video signal from Walter Banks's neighborhood in Jamaica.
"Banks, there's a taxi waiting on your block. Did you call a blue taxi cab? Are you going someplace? Did Rude Buay show up earlier than planned?" Chelo and images of the blue cab are now affixed to the TV monitor. He zooms in for more clarity.
Finally, the monitor goes blank.
Chelo fiddles with a few gadget antennas while still talking on the phone.
"I saw that taxi outside your home. The driver just sat there waiting. Your house lights were on. So, I figured you were at home. Now I lost that … signal. I don't see

it anymore. Let me try fixing the signal router. I will call you back."

Banks' phone rings again.

It's Chelo,

"Sorry, Banks, no more pictures. I lost it. I saw it a few minutes ago. Conyo! The blue taxi cab was there. I did not get the driver's profile, though. He looked … It happened so fast."

"Is he black? What does he look like?"

Banks inquires as he grabs his gun.

"I'm not sure. I didn't get a close-up of the driver. The image was just a flicker," Chelo responds.

"Darn, if Rude Buay changed his itinerary, why didn't he inform me? He knows where I stand with surprises. I hate them. He'd better not be pulling a fast one on me. I'll blow his brains out."

Banks states as he ensures that his gun is fully loaded.

"If he did, that's a big NO. Even if he offers you a bonus, you never know with those Americans."

"Got picture! Got Picture!"

Yells Chelo.

Continuing,

"It looks like the Don. Don Alberto, it is. He just stepped out of the taxi."

Banks finally gets a picture. It reveals Alberto coming toward the house and carrying a sack large enough to hold a UZI.

FLASHBACK:

Rude Buay calls a taxi and leaves. Later, Banks is sitting at the table at home having coffee while he reviews the blueprint. Suddenly, a bullet coming through his glass window pane strikes him. He blacks out.

BACK TO PRESENT:

Seeing this, Banks, knowing that a UZI will outmatch his arsenal of weaponry, turns off the light and exits through the back door, carrying his cell phone and semi-automatic gun in hand.
Alberto shows up outside the house. He removes the UZI from the sack, attached with a silencer. He knocks on the front door. There's no answer. He blows out the lock and enters the house. He switches the light on and rummages from room to room. There is no Walter Banks.
Noticing Banks' espionage gadgets, he kicks most of them over and unplugs the multiple TV monitors.
Meanwhile, Banks dials 911 for emergency backup before returning to the house, just in case he confronted Alberto. Don Alberto sees Banks' shadow entering the yard. He unloads several rounds on the Jamaican agent. Nothing connects. Banks fires back also missing the agile Alberto. The neighbors are alerted by the sound of firearms. Suddenly, the once quiet neighborhood, except for the sound of ships, is awakened to the sound of gunshots like popping corn.

Alberto gets inside the taxi and drives away before the community can converge on him.

Moments later, late-arriving Jamaican police flood the area in squad cars. They are too late. Alberto has already fled the area.

Chelo, losing signal once again in the satellite-unfriendly community of Port Antonio, is unable to capture Alberto's getaway.

Alberto Gomez later abandons the car in a ravine and joins forces with his partner in crime, Johnny Too Bad. Together they drive away with the Commissioner, taking him hostage.

17

The shaken-up Walter Banks nevertheless shows up solo and on time to meet with Rude Buay and Rude Buay's partner, Miles Tate. Rude Buay greets Banks and then introduces him to agent Miles Tate. "Glad to know you've escaped, " says Rude Buay. "Thanks to Chelo and his high-tech gadgets. His work will no doubt be in the Smithsonian Institute someday."
Banks replies,
"The Dragon Drug Cartel's MO indicates that they were planning a clean sweep operation. By kidnapping M ldred, the Commissioner, and then you, they would not have only left us ill-equipped to compete effectively - short-staffed to combat their onslaughts." A waitress seats the three men at a table.
Rude Buay asks,
"Which of the locals do you confide in, anc can be made ready soon?"
"Not sure about that. Most are still upset about how America handled the extradition of Johnny Too Bad.
States Walter Banks,
"Ah, they should let sleeping dogs lie. The man is a menace, always has been."
Interjects agent Tate,
"Banks, we will find the kidnappers along with your team members. *We may lose some battles, but rest assured we will win this war*.
Rude Buay cleverly responds.

The waitress serves up some roast breadfruit ting and saltfish with ackee. Tate looks as if he is not sure about the food.
Rude Buay in confidence,
"Eat up, man. It's all good. Ital food! Don't bite your fingers when you are finished."
Tate obliges and relishes the savory dish. Banks interjects,
"Maybe the doctor will, seeing she knows so much about our last mission."
Rude Buay responds,
"I am afraid it's not her thing. They said if little Leticia was able to get to the hospital on time, her life might have been spared."
"The doctor is that good, huh?" Tate responds.
"Yes, Tamara is great at what she does."
Claims Rude Buay,
"Do we get to...?"
Tate interjects as he is interrupted by Banks.
"Yes, there is a great spot we can go after sunset."
"I haven't had a chance to talk with DEA headquarters about these kidnappings along with other new developments. By sunset, the kidnappers could ask for ransoms,"
States agent Rude Buay.
"You think?"
Tate replies,
"... and after sunset, no partying?"
Says Banks.
Rude Buay responds,
"I'd like to ask for a rain check on that one."
"You could invite TAMARA. Jamaica got to mix business with a little bit of pleasure. You never know who is connected to..."
Rude Buay reflects.
"Agent Tate is too wet behind the ears to deflect."
Banks inserts,
"Plus, he is missing his tattoo."
Tate looks at both men in response,

“I must say that I have read the entire account. I love it!”
“Good! I don’t want to have to take you fishing for
Jacks.”
“Is Jack your favorite fish?”
Tate asks.
“Every snitch finds out the hard way.” Rude Buay states as he
excuses himself from the table.
Tate follows Rude Buay.
While Banks stays behind.

18

At the Crows' Nest, an upscale restaurant nestled between the coconut trees and the beach in MO BAY. Rude Buay, Tate and
Banks are at a table having a few drinks. There is one vacant chair across from Rude Buay. The soulful Reggae artist performs a combination of dancehall favorites and ballads.
The three men are enjoying the ambiance of the festivity.

TAMARA ROSS, the stunningly eye-catching 26-year-old beauty, walks in. She has never looked so hot publicly. Eyes in the semi-lit room are focused on her, and the turning of the necks of all genders indicates multiple double-takes. If a massage therapist was present, that individual was about to cash in big time with some deep tissue and double sessions. Rude Buay acknowledges Tamara while admiring her sensuality.
Rude Buay gets up from his seat and pulls out her chair.
She sits.
He slides that chair in a little closer to the table.

Tamara is flattered.

He pats her lightly on the shoulder area.

She smiles.

He responds in kind.

Rude Buay introduces her,

"Glad you could join us. This is my partner agent, Miles Tate. Agent Tate, meet Dr. Tamara Ross."

Tate, drinking Guinness Stout, possibly for the first time, could not contain himself. The bottled drink slips out of Tate's hand and spills toward Walter Banks, some splattering on Banks' evening attire.

"Sorry, my gosh. I am so sorry."

Banks responds,

"Hey, calm down. You only had half of the bottle. What is the matter…?" Rude Buay interjects,

"I don't think it's the drink. Maybe…" The Maître D. darts in with a mop and wash rag. He begins cleaning up the spill.

The waiter aids him while he evacuates the guests to a table close to the stage.

The artist delivers another hot number. Tamara wishes Rude Buay would do this dance. Even so, all eyes at the table are focused on Miles Tate. Tamara, the lady she is, has been somewhat taken aback by Tate's naivety.

Banks look at the ruin caused by his "Threads."

Rude Buay jesters,

"Tate is so on top of his game that he memorized our last account verbatim in less than a day." Banks stares at Tate in amazement.

Rude Buay continues,

"He said if he was going to be efficient, he needed to prepare himself by learning from those who have gone through the minefield against the Dragon Drug Cartel. But he still has a lot to prove…'

Tamara interjects,

"Don't be so hard on him, Rude Buay. Tate, you are going to love it here in Jamaica. Watch out for those Hotties!"

Tate regains his presence of mind and addresses Dr. Ross,

"Thanks. So, how does that voodoo work? Is lighting the candle and creating a periphery a part of the ritual? Or is that just something you do? "

Dr. Ross responds,

"It doesn't matter, light or no light, a circle or a square, it's all in the belief mechanism. You can if you believe you can."

Tate focuses on Rude Buay, who responds:

"Never practiced, don't care for its workings." The artist takes a break, and the DJ spins some vinyl. Suddenly, a woman in her late 50s wearing a head tie shows up at the table. She interrupts. In Rude Buay's mind, he visualizes Maude Davis, his long-gone godmother.

The woman hands Rude Buay a folded piece of paper and departs. Rude Buay opens it. The others are oblivious concerning what's contained therein.

It says:

"Your friends are in Tivoli Gardens, West Kingstown. Seek, and you shall find. Knock, and it shall be opened unto you. Ask, and it shall be given to you."

Immediately, Rude Buay's phone rings.

He answers.

It's his boss, Michael Ortiz.

"Rude Buay, I have great news: Heidi Hudson has been reactivated. She will resume active duty tomorrow and team up with you and Tate in Jamaica. Now, promise me one thing. All three of your asses will be coming back alive to Miami when this is all over."

Rude Buay responds,

"Great move! I can't promise that second part, though. It has much to do with the playing of the hand versus the one that's been dealt."

All eyes at that table are fixed on agent Rude Buay.

They all anticipate him breaking the news.

He does,

"Hudson will be joining us in the morning!" "That is awesome!" Says Tamara.

She continues,

"Now I don't have to spend my night at the shooting range."

Banks jokingly,

"I won't be surprised if you are strapped right now."
They all celebrate with cheers.
Moments later, they wrap the event.
Rude Buay takes Tamara up on a much-celebrated nightcap.

19

Outside the small airport hangar at Kingston Airport, agent HEIDI HUDSON, Caucasian, is in her early thirties, wearing dark sunglasses, street clothes, and deplanes. Two full-size minivans wait. Agent Rude Buay and Tate step out from the black minivan, and Banks step out from the gray minivan. The three men greet Agent Hudson. After this, Rude Buay directs her to Walter Banks' vehicle. She gets inside.

The hatch of the aircraft opens up, and with the aid of the pilot, the three men load eclectic assortments of ammunition, including UZIs and AK 45s, into the rear of both minivans.

The black and gray vehicles enter their low rider modes and take off in "rhythm and soul through Kingston."

Inside the gray minivan, Banks, under the wheel, is poised for battle. Hudson, in the front passenger seat, though buckled in, holds on for her dear life.

Banks reiterates,

"Welcome back, Agent Hudson."

Hudson replies,

"I love this place! I must say that things have changed since our last visit. Do you think we will be able to find Mildred and Baptiste with all the going on?"
"Where there is a will, there is a way."
Banks continues,
"That's what agent Rude Buay believes."
Hudson responds,

"He is so resilient, charismatic, and at times untouchable. Rude Buay cares so much about his people. It is contagious." "We so appreciate him," Replies Banks.
Both vehicles are approaching West Kingston. Rude Buay tunes the car radio to 100.9 FM Radio Jamaica. The reggae music fades abruptly. The crisp, articulate announcer says: "We continue to follow information regarding the death of the three-year-old Leticia Hastings, who died of a cocaine overdose last week." Rude Buay presses the transmit button on the stereo, and the gray minivan picks up the timely audio feed. "News just in states: over one million cartons of powdered milk are feared being recalled worldwide, according to the FDA. This happened after a three-year-old girl lost her life as a result of being accidentally fed contaminated milk. It was alleged that a Ziploc bag containing almost eight kilos of cocaine ruptured in a container of milk. Leticia was innocently fed the milk by her mother, Beverly Hastings. Leticia died later as a result of that drug overdose.

In other related news, the police commissioner and his one-time partner in crime, Mildred Simms, have still not been found after they were both kidnapped by alleged members of the Dragon Drug Cartel last week. Walter Banks, a member of their team, was reported to have survived kidnapped attempts by the cartel. Stay tuned for the weather forecast when we return." With a mountainous backdrop, the street sign reads Approaching Tivoli Gardens.

Moments later, the two minivans roll into Tivoli Gardens. Gunmen on multiple rooftops are alerted. Even so, they are mesmerized by the hydraulic movements displayed by both vehicles. As a result, the vans proceed unscathed and with celebrated applause. Rude Buay addresses his colleagues via stereo in the gray minivan.

"Our objective is to rescue the kidnapped. If blood is to be shed, let it be that of the kidnappers and not ours. We are a team. 'United, we will stand. Divided, we will certainly fall.' Our only burning desire is to win. Whatever it takes, remember, we all come out of this alive. Welcome to TG, better known as Tivoli Gardens."

20

Back at the Commissioner's house, a FedEx package arrives. Christine Baptiste signs for it. The senders' address seemed ineligible to her. Anyway, she opens the package and discovers Richard's wallet. Inside the package, she finds a note that reads RB—RIP.
Christine rushes for her cell phone. She immediately calls Rude Buay. He answers the cellular phone call. Rude Buay, this is Christine, Richards' wife. I know you are very busy, but I was asked to update you about the kidnapping of my husband Richard. A package was just delivered to me by FedEx. In it was Richard's wallet and a note which read: RB - RIP. Have you heard anything from the kidnappers? Did they mention anything about a ransom as yet?" Rude Buay responds,
"We have not heard anything as of yet. As soon as or when we do, we will inform you. Mrs. Baptiste, are those hidden cameras installed at your home working efficiently?"
In tears, Christine says,

"Yes! Thank you for making that possible." The four agents continue on their quest through Tivoli Gardens. Rude Buay asks Agent Tate, "What would you say are the three things that make you tick as a DEA?"

Miles Tate responds,

"Search, Seizure, and Arrest, I'm still waiting for the latter … "

Many teens line the streets, buyers and sellers alike.

Rude Buay pulls up to the curb.

Banks follow the suites and corners of the sellers.

Hudson jumps out to assist.

Rude Buay chases after the Buyers. Tate catches up, grabs one of the teens, and confiscates several marijuana spliffs.

Rude Buay senses the potential buried inside the more than a dozen teens. He addresses them,

"My name is Agent Rude Buay, and these are my colleagues. Don't ever let us see you all out here again."

The agents release the youths and immediately vacate the area.

The agents return to their car. Tate is mesmerized by the giant size of these confiscated rolled-in newspaper marijuana joints. He is tempted. Rude Buay looks across at him. Rude Buay cautions:

"Not on my watch."

Tate changes that mindset.

Banks keep up with Rude Buay. Agents Tate and Hudson get an eyeful of the weaponry displayed by some guards outside a wooded house. Rude Buay pulls up and stops in front of the battalion. Tate is terrified.

"Are you okay?"

Asks the veteran agent - Rude Buay.

Without waiting for an answer, Rude Buay says,

"Follow me,"

Banks and Hudson wait inside their greatly admired minivan. Rude Buay asks the armed guards:

"Where is Levy? Need to see him."

One of the guards responds,

"Nobody sees Levy."

Rude Buay flashes his badge, pushes the guard out of the way, and barges in, followed by Tate. LEVY is a bearded man in his 50s, wearing a knitted hat in the colors of the flag. His dreadlocks are rolled up underneath the black, yellow, and green. There is a wide assortment of narcotics and money in the now-entranced living room of the house.

Levy greets.

"Hey, Rude Buay, not because you are wearing a badge, it doesn't give you the right to barge in on me, and I like that. Chua? Anyway, let's get down to business.

What can I do for you, mon?

Rude Buay responds,

"I am looking for Mildred Simms and the Commissioner. I heard that Johnny has them."

"Who told you that?"

Asks Levy.

"Come on, you know that the commissioner helped by having him extradited to the U.S. If you were in his shoes, who would be one of the first people to exercise vindictiveness? Plus, his fingerprints were found on the commissioner's vehicle after the kidnapping occurred."

"America has given Johnny a bad rap. We run things in Tivoli Gardens, and he might be referred to as

Johnny is too bad, but he doesn't have your people. Plus, you just touched my door with your bare hands on your way in. If I wanted to plant your fingerprints at the crime scene, I could hire the experts to do so. Money is power, and when you don't have any, it not only stinks, it sours,"

Says Levy,

Rude Buay doesn't believe a word he says. Even so, he notices the AKA 45 sitting on Levy's table.

Meanwhile, the guards outside Levy's establishment focus on the waiting gray minivan with Banks and Hudson inside.

Rude Buay turns to leave.

Levy says,

"Happy Hunting!"

Rude Buay eyes Tate.

Tate draws and points his gun in Levy's face.

Levy asks,

"What is this, Rude Buay? You didn't get what you wanted. You are afraid of what the Jamaicans will do

to you, so you are going to have the White Man shoot me." Rude Buay responds,
"No, I am not. I want answers."
Rude Buay grabs Levy in a chokehold. He drags him to the restroom and sticks his head deep down in the unflushed toilet. Rude Buay demands,
"Now, will you tell me where my people are, or must I make you drink first?"
Levy replies in hardcore patois, "That is I, and I piss. No problem if I drink it. That would not resurrect your brother Clifford. Is harden him been hardened!"
Rude Buay again demands.'
"Give me a location. Do you want to live, or do you want to die?"
Rude Buay submerges Levy's head a second time into the toilet bowl and then releases him. Levy spits out a mouthful on Rude Buay.
Rude Buay punches him hard in the face. Levy rocks back. He launches a fist at Rude Buay. The agent ducks out of it and shoots Levy in the face. Levy's Posse on the outside is alerted by the gunshot. In their mind, they think that Levy shot Rude Buay.
Rude Buay barges out with Tate behind him. The surprised guards try training their weapons on the agents. Banks and Hudson jump out of their vehicle to assist Rude Buay and Tate in the onslaught of the guards.
The death count at Levy's establishment equaled eleven, ten guards and Levy.

Looking out his window from across the street, an old man sees the body count. He yells from his window in some hardcore patois,

"Are you looking for Johnny? He is at Chin Chins Bar and Grill on Friday nights, right up on Mannings Hill Road. I hope you speak Chinese."

Rude Buay steps out and puts a hundred-dollar bill under a rock.

The old man clues in and hurries down to get it.

The four agents proceed to Chin Chins Bar and Grill.

21

The agents merge onto Kent Street and pull up next to Chin Chins. Rude Buay and Tate barge inside the bar and grill restaurant. Banks and Hudson wait outside in surveillance mode. It's dinner time inside Chin Chins. Some people are dining, some are drinking, some are just listening to music, and others are shooting pool.

In the agent survey, there is no glimpse of Johnny. Rude Buay walks up to the bar. The bartender, whose name tag reads JIM, is busy tending, so Rude Buay waits his turn.

"Hey, Jim, I am looking for Johnny. Have you seen him lately?

"No, mon, sorry."

The bartender returns to his duty.

Tate yells at him,

"Seen or heard anything about the two people he kidnapped?"

"I wished I could help you guys! I mind my own business around here."

Says uncooperative Jim,

One man at the pool table getting ready to shoot for the eight-ball overhears and responds.

"The Americans took him out of here months ago. Then he escaped to China. He must love those Chinese women. Try Beijing!" Rude Buay and Tate head out to their vehicle. They wait and survey.

Rude Buay notifies his other agents in the accompanying minivan through the stereo system.

"Nothing there, everyone is so tight-lipped. Except for one drunk who said he's in Beijing."

Hudson asks,

"So, what do we do?" Rude Buay responds,

"We will persist until we find him. We will scratch him like a crayfish, even under a rock."

Hudson responds,

"I've never been to China before. I am all in!"

Tate looks over at Rude Buay and asks,

"Is that the same as shrimp?"

Rude Buay answers,

"Close!"

Tate continues,

"You did say China? Do you think Ortiz would Greenlight such an expedition? Why aren't these locals leading us to him?"

Rude Buay responds,

"In West Kingston, no one trusts anyone. Johnny is like a politician. He has been so good to those people; no one wants to bring him down." Tate responds,

"But he is wanted. Why don't they?" "He performs his dirty work. Then, they are treated like modern-day

Santa Claus would. He has learned a lot from Alberto in that regard...."

Rude Buay says.

Banks and Heidi Hudson overhear Rude Buay and Agent Tate's conversation broadcast through the van's stereo.

During this interlude, two local men, fully armed, come up to Banks' minivan and address Banks.

Banks rolls down the window to hear them.

"Got to move these supped-up minivans, can't park them out here."

They both focus on Heidi Hudson. Rude Buay and Tate are alert and poised to assist if necessary.

"Is that your pimp...?"

One of the men asks,

Hudson acts as if she isn't sure what he's talking about.

Looking at Banks, they continue,

"If he is pimp daddy, I would like to..."

One of the men grabs Hudson's arm while aiming his gun at Banks.

Hudson blasts the gun-carrying man, who falls dead onto the street. Before the other man could release Hudson's arm and reach for his gun, Banks caps him in the head. He, too, falls onto the street a dead man. Meanwhile, Rude Buay and Tate stand erect and ready to unleash. Both agents return their guns to the holsters and hop inside the minivan.

Banks and Hudson follow suit and drive off.

22

The following morning, the agents continue combing through West Kingston for the hostages.

Hudson notices a gathering as they cross an intersection. She notifies Rude Buay through the stereo system.

"Rude Buay, pull over, these kids are way too young..."

Banks parks and Hudson rushes out, leaving the door ajar.

Rude Buay complies.

Rude Buay's vehicle makes a quick U-Turn. Heidi Hudson is already out of the car in pursuit of the teenage crowd. Now, the other three agents are on foot, heading in Agent Hudson's direction. Agent Hudson is catching up to a 14 - 15-year-old Afro-Asian girl, Tasha.

On one hand, the almost subdued Tasha carries two Milky Way cans and a switchblade on the other.

Hudson catches up with her.

She confronts Heidi Hudson.

Hudson kicks the opened knife out of Tasha's hand. Tasha rolls over on the ground. The two cans hit the pitched road and open, revealing a Ziploc bag with at least one eight of a kilo of cocaine underneath the powdered milk.

Banks covers Hudson while Tate confiscates the narcotics.

Rude Buay looks on.

Agent Hudson addresses Tasha:

"What is your name, young lady?"

"Tasha Ching,"

"How old are you?"

"I am almost 15,"

"Why aren't you in school?"

"Please don't tell my parents, they will kill me."

"How long have you been doing this?"

"One and a half years,"

'Why"

"The money is good,"

"How did you get involved?"

"Johnny introduced me on my 13th birthday. He said I would get rich doing the streets like him,"

"What is your address?"

"I don't have one,"

"Where do your parents live?"

"I can't tell you."

Rude Buay walks over into Tasha's space. "Tasha, my name is Agent Bascombe; some call me Rude Buay.

"You mean like in Rihanna's song?" Tasha immediately begins to sing and dance to the hit song by Rihanna:

Come here rude boy,
boy Can you get it up Come here rude boy,
boy Is you big enough Take it, take it Baby,
baby Take it, take it Love me, love me.
Tonight I'mma let you be the captain
Tonight I'mma let you do your thing,
yeah Tonight I'mma let you be a rider
Giddy up
Giddy up
Giddy up, babe

"The name is the same. We are here to help you and will handle this intelligently."
"You don't know my parents. They will KILL me."
Hudson interjects,
"We will ask them not to."
"I don't know why you all want to help me I am nobody…"
Rude Buay interrupts,
"That's what society makes you think. You are filled with potential, Tasha."
"My parents are not together,"
Hudson questions,
"You live at home, mom?"
"Yes,"
Tasha replies,
"Where is Johnny now?"
Rude Buay asks,

"I have not seen Too Bad in almost a week.
They said that he went to China."
Tasha says,
"How did you get here?"
Rude Buay inquires,
"I took the bus from Kingston."
Tasha responds,
"Okay, we will give you a ride," Says Rude Buay.
"You all promise. This is not some kidnapping, right?
I don't want to end up in Bermuda..."
Tasha says.
The four agents give Tasha a reassuring look.
Hudson leads the way.
Tasha follows Hudson and boards the gray minivan.
The two minivans take off, and the gray van leads the way towards Kingston.

23

The agents arrive in Kingston. Tasha points out the house on the hill inside a cul-de-sac. Both minivans pull up and park. Rude Buay and Tate get out and head up the hill towards the house. Rude Buay knocks on the door. A dark-skinned Jamaican woman answers. My name is Agent Bascombe; this is my partner Miles Tate. Agents Heidi Hudson and Walter Banks are inside the other van. We are here on a matter that we feel concerns you.

"The man and the woman who got kidnapped are not here, agents Bascombe and whatever your name is, Tate? And we are sure not hiding Johnny Too Bad."

"May we call you Miss or Mrs.…?"

"You may call me Mrs. Ching. It doesn't matter he is gone. I sang him hit the road, Jack. Don't return anymore… when he decided to walk out on Tasha and me."

Rude Bauy continues,

"Mrs. Ching, it is about your daughter. We found her at a location where she doesn't belong." "Where is Tasha? I thought she said that she was going to live with her father. That…" "We found her on the streets of West Kingston dealing narcotics." States Rude Buay,

"I will KILL Tasha…"
Mrs. Ching responds,
Rude Buay interjects,
"That's what she told us."
Rude Buay continues,
"But we assured her that if she would cooperate by letting us bring her home, you wouldn't hurt her. Additionally, we would make sure that this is handled intelligently."
"Where is Tasha?"
Agent Heidi Hudson, overhearing the conversation via the "wired" Rude Buay with Banks and Tasha listening in, steps out of the gray minivan and hands over Tasha to her mother." "Thank you very much, agents Hudson, Bascombe, and Tate, and will you let Mr. Banks know that I say thanks? Is he the one who escaped getting kidnapped?" Banks steps out of the minivan to deliver Tasha's forgotten sweater.
Mrs. Ching gets a closer view of the Jamaican agent Walter Banks.
"I am sure I heard about him on the news last week. Yes, that's him. You all be careful now. It is like a jungle out there…"
Tears well up in Tasha's eyes.
"Thanks, and goodbye,"
Tasha says.
The agents depart.

24

Meanwhile, a submarine surfaces at an abandoned dock in Shanghai, China. There are no on-lookers, so the five individuals get off undetected: Denise, Shelly, Amanda Johnny Too Bad, and a blindfolded woman. They escort the blindfold to a waiting van and seat her inside; the van takes off with David Lee at the driver's wheel. The van pulls up outside the Torture House. They exit, remove the previously blindfolded Mildred from her seat, and amble towards the house's interior. The move descends to the desolate basement. Nothing there except for the four walls, a chair in the middle of the room, and a noose from a rope dangling from the extended roof. With her mouth still covered with duct tape, Shelly removes the blindfold that clothed Mildred's eyes. Mildred's face shows a sense of frustration of wanting to speak and being unable to. The three women bind Mildred's hands and feet to the chair with ropes. Johnny, overseeing, grabs the slow-moving extended noose and slips it around Mildred's neck. He adjusts the chair downwards so the rope around her neck tightens. They feel satisfied with the

proper functioning of their mechanism. They depart and board the waiting van. The van drives off.
Rude Buay checks in with the Chinese immigration authorities, but they are unable to verify that Johnny, along with other members of the Dragon Drug Cartel, had entered the country.

MEANWHILE, VULTURES FLY LOW over a small reservation as the morning sun begins to cast its rays on the outskirts of Tivoli Gardens. In the interim, in TG, Rude Buay, Miles Tate, Heidi Hudson, and Walter Banks continue searching for the kidnapped. Even so, they are still oblivious to Mildred's whereabouts.
The four agents continue to search huts, houses, tenement yards, bars, and other buildings. Jamaican police with dogs now join them in the search.
Rude Buay pulls up at a Barber Shop. He gets out of his car and is followed by Tate.
In the meantime, Hudson and Banks visit the restaurant across the street.
Inside the barbershop: Some men get their hair cut while others wait their turn.
Rude Buay surveys and then addresses:
"My name is Agent Bascombe, and this is Agent Tate. We are with the Drug Enforcement Agency. We are looking for Johnny Too Bad and the kidnapped Mildred Simms and Baptiste."
One man who is baldheaded and certainly not there to get a haircut says nonchalantly,

"We heard about you, Rude Buay! You have more significant issues in America, like Child Care, Recession, and Abortion. I hope Jamaica's Prime Minister isn't paying you out of our hard-earned tax dollars. That man Baptiste deserves to get what he received. The woman Simms, her past is what got her in trouble. Nobody in Tivoli Gardens is going to help you, mon.

You came to the wrong place."

Rude Buay continues,

"Has anyone seen any of the hostages or know of their whereabouts?"

Everyone is mute.

"And for you, sir,"

Rude Buay looks directly at the "smart mouth" local.

"Empty all your pockets and place the contents on this table."

Fritz hesitates to fulfill agent Rude Buay's request and suddenly looks down at the barrels of two guns, Rude Buay's and Tates' semi-automatics. Out of his pockets come a switchblade knife, vials of crack, and packets of cocaine.

Tate immediately cuffs him and waits for the Jamaican police to arrive in their squad car and take him away—two officers who previously abandoned the search return and took Fritz to jail.

In the meantime, at a restaurant across the street, Hudson confronts the MANAGER on Duty.

Heidi Hudson addresses,

"Good morning! My name is Agent Hudson. I am looking for Johnny Too Bad. Have you seen him lately? Or heard about the whereabouts regarding the kidnapped Simms and Baptiste?" The Manager serving beef patty and cocoa bread to a customer responds,

"Fire!"

Hudson asks,

"What do you mean?"

The woman reiterates in patois,

"Fire ah go burn them. They hurt poor Johnny's feelings."

Banks responds,

"Does he have feelings?"

Unfortunately, leaving that for the woman to massage and marinate Banks and Hudson left the Jamaican restaurant unaccomplished.

25

Rude Buay's phone rings. He answers it on the second ring. "Hello, agent Rude Buay,"
The female voice echoes,
"This is Christine, the Commissioner's wife. Has there been any word yet on Richard's whereabouts? If no ransom has been requested, the chances of him still being alive are slim. It has been a few days now."
"Mrs. Baptiste, we are doing everything possible to try and locate your husband, Richard, as well as his kidnappers.
We hope that we'll find Richard alive. So far, I hate to inform you, but nothing has turned up positively except that the Jamaican police a short while ago claimed that they could trace the FedEx package that was sent to your home as being sent from Tivoli Gardens. However, as you had seen on that package, the sender's name was ineligible. I am very optimistic that we'll find him. We will notify you as soon as we locate your husband."
Christine hears Agent Rude Buay but doesn't believe a word he says. In tears, Christine continues, this time talking to herself.

"I don't know what they want my husband for. Whatever political party gave power to this drug cartel, is putting our country to shame. We used to be one love, but now it seems like one hate. Innocent people, including kids, die for nothing. Who gave drug dealers power over civilians? The government and their MPs! Richard always believed in ONE Jamaica. Now, the same team he assembled to protect and serve. They all are sitting on their butts so that vultures can devour their body and ants their bones. In the country, he has worked

so hard to defend has allowed the oppressors to oppress continually…Like Bob Marley said: 'Who the cap fit to wear it.'

Those wicked politicians!"

Christine aborts her call to agent Rude Buay. Suddenly, her house phone rings. She tries catching it on the second ring, misses it, but grabs it on the third.

"Hello, Hello, Hello!"

Christine addresses.

There is no answer.

The only sound she hears is "Click. Click"

Terrified, Christine bolsters herself and rushes to the bedroom. She removes one of the pillows and pulls out her husband's automatic weapon. She checks to make sure that it's loaded. Satisfied, she sits on the couch facing the door and waits.

Two Jamaican police officers hide out up the street, oblivious to her and out of view of her property's surveillance cameras.

These watchers, dispatched earlier after a government official and ally of Johnny and Alberto Gomez determined the tracking location of the FedEx package, continue to wait.

Already tapped into Christine's phone line, they gather information.

On their TV monitor, the police could see Christine waiting for the kill.

It's dawn. The policemen look at each other, but none dare to become casualties, so they unwillingly vacate the area.

26

Back in Tivoli Gardens, Rude Buay, not giving up, continues to follow his instincts. Driving further along Mannings Hill, they come upon a blockage on the street. The blockade comprised abandoned iceboxes, car tires, tree trunks, bed mattresses, old furniture, tree branches, a skeleton of stripped vehicles, and oil drums. Rude Buay, Miles Tate, Walter Banks, and Heidi Hudson exit their car and make a clear path. They re-board their vehicle and proceed along the same street.

At an undisclosed location in Tivoli Gardens, Alberto reclines in a black leather chair and sips an almost full cup of robust black coffee. He then reaches for his phone and dials.

Rude Buay and his agents are combing the streets, looking for evidence that could lead them to the finding of the hostages.

Rude Buay's cell phone rings, and he answers:

"This is Rude Buay."

Rude Buay realizes Alberto Gomez's number and goes to the full-circuit stereo. The two agents in the other minivan listen in. The voice on the other end greets. "Rude Buay, this is Albert Gomez. You and your agents will not take a back seat by letting me do my thing as I see fit. First, I must inform you that the man you are looking for is sitting under my thumb. And very soon, you could be accompanying him if you continue pursuing my enterprise. Don't forget we do not only control Tivoli Gardens, but We are also global…"

Rude Buay interrupts:

"All that you are saying is old news. Understand that every seed you've planted can sprout, but that doesn't mean it will. I am interested in the two hostages, not what you and David Lee have put together globally."

"That won't happen unless you and your agents are willing to comply with our demands."

Alberto says,

"Try me!"

Rude Buay answers courageously.

"You failed at living up to demands back in Port Antonio. Not sure you are capable of keeping your word."

States Alberto.

"You are nothing but a prick!"

Rude Buay responds.

"You have one hour to withdraw your antagonistic pursuits of the Dragon Cartel. I have a private jet waiting at a hanger outside the Kingston airport and a van, plus a motorcade, waiting to escort you to it if you so desire. After you and your peeps clear Jamaican airspace en route to America, I would happily release

Simms and the Commissioner, one at a time." "Why are you doing this? If you have gotten your wish, why drip on the releasing process of the hostages?"
Alberto continues,
"You don't ask questions at this point, Rude Buay; you fulfill demands. That's the way I choose to lay my safety net. Additionally, I am sending a message to Washington that if they mess with us any further, we will not only expand across the five oceans but cause some of the most devastating recalls that country has ever experienced." Alberto continues,
"As for you? If you screw up, vultures will enjoy fresh meat of you and your agents."
Rude Buay weighs the consequences and asks,
"Where is that van located?"
"You are thinking on your feet."
Alberto's coffee cup is refilled by a tall Jamaican woman. His UZI is present and close to his reach. Money and milk can create a decorative aurora of drug dealing spectacle. Alberto snorts two lines of coke, one per nostril. Alberto fetches his gun and car keys. He leaves. Even so, he continues his phone conversation with Rude Buay. Alberto continues,
"It's located at the entrance of Tivoli Gardens, on the Southwest corner."

BACK AT THE ENTRANCE TO TG, the van waits, along with a pair of motorbikes and two men standing guard.

ON ANOTHER TIVOLI GARDENS STREET, the agents park their cars.

Rude Buay puts Alberto on hold and commissions his other agents via the stereo.

"Banks and Hudson, I need you to cover the outside of this property while Tate and I engage in this investigative pursuit."

Rude Buay releases the hold button and continues his conversation with Alberto.

Rude Buay replies,

"Alberto, it's a deal. How soon can we take custody of Baptiste and Simms?"

Alberto responds,

"They belong to the Jamaican Government. You have my word that they will be released simultaneously to their government."

Rude Buay does not believe a word Alberto says.

Alberto continues,

"Good! That private jet flies in 48 minutes." The agents continue their search of West Kingston.

Rude Buay sees a house with an outdoor sign saying, "Beware of dogs." He pulls over. Banks follow suit. Alberto's guards are unaware of the agents' entourage forming outside the front door.

Upon noticing the black and gray vans parked outside the house. The guards release a few rounds from Uzis in the vehicle's direction.

The vans are empty as the four agents have already dispersed and taken up positions on the other side of the house. One of the guards fires at Rude Buay. He misses and takes a bullet from Rude Buay's' gun instead. That guard hits the ground, dead.

27

Heidi Hudson enters the house through the already-opened front door amidst barking dogs. The tall Jamaican woman attempts to escape. The agile Heidi Hudson pushes her back inside with a vengeance. Heidi Hudson asks,

"Where are Simms and Baptiste?"

The Woman does not respond. So, Hudson handcuffs her.

"You are going with us."

"Hudson says as she pushes the woman in front of her like a human shield, proceeding through the house's interior."

In the interim, Rude Buay and Tate exchange firepower with the other guard. Rude Buay shoots. The Guard runs for the parked car. A bullet catches the guard disconnected and cuts him down.

MEANWHILE, OBLIVIOUS TO the agents, Alberto boards a waiting submarine from an abandoned dock in Kingston.

Back at the House in Tivoli Gardens, Rude Buay, Tate, and Banks catch up with Heidi Hudson as they penetrate deep inside that house. Rude Buay observes the handcuffed woman. Like a man possessed, he asks, "Where are Baptiste and Simms?" The woman now hears this asked of her by two separate agents. Yet, she still refuses to cooperate. Money and milk can create a decorative and auroras drug-dealing spectacle inside the living room. The agents move deeper inside the strange house. Walter Banks is already leading the way, followed by Rude Buay, Tate, Hudson, and the Jamaican Woman.

The barking sounds of multiple dogs alert the agents to open a locked door. Rude Buay blows out the lock with a bullet from his gun.

As they enter take-down styles, three chained bloodhounds form a periphery plunge in desperation towards them.

The starving, chained dogs intermittently salivate at their prey, which is chained to an electric wired chair. Bones and blood residue add to the presence of recent carnivorous activities.

When the dogs plunge fully forward the extent of the chains, place their mouths at least three feet in front of the chained victim.

Walter Banks recognizes the victim and yells out,

"It's the Commish!"

Rude Buay advises,

"Let's get him out of there swiftly."

Four guns are pointed at the three dogs. As the agents get ready to take the drooling dogs out of their misery, the Jamaican Woman yells,
"Cease fire!"
The animals lock eyes with the Jamaican Woman and retreat. Not leaving anything to chance, the agents maintain their aim on the three bloodhounds. Heidi Hudson assesses the situation.
"I got it!"
Hudson marches amid that "dog's den."
She notices the Commissioner wired to the max.
Walter Banks senses trouble and says,
"Be careful, Hudson; I hear a ticking sound. Any wire you touch could send us all up in smoke." Banks gets on his cell phone and dials Chelo in Bogota, Colombia. Chelo is fast asleep. He jumps up and grabs the phone.
"Chelo! I am sleeping."
Says Chelo,

"Wake up, man. We are under a time crunch. I need your help. We found the Commissioner. He is wired to the max, with multiple red, blue, and black wires."
Relays Walter Banks,
Chelo asks,
"What is the address?"
Banks replies,
"No address, a great big house in Tivoli Gardens off Mannings Hill. Come on, Chelo, give us your best shot."

Chelo fumbles around with various monitor screens.
He claims,
"I got it! Wait."
Ticking decibels increase.
Heidi Hudson responds,
"There is no… time to wait; we could all get killed."
Chelo replies,
"Banks, tell Hudson not to touch anything on that man, not even his clothing. The only way out is to turn off the power switch located at the circuit breaker."
Banks looks over at the Jamaican woman and asks,
"Where is the darn circuit breaker?" The Jamaican Woman reluctantly points towards an adjacent room across the hall.
Chelo assures,
"She is right! Move quickly. Time is running out!"
Rude Buay pulls out another automatic from under his trousers. He points it to the dogs where Banks' aim was directed.
Banks tugs the woman to the room where she indicates the power turn-off switch is. In the interim, the dogs plunge forward at Agent Hudson with the entire length of their chain.
Tate yells,
"Cease fire!"
There is no response from the dogs. Rude Buay and Hudson follow up using the same command to no avail.

Total darkness now engulfs the room, mixed with the sounds of barking dogs and the agents' mumbling. Banks and the woman return with the aid of his mini-emergency flashlight.

The Jamaican woman again yells,

"Cease Fire!"

The dogs retreat. With the aid of Banks' flashlight, he and Hudson remove the Commissioner, who is still wearing the clothes he did when kidnapped. Together, the agents make their getaway from inside the house.

Rude Buay asks the woman,

"Any information on Mildred Simms' whereabouts?"

The Jamaican woman replies,

"Try Shanghai."

As the agents make their exit on the house's terrace, Banks pulls out five U.S. one hundred dollar bills and attempts to hand it over to the woman, who is still handcuffed. Hudson grabs the cash and sticks it inside the woman's bra. Meanwhile, the agents quickly remove the duct tape from the Commissioners' mouth.

The Commissioner now vocal,

Thank you, Mr. Rude Buay and...

Rude Buay assists Tate and my partner, Miles Tate.

The Commissioner,

"Tate, it's so great seeing all you good people once again. I missed the debriefing. Thanks, Hudson. Great intuition. Banks, we appreciate you!"

Rude Buay states,

"No problem, we got you out of there safely. Now we've got to go and find Mildred Simms." The Commissioner asks,
"Where is Mildred? They got her, too?"
Rude Buay expounds,
"Yes. Also kidnapped by the Dragons on the same evening as you ..."
They load up, place the Commissioner inside the gray minivan, and depart from the premises, leaving the woman behind still in handcuffs.

I

28

It's nightfall. At the Tivoli Gardens entrance, the cube van waits. The agents get ready to board. A
RASTAFARIAN GUARD accompanied by the driver ushers in Rude Buay and his crew.
The Rastafarian Guard says to the driver.
"Overload!"
Driver asks,
"What you mean overload?"
The Rastafarian Guard answers in deep patois,
"Me, say overload, one too many mon."
The Driver and Guard stare at the Commissioner, who is bearded and outfitted in street clothes, wearing a Rastafarian wig and dark sunglasses. His chic tie is hanging out from his side pocket. Rude Buay argues,
"We've got to take him, or we don't go." The driver continues staring at the Rastafarian Guard and Baptiste.
The Rastafarian Guard responds,
"That man is not getting inside this van. I was told four people now five show up. Not another thug!"
The driver and the guard continue arguing, creating a stand-off against the agents and the Commissioner. The Guard senses trouble not knowing what to expect at this point from the agents. So, he commands, "Drop your weapons!" The agents comply.
While the Guard moves the four guns to the side and out of the way. Rude Buay kicks him hard in the stomach. The Guard falls to the ground gasping for air. The Guard quickly regains his presence of mind. He aims at Rude Buay and shoots. Rude Buay

dodges out of his onslaught and reaches for the gun under his left trouser leg. He gets a successful shot off, which caps the Rastafarian Guard. The driver swings at Rude Buay. His swing is blocked by Rude Buay using his left hand and his right hand to punch him hard in his face, as a result, knocking him out.

The four agents and the Commissioner swiftly load up ammunition and luggage from the minivans onto the cube van. They board the van. The Commissioner, under Rude Buay's instruction, takes the wheel.

The van departs through the streets of Kingston.

Suddenly, Rude Buay's phone rings. He answers.

"My pilot flies in ten minutes."

Says Alberto.

"Blame it on your drivers."

Rude Buay responds.

"We'll make it anyway."

Rude Buay continues and then hangs up.

Later they arrive at the airport hangar in Kingston. The Cube van pulls up next to the waiting Jet aircraft. They disembark and come face to face with the Pilot and his co-pilot.

The Pilot's eyes are focused on the Commissioner. Something doesn't seem right to him. Looking at Rude Buay he says,

"You are late Rude Buay, this plane should have flown five minutes ago, David Lee wouldn't be very happy with this." Says the Pilot.

Richard Baptiste, the Commissioner responding to the name drop, asks.

"I thought it was ... Alberto?"

The Pilot answers as a matter of fact,

"On his way to ... Asia! Got to move it ...!"

Looking over at the Co-Pilot, the Pilot instructs,

"Frisk them down and get those bastards on board."

The Co-Pilot complies.

They are clean except for Rude Buay, still carrying that gun in his left trousers leg.
The Pilot removes Rude Buay's gun, removes the bullets, and tosses it away.
The Commissioner attempts to get on the Jet last.
The Pilot is alerted.
"We are not taking you. Trying to get into America illegally?"
He continues,
"Not going to happen. Plus, we don't have an extra seat anyway. You could ride on the wing."
Says the Pilot.
In protest, the four agents, headed by Rude Buay, deplane. The Pilot is confused. He commands.
"Get your asses back on that plane. I'll take you to Miami, dead or alive. It's your choice." He aims his gun at them.
The Co-Pilot's back is turned against the aircraft. Rude Buay grabs him behind his neck and lifts him off the ground while his feet dangle. He drops him hard to the ground, takes away his weapon, caps him several times, and then aims a gun at the pilot.
The Pilot has a change of heart. "It's okay we will take your friend if that's what you want."
Rude Buay commands,
"Drop your weapons!"
The Pilot is flustered, but he complies.
Tate and Banks check the Pilot for additional weapons. There is none.
Rude Buay shoves the Pilot aboard the Jet and commands,
"Open up the hatch."
The Pilot does as commanded.
Rude Buay keeps an eye on the pilot while the Commissioner and the other agents load their weapons and luggage onto the aircraft.
Everyone is now on board.

The pilot sits in control of the Jet.
Rude Buay announces,
“Change of plans! We are going to Shanghai, China.”
The Pilot remarks,
“Never been there before. Navigation could be problematic. Plus, I don't speak their language.” Rude Buay weighs his options.
Richard Baptiste gets up from his seat,
“Don't worry, I got this! I've taken off and landed in Shanghai on numerous occasions.”
The pilot gets up, relinquishing control to Baptiste. Rude Buay grabs the pilot and pushes him through the door and off the plane.
He tries to get away on foot. Several rounds from Rude Buay’s gun cut him down as he collapsed to his death.
The plane taxis and then takes off.

29

It's a crisp, busy morning. The hustle and bustle of the white-collar workforce resemble New York's Wall Street before the sound of the big bell and the Wall Street protests. Retrospectively, across the way, an African American freestyler draws a crowd of Asian supporters like a vacuum in motion. Chu Ling joins the mesmerized audience.

Up the block, two Chinese Police Officers converse while looking toward the crowd. Their eyes are now fixed on Chu, who seems mesmerized by the artistic performance. The officers proceed toward the gathering and confront Chu Ling. The senior Chinese police officer questions,

"Miss, what are you carrying in that bag?"

Chu Ling replies,

"Groceries!"

The Junior Officer is "gun-happy" while his partner continues the investigation. The senior CHINESE POLICE OFFICER asks,

"Do you mind if we take a look?"

Chu Ling reluctantly hands over the bag.

The senior officer opens it. He sees an entire container of milk. Nevertheless, he looks at Chu and asks as he approaches the trash can.

"If there is nothing but milk inside, we will replace it."

The senior officer pours the milk out into the trash can. A Ziploc bag with a powdery substance falls out on top of the milk. He retrieves it and asks,

"Miss, what is your name?"

"Chu Ling."

"Chu - Ling!" He continues,

"I am afraid this is not all milk. We are going to have to arrest you for cocaine possession." The junior officer handcuffs Chu Ling and escorts her to their parked cruiser.

The crowd, as well as the freestyler, scatter as the arrest is conducted.

Moments later, the Drug Czar David Lee meanders through a dense crowd of pedestrians looking for his wife Chu on that same street. In the meantime, at a prestigious law firm in downtown Shanghai, on the top floor of a high-rise building, twelve lawyers of the Chins Law Firm engage in their early morning free-basing ritual. Some freebase while others chip away from the cocaine mound. Others assemble and snort—consequently, severe vomiting and giddiness set in later. The Law Firm's Green Room is now full of panic and pandemonium. Less than an hour later, ambulances arrive, whisking all twelve lawyers to a downtown Shanghai hospital. Several blocks away, the news is live on a big TV screen regarding the recent Chinese Drug Bust. People outside a bus station are glued to that early morning news in various languages worldwide. ONE AMERICA TV station delivers the following newscast along with footage:

"This is your early morning late-breaking news from ONE AMERICA TV:"

A female American TV announcer sinks her teeth into it.

"Earlier this morning, at least a dozen lawyers from Chins Law Firm in downtown Shanghai were rushed to the hospital after an apparent free-basing session.

Chinese Police discovered two milk cans containing cocaine residue under the table of the office where the alleged free-basing session occurred.

Meanwhile, over ten thousand cans of milk believed to have been packed with Ziploc bags of uncut cocaine were discovered in a submarine down the Chinese River bound for the Caribbean. The estimated street value of the cargo is over $10M. A Drug Lord, Salvador, was arrested and detained by Chinese Police in conjunction with the drug bust.

Meanwhile, the FDA in Washington, DC, has scheduled a meeting for the following Monday to discuss the possibility of a recall of all powdered milk products, including baby formula. According to analysts, if this recall goes into effect, millions of kids around the world could die of scurvy and malnutrition. Many mothers are resorting to breastfeeding to protect their young ones from death or malnourished-related diseases.

China, emerging as one of the largest industrial nations, is now under pressure. Anything shipped from that country is subject to search by Chinese authorities and levied with massive tariffs.

Besides, random searching of packages on all public transportation is now in effect in China. This morning, Chinese police also arrested and detained Chu Ling, the mistress of the Drug Lord and Entrepreneur David Lee, on drug trafficking charges. It is believed that Ling sold narcotics to the Chin Law firm earlier this morning."

Many mothers around the world are stunned by these latest revelations: One woman in Utah rushes to her bedroom to see if her four kids, all under five years old, are okay. She is satisfied as they are all playing with toys. She overlooks the powdered milk products on the kitchen counter and instead grabs the youngest and prepares to breastfeed the infant. One woman in Hollywood, California, wishing she had kids, breaks out in tears upon viewing the news.

On the other hand, one starving writer in Seattle takes copious notes in the hope that he could someday profit from the story.

30

An intense free-basing, get-high interlude inside David Lee's house unfolds around the dining table involving David Lee, Alberto Gomez, Denise Gomez, Shelly Hall, Amanda Kingsley, and Johnny Too Bad. Johnny methodically rolls a giant-sized marijuana spliff on the cover page of the local Chinese newspaper that covered the drug bust. He lights up, partakes, and passes it off to Alberto, who takes a considerable toke before passing it along to his associates.

Everyone partakes except for David Lee, who is busily separating his upcoming dosage from the vast mound of cocaine with the use of a razor blade. Then, with a straw, he attacks and snorts that entire line like clean air.

David is now relaxed.

He addresses his associates,

"We have got to do something about Rude Buay. That jet still has not arrived in Miami."

"Orders must be carried out. Once again, he reneged on..."

Responds Alberto.

Johnny interjects,

"It should be clear to him in my note that I want him out of TG." Shelly chimes in,
"Out of Jamaica. Period!"
David Lee states,
"That private jet left Jamaica with two sets of casualties behind. One at the ground transportation pick-up site in Tivoli Gardens, and the other at the airplane hangar in Kingston." Shelly reaffirms,
"Rude Buay doesn't know how to fly an airplane."
Alberto responds,
"I don't think that any of the others do …" Johnny interrupts,
"The Commissioner attended aviation school in China. That's where he met his wife." Eyebrows are raised.
Johnny Too Bad asks,
"Boss, enough respect, but how did you let that PIG getaway? I thought that we had him inside the net."
Alberto responds,
"Blame it on those … guards. Too many loose ends!"
David opens his loaded wallet. He removes Chu Ling's picture and reflects. He has a moment, pondering whether she would be released from within the prison walls in that mediatory event with his wife. Everyone in the circle is now silent.
David Lee continues,
"Guys, we need to figure out where that plane landed. There has been no communication from that pilot as of yet."
Johnny is in deep thought.

Johnny Too Bad states,
"They took Tasha back home to her mother. I wonder if she told those bastards that I went to China."
David Lee questions,
"Who the heck is Tasha?"
Johnny Too Bad replies,
"She worked for me."
Amanda Kingsley is peeved. "Risking our lives with a minor …?" She asks.
Alberto picks up his gun and car keys off the table in preparation to depart. His wife, Denise, gets in his way.
"Where are you going to Papi?"
Alberto responds,
"Let's go to the airport!"
They all look at each other as if Alberto's decision was the expected magical wand to be waved to conclude the Rude Buay saga.
The get-high session escalates into a massive conclusion.
They make their exit…

31

The plane arrives in Shanghai, China. The agents and Commissioner deplane. With the newly acquired cell phone from Walter Banks, Baptiste dials his wife, Christine, for the first time after being kidnapped. Christine Baptiste answers,
"Hello, who is this?"
"This is Rich, Richard. I am free, Chris! Free at last. Meet me in China. I will text you the exact location when we check in."
Christine Baptiste asks,
"WE?"
Richard Baptiste responds,
"I am with Banks, Rude Buay, and the rest of their team. You remember telling me that you wanted to fly with me someday. I may consider taking up piloting … you and me, Chrissie."
Christine Baptiste responds,
"Please send me your location soon. I can't wait … !"
A distinguished Asian Official dressed in white attire interrupts the celebration.
He meets and greets them at the airplane hangar. He bows in acknowledgment and points to a van in a

parking spot. Rude Buay ambles towards the vehicle and looks it over.

The Official hands over the keys to Rude Buay and a folded piece of paper. They load up their luggage and weaponry. Rude Buay reads the address: The Lounge, 17 Chamber Lane, Shanghai. The distinguished official looks at Rude Buay with concern. A distinguished gentleman asks,

"Mr. Rude Buay, how is your Kung Fu?"

Rude Buay thinks it through and replies, "What I lack in skill, I will make up for inactivity. And where there are no roots, sprouts will appear." The Asian Official gives him a thumbs up and smilingly departs.

The agents board the van. The Commissioner takes the wheel.

The van departs.

32

Rude Buay and his entourage arrive outside David Lee's house. Covert and desolate The Lounge sits on a hill. Rude Buay, Walter Banks, Heidi Hudson, Miles Tate, and Commissioner Richard Baptiste jump out. They are instantly alerted by the pacing guards on the grounds of the property, as well as the roof of that house. It's now nightfall, so Rude Buay and his men disperse and manage to surround the house. Even so, one of the patrolling guards notices the five intruders.
A patrolling guard yells out,
"We are under attack, Americans! Americans! Jamericans!"
Other guards jump off the roof. They emerge, running through the back and front doors in confrontation.
All armed agents, including the Commissioner, unload several rounds on the guards.
The skilled guards retaliate and dodge out of the agent's firepower until there are no more bullets left in their guns.
Sensing their vulnerability, a petite guard viciously approaches them, Kung Fu style. No one dares take him on except Rude Buay.

Moments later, Rude Buay leaves the elfin martial32artist on the ground, paralyzed.

Another agent, realizing the affliction rendered to his coworker, violently attacks Rude Buay with the "crane" move before Rude Buay can even compose himself. Rude Buay quickly unravels that guard and gets confronted by yet another. This agile guard quickly shows up the agents' Kung Fu deficiencies. Witnessing Rude Buay's manhandling, his team rushes to the parked van down the hill to acquire more bullets.

Upon returning, the guard has Rude Buay held upside down and about to smash his head on top of the paved concrete driveway.

Agent Heidi Hudson gets a shot off from her reloaded gun and shoots the guard directly in his forehead. The guard topples over, with Rude Buay falling on top of him.

Rude Buay gets up and steps on top of the guard en route to the house's interior with his team in tow. The other guards fail miserably to make a comeback and try to flee past them. They all get capped by Rude Buay's team.

Rude Buay reloads his gun upon entering, thanks to Walter Banks's generosity in providing him with bullets.

The agents, along with the Commissioner, are now inside the living room. A maid wearing an apron comes flying out of the ceiling through the manhole.

Hudson sees her and, instead of shooting her, changes her mind and engages in hand-to-hand combat.

As they go at it, Hudson asks the maid,

"Where is Mildred Simms?" Instead of getting an answer the maid engages in more Kung Fu action. Hudson hones her skill of the craft on the maid via on-the-job training. In the meantime, other members of the agents' team rummage through the house.

In a room adjacent to the living room, they discover stacks of Jewish bankroll, millions of dollars in U.S. currency, Chinese currency, hundreds of Ziploc bags with at least one eight-kilo of uncut cocaine each, American passport, grenades, survival kits, along with a massive gun collection. Inside the next room, they enter the take-down style. No one is there, but numerous milk cans are arranged like they are on an assembly line. Rude Buay, Walter Banks, Miles Tate, and The Commissioner enter another room searching for Mildred Simms. She is not there. Another room beckons, so they enter in search of Mildred.

33

At the same time, outside the airport hangar, a convoy of cars pulled up led by David Lee's BMW. Alberto's Mercedes Benz follows. Shelly, Denise, and Amanda follow in their Hatchback and Johnny Too Bad in his Escalade. They surveyed for a while, trying to determine if the Jet arranged to take the agents back to Miami and was flown to Shanghai instead. It's tedious, as most of the jets look alike. Finally, they stumble into it. Alberto opens the door and enters. The others wait outside.

Inside the jet's cockpit, Alberto discovers the tie Commissioner Baptiste wore when he was kidnapped. He alerts Johnny Too Bad and his other associates. They clue in. Shelly, Amanda, and Denise take off speedily in their Hatchback. The others board their vehicle, preparing to leave.

However, before the men take off, a van pulls up. Four Henchmen jump out. David Lee gets out of his car with his gun aimed at the four men. David Lee yells,

"You are late! …Late!"

The men bow apologetically. David Lee hands a wad of dollar bills, which he retrieved from his pocket, along with an address on a sheet of paper. The Henchmen take off speedily. The Drug Lords take off in the opposite direction.

MEANWHILE BACK AT LEE'S HOUSE. Oblivious to Hudson's partners, agent Hudson is now confronted by Amanda Kingsley, her newly arrived combat. The tired maid whimpers, bloody in the corner as a result of Hudson's spanking.

Shelly and Denise wait with the car door still open after Amanda's exit. Amanda Kingsley outdoes Agent Hudson with her kung-fu skills.

Finally, Shelly yells out,

"Let's take that … to Torture House! Amanda puts the agent in a chokehold and drags her outside to the waiting car.

Upon arriving, Amanda, with the help of Shelly and Denise, bound Hudson with ropes, tied her hands behind her back, and threw her in the back of their tinted windows vehicle.

Shelly takes the wheel. Looking in the rearview mirror, she addresses Agent Hudson:

"Welcome back, bitch you never learn, huh? You had your chance to be free. Stay in America with your son. Instead, you are determined to mess up our livelihood." Heidi Hudson asks,

"What do you want from me?"

Shelly responds, "You will find out at the Torture House." The car continues on its way.

Meanwhile, back inside The Lounge, one of Lee's other houses, the agents and the Commissioner return to the living room and notice the maid on the floor coughing up blood.

Additionally, to their surprise, they realize that Agent Hudson is missing.

Looking outside, the fresh tire marks leave an imprint on the dust-laden pavement. The men hustle to their vehicles to embark on a search for the missing Agent Hudson.

Meanwhile, the Hatchback carrying Hudson turns the corner up the street.

Denise had never seen smoking in public before. She turns to Amanda and asks for a cigarette. Amanda grants her request. Denise lights up, stating:

"I'll put that bitch out of her misery."

34

Torture House is located on a cul-de-sac in the hills of northern Shanghai. The grounds are fit for entertaining, with several barbeque pits and a large swimming pool.

The three women drag Hudson inside and tie her up just like they did to the kidnapped Mildred Simms. Creating a huddle around Hudson, they continue to terrorize the agent. Shelly could have addressed any other issue to open up the interrogation process for Heidi Hudson. Still, she chooses to return to the last question she asked of Agent Hudson during the interrogation session back in Jamaica on the previous mission.

"Who did your dad pay to take out my man in Bogota?"

Heidi Hudson responds,

"Will you just let my dad rest in peace?"

Shelly responds,

"No Bitch, he is not going to rest, neither are you until I find out who snuffed out Mike."

Heidi Hudson replies,

"Dad had nothing to do with your boyfriend's death," Shelly states:

"That's what you said the last time. Your dad had every reason to hurt him. Mike decided not to split his cocaine profits with your deceptive, corrupt, deceitful dad. Therefore, your dad, one of the wealthiest DEA to ever work in Miami, hired someone to kill Mike."

Heidi responds,

"I am not my father's keeper, just his daughter. You are asking me questions I can't answer." Denise steps right into the frame. She hands over a journal to her counterpart, Shelly.

Shelly removes the bookmark and begins to read silently at first. Shelly continues,

"You wrote in your journal the day Mike was killed: 'My dad did what he had to do to get where he needed to go.' Did you not?"

Hudson, feeling like she is being put on trial, responds, "My dad was paid to do a job as a DEA. Like every loyal agent, he was obligated to report the facts to his superiors. Your man was a Drug Lord, and dealing drugs was, and still is, against the law."

Denise interjects,

"Is that the eleventh commandment because I never saw it in the Ten?"

Heidi replies,

"Everything wrong was not included in those two tablets of stone..." Amanda interrupts,

"Alright, Hudson, enough of that Bible stuff. This is not Sunday school. Besides, my sister was too easy on you the last time."

Amanda continues,

"May … Agnes Richards R.I.P." Hudson reflects on the torture she encountered by Agnes and Shelly during the previous operation.

Amanda locks eyes with Agent Hudson,

"FYI, I will push the button for you to hang out on the Sabbath. You can pray all you want. There won't be any miracle."

Amanda approaches the chair in which Hudson sits, slaps her twice hard in the face, and then tightens the noose hanging around the agent's neck.

The women open a closet filled with an eclectic assortment of weapons. They arm themselves to the massive.

Shelly, looking back at Hudson, threatens,

"We will be back! Your countdown begins right now."

BACK AT THE LOUNGE in Shanghai, Rude Buay, Miles Tate, Walter Banks, and the Commissioner all race to their vehicles. Before the men could board their van, Rude Buay noticed that all four van tires had been slashed as the truck sat on its rims. Rude Buay kicks the tires in disgust. Thinking it through, he then advises, "There is an option! I am going to check that parked car in the back driveway."

Rude Buay leaves the other men and departs in that direction.

He breaks inside a parked car and tries to start it. The car does not respond, so he opens the hood only to realize that the battery is missing. Rude Buay leaves, searching for options.

In the meantime, a van pulls up next to the truck with the slashed tires. The four Henchmen jump out. They surround Banks, Tate, and Baptiste. The three men are no match for these four henchmen. So, the quartet captures the trio, strips them of all their weapons, and throws them inside their van. They jump inside the truck. The van departs up the hill, following in tow of the femme Fatales.

Moments later, Rude Buay, after locating no other form of transportation, returns down the hill to the scene of that abandoned van. There is no one there. Even so, he surveys but in vain. The smell of hay and the neighing of a horse alert him to a nearby barn. He rushes to the horse shed. There, he finds a horse kicking up its heels. He takes it for a ride through the village, searching for Tate, Banks, and Baptiste.

35

Tate, Banks, and Baptiste are escorted inside an office. For the first time, they are face-to-face with Alberto Gomez and David Lee.

Alberto, staring at Banks, states:

"Walter Banks, I knew you would show up voluntarily." Banks pleads the fifth.

Alberto continues,

"Commissioner, you can run, but you can't hide. How do you like your Déjà Vu?"

Alberto shoots at the Commissioner. The bullet misses his head. The Commissioner can't believe what he has been drawn into for the second time in less than a month.

Alberto looks across at his Henchmen and commands, "Take them to the Torture House and leave the white guy."

The four men comply.

Tate is now on center stage in front of David Lee and Alberto Gomez.

Alberto asks,

"Agent Tate, how long have you been an agent?"

Tate responds,

"Less than one month!"

Alberto continues,

"Someone suckered you into interrupting the flow, huh? You sure handle yourself like a pro."

Tate responds,

"Thanks, I've always wanted to be a DEA. A great one!" Alberto questions,

"How much do they pay you?"

Tate answers,

"I am not really in for the money."

Alberto says,

"You are such a deceitful bastard. No wonder you always wanted to be a DEA. What are you in for, Drugs and Hotties?"

Tate responds,

"None of those things matter!"

David goes inside the closet and retrieves an attaché case. He brings it out and displays it on the table in front of Agent Tate. He then opens it. Inside the attaché:

Stacks of crisp U.S. one hundred dollar bills. Tate's eyes light up.

David Lee addresses,

"Tate, we are expanding rapidly and need someone like you to head up operations at the U.S./Canadian Border. You have the right complexion and the perfect age."

David Lee hands over the attaché and encourages,

David Lee encourages,

“This is a "draw."

Tate counts the money. He is excited but confused.

David Lee states,

“If you change your mind, just return the cash as-is. Here is my business card.” Tate accepts the bribe.

Alberto says to Tate, You are free to go, Agent Tate.

Tate departs.

Shelly, Denise, and Amanda bring in Heidi Hudson, who is bruised, battered, and tied up.

Alberto addresses:

“Agent Hudson, it is good to see you again. I must say that you are either stupid or Rude Buay must have brainwashed you, hypnotized you, or... Is it your resilience, or do you get your high from being abused?” Hudson maintains her silence.

Alberto interrogates,

“I desire to get you out of this situation you have locked yourself into. You had so many opportunities to be free. Yet, you won't leave the DEA business. It seems like you are trying to cash in.” David goes to the closet and returns with an attaché. He opens it on the table in front of Agent Hudson.

The case is stacked with U.S. one-hundred-dollar bills.

David Lee argues,

“Agent Hudson, here is what we can do for you. We are expanding and need your expertise at the Nogales border in Arizona. You fit the profile of the person we seek to head up that operation. We don’t want to use

one of us, just not yet." Agent Hudson stares at the loot. "No thanks, I will not be bribed." Says Hudson.
Alberto continues,
"Agent, are you sure you want to pass this on with bonuses and incentives added? We would also be willing to bury the hatchet - your dad's."
Alberto looks across at Shelly Hall for validation.
Heidi Hudson reiterates, "I am not interested even if it cost me my life." Alberto looking across at Shelly.
"Take her back to the Torture House! We'll hang her tomorrow."
Denise asks,
"What do we do with Mildred Simms?"
Alberto responds,
"Leave her for Johnny, along with Banks and Baptiste. He wants them for Jamaica. Bring us Rude Buay alive. Hudson?... We'll hang her ass tomorrow!"

36

The three female Drug Lords, Shelly, Denise, and Amanda, rough up Agent Hudson excessively as they take her to the car. They push her inside and drive off back to the Torture House.

In the meantime, Rude Buay continues riding briskly through the villages of northern Shanghai in search of the other members of his team. He dials Banks, Baptiste, Hudson, and Tate in succession. He does not receive a response from any of them, so he dials Chelo and gets a busy tone.

Chelo is on the rooftop in Bogota, busy rewiring his equipment, and misses that call.

Rude Buay hangs up and redials as the horse gallops along the narrow streets. Still, no one picks up his call. From the streets, he can see Chinese kids playing at the park. They are now focused on him. They were thrilled to see a man riding a horse through their neighborhood. One kid yells out,

"Holy Grail!"

Finally, Chelo aborts the rooftop equipment renovation and re-enters his shack. He sees the blinking light and responds to the missed call.

Rude Buay picks up.

"Rude Buay, I have been working all day on the roof installing a new antenna, señor. Now I have the video for you."

Rude Buay replies,

"I am not in a vehicle right now, Chelo. You are going to have to describe the visuals for me."

Chelo asks,

"What is your location, Agent Rude Buay?"

Rude Buay responds,

"On a horse, Chelo, in northern Shanghai, give me what you got, Chelo,"

Chelo replies,

"I have some recent footage from inside a building called the Torture House. Shelly, Denise, and Amanda were viewed as terrorizing Agent Hudson. Walter Banks, the Commissioner, Mildred Simms, and Hudson possibly await their hanging. I was able to track Johnny Too Bad. He just left the dock and boarded a taxi. He could be heading to the hanging or pursuing you."

"Where is that house, Chelo?"

"In a Cul De Sac in Northern Shanghai, no address listed. That is a very remote location."

Says Chelo.

"Thanks. Anything on agent Tate?"

"Nothing, Zip, Nada. He could have been kidnapped and sent to a different location or already killed by the Dragon Cartel."

Rude Buay responds,

"Thanks, Chelo …"
Rude Buay hurries through the remote village. His phone rings, and he gets it.
"Rude Buay, Johnny just made a stop a mile east of your location at the Wood House. It is situated one mile north of your location."
Chelo advises.
Rude Buay challenges the horse to speed up and rides in that direction.

37

RUDE BUAY pulls up on the horse outside the Wood House. The street is swamped with expensive automobiles. He enters the house armed in search of the DRAGONS. Johnny makes a transfer of cash with two drug dealers earlier, who now leave, oblivious to the agent. Johnny proceeds towards the door with the attaché filled with money. He unexpectedly runs into Rude Buay, who is waiting for him on his way in.

Johnny shoots at Rude Buay and darts back to the office where that transaction was made. Rude Buay pursues and is confronted by Johnny's bodyguard. In the interim, Johnny loads two guns and sticks them in his waist. At the same time, additional BODYGUARDS hurry to the rooftop and position for battle. Rude Buay, in Terminator style, eliminates the first bodyguard.

There's movement on top of the building. The fast-paced footsteps on the roof alert Rude Buay that he is about to be cornered and possibly terminated by such an entourage.

Johnny emerges from the office. He opens fire on Rude Buay. Rude Buay eludes Johnny's onslaught and makes his way to the roof of the building to gain an advantage.

Rude Buay confronts one of the roof-top bodyguards. They engage in a massive shoot out at each other. The bodyguard searches for a perfect aim and settles after succeeding. Yet, he misses as Rude Buay dodges out of it. Rude Buay finally gains the upper hand when he caps the bodyguard between both eyes. Suddenly, Johnny emerges on the rooftop. Just before Rude Buay fires, a hail of bullets rain from Johnny's gun and ricochet behind the wall, protecting Rude Buay.

In the heat of battle, Rude Buay shoots several rounds and hits Johnny in his right upper arm. Johnny's gun, previously in his right hand falls to the ground. Johnny Too Bad quickly engages in the continued attack on Rude Buay using the weapon in his left hand. He fires off several rounds, but nothing connects. The gun is now empty, unknown to Rude Buay.

"Come, Johnny Too Bad. Show me what you got."

Rude Buay says, "I and I rule, Rude Buay."

Says Johnny in Patois.

While shooting with the left hand, Johnny kneels and retrieves the fallen gun.

Meanwhile, Rude Buay reloads his empty guns amidst the dodging of bullets.

Johnny is now holding two guns once again but shoots using the weapon in his right hand—rude Buay clues in. Rude Buay continues shooting at him.

Finally, Johnny's gun is empty. Rude Buay senses Johnny's vulnerability and shoots Johnny in the forehead. Johnny falls off the building and onto the ground, two stories below. Rude Buay retrieves the note from his breast pocket. He folds it many times, creating a paper airplane. He later shoots it in the direction of Johnny's corpse. The object falls on top of the wasted Johnny.

At the same time, back at the Torture House, Shelly, Denise, and Amanda continually terrorize Agent Hudson. Upon learning of Johnny's death, though, the three women rush to their Hatchback and depart speedily towards the Wood House to meet the Drug Queen.

They notice Johnny's body in the street.

"I will take on Rude Buay."

Says Denise.

"This is my turn, Shelly. You faced off with him last time."

Amanda says,

"I have a spanking for his ..."

She continues.

Rude Buay comes down to the ground level of the Wood House. The three women confront him. Realizing that his gun is out of bullets, Amanda decides to take him on in hand-to-hand combat. She envisions taking Rude Buay alive after the severe spanking she's about to give him.

"Go, girl! Show him what you got!"

Shelly and Denise yell out to their female counterpart. Sensing that Amanda has the upper hand and is unaware that Agent Rude Buay has honed his martial arts skills, they leave Amanda to humiliate Agent Rude Buay before taking him hostage.

38

Heidi Hudson wrestles with the rope that binds her hands and feet inside the Torture House. Using her teeth, she gnaws away at the remaining strands. Finally, she manages to break herself free. She hustles to the next room, where Mildred Simms is tied up on a chair. She sets Mildred free, and they try to make their getaway together.

Agent Hudson notices Walter Banks and the Commissioner tied up in a room on their way out.

While Mildred also notices something: three guns on the table. She grabs two, and Hudson grabs the other. Suddenly, the Hatchback carrying Shelly and Denise pulls into the driveway.

Mildred frees Walter Banks inside the house, while Agent Hudson frees the Commissioner. All four exit the building hastily, passing the four dangling nooses. Shelly and Denise are now inside the house, entering through the back door. They miss the quartet. Heidi Hudson shoots at the multi-propane tanks in the Barbecue pit, while Mildred blows up the Hatchback with several rounds. The house goes up in flames progressively.

Rude Buay and Amanda still go at each other in Kung Fu style at the Wood House. Amanda is putting a whopping on Rude Buay; she is taking him to 101 Kung Fu School. Just when it seems like her vision is close to becoming reality, the sound of a speeding vehicle summons her.

On the outside, David Lee is racing in his BMW towards the SCENE. His car pulls up outside. He darts out and heads to the interior of the Wood House. David Lee notices as Rude Buay sends Amanda to the ground with a flying kick to her upper rib cage. Wasting no time, David Lee sees this as an opportunity to capture Rude Buay. So, he joins in for a possible two-on-one takedown of the agent. However, before he can make a go at Rude Buay. Amanda gets back up but succumbs to a broken neck by another kick from the agent, landing her on the ground. This infuriates David Lee, and he attacks Rude Buay with a vengeance. His first kick sends Rude Buay flying. The agent artfully lands on his feet like a cat falling on all fours.

David Lee continues his flying kick tirade on Rude Buay. The agent shows signs of exhaustion, resting against the ropes like a boxer. There is no bell, so the duel continues anyway.

There is a sudden crash, and like the effects of an earthquake, the building rocks back and forth. Alberto Gomez's cube truck, fully loaded with cans of milk, slams into one of the main pillars supporting the Wood House.

Finally, the truck comes to a complete stop. As a result, not only is Wood House lodging the penetrated truck, but David Lee's attention is diverted by the crash.

Rude Buay seizes the opportunity and lands various flying kicks and jabs into David Lee's body. One kick strikes David Lee in his groin area. The drug czar is shaken up and hobbles to the corner, foaming through his mouth.

Rude Buay, not letting up, comes at him again with an arsenal of hits. The final part puts David Lee's head into a fix. The drug czar falls over with a broken neck.

Rude Buay, not taking any chances, delivers a series of kicks into David Lee's stomach, finishing him off.

Alberto Gomez hurries out of the wreckage and center stage, just in time to witness the demolishment of his associate David Lee. He is peeved. Not sure if he should confront the agent in hand-to-hand combat, he resorts to shooting at Rude Buay, although he would instead take him alive.

CLICK! CLICK! CLICK!

Alberto realizes that Rude Buay's gun is now empty, so he engages him in hand-to-hand combat.

The brawl ensues as Rude Buay lands beside him, knocking Alberto Gomez to the ground. The two men go at it for a while, attempting to punch each other's daylight.

The exhausted Rude Buay begins attacking Alberto with a vengeance. Suddenly, there's a creaking sound as the Wood House starts to give way. Alberto wants Rude Buay alive, but the agent is too much for him to handle. Sensing the mayhem, Alberto runs for the side door's exit. Rude Buay is exhausted and staggers around the room. He goes back in time.

FLASHBACK:

MILDRED KEEPS DODGING Axel James' bullets. Rude Buay, with blood on his vest, rolls over onto his stomach and gets a good aim at Axel. Rude Buay Discharges. The bullet HITS Axel right between his two eyes. He falls backward thunderously onto the deck. Niki, the 14-year-old, plunges forward into the deep. A mountain-like wave beckons. It hits the Catamaran viciously. Alberto, dressed in a wet suit, jumps overboard into the wave, unnoticed by everyone on the other ship. The Catamaran sails speedily towards an unavoidable collapse onto the island of Cuba. Mildred dives into the deep and clutches Niki around her neck. Rude Buay throws out the life rope. Mildred catches it. Rude Buay reels them in. Another mountainous wave hits the Catamaran. It slams into Cuba at full speed, bursting into flames, debris, spikes, and fragments of lumber.

BACK TO PRESENT:

Agent Miles Tate enters the Wood House through the front door. Rude Buay, exhausted than ever, senses a sigh of relief upon Tate's entrance. Rude Buay yells to Agent Tate, "Shoot him! Shoot the Philistine, don't give him another chance."
Miles Tate shoots, but instead of shooting Alberto Gomez, he shoots Rude Buay—the bullet lodges in Rude Buay's upper left leg. Rude Buay falls to the ground. Simultaneously, the Wood House caves in on Rude Buay while Agent Tate escapes.
Outside the Wood House, two vehicles raced to the scene. First, the taxi pulls up, and out jumps Walter Banks,
Mildred Simms, agent Heidi Hudson, and the Commissioner (Richard Baptiste).
Right behind it, a black limousine pulls up. Dr. Tamara Ross steps out, followed by Christine Baptiste, who is all dolled up.
Noticing the collapse, many tears are shed at the scene.

THE HORSE AUTOMATICALLY, released from its post, trots and scrapes on the other side of the street.

BOOK # 3

"The things I've been through give me fortitude. I'm not easily broken. Not only have I seen too much, but I've also been through too much. Selling out is not in my greasepaint. You may hang my body tomorrow, but you will never hang my backbone, a slice of which I have embodied in this character, Rude Buay."

- JOHN ALAN ANDREWS

RUDE BUAY

SHATTERPROOF

TABLE OF CONTENTS

1

In a chic Cul De Sac located in the covert hills of Northern Shanghai, smoke, debris, fire, and ashes continue to rise from what's left of the sweltering Torture House.

Less than 24 hours ago, this domicile had housed some high-profile hostages, four of the most efficient agents the world has ever seen. Fighters against narcotics, these adept drug enforcement agents who hailed from the U.S. and Jamaica have been tortured immensely by the invincible Dragon Drug Cartel. A descendant of a former special drug enforcement agent, HEIDI HUDSON: she's Caucasian in her late twenties. Hudson steps off the plane in Miami. Jamaican-born.

MILDRED SIMMS, in her late twenties. She is a drop-dead gorgeous, sophisticated African American beauty, every man's heart's desire, and employed by the Ministry of Tourism in Jamaica.

WALTER BANKS, a Jamaican-born African American in his late fifties with salt and pepper hair, is a veteran D.E.A. who served for many years in Colombia.

The Commissioner of Police in Jamaica is RICHARD BAPTISTE, a tall, slim, kingly man in his forties.

These agents miraculously and cleverly not only made their escape before two femme Fatales of the Dragon Drug Cartel returned to kill them but were also instrumental in setting the house on fire. Agents Heidi Hudson and Mildred Simms were the ones who pulled the detonating gun triggers, which set this Torture House ablaze, sending fumes of Ganja and mahogany wood into the universe as soon as those two women entered through the garage.

Later that day, fire trucks with idle engines and flashing lights continued to pour water on the remains of the burning building. While they dowse a room filled with sacks of weed, suddenly, as if by a stroke of luck, an enthusiastic Chinese firefighter notices some movements nearby in the large outdoor swimming pool.

The pool is partially covered with fallen burnt roofing and mahogany scaffolds, some of which still fall into the water and are extinguished.

In haste, multiple firefighters extend a ladder into the pool between the scaffolds while concentrating the water hose nearby.

Two exhausted women accept the aluminum ladder's invitation and begin climbing out in what's left of their street clothes amidst the burning inferno.

First on the ladder is DENISE GOMEZ. Denise is an Asian trophy woman in her late twenties. Her engagement ring, still touching her wedding band, is to be significantly desired by any woman. The blinding rock speaks for itself, despite her partially covered, with ash, appearance. The first firefighter rescues her. This agile fireman grabs her and escorts her to the sidewalk. They're a team of firefighters who emerge and proceed to pump water out of Denise Gomez's lungs.

Another agile firefighter quickly grabs the ascending WWE-type SHELLY HALL and pulls her swiftly to safety before the building's roof caves in atop the pool. Shelly Hall, partially covered with ash, is a tall Caucasian woman in her 30s. Soon, she is lying on the sidewalk. With the aid of mouth-to-mouth resuscitation performed by a firefighter, water pours out of her mouth and nostrils like a spurt as she coughs up some more intermittently.

Soon after, both rescued femme Fatales are placed on separate gurneys and rushed into idling ambulances. The ambulances depart speedily while the fire trucks continue to dowse water on the smoky remains of the almost diminished Torture House.

MEANWHILE, IN A NOT TOO DISTANT Shanghai village, a white car cruises down the street.

Inside, the driver MILES TATE navigates while surveying through the narrow Shanghai roadsides. Tate is Caucasian in his early 30s. Next to him on the front seat is a half-closed attaché case.

At the same time, ALBERTO GOMEZ, drug Czar and leader of the Dragon Drug Cartel, is on foot going down that same street. Alberto Gomez is dressed in a tattered, expensive business suit and tinted sunglasses. He's in his mid to late 30s, of descent. Alberto Gomez is bruised and bloodied over most of his body. He's been involved in a big fight or scuffle. Miles Tate stops the car and pulls over to the curb. He puts the attaché case on the rear seat and opens the front passenger door to accommodate the drug, Czar. Alberto Gomez boards on the front seat when the passenger door swings open.

"Thanks! Always on time, huh?"

Says Alberto Gomez.

"Like they say in Jamaica: No Problem. No problem mon!"

Says Tate.

Alberto Gomez seems focused.

Tate continues,

"He almost ate your lunch, huh?"

Alberto Gomez is keeping it all business: questions,

"So, you finished him off, yeah?"

"One shot straight for the bull's eye. He went down, and Wood House subsequently caved in on him."

Tate responds.

"Nice finish to that pain in the A…!"

Says Alberto Gomez.

The two men high-fived each other while waiting for the stoplight to go green.

"What about the hostages?"

Asks Tate.

"Without Amanda…I'm sure Denise and Shelly Hall have them bound and ready for tomorrow's hanging."
Alberto Gomez responds:
"Our first order of business will be to affix your Dragon signature as soon as I find some new gear and a local tattoo shop. We have to make you official for that group hanging."
Later, Alberto Gomez pulls up at a tattoo shop. They enter the establishment run by the Tattoo King, who is extravagantly tattooed all over his body. His lavish tattoo décor clearly states I am tattooed on my hands, tattooed in my heart, and tattooed on my brain.

2

In Montego Bay, Jamaica, investigators and the news media ambitiously converge on the Ministry of Tourism building. They swarm around Mildred Simms, gleaning for every bit of news regarding her escape. The Caribbean beauty has just returned to the office at the Ministry of Tourism for the first time after being kidnapped by members of the high-ranking Dragon Drug Cartel. While the gathering media pry the information relevant to her capture and escape from the Torture House, it sends shockwaves through the hearts of her coworkers, awaiting their opportunity to console Jamaica's Mildred. TV cameras keep rolling, lights flashing, and boom mikes extending as eager reporters recapture this remarkable hostage recovery story. They lament her bravery in pulling the trigger, which sets the Torture House on fire. A few blocks away at the Police Barracks, a similar scenario unfolds: the overzealous news media glean information from ex-hostage and Jamaican Police Commissioner Richard Baptiste. Standing across from the commissioner is his wife, CHRISTINE BAPTISTE. Christine, a stylist in her own right, is dressed to the nines. Additionally, she glows, basking in the

happiness of being back in Jamaica and by the side of her ex-hostage husband, Richard.
Standing next to Christine is the Governor-General Dr. Bradford Wiley, who is intellectually sound and in his sixties. He beams with joy to see Richard alive and well. The two men have been responsible for making multiple important decisions in fighting the war on narcotics, not only in Jamaica but also in the other Caribbean Islands, Asia, the U.S., and Mexico.
The news media continue to garner information while the TV cameras roll excessively. One Spanish reporter from a Mexican affiliate radio station steps up and etches notes on a yellow pad.
Many Jamaicans are glued to their TV sets at home, soaking up the news.
At the Police Barracks, a microphone extends on a boom towards The Commissioner. One reporter asks:
"How did you survive this ordeal and come out of it alive after being kidnapped by the Dragon Drug Cartel twice in one month?"
"I don't know. It was more than a miracle. ... thanks to Rude Buay and his awesome team, or else we would be..."
"And ... where is Rude Buay now?"
Another reporter asks as the camera zooms out.
"Not sure. According to reports, he is feared dead. After the building, in which he single-handedly eliminated several members of the Dragon Drug Cartel, including Johnny Too Bad, collapsed on top of

him. How would you categorize the presumed dead agent
Rude Buay?"
Asks the reporter.
"We owe a sincere debt of gratitude to agent Rude Buay. He wanted to create a better world for all. We were happy to be part of his mission."
Says Richard.
Before another reporter could quiz the Commissioner, two double-breasted jacket-attired police officers escorted him and his wife out of the room and into a waiting limousine. Microphones attached to booms were still against the limousine's window. The vehicle drove off, leaving them hanging.

MEANWHILE, IN KINGSTON, the capital city of Jamaica, drug lord MARCUS RANKS, wearing his dreadlocks hairstyle, is on a tirade. Ranks, an ally to the Dragon Drug Cartel, has ordered his men to block off all streets east, west, north, and south of Kingston. The Jamaican Drug Lord vowed that he would avenge the U.S., not only for extraditing Johnny Too Bad to America but for setting pigs on Johnny like a pack of dogs to snuff him out.
With water dowsed on the Tivoli Gardens riot, the extradition of Johnny Too Bad, and the Drug Lord's death, the Jamaican Law Enforcement had lapsed back into their comfort zone regarding TG.

Ranks, on the other hand, was planning a major comeback for the Dragons in TG, moving their new drug, methamphetamine, in large quantities into West Kingston. Therefore, Ranks ordered those streets heading into Kingston to be blocked off. If the police were ever to join forces and enter into Tivoli Gardens, they would be slowed down, robbed of their weapons, and then beaten to death.

The Jamaican Police Department, which was somewhat shorthanded at this point, had to cool its heels when it came to apprehending drug smugglers in Tivoli Gardens.

3

Alberto Gomez and Miles Tate are still at the upscale Shanghai tattoo shop. Alberto admires as the petite, in-stature attendant affixes the signature of the dragons behind Tate's right ear. Miles Tate is elated as he now sports the Dragon cartel's signature. Alberto Gomez, now neatly attired, looks clean again except for multiple facial bruises. He is always the businessman, suave and debonair, sporting his dark sunglasses. He is focused like a man on a mission.

"So, based on expansion plans, where would I be stationed, Vermont or Vancouver?"

Asks Miles Tate.

Alberto Gomez's cell phone rings, and he gets it.

"Papi…!" Exclaims Denise Gomez.

Denise is lying on a Shanghai hospital bed, sadly affected by second-degree burns over most of her body as a result of the Torture House fire. Across from her is her partner in crime, Shelly Hall. With multiple burns to her body. Shelly Hall is in the same uncomfortable condition. Overwhelmed in pain, the veteran drug lady tries masking it. Denise Gomez is dying to report.

Sensing the somber tone in Denise's voice, Alberto Gomez questions,
"Why? Where are you, at the Torture House, planning those hangings for tomorrow?" "No, we are at the hospital and badly burned up. The Torture House burned down last night. However, thanks to the swimming pool, Shelly Hall and I are still alive but badly burned up, Al."
"You got to be kidding! The Hatchback caught on fire? What happened to the ... hostages?" Asks Alberto Gomez.
"Too Bad! When we arrived at the Wood House, several bullets fired out, and the building exploded in flames. They got away. All four of them! Those ... bastards escaped. It seems like it was a collaborative effort. Don't know how they pulled that one-off. Where is Rude Buay? Did you get him?"
Denise asks.
"Escaped huh? They may run, but they cannot hide. They are such a minority in this city. They ought to know that. Those agents won't have a ... chance. When we catch them, we will hang their ... high!" Regarding Rude Buay, we finished him off at the Wood House.
States Alberto Gomez.
Tate eavesdrops and reacts negatively to the survival story of the hostages. He can't wrap his mind around it. Tate had envisioned joining the Dragon Cartel with a significant advantage over its opposition - the D.E.A. and its allies. This would be his first big celebration

after deflecting back in Shanghai. He so wanted to witness the hanging of agents Mildred Simms, Walter Banks, Heidi Hudson, and the Jamaican Police Commissioner Richard Baptiste. Being disappointed is an understatement.

"We are heading to the hospital ... We'll be there soon." Alberto Gomez says.

The two men look at each other in total disbelief. They reluctantly digest this latest breaking news from Denise and Shelly Hall. Distasteful as it has been, finally, Tate is the first one to speak:

"How the heck did they get out of there alive? It's like a miracle! I mean Denise and Shelly Hall. Are they half-fish, half-human? Sounds like Déjà vu to me. Are they mermaids?"

"They met in swim school. They handle water situations well."

Says Alberto Gomez.

"No wonder they could have boiled in that swimming pool."

Says Tate.

"Who knows what condition they are in? It could be more serious than they are claiming…"

The car with the two Drug Lords on board pulls up at the hospital ER entrance and comes to a halt. Tate puts the car in park. Tate and Alberto Gomez step out and hurriedly enter the hospital compound like men on a mission.

4

Meanwhile, at the hospital, after looking at their grossly burnt bodies, Alberto Gomez, Miles Tate, Denise Gomez, and Shelly Hall embark upon laying plans for a massive comeback. They envision capturing all the DEA agents and hanging them one by one from the gallows. They also discuss plans to set up the Dragon Drug Cartel headquarters in the sister cities of Nogales in Mexico and Arizona. This would mean, however, truncating themselves from Colombia after five years of narcotics operations on its soil.

About 60 miles south of Tucson lie the sister cities that share that same name - Nogales. One is in Arizona, and the other is in Old Mexico. Many years ago, groves of walnut trees covered the mountain pass that bridged the two enclaves, leading to the name Nogales, derived from the Spanish word for dark walnuts. Today, not only do many Americans cross the border into Nogales to acquire less costly medical care and over-the-counter drugs, but drug smugglers experience much ease trafficking narcotics from the Mexican border city across to the American side. The Dragon Drug Cartel, by now, was beginning to feel the need not only to capitalize but to dominate in Mexico as well. Even so, they had to move swiftly as other drug cartels also wanted to take advantage of this narcotics trafficking accessibility. Alberto Gomez pulled out the stops as he addressed his team at the hospital double room briefing:

"Tate, as David Lee requested, you will be set up in Vermont, on the U.S.-Canadian Border. Shelly Hall will monitor those operations when you return to active duty.

Denise and I will handle the Nogales Border between Mexico and Arizona until we can find a competent replacement. Our priority will be to expand trade between Mexico and California and Mexico and Arizona. This new venture will be very challenging, as we will also have to deal with other D.E.A. agents and competing cartels."

Alberto Gomez continues,

"I have already contacted Johnny Too Bad's protégé Marcus Ranks. He will head up the Tivoli Garden operation, thus putting it back on the map. We cannot leave Jamaica out of the mix. It is still our breadbasket, our bread and butter. We miss Johnny Too Bad, but we have to move on; that is the trend of this business."

SAMMY CHIN, an ally of David Lee, will head up China, along with the rest of Asia. GRACE McCloud will replace Amanda Kingsley and monitor our Miami operations. SALVADOR will be ready to start shipping soon. We may need him temporarily in Bogotá at this point."

"I thought Sal was in…" Questions Miles Tate.
"I have a connection with some of the authorities at the Shanghai prison. We stand an excellent chance of getting him out of there. You are in good hands with us, Tate."
Responds Alberto Gomez.
"We could be back in the trade in less than two weeks. Denise's and Shelly's wounds will heal soon, and we will be back in business for good."
"I can't wait to get out of here, guys. I can't wait to join you."
Chimes Shelly Hall.
"You and me, both of us,"
Adds Denise Gomez.
Before that brief emergency meeting of the smuggling minds is about to be adjourned, a piece of late-breaking news, far too coincidentally close to their train of thought, from the ABC News channel catches their attention. They all glued onto the two small TV sets inside the double hospital room. The news is turf-worthy:
"Five people found burned beyond recognition in an abandoned SUV in an area of Arizona frequented by smugglers were likely the victims of one of the same drug cartels that have ravaged parts of Mexico with their rampant violence, the local sheriff said today. A border patrol agent noticed a white Ford Expedition stopping around 4:30 a.m. Saturday in Vekol Valley, a desert area that's a well-known smuggling corridor for

drugs and illegal immigrants from Mexico. Suspecting the car stopped to pick up drugs, the agent tried to contact the vehicle, but the vehicle fled. When the sun rose, the agent noticed car tracks leading off the road and followed them for a few miles into the desert. The agent found a smoldering vehicle and called for backup. When other agents arrived, they used fire extinguishers to put out the fire and found five charred bodies inside the car, say the police."

"This is pretty significant,"

Pinal County Sheriff Paul Babeu said when interviewed.

"Given all these indicators, you don't have to be a homicide detective to add all the information."

Says the Journalistic informer as he buttons it up.

According to investigators, One victim was found in the sedan's rear passenger seat and four others in the back cargo compartment, their bodies burned beyond recognition. Investigators have not yet determined whether the bodies were bound, the sheriff said. Babeu told ABC News that it was likely that others had fled the scene.

"There wasn't anyone in the front driver's seat or the front passenger's seat, and the position of the bodies led us to believe that it's most likely that other people were aboard it,"

Babeu said and continued:

"The deaths are being investigated as homicides. The vehicle was stopped in an open area. It did not crash into something. Whoever murdered these people did it intentionally." Like a water mouth, he rambles on: "They brought them there either alive or dead and torched the vehicle to conceal the evidence." The incident is likely a case of drug cartel violence. This is more than likely connected to drug smuggling. It's most likely not human smuggling because most of the time, if the illegal person is no longer of use or too slow for the rest of the group, they're left to fend for themselves or die. We don't see many cases where illegal people are killed. They're usually only killed if they put up a fight as they're being robbed. This is more likely punishment on criminals who tried to steal from the cartels or some competing interest in a criminal element."

Babeu states further that investigators will try to determine whether the victims were dead before the fire was started or whether they were alive when the SUV was set ablaze.

Shelly Hall tossed in bed, aggravating her injuries:

"BS…total BS! Way too many Private Eyes!"

Denise concurs and uncomfortably reaches for her iPad and research.

The Vekol Valley is located 70 miles north of the U.S.-Mexican border. Babeu called the area a "hotbed for human and drug smuggling."

The federal government put up 15 billboards that read: "Danger Warning, Travel Not Recommended, Drug

Smuggling, Active and Armed Gunmen" in the area along Interstate 8.

Last year, the Vekol Valley was the site of the largest drug bust in the history of Arizona.

Seventy-six members of the Sinaloa cartel were arrested in the bust, known as Operation Pipeline Express. The suspects had 108 weapons, including scoped rifles, AK47s, and two weapons from the U.S. government's Fast & Furious program.

The controversial program, run by the Bureau of Alcohol, Tobacco, Firearms, and Explosives, was designed to track guns bought in the United States by straw men and delivered to drug cartels in Mexico in an attempt to catch the cartel higher-ups. Begun in 2009, it was shut down after the December 2010 murder of U.S. Border Patrol agent Brian Terry, who was killed with a weapon sold through the program.

Babeu said the fact that the Fast & Furious guns were found in the possession of the Sinaloa cartel members is a sign that the program is "criminal."

The Journalist on screen confirms what Denise researched and, before taking a commercial break, says:

“We will be back with more in a minute.”

The attending nurse walks in, sees Denise Gomez and Shelly Hall in surprise, and signals five more minutes. She then departs.

Tate looks across at Alberto Gomez, so do Denise and Shelly Hall as they reminisce and integrate that report:

The astute Journalist/News Reporter returns:
"Ten suspected gangsters were killed Thursday morning during a running gun battle in the Mexican border town of Nogales, just one week after the U.S. State Department warned of growing violence among narcotics rings. Mexican media said Sonoran justice officials confirmed the number of dead and reported that several police officers were injured by shrapnel when fleeing suspects tossed grenades at them. No law enforcement agents were reported dead. The events in Nogales were part of a bloody day along the nearly 2,000-mile Mexican border, where 21 people died in 24 hours of violence involving drug traffickers and other criminal syndicates.
Sources reported that four men were shot dead in front of a crowd at an amusement park, and a toddler died when the car he was in crashed during a gun battle. Also, a businessman was murdered after leading a protest against violence."
Eyes in that hospital room connects.
Reporter continues:
"This is a very, very dangerous time to be a drug agent, said Beth Kepshall, special agent in charge of the Drug Enforcement Administration in Phoenix. The stakes are more significant here in Arizona than I've seen. Kempshall said the situation in Nogales was still unfolding Wednesday afternoon, and information was sketchy. The number of bodies was still in chaos, she noted. It wasn't a good situation down there..."

"Scare tactics?"
Asks Alberto Gomez.
"Is he making a Documentary? There is way too much exposition."
Contend, Denise Gomez.
Even so, the Reporter has found a captive audience from his perch to theirs.
Feeling it, he continues: "Tucson Sources reported that shootings began around 6 a.m. as police stopped a pair of vehicles containing suspected gangsters. It was not immediately clear whether that incident was preceded by fighting between narcotics groups or something else. Officers pursued the suspects along major Nogales streets, with at least two battles occurring a few miles from the border. Four suspects reportedly died after officers shot out a vehicle's tires, causing it to crash. Others were killed by gunfire. Three civilians also suffered minor injuries during the fighting, according to the Sources.
Just last week, D.E.A. officials said violence in Sonora is growing because outside narcotics organizations are challenging the so-called Sinaloa cartel, which for years claimed dominion over smuggling routes into Arizona. Kempshall said a crackdown by the Mexican government and increased pressure by U.S. agents had added friction: They're fighting over the routes into the United States, and over control of the border area.

Brian Levin, a Customs and Border Protection spokesman, said U.S. entry ports are always prepared for violence, so no additional security measures are in place.

The State Department alert said Nogales is among several border cities that have recently experienced public shootouts during daily hours. Conflicts involving heavily armed gangsters claimed about 3,000 lives in Mexico this year. In September, there were at least five public gun battles, including the murder of a man next to a school. Last week, gunmen fired hundreds of rounds into the home of a Nogales reporter, who was not injured.

On Wednesday in Ciudad Juarez, four men were shot inside an amusement park where teenagers were riding bikes through obstacle courses, skating, and rappelling. Elsewhere in the city, a used car salesman was shot to death while driving down the main boulevard hours after leading hundreds of other business owners in a protest against kidnappings and extortion. The demonstrators had threatened to close their businesses or stop paying taxes because so many were being targeted by extortionists demanding up to $500 a week for protection against crime. In Tijuana, a 1-year-old boy was killed when the car he was riding in crashed as the driver tried to flee a gunfight late Wednesday between the police and three armed men, officials in the state prosecutor's office said. The toddler had been sitting in his mother's lap…"

"That's enough!"
Says Shelly Hall, propping herself up on the bed.
Alberto Gomez chairs:
"There is no more Agent Rude Buay to interfere, and whoever Michael Ortiz puts in his place is not ready for such a force as us. Neither is the Sinaloa Cartel. The bozo heading it up doesn't even know his left hand from his right and operates on one half a brain."
Miles Tate proclaims in support of his Boss' epiphany.
"As for Rude Buay's replacement, there is no one to put in Rude Buay's place as far as I know. Heidi Hudson is not ready for such a task. He was her strength, a shoulder she leaned on. Those Jamaican agents are nothing, very incompetent."
"Michael Ortiz would not take us on by himself. I doubt he would use them."
Adds Denise Gomez.
The nurse returns to the room. They abruptly adjourn the meeting. Alberto Gomez kisses Denise on her lips. He then quickly departs with ex-agent and now ally Miles Tate.

5

METHAMPHETAMINE, cocaine, and heroin, along with other narcotics, pour into Nogales - Arizona, El Paso, San Diego, Canada, Miami, China, and the Jamaican cities of Tivoli Gardens, Kingston, and Port Antonio - originated from Nogales, Mexico. Truckers carefully unload their cargo in these major drug smuggling cities. The dealers arrive and pick up the drugs in their high-end automobiles. They distribute them to buyers at parks, grocery stores, clubs, parking garages, yachts, and airplane hangars. At the same time, some deliver at more secret locations like back alleys and business offices.

Getting high on the streets from cocaine, meth, and other drugs has become the thing to do as if drugs have been legalized. You could walk down almost any street and buy narcotics just like you would candy or bottled water. For so many drug addicts, their new long-lasting high comes from the drug Methamphetamine.

On the street; this brain and body killer drug Methamphetamine or Meth; is more commonly sold under names such as crank, speed, crystal, or ice. This whitish or pale yellow crystal-like powder is usually

chewed, ingested, injected, snorted, or sometimes smoked.
Methamphetamine, sold in large quantities, is a powerfully intense stimulant that creates a euphoric and energetic feeling. It releases high levels of the neurotransmitter dopamine, which stimulates brain cells, enhancing mood and body movement. While a cocaine high lasts about 15-20 minutes, a meth high lasts 2-14 hours. The Dragon Drug Cartel uses this opportune sales pitch to push Meth like none other. Drug users and pushers alike trading on the streets seem to have no respect for law enforcement. The plea of most drug users is: "Legalize drugs so the price would drop."
Many even say:
"Legalize drugs so people can have easy access without interference from the police."
On the other hand, most Jamaican law enforcement authorities have seen enough living through the Tivoli Gardens riots and with the streets in Kingston being blocked off recently. They wouldn't fall for that legalization phenomenon. In Jamaica, the police beef up their operation and arrest many narcotics offenders, including several young adult drug smugglers.

IN THE INTERIM, while Denise Gomez and

Shelly Hall recuperates from their injuries, and profits from Methamphetamine around the globe soar at a fantastic pace. Unfortunately, though, these profits do not flow to the Dragon Drug Cartel; they had previously focused their efforts on the profits from the drug cocaine in Colombia.

Alberto Gomez realizes that despite their worthy plans and past successes, they have only been playing from the game's periphery. Miles Tate and Gomez concentrate on playing "catching up" to the Sinaloa Drug Cartel, who outshone them in every way possible.

Hence Gomez decides to revert to the young, the innocent, and the gadded to move meth expediently from Mexico across the U.S. borders to catch up with his competitors.

MEANWHILE, ACROSS THE U.S./MEXICAN El

Paso border, a stand-off ensues as U.S. Border Patrol Officers confront and seize over 500 pounds of Methamphetamine, a street value of over $20,000,000.00 (20 million dollars) in Miami.

Several smugglers transporting the substance in cars were detained and arrested as they tried to transport them across and into the U.S. illegally. Even as these smugglers were placed in handcuffs by U.S. border patrols, the Dragon Drug Cartel sent in over two dozen pre-teenagers, recently trained at a firing range, to combat the attacks made by the border patrols on those smugglers.

In the interim, while the El Paso border patrols were busily conducting their investigation of the smugglers, those same over two dozen kids ages 11-12 stormed through the Mexican city of Nogales and across the U.S. border into the Arizonian municipality of Nogales, demanding a release of the smugglers and their seized narcotics.

Armed with AK47s, they confronted the investigation-focused border officers, shooting and killing many. It was said that the El Paso border patrols did not even the score. Instead of retaliating, those officers chose not to return fire because they realized that they were dealing with a bunch of minors or what some may call Generation K2-10.

By the time those border patrol officers reverted to tear gas to restrain the kids, many of them were already gunned down by the antagonistic pre-teenagers. The arrested smugglers were then released by the efforts of the minors, who stormed into the border's detention center. Using keys found at fallen border patrols' desks, they unlocked the handcuffs of the detained and set them free.

Upon their release, the smugglers continued on their trafficking routes throughout the U.S. as well as Canada.

After the vicious shoot-out, which left many border officers dead, the kids were reinforced with other minors as back-ups penetrating the Mexican city of Nogales in SUVs, spraying bullets like rain from the machine and sub-machine guns.

It wasn't until their bullets ran out that the still-alive officers stationed at the border and those who were rushed in to defend as well were able to catch up with many of these pre-teenagers trying to flee back into Mexico. At the end of this standoff between the minors and border patrols, over one dozen minors were arrested.

The others took flight and fled into the hills of the Mexican desert. For days later on, the Mexican Police combed through the desert equipped with tear gas in search of those remaining kid shooters. Unfortunately, days of searching produced negative results as the police returned empty-handed.

On the other hand, the kids had returned safely to the base camp of the Dragons in Southern Nogales and sought refuge. There, they continued their combat training under the auspices of Drug Czar Alberto Gomez, leader of the infamous Dragon Drug Cartel.

6

Greg Bascombe, an African Jamaican in his mid-40s, is the dad of two daughters. He lives in Jamaica with his family. His wife, BRENDA BASCOMBE, is Caucasian and in her late 30s. Together, the Bascombe family is raising their twin teenage daughters, GLENDA and THELMA.

Greg is one of Jamaica's finest at the Port Antonio Police Department. His tenure in law enforcement dates back almost a decade. He is also a leader in his church, revered by the young and old alike. Greg is the youth pastor and the church treasurer. His wife, Brenda, is a church elder who sits on the church board and is involved in every major decision that the organization makes.

At fourteen, the girls are straight "A" students. Thelma wants to become a doctor, and Glenda wants to become a missionary. Additionally, they are the talk of their church and the community. They excel in just about everything they touch. Subtly, the girls are evolving into Port Antonio's Model Citizens.

Lately, though, Greg has diverted into a slump. His ways are uncanny. Not only has he been missing necessary appointments, but he has been hanging out with his high school buddies at regular freebasing and meth consumption sessions.

Brenda, noticing Greg's unaccountability, suggests that they start attending counseling with their senior pastor, Douglas Cambridge. Greg has a big ego and refuses, not wanting to submit his ego to another man. At church, although the Bascombe's put on a façade of a tight-knit family with all of their ducks in a row, at home, the family is falling apart at the seams.
One Sunday afternoon after church, Greg leaves his car at home and asks one of his high school buddies to pick him up. Together, they drive to a house where three of their other ex-schoolmates join them for a freebasing session.

IN THE INTERIM, Glenda visits her dad's car parked on the street. She rummages through the car. In the glove compartment, she discovers not only almost one gram of cocaine but methamphetamine, along with freebasing utensils. She is ecstatic and indulges. Narcotic usage has been an evolving habit for young Glenda. For several weeks, she has been sneaking into her dad's car every time he's away and subsequently acquiring her fix. Additionally, some of her peers had, on several occasions, brought meth to school. The young teen has gradually become an addict and would often join her classmates for their regular get-high sessions during lunch breaks. Then, they would return to class, flying on cloud nine.

This time around, her high gives her the cravings for more and more methamphetamine. She finds herself licking the foil paper clean of all residues with her tongue, not fearing that her dad would realize his product has been tampered with.

Gradually and oblivious to Glenda, the meth intake had been wearing on her brain and body over time, causing both to deteriorate.

Later, Glenda walks the streets solo in high spirits. She enters the ramp and onto the major highway. Several vehicles are traveling at high speed. The driver of the oncoming eighteen-wheeler tractor-trailer sees her staggering across the road. He applies brakes. Even so, unable to stop the trailer he runs her over, crushing her under the vehicle's wheels.

Other vehicles crash into the trailer, creating a multiple-vehicle collision. Many injuries occur. Lives are lost in this multiple-vehicle accident, including the driver of the trailer. As the vehicle slams into the median upon impact, the driver is tossed from inside the truck and onto the street. It is a massive automobile pile-up with multiple vehicles colliding and forming a heap. There's unrest in the chicest community of Port Antonio as neighbors rush to the scene. Brenda and Thelma are making dinner, getting the sad news, and hurrying to the scene on foot and in tears. In the meantime, Greg bathes in remorse after hearing the tragic news and gets dropped off at the house in a taxi. His colleagues, so high on meth, were unable to drive him home.

Greg gets to his car and decides to drive to the scene. He notices the foil paper on the seat and clues in on the scenario: His narcotics, which he had confiscated during a recent drug bust and which had intentionally not been transferred to the station, had been tampered with by his daughter. He races to the scene of the accident, still under the influence. Upon arriving at the scene and noticing the mayhem, Greg Bascombe, armed on his off day, reaches inside his gun holster. He removes his gun and shoots himself in the head.

The sound of the gunshot alerts those at the scene, including his wife and daughter, along with his neighbors and other attending police officers. It is too much for his family and the small community of chic Port Antonio to unravel on that Sunday afternoon. There is wailing and lamentation in the community. Brenda and Thelma are discombobulated. Many cries go out on their behalf. Their church members show up in droves, providing comfort during double grief.

7

Through the upscale Port Antonio community, traffic is at a standstill as funeral-goers by the hundreds proceed to the cemetery. Some mourners, traveling in buses, cars, on motorbikes, and others on foot, are still saddened by the shock of the double narcotics-related suicide.

Leading the procession is a motorcade of Jamaican police officers on motorbikes displaying Green, Black, and Gold, followed in tow by two wreath-covered hearses. Spectators sitting on their porches, verandas, and patios are bathed in tears as the procession passes the village. Motorists yield and give way to the saddened procession in a tear-shedding homage to the dead.

Meanwhile, the regretful multicultural, multiethnic, multiage procession, singing songs of praise, wipes their crying eyes as they travel along the streets of Port Antonio.

Even while the news media in Jamaica are lashing out against the Mexicans for infiltrating their country with Methamphetamine, multiple kilos of coke and other drugs rapidly continue to contaminate the Jamaican community. Getting high has radically become the "thing" to do. Not doing it says you are square or have a severe problem with the most important person - YOURSELF.

While some maintain the stance that if there are no customers to buy drugs, no drugs will get sold—something no drug dealer wants to hear, knowing fully that the buck stops with the client. The funeral procession arrives at the cemetery. Glenda Ann Marie Bascombe is laid to rest. While the grave diggers fill that grave with soil, the minister prepares for the burial service of her dad, Police Officer Greg Patrick Bascombe, the cousin of agent Randy Bascombe, adjacent and a few feet away.

The black, green, and gold Jamaican flag covering his casket is removed by a fellow Jamaican police officer. His casket is then lowered into the grave.

It is a dual solemn occasion as mourners shed more tears. Glenn's wife, Brenda, and daughter, Thelma, standing at the head of the gravesite, break once again and are comforted by a group of consoling women.

At the end of the ceremony, the gravediggers fill this other grave also with soil as the mourners amble away from what will go down in history as the most tragic twin burial in Jamaica.

8

A black BMW pulls up outside a house in MO Bay. TAMARA ROSS, the stunningly eye-catching mid- to late twenty-year-old beauty, steps out. She proceeds to retrieve her keys to unlock the house door. Her cell phone rings at the same time. She answers it. The call creates a sense of urgency as she heads back to the car and takes off speedily. The automobile screeches around the bend in the road as Dr. Ross puts the pedal to the metal.

From many miles away, the sound of a speeding ambulance siren echoes. Meanwhile, a Chinese Private Jet makes its presence felt as it takes off to the skies from MO Bay airport. Earlier a passenger on a gurney was seen deplaning from that aircraft.

The early morning traffic is now bumper to bumper as the BMW navigates its way through the huge traffic gridlock.

Suddenly, the driver of a tailgating minivan loses focus and rear-ends the BMW. This mayhem brings traffic to a standstill as the drivers of both vehicles involved are now caught up in assessing the damage done to their vehicles. After the settlement with the exchange of information the standstill traffic proceeds. Tamara continues her journey.

Dr. Tamara Ross' car pulls into the parking lot of MO Bay Hospital's ER entrance. She races to the emergency room. The nurse on duty says to her, "He's in room #26!"

Dr. Ross rushes upstairs to that room. The patient lying in bed is no stranger to her, but this is the first time that she has been entrusted with the responsibility of possibly doctoring him back to health.

Agent RANDY BASCOMBE, better known as RUDE BUAY and colloquially "Rude Boy," is of Jamaican descent. He opens his eyes and smiles at Dr. Ross. Rude Buay, in his early forties, is adorned with a scorpion tattooed to his bald head, with its fangs upstaging his forehead, and a tail extending towards his right earlobe. He is also badly bruised and battered.

Dr. Ross returns the smile. "How are you felling agent?"

She asks coyly.

"How soon can you get me out of here?"

Rude Buay asks.

"I am going to have to diagnose your condition first before I can determine the length of your recovery. From what I can tell: you seem to have been badly hurt. I don't know how you survived. As far as I know, there isn't a quick-fix recovery method in medicine for a building falling on someone. I saw that collapsed building. You got out of there alive, that's a miracle in itself!"

Rude Buay smiles again.

"So, how soon?"

Asks Rude Buay.

Dr. Ross continues.

"Why didn't you get fixed up in Shanghai or the United States? They can rush the healing process. Are you here for treatment or some TLC?"

"I picked Jamaica because of your expertise… I wouldn't trust anyone to put me back together again."

Tamara is flattered. She leans in and kisses Rude Buay on the cheek.

"Don't worry. I'll get you out of here in record time."

She assures Rude Buay.

Tamara checks the chart and begins attaching I-vies to the agent's body. As Rude Buay falls asleep, she administers to his many wounds.

At the Emergency Room, a patient is wheeled in suffering from gunshot wounds. Dr. Tamara Ross gets the call. She concludes the dressing of Rude Buay's wounds and heads to the E.R.

FLASHBACK:

At the Wood House, Rude Buay finally wakes up. He rolls over and realizes that he's been trapped beneath the rubble. He immediately embarks on setting himself free. It is a tedious task as multiple wood timbers press their weight against his body. He twists and turns continuously.

Finally, Rude Buay manages to force his way out of the rubble. He sees a lighted area and crawls to it. He hears a neighing sound and reflects on his first encounter with the horseback at The Lodge. To Rude Buay's surprise, the horse is also trying to remove objects with its mouth to access the interior of the collapsed building where he is trapped. It finally gains access. Rude Buay, in pain, climbs upon its back and rides across the street. Two Chinese Policemen guarding the structure notice him drenched in blood and rush to his aid.

Later, upon Rude Buay's request, they put him on a private jet bound for Jamaica.

BACK TO PRESENT:

Dr. Ross re-opens the door to Rude Buay's room. She notices he is still fast asleep. The doctor smiles, closes the door, and departs.

9

Later, agent Rude Buay sits up in bed at MO Bay Hospital, gleaning through the Jamaican Gleaner newspaper. The extended headlines read Jamaican Police Officer Glen Patrick Bascombe and Teen Daughter Commit Meth-Related Suicides In Port Antonio. Rude Buay gives the page heading multiple second looks. He knows Glen. Not only are they related cousins, but they also went to High School together. As he reads the front page news horrified, Rude Buay can't help reflecting on the death of his brother Clifford over a decade ago in a drug-related incident outside their tenement yard in Jamaica. He can still see his mother holding his blood-drenched brother in her arms before the Jamaican police conducting their investigation and him standing next to her along with his godmother, Maude Davis. Rude Buay tosses the newspaper aside and focuses on the I-vies still attached to his body as he tries to roll onto his side but feels trapped. Suddenly, the screen opens, and Dr. Tamara Ross enters. Looking at Rude Buay, she says,

"How was your rest?"

"I guess my thoughts were so centered on getting out of here, and I don't recall resting except that it was a mixture of dreams and nightmares."
Says Rude Buay.
"You've got to follow the doctor's orders. Rest is necessary if you want a speedy recovery, my dear."
Tamara encourages.
She continues,
"So, what was the dream?"
"I had a dream about you but then woke up and began reading the front page of the Jamaican Gleaner. There, unfortunately, I learned about my cousin and his daughter's drug-related suicide."
"Which copy was that?"
Asks Tamara.
Tamara picks up the paper and stares at the headlines.
"No wonder you missed his funeral. I had no idea you all were related."
"Good guy, bad situation."
"Yep. I am glad that you survived."
She comments as she puts down the newspaper. As she cleans and dresses Rude Buay's wounds, she probes,
"The dream? … and about me?"
Asks Tamara,
"I'll save that when I can stand on my own two feet."
Says Rude Buay,
"Why do men always want to make women wait?
Asks Tamara,
"Why? Because … you all do the same thing to us."

Says Rude Buay.

"I am not sure that is medically correct."

Responds Dr. Ross.

"I want to let you know that as your physician, my duty is two-fold. I still don't trust any nurse taking care of you."

Adds Tamara Ross.

Rude Buay admires Tamara as she unfolds her thoughts.

"I don't blame you, after that previous dilemma with the nurse and Axel James several months ago at the Port Antonio hospital; one never knows who is connected."

Tamara reattaches Rude Buay's life support and reaches inside her purse. She removes her cell phone and shows Rude Buay pictures of Jamaican Policemen guarding the corridor and the checkpoint at the hospital's entrance.

She then retrieves a semi-automatic gun from her more oversized purse and hands it to Rude Buay.

He checks the gun and sees that it has a silencer attached and is fully loaded. He carefully puts it underneath his pillow.

Dr. Ross answers her cellular pager. She has to go. She blows Rude Buay a kiss and departs.

10

Tamara strolls through the hospital's parking lot. She gets inside her car and drives to the hospital's security checkpoint. There, she is stopped, although still attired with the stethoscope around her neck and scrubs, she is detained. Two Jamaican Police Officers also search her car thoroughly. She is given the green light. Tamara views the situation as just a routine check and continues unaffected by their oversight.

Several miles up the road, she notices something through her rearview mirror and senses being followed. This vehicle has been tailing her BMW for more than a mile. She speeds up, and her perpetrator does, and vice versa. She accesses her car phone and immediately dials 911. A rookie officer picks up the call at Montego Bay Police Station.

Tamara reports the facts of the matter to the officer, who asks:

"What is your location, Miss Ross?" "Heading west on Overlook Way," She responds.

"What is the make and model of the vehicle trailing you?"

Asks the police officer, who is still wet behind his ears. "It's a black SUV. No front license tags." Responds Dr. Ross. "What does the driver look like?"
Asks the officer.
"It looks like two men wearing dark sunglasses and dark suits." Dr. Ross responds. "Where are you now?" The officer asks.
"At the peak of Hilltop Road, I pulled off from the regular route to my house, and they are still in pursuit. You need to send in a response team right away!"
Explains Dr. Ross.
"Miss Ross …"
Responds the Police Officer…
Dr. Ross interrupts,
"Why… all of these questions? Don't you understand that I am being followed for several miles by a pursuer who will not let up?"
A female Officer interrupts and intercepts the conversation.
"Miss Ross, Don't you panic. Drive normally. We are on our way. That is a lonely stretch of road. However, a shopping center is two miles up the road, so you may want to pull into that busy mall. We will be there soon." Dr. Ross speeds up and sees the colossal shopping mall beckoning in the distance. Before she could exit the mall, the trailing SUV sped up, passed, and appeared before her BMW.
Dr. Ross stops her car and attempts to make a U-Turn. Before she could position her car for that getaway turn,

the two armed men jumped out and surrounded her vehicle. The doctor makes sure her doors are locked. One of the men breaks the driver's window using a crowbar. The Doctor yells for help. Her cries are not heard by anyone except the two men as she is still a great distance away from that mall.

The two men drag her out of the car. They tape up her mouth. They bind her with ropes, throw her in the back of their SUV, and re-board their vehicle. The speeding SUV departs from the scene, continuing on its recent path.

11

A Jamaican Police Officer sneaks into Rude Buay's room. The officer looks around the room. Rude Buay's eyes are closed. The officer attempts to remove the life support attached to the agent's wrist. Rude Buay opens his eyes and senses the officer's motive. Realizing that the agent is helpless and unable to defend himself, the officer removes the life support attached to the monitor and reaches for the one attached to the agent's arm.

In the interim, Rude Buay reaches underneath his pillow and retrieves his gun. Before the officer could bring out and engage his pistol, Rude Buay shoots him in the face with the silencer-attached weapon. Time elapses as Rude Buay tries to make his way out of bed. The other officer, realizing his partner has not returned, barges inside Rude Buay's hospital room. Rude Buay hears his footsteps and sees him coming. Rude Buay, though in pain, arms himself and slumps back in the bed. He fires off a round that hits the police officer in his head. The officer topples over to the ground a dead man. Now, two officers are lying bloodied and dead on the floor of his hospital room.

Rude Buay makes another effort to get out of there. He is not even focusing on the detached life support which hangs from the machine. Even so, it seems like he is trapped inside that room.

MEANWHILE, A NURSE filing away papers in her office, notices a stack of fresh sheets undelivered to room # 26, the same room in which Rude Buay resides. So, she checks the housekeeping records.

Additionally, she checks the records more in-depth and realizes Dr. Tamara Ross has not reported for work in some time.

"If she did show up, those bedsheets would not sit in that room."

Says the nurse as she picks up the bedsheets and heads swiftly to room # 26.

Upon entering the room, she notices a silhouette sitting on the agent's bed with a pointed gun in his hand. Not only is the gun pointed at her, but she also notices the two dead bodies on the floor. The site of the blood-drenched uniformed police officers makes her quiver. Retracting the curtain, she notices agent Rude Buay sitting up in bed with his gun pointed at her. She screams out:

"Help!"

She drops the bedsheets on the ground and darts out of the hospital ward and back to her office. She goes to her desk and calls the hospital security. There is a male patient in another bed in that hospital ward, his leg propped up in a cast. He hears the cry for help and tries moving off the bed to assist in the situation.

In the meantime, Rude Buay looks out the window and back inside the room. The distance between his room and the ground level descends many stories. In a state of panic, he grabs the blood-stained bedsheets off the floor, picks up his gun, and ties it around his neck using the pillowcase.

He gets out onto the ledge of the window. Finally, he ties those sheets together like a rope and attaches one end to the window's bar. He is holding on to the strung-together sheets as he makes his descent.

Inside the hospital, security guards are alerted. They emerge, racing to his room, followed by the same nurse. The patient with the leg in a cast aches as he hurts his leg while getting up to assist. By this time, the security guards arrive at Rude Buay's room and look through that opened window; Rude Buay has already made it to the hospital's ground level. They race out in pursuit.

Rude Buay sprints to the morgue area. He sees a hearse parked next to the dead house. He tries the driver's door. It's open. The agent looks inside for the ignition keys. There are none. His bullet wound in the leg begins to bleed severely. He runs inside the morgue. There is nothing to stop the bleeding. A dead man lies on a gurney with a sheet wrapped around him. Rude Buay removes the sheet. The dead man is dressed in black trousers, a white shirt, and a bow tie. He rips the sheet and uses a portion of it to wrap around his wound. He then removes his hospital attire, throws it on the floor, and rids the dead man of his clothing. He puts them on. He finally discovers a pack of bandages while getting dressed. He grabs it and returns to the hearse. Rude Buay pulls the vehicle's hood lever. The hood pops open. He hot-wires the car and makes his getaway through the back streets of the hospital, merging with the flow of the primary street traffic.

Meanwhile, the security guards at the hospital return to their posts unaccomplished in their pursuit of Rude Buay.

12

Rude Buay pulls up across the street from a church. He parks the hearse and walks to the hotel up the block. He gets a hotel room. Once inside, he begins to attend to his wounds using the bandage. His phone rings. It's Michael Ortiz, his boss in Miami.

"Rude Buay, how is the recuperation process?"

"My wounds are being attended to as we speak."

Says Rude Buay.

"Can you speak now?"

"Yes. I am by myself."

"Really?"

"Go ahead!"

"How soon can we expect you back in Miami?"

"Are you asking me to return to Miami or suggesting I return while I am still…?"

Rude Buay notices that his wound is bleeding more than before.

"Medical conditions here are superb. Plus, we have drug-related issues here in the U.S., too, you know."

Says Ortiz.

"Boss, I still have dual citizenship and always will. The drug crisis here has expanded tremendously.

Methamphetamine is on the rise. I recently lost my cousin and his daughter. The Dragons are not letting up. We are in a situation where this country needs a lot of help to fight this war on drugs. What is the availability of agent Hudson?" "Rude Buay, I am afraid that you've gotten in way too deep. You were only on loan from the U.S. remember? And now you are asking to have agent Hudson join you again? Since you took on this Caribbean vacation, we have lost three agents. Two of them you shot and killed yourself and one who has recently deflected."

"Boss, if you ask Agent Hudson if she would rather be working in the Caribbean than Miami, I can bet she would say the Caribbean any day. Plus, it's ludicrous, I must say, to blame me for others' misdeeds. They were traitors…"

"Apparently you've brainwashed her enough that she will cover for you as she has always done, Rude Buay."

"If the war on drugs is ever going to be won, at our level, I would say we need the best fighters, those who would not whimper but fight to the … end. You have read it in the news: The cartels are now getting their guns from the Fast & Furious program. What's next?" States Rude Buay.

"I will ask her tomorrow and get back to you. But I am not going to twist her arm."

Rude Buay hangs up the phone, expecting Agent Hudson to buy into his concept.

He continues to freshen up and administer to his wounds. That same evening, a rental car company dropped off a car for the agent. He picks up a pair of shoes at a nearby store and drives through the city hoping there's a chance he would run into Dr. Tamara Ross. His search for her is in vain. So, the agent returns to his hotel room unaccomplished. Rude Buay calls Chelo, his counterpart, to see if he could be of any assistance in tracking down Tamara's whereabouts using his intel with his sophisticated spy gadgets.

13

Chelo, who is in his mid-30s and of descent, is fiddling with his multiple spy gadgets. He takes a break and answers the phone.

"Rude Buay! Man, it's sure good to hear from you. Sorry about that satellite failure in Shanghai. Anyway, I heard you survived according to Ortiz. How can I help you?"

"The Dragon Drug Cartel has possibly kidnapped Dr. Ross. She has been missing from the hospital for several days now. I need some help to track her whereabouts."

Says Rude Buay.

"You know how tough it is transmitting signals out of Jamaica. Too many … interceptions! Plus, since Miles Tate shared the 411 regarding our operation with the Dragons. They could clue in on our whereabouts easily. Try Walter Banks he might be able to assist better in the present circumstances."

Rude Buay hangs up that call and dials.

WALTER BANKS, the veteran agent, is reading about a Mexican drug account in the Jamaican Gleaner.

Banks is an African American man in his fifties with salt-and-pepper hair.

"Good to hear from you, Rude Buay. I thought the doctor was looking after you. At least that's what Mildred conveyed to us before our planned meeting with the Commissioner to honor you with a eulogy."

"Mildred always seems to know where I am. Doesn't she?"

States Rude Buay,

"The Commissioner and I had already discussed the tragedy and felt there was no way you would survive the collapse of the Wood House. Now that you are unbreakable like that "Six Million Dollar Man," I know it won't be long before we team up again." I'll see what I can come up with through my existing local connections. As you may have already learned our main satellite source has become problematic."

Says Banks.

"Let's do it sooner than later."

Says Rude Buay.

"Nothing from Chelo, huh?"

Asks Banks.

"It has become very problematic for him since they took out our satellites in Bogotá."

Says Rude Buay.

"Okay, I'll see what I can find."

Says Banks.

"I will be counting on you!"

States Rude Buay.

14

Later, Rude Buay is alerted by an email on his laptop. He checks it. The email is from Tamara. He is somewhat relieved. Until he starts reading it, It states:

Dear Rude Buay,

I hope you have stopped pursuing the Dragon Drug Cartel. It's a waste of your time. Any day now I could be hanged and fed to vultures. I miss you, Rude Buay. Thanks for the times we've shared. All the best with your recovery.

XOXO Tamara.

Sandals, MO Bay.

Rude Buay is confused. This is not like Tamara. He ponders: "Is that all she wrote? Did fear tactics from the kidnappers pressure her; forcing her into writing this twisted style of email?"
These questions and other similar ones riddle his mind. At the same time, he applies a fresh bandage to his wounds and gets dressed. He takes up the gun which Tamara left him at the hospital. He looks it over. He is satisfied; the gun is still loaded, minus the two

used bullets. He straps the gun underneath his pullover jacket. Sandals? He retrieves another weapon that belonged to one of the fallen officers at the hospital and straps it around his leg underneath his trousers.

Rude Buay's phone rings. Walter Banks is on the line. Banks alerts Rude Buay that Tamara was reportedly seen at Sandals in Montego Bay. With that confirmation of her location, he ensures his weapons are intact. He heads out speedily and asks Banks to cover him as backup.

Banks agrees.

RUDE BUAY PULLS UP outside Sandals. This famous Hotel and restaurant are buzzing with activity. Parking attendants valet cars in rapid succession. Patrons mingle all over the compound. He moseys inside the resort with caution. As soon as he enters the lobby an armed man approaches him and sticks a gun in the back. Still, he manages to bring out the gun underneath his pullover in confrontation. The man proceeds up through the hotel's stairway. Rude Buay follows, looking for another excellent aim to blast the perpetrator.

Before he could make his way up the second set of stairs, a door from that floor level opened; he tried to reach for the other gun under his trousers. Another man grabs him from behind and wrestles the gun away from him. The man manages to floor Rude Buay. Instantly the other perpetrator runs back down the stairs. Together, they drag him back outside through the exit door. They have a hard time restraining the agent who is valiantly putting up a fight. One of the men lets up and reaches inside his jacket pocket and pulls out a syringe. He sticks a needle in his arm and injects fluid into that arm.

Unknown to Rude Buay, the two men were also involved in authorizing the email sent by Tamara earlier.

They escort Rude Buay to the parking lot. Before getting to their vehicle, he is partially knocked out. They drag him, toss him inside the trunk of their car, and drive off. Rude Buay struggles to stay in a conscious state of mind. But all he can see is a flashback to almost a year ago when Axel James and Ian Baynes, two members of the Dragon Drug Cartel, tied him up and put him inside the trunk of their car and then drove him through the hills of Jamaica for the kill. Finally, the drug sets in, and the agent snaps into a semi-unconscious state.

15

During the night, Rude Buay sleeps like a baby in the private Jet aircraft manned by the Dragon Drug Cartel. The following morning, he wakes up in Nogales, Mexico. The airplane in which he was transported touched down and taxied to a private hangar. They transport Rude Buay to a guest house strapped inside a customized van. This wooded building is located deep inside the rugged hills of Nogales, Mexico, and overlooks the city.

Later, one of Alberto Gomez's guards drags Rude Buay from the guest room and into the makeshift meeting room. A big table in the middle of the room is surrounded by six chairs. The aura inside that room is so tense that you can cut it with a knife. Seated at the head of the table is Drug Czar Alberto Gomez. On his right, in the anticlockwise direction, is his wife, Denise Gomez. Next to Denise is seated Shelly Hall. Marcus Ranks sits to her right. Next to Marcus and facing Alberto Gomez is Miles Tate! Sitting next to Tate is Grace McCloud. Seated next to Grace is Sammy Chin.

The guard escorts Rude Buay to that vacant seat at the table next to Alberto Gomez. He plops the agent down on the chair.

The door, in two halves, swings open in unison. Two Hispanic men in male nurse attire enter, closing the door effortlessly behind them. One guard places a tray on the table before Rude Buay and grinds his enormous bicuspid teeth. The other places a pair of pliers and a washcloth next to the tray and grunts doh, ray, me, fah, soh, la, tee, doh. As if to say this is my song, soon we are going to kill you if …, Alberto Gomez presides:

"Welcome Agent Rude Buay!"

Rude Buay is still groggy but can still hear the echo of the last doh!

Alberto Gomez slaps Rude Buay in his face.

Rude Buay feels it. He evolves into an alert stance.

"Are you with us, Rude Buay?"

asks Alberto Gomez.

Rude Buay stares at him as his intellect drifts in and out like a rolling tide.

"You must remain alert during this meeting as this could determine if you should live or die."

Rude Buay nods in unconscious agreement.

"While we have your undivided attention, Rude Buay, I might as well cut straight to the chase. I must let you know that you are a fortunate man who is still alive. We could have had you killed, but instead, we brought you to Nogales to allow you to team up with the fastest-growing cartel ever orchestrated. You are hardworking, which means you get the job done. It would benefit you and us both if you would join our extension program with the organization. You would benefit from an unmatched salary. Plus, you'll receive bonuses from our annual profits. In the first year, a whopping 5% will go to you, the second year 10%, the third year 15%, and the fourth year 20%. I know how much you make as a U.S. D.E.A. I would say it's peanuts compared to what you can earn just on salary alone in the narcotics trade.

Rude Buay hears Alberto Gomez but isn't assimilating nor digesting the team player mindset strategy or the Czars' monotonous trade philosophy.

"You will be working with the border patrols, acting as if you are completely on their side. We need an inside man on our side. You will let our dealers into the U.S. unscathed. If there is a sticky situation involving our men, you will work it out in our favor. Of course, with you being the head honcho, you will step in and put out the fire. Our men are well trained. They know the border lingo, and even dealing with the meter maids on the other side, they are adept. With you as the "top dog," we will be a force to be reckoned with.

It's no incident that the lead Border Patrol Officer position is open. With your credentials, you shouldn't have a problem nailing that prestigious job. The U.S. government would not turn you down; you only need to apply. Look at what you've done for them. Your résumé speaks for itself, agent." Rude Buay is somewhat flattered. "You will fit in so well that no one would even know you are working for us. After five years, you can feel free to walk away, no strings attached!" There is silence. All eyes are now focused on Rude Buay anticipating his acceptance of the deal. Instead, he composes himself but remains silent.

Alberto Gomez quickly states:

"If you refuse the job, we'll have no choice but to execute you by hanging based on charges of treason, along with all the trouble you have caused us in the past. So, while the noose waits to dangle for your neck at the gallows, those two gentlemen standing over you have been instructed to extract one of your fingernails daily, leaving your pinky fingers for the last days leading up to your hanging."

Once again, all eyes are focused on Rude Buay, expecting him to give in. Finally, he composes himself.

"The things I've been through give me fortitude. I'm not easily broken. Not only have I seen too much, but I've also been through too much. Selling out is not in my character. You may hang my body on that gallows, but you will never hang my character!"

States Rude Buay.

"I'll give you ten hours to think it over and make an intelligent decision. The initial nail removal process could begin at sunrise tomorrow. First, they would start with your right thumb and then your trigger-holding finger the next morning."

The meeting adjourns. Not before the Dragon Drug Cartel performs its freebasing get-high ritual.

16

It's almost sunrise the following morning and almost ten hours since the Dragon Drug Cartel wrapped their meeting with Agent Rude Buay. The agent still doesn't accept the offer to team up with the Dragons. So, to put seasoned salt in Rude Buay's wounds, the Dragons put Dr. Tamara Ross on a Jet bound from Jamaica to Nogales, Mexico. The objective: to arrange for her hanging before Rude Buay's trip to the gallows.
Dr. Ross has no idea what their plot is about. The flight crew speaks using codes, none of which are familiar to her.

BACK IN JAMAICA, Banks shows up at Sandals as backup for agent Rude Buay. The traffic heading to Sandals was full of gridlock and bottlenecking. Somewhat slowed, he arrived there late. Now, he is surprised that he didn't get a progress report from Rude Buay.
Upon arrival on the hotel compound, Banks learns from his inside source at Sandals that Dr. Ross has been moved to a facility in Nogales, Mexico. His source, an elderly woman, had heard them speaking in Spanish and listened to their planned destination for Dr. Ross. Also, agent Rude Buay was seen accompanying two men to their car hours before. Upon returning home,

Walter Banks gets a phone call from Chelo informing him that the Dragons had moved operations from Colombia and set up base in Nogales, Mexico, to better facilitate their Meth trade. Chelo and Walter Banks later pack some spy gadgets in boxes and suitcases. They head out separately to the Arizona, Mexican border town of Nogales, and later to Nogales, Mexico.

IMMEDIATELY AFTER SUNSET, the following day, the door to agent Rude Buay's makeshift prison cell opens. The room is exactly 10 feet by 5 feet. Inside, there is a cot on one side against the wall. On the other side is a small wooden table. Next to the table is a small trash can. The dangling light bulb on a hanging electrical cord in the roof is illuminated. The two men, seen before dressing in a nurse's uniform, barge inside. Rude Buay is lying on the cot with both hands and feet tied with nylon ropes.

One of the men is carrying a tray and a large pair of pliers. The other man holds a small damp towel and a box of latex gloves. He is also wearing an apron. He passes a pair of transparent latex gloves to his partner, who puts them on methodically as if he's a surgeon preparing to perform a particular surgical operation.

Moments later, the apron-wearing man grabs Agent Rude Buay's hands. Together, they tie down Rude Buay's right hand on the table, securing the ropes around the wooden table's legs.

Rude Buay knows what's about to go down any minute; he flinches not only in his mind but also in his body. The agent's right thumb is the main focus of the pair of pliers.

One attendant presses down on Rude Buay's right hand using both of his hands, while the other brutally removes the agent's right thumbnail using the pair of pliers. Rude Buay yells out as the pain surges through his entire body.

The thumbnail, with some flesh attached to it, gets deposited in the trash can. The attendant then uses the damp rag to wipe the blood from the table including the vast amount flowing from the agent's bleeding right thumb.

From inside his apron pocket, the attendant grabs a bandage and wraps it around the nail-less thumb, tying it around the agent's other four fingers on that hand and tying it around the wrist.

Rude Buay is then escorted to the cot in his room. The two men finish cleaning up the blood residue and depart.

The following evening at sunset, they return and extract the thumb on his left hand. Each day for ten days, these men remove one of Rude Buay's fingernails, leaving those on his two pinky fingers for last, as ordered by Alberto Gomez.

17

With the ten-day fingernail removal ordeal completed, Rude Buay remains all drenched with blood, as blood from his ten fingers drains into a cloth bag wrapped around both of his hands like a muzzle. The bag is tied at the wrists. The two men dressed in bloodied nurse uniforms strap Rude Buay onto a truck. Before they send Rude Buay to the gallows they ask the agent what he would like before he dies.

"I would like to see Dr. Tamara Ross again."

Says Rude Buay.

Attempting to get the agent to buy into the team concept of the Dragons for one last time and avoid being hanged, Alberto Gomez requests a laptop computer brought to the truck with video clips of Tamara. The two male attendants bring out the laptop and show Rude Buay video clips of Tamara being beaten and spat upon by several Mexican maids.

The videos are very horrifying and are more than what the agent wanted as a dying wish. He tugs at the ropes to escape but is restrained by the two men.

In the interim, the driver arrives and checks the truck and the ropes that bind Rude Buay to ensure the agent is securely tied up.

The truck departs during the wee hours as the clouds give way to the sunrise in Nogales hills. Alberto Gomez, Denise Gomez, Miles Tate, Shelly Hall, Marcus Ranks, Grace McCloud, Sammy Chin, and the two male attendants celebrate during an intense freebasing event in the upper room of the Casa. At this meeting, Alberto Gomez also introduces newcomer Victor Crip a Mexican native in his mid-30s, to head up operations in Nogales - the position which Rude Buay had recently turned down. As part of Victor's initiation, the newbie pulls out a glass pipe, similar to a crack pipe. He pours in about 0.2 grams of methamphetamine. Holding the pipe on his lips, he starts to gently heat the bottom part of the pipe to allow the drug to vaporize. He slowly inhales. He passes the pipe along with the crystal meth folded in an aluminum foil. The others partake in the chasing of the white dragon, a term used amongst drug dealers for meth smoking. They all are now as high as kites. They laugh and cut up, detailing what Rude Buay will say and do as the noose tightens around his neck. Rude Buay couldn't help but hear and notice their taunting from the window across the way as he was driven to his hanging by the Mexican truck driver. In a celebratory and festive mood, the drug lords synchronized their watches, as the hanging was set for 9:00 AM sharp.

CHELO HAD ARRIVED IN NOGALES, MEXICO, on the afternoon of the previous day before the scheduled hanging and set up his spy operations in that city. After working tirelessly rigging several antennas from his wooden hut, he was able to pinpoint the location where the Dragons detained agent Rude Buay. On foot, he hustled to the area. Everyone was still asleep at the Casa.

Later, the truck took off and went through the rolling hills and dirt roads of Nogales, Mexico. The journey continued as multitudes of vultures swarmed overhead, sweeping down momentarily to feed on the remains of human bodies littered like a mass execution through the hills. Rude Buay had never been to war in this country but imagined that at least they buried the bodies. The milieu was horrific! The hissing musical sound of maggots indicated that no graves were prepared for those who perished, not even trenches. The stench is overbearing. The truck finally stops on top of the hill close to the gallows. From that vantage point, a swinging noose awaited the agent. Two men dressed in coveralls await his arrival: One to hang him and the other standing next to the grave to bury him in that seven-footer open shallow trench. The driver steps out, focused on the task at hand.

Chelo takes a portion of the page from the book by Walter Banks, who had rescued him when he was driven to the gallows in Colombia over a year ago. Chelo promptly unties himself from underneath the truck's chassis and swiftly kicks the driver in his lower stomach region. The driver falls over, gasping for air. As a result of the blow, the driver's rifle falls and is lying on the ground. Chelo kicks the rifle in Rude Buay's direction. Rude Buay's hands are still muzzled in that bloodied cloth sack. Using his teeth, the agent speedily unties the sack, crawls on his stomach, and elbows towards the fallen rifle. The barefooted Chelo kicks the driver one more time. This time, he kicks him hard in his stomach. The driver once again crouches and gasps continuously for air.

Forgetting how painful it could be to lose all ten fingernails in less than two weeks, Rude Buay picks up the rifle and forces his bloodied, swollen trigger finger inside the trigger slot. It bleeds as he pulls the switch. He blasts the driver.

The hanger and the undertaker hear the sound of that single gunshot and depart speedily from around the hanging site. The undertaker drops his shovel in the process. It falls into the trench. They race to the truck that transported Rude Buay to the set. Rude Buay shoots again and kills both men while Chelo positions himself as a decoy. Chelo and Rude Buay hurry on their feet.

Moments later, after their departure, the truck in which Rude Buay was transported exploded at exactly 9:05 AM into a ball of fire.
Now free, Chelo and Rude Buay continue on foot for many hours through the rugged hillsides of Nogales.

CHELO, EARLIER before the truck was scheduled to leave for the gallows, ever alert, while under the truck's chassis and waiting for it to depart from the Casa, was fortunate to eavesdrop on the conversations of the two male attendants. They had mentioned Tamara's whereabouts, about two miles from the Casa. Also, she was next on the list to be hanged, and she was supposed to be hanged before Rude Buay, but Alberto Gomez had wanted to welcome Victor Crip with the hanging of Rude Buay on the following day instead. They even articulated her beauty and implied doing a twosome or a watch while I do it with her if time permits. They even joked about the latter and suggested tossing a coin upon arrival for supremacy. Immediately after their conversation, Chelo was able to pick up the house where Tamara resided on his pen radar. Now, he and Rude Buay move swiftly in that direction through Southern Nogales.
The terrain is rough, and it is difficult to get through the hills, more so for Rude Buay, who has not been exposed to that mode of getting around since his days in elementary school when he sometimes went to school barefooted. Chelo, though barefoot, can deal

with the blisters and bruises on his feet. At this point, rude Buay, still in those shoes he wore to locate Tamara back at Sandals in Jamaica, has almost worn them out. Their soles give way, leaving him with not only multiple calluses but severe bruises and blisters as well. The thorns from the failed cactus add their punch to both men's feet.

While traveling through the hills, they discover many chopped, dismembered bodies as vultures continue to feed, and the unpleasant odor surfaces. The stench remains unbearable, coming from the corpses made up of men and women and children and celebrated by maggots. Even so, they must hurry as time elapses and the high stakes increase. Rude Buay falls between some waist-high shrubbery but gets up and continues tirelessly.

18

Nearing the house, a small dog begins barking as Rude Buay and Chelo close in on the domicile.

A guard keeping watch is alerted and trains his weapon on Rude Buay and Chelo for several minutes, accompanied by dogs. After an extensive cat-and-mouse ordeal, the guard's gun runs out of bullets. Now, the switch: Rude Buay, on a foot race, is in pursuit of the guard. The dogs cool it by wagging their tails. Using his rifle, he cuts down the guard, whose dodging skills and agility on foot speed run out. He enters the house in take-down style with Chelo in tow. Inside, he discovers Dr. Tamara Ross. She is tied up, hands and feet, kneeling at the bedside. Chelo finds a kitchen knife and quickly cuts the ropes. Together, the trio journeys into the city and takes refuge in a hotel after sundown. The following morning, at sunrise, Chelo says goodbye to Rude Buay and Tamara.

TAMARA PROCEEDS TO BANDAGE Rude Buay's ten nail-less fingers and attends to his gunshot wound suffered in Shanghai. The regular program on the TV is interrupted as the reporter comes on with breaking news:

"Almost two dozen kids under the ages of 12 and involved in the trade of Methamphetamine were involved in yet another standoff with border patrols in Nogales, Arizona earlier today. As a result, many officers were left dead, and more than half of those kids were captured and their AK47s confiscated. However, the other kids fled to safety through the Mexican Nogales hillsides. Mexican police are now combing through the desert, looking for these bandits. More news to come on this evolving story."
Rude Buay asks,
"What's up with these kids?" They have no epiphany as to what they are into." "Not only that,"
Says Dr. Ross.
"What's your take on Meth?"
Asks Rude Buay.
Dr. Tamara Ross voices her concern:
"You lost your cousin and his daughter."
"Don't remind me,"
Says Rude Buay.
She continues,
"According to the National Institute on Drug and Abuse, National Institutes of Health in regard to how Meth affects the Brain and the Body: No matter how methamphetamine is used, it eventually ends up that it can affect lots of brain structures but the ones it affects the most are the ones that contain a chemical called dopamine. The reason for this is that the shape, size, and chemical structure of methamphetamine and

dopamine are similar. Before I tell you more about dopamine and methamphetamine, I'd better tell you how nerve cells work.

Rude Buay is all ears.

The human brain is made up of billions of nerve cells (or neurons). Neurons come in all shapes and sizes, but most have three important parts: a cell body that contains the nucleus and directs the neuron's activities; dendrites, short fibers that receive messages from other neurons and relay them to the cell body; and an axon, a long single fiber that carries messages from the cell body to dendrites of other neurons.

Axons of one neuron and the dendrites of a neighboring neuron are located very close to each other, but they don't touch. Therefore, to communicate with each other they use chemical messengers known as neurotransmitters. When one neuron wants to send a message to another neuron it releases a neurotransmitter from its axon into the small space that separates the two neurons. This space is called a synapse. The neurotransmitter crosses the synapse and attaches to specific places on the dendrites of the neighboring neuron called receptors. Once the neurotransmitter has relayed its message, it is either destroyed or taken back up into the first neuron where it is recycled for use again."

Rude Buay senses that Dr. Ross is on a roll and chooses not to interrupt the flow of such vital information but nods to assure her that he's still listening. "There are many different neurotransmitters, but the one that is most affected by methamphetamine is dopamine. Dopamine is sometimes called the pleasure neurotransmitter because it helps you feel good from things like playing soccer, eating a big piece of chocolate cake, or riding a roller coaster. When something pleasurable happens, certain axons release lots of dopamine. The dopamine attaches to receptors on the dendrites of neighboring neurons and passes on the pleasure message.

This process is stopped when dopamine is released from the receptors and pumped back into the neuron that released it where it is stored for later use. Usually, neurons recycle dopamine. But methamphetamine can fool neurons into taking it up just like they would dopamine. Once inside a neuron, methamphetamine causes that neuron to release lots of dopamine. All this dopamine causes the person to feel an extra sense of pleasure that can last all day. But eventually, these pleasurable effects stop. They are followed by unpleasant feelings called a "crash" that often lead a person to use more of the drug. If a person continues to use methamphetamine, they will have a difficult time feeling pleasure from anything. Imagine no longer enjoying your favorite food or an afternoon with your friends!

Methamphetamine has lots of other effects: Because it is similar to dopamine, methamphetamine can change the function of any neuron that contains dopamine. And if this weren't enough, methamphetamine can also affect neurons that contain two other neurotransmitters called serotonin and norepinephrine. All of this means that methamphetamine can change how lots of things in the brain and the bodywork.

Even small amounts of methamphetamine can cause a person to be more awake and active, lose their appetite, and become irritable and aggressive. Methamphetamine also causes a person's blood pressure to increase and their heart to beat faster."

(She pauses for breath and then continues) Long-Term Effects of Meth:

Scientists are using brain imaging techniques, like positron emission tomography (called PET for short), to study the brains of human methamphetamine users. They have discovered that even three years after long-time methamphetamine users had quit using the drug, their dopamine neurons were still damaged. Scientists don't know yet whether this damage is permanent, but this research shows that changes in the brain from methamphetamine use can last a long time. Research with animals has shown that the drug methamphetamine can also damage neurons that contain serotonin. This damage also continues long after the drug use is stopped.

These changes in dopamine and serotonin neurons may explain some of the effects of methamphetamine. If a person uses methamphetamine for a long time, they may become paranoid. They may also hear and see things that aren't there. These are called hallucinations. Because methamphetamine causes big increases in blood pressure, someone using it for a long time may also have permanent damage to blood vessels in the brain. This can lead to strokes caused by bleeding in the brain.

Tamara adds:
Researchers are only beginning to understand how methamphetamine acts in the brain and body. When they learn more about how methamphetamine causes its effects, they may be able to develop treatments that prevent or reverse the damage this drug can cause."
"Really?"
Asks Rude Buay as he picks up his car keys and automatic rifle.
"That's why Glenda, at an unconscious level and state of mind, walked onto the Freeway and committed suicide by having that eighteen-wheeler run her over, and Glen later blew out his brains," Rude Buay continued.
"She must have been so brain-dead, her body had to follow its leader,"
Informs Tamara Ross.

"Thanks for the invaluable research. Maybe you'll make the next breakthrough…, " says Rude Buay.
He kisses Tamara on her lips as he walks towards the door.
"Go get them! They can't stop you! You're UNSTOPPABLE, you're
UNTOUCHABLE but most of all … Randy, you're SHATTERPROOF! And much more!"
Tamara challenges Rude Buay.
He slips two pairs of ventilated gloves provided by Tamara over the fresh bandage on the five fingers of both hands. Rude Buay makes his exit from the hotel room door in terminator style. "I'll get you out of here soon!"

19

The Methamphetamine trade continues to expand rapidly, not only in Mexico and Arizona but has also diversified to Jamaica, Asia, Los Angeles, and New York, as well as the U.S./Canadian border. Several dominant cartels, including the Dragons and the Sinaloa Cartel, compete viciously for drug territory, resulting in many killings, particularly in Mexico.

Many traders in Mexico distribute the drug on multiple levels of trade. Chelo, one day, while collecting video feed through his high-tech satellite equipment, discovered what Rude Buay later described as one of the most successful and amazing ways, though on a small scale, to smuggle drugs across the border.

The Dragons smuggled narcotics through these tunnels from Mexico to Arizona every day, including Saturdays, Sundays, and Holidays.

Methamphetamine smugglers in the border town of Nogales, Mexico, continue to bring drugs into the U.S. through Nogales, Arizona, as some would say, for the cost of a quarter.

They habitually use parking meters on International Street, which hugs the border fence in Nogales: These meters cost 25 cents. So, the smugglers in Mexico would tunnel under the fence and wind up under the metered parking spaces. There, they would carefully cut neat rectangle-type manholes out of the pavement. Their associates in Nogales would park false-bottomed vehicles in the spaces above the holes, feed the meters, and then wait while the underground smugglers stuffed their cars full of Meth and other narcotics from below. This was done multiple times per day. As soon as this exchange was finished, the smugglers, utilize vehicle jacks to put the pavement plugs back into the manholes. The cars then drive away loaded with a variety of narcotics, mainly methamphetamine.

Additionally, some smugglers were caught on video using catapults which launched bales of drugs across the border fence. If it was going to get across the border those Mexicans found a way.

Methamphetamine became very popular also in Jamaica even though the effects of Glenda Bascombe's death were still felt and talked about by many during their daily routines whether on the street or in their homes. To many concerned parents, it stuck out like a sore thumb.

IT IS WELL KNOWN in the drug world that the cartels control the trafficking of drugs from South America to the U.S., a business that is worth an estimated $ 13 billion (£9 billion) a year. Their power grew as the U.S. stepped up anti-narcotics operations in the Caribbean and Florida. A U.S. State Department report estimated that as much as 90% of all cocaine and methamphetamine consumed in the US comes via Mexico.

Meanwhile, many are killed both in Mexico and neighboring U.S. border towns like Nogales by the Dragon Drug Cartel, not only because the demands for narcotics increase but also because smugglers fail to carry out their assignments and creditors fail to pay up for their drugs.

The Mexican government issued partial figures on 11 January 2012. These showed that 12,903 people had been killed in violence blamed on organized crime from January to September 2011. Added to the previous overall total, this means that 47,515 people had died in the five years of Mr. Calderon's presidency. Although there is no breakdown, the victims include suspected drug gang members, members of the security forces, and those considered innocent bystanders.

Reported one source, While another source stated:

Violence was first concentrated in Mexico's northern border regions, especially Chihuahua, as well as in Pacific states like Sinaloa, Michoacán, and Guerrero. Ciudad Juarez (just across from El Paso in Texas) was the most violent city. In 2010, some 3,100 people were killed in Juarez, which has a population of more than a million. But since 2010, violence has spread to other regions, including Nuevo Leon and Tamaulipas states. One of the focal points for violence has been Mexico's third-largest city, Monterrey.

The year 2011 also saw new areas hit. For example, VeraCrip on the eastern coast saw a series of mass killings. The Government of Mexico feels the police cannot be trusted. Drug cartels with massive resources at their disposal have repeatedly managed to infiltrate the underpaid police from the grassroots level to the very top. Efforts are underway to rebuild the entire structure of the Mexican police force, but the process is expected to take years.

RUMORS SPREAD QUICKLY in Jamaica amongst Rude Buay's peers that the agent was still alive and stationed in Mexico fighting the war on drugs. Meanwhile, many Jamaicans, as well as meth users, were becoming mentally paralyzed from the use of Methamphetamine. Jamaica was rising rapidly in the meth using stats.

At the same time, Commissioner Richard Baptiste, in his 50s, and Mildred Simms, who had previously teamed up with Rude Buay in Jamaica and China against the Dragons, for a while believed that the agent Rude Buay had turned his back on his people.

Mildred Simms and the Commissioner also accused Rude Buay of forsaking his Jamaican people when they faced similar drug problems. Tivoli Gardens stated it was like a simmering volcano and could erupt again, spewing many more Johnny Too Bads.

Not sure how to handle this dilemma, they even took things a step further and discussed Rude Buay's elimination proceedings with the Governor-General of Jamaica, Bradford Wiley.

In this plot, they would secretly deliver Rude Buay into the hands of the Dragon Drug Cartel, just like the Philistines, in the Bible days, did to Samson.

Even so, Governor-General Wiley, a man of peace and tranquility, saw things differently and suggested to the Commissioner and Mildred Simms that they team up with Rude Buay to fight against the Dragons. His wisdom led him to believe that Rude Buay was about *One Love for Jamaica.*

Was that enough to change their perspective on the Rude Buay's situation? At least they let it rest for a while as they came to grips with convincing themselves that if Rude Buay was involved, it had to be a worthwhile cause for Jamaicans and the whole world.

20

A dark-colored jeep speeds through the dirt road surrounded by trees and shrubbery in the hillsides of Nogales, Mexico. A blanket of dust follows it in tow. Finally, the vehicle stops on top of a hill overlooking Nogales, close to the Mexican/U.S. border. Another jeep is parked on top of that hill.

Out of the newly arrived vehicle, step out Denise Gomez, Shelly Hall, and Grace McCloud. The three women are dangerously armed with rifles. They move towards the other parked jeep.

Inside that parked vehicle is Victor Crip, the newly appointed drug lord to oversee trade between the twin cities of Nogales. Using his binoculars, Crip surveys the border. Noticing the three femme Fatales, Crip discards his binoculars and picks up his semi-automatic. He senses some rivalry. The women continue to pursue Victor Crip with aimed rifles aggressively. He now senses more than ever his life is being threatened. He notices their dragon tattoo signature. He knows them.

"¿Cómo eta? What's up, ladies? We are on the same team." Crip addresses,

No one responds verbally, neither in Spanish nor English. Instead, they maintain their stance with weapons pointed at Crip.

"Mistaken identity? We work for the same boss. Are you locas?" He questions.

"Con man, this is not our first Rodeo. What's up with the Nogales shipment?"

Asks Denise.
"That's right! The Nogales shipment?"
Restates Shelly Hall,
"Muchos problemas señoritas. The Blackman! The Blackman! Let me explain."
Says Victor Crip.
"Explain?"
Asks Grace McCloud.
Denise continues,
"Do you see all the cars parked on meters over on Independence Street? They have been there all day. If those drivers run out of quarters to feed those meters, do you know we could come up against the policia? They will instantly shut down our tunnel meter operation if we fail to get them to accept a bribe."
"That's right! Los Angeles and Canada are still waiting for their supply of Meth. You are pissing off, Miles Tate. Who thinks we are dropping the ball!"
Says Shelly Hall.
Victor Crip looks at his pair of binoculars on the floor of the jeep with its driver's door still ajar. He then looks at the women still maintaining their offensive stance.
"You are causing problems on Independence Street, Victor Crip."
Says Grace McCloud,
"What were you looking at inside that gadget when we showed up? Shades of...? You are not doing your job. Goddammit!"
"Dios made the man, and he made the woman. If you all will let me speak, I can certainly explain." "And your name is JESUS? You mix Spanish with English like you aren't sure which one you want to or can speak," states Grace McCloud.
"No. I was looking through those binoculars for a black man carrying a rifle and sporting a scorpion tattoo.

Didn't you hear? Last night, they said he shot up the tires on all the eighteen-wheelers heading for the parking lot and then called in the police, who made several arrests. We don't have his entire identity. The only evidence is that he is black and had a rifle, according to one of our drivers who made his getaway."
"Why the heck weren't we notified? Did you inform Alberto Gomez?" We could have already caught the bastard. On the other hand, I think you are dreaming." Says Shelly Hall to Victor Crip.
"I just got the word, so I decided to find that man before he strikes again. I want to kill him myself. Go down as the real Victor - Numero Uno!"
Says Victor Crip.
The women reboard their jeep and drive back down the hill, on their way back into the hills and into Mexico.

MOMENTS LATER, Rude Buay, on the other side of the hill, oblivious of the fact that Victor Crip has visitors in the form of Hall, and Gomez, kept crawling on his stomach toward the summit. He finally sees Victor outside his jeep, looking through the binoculars. Victor's back is turned toward the agent as he is focused on binocular surveillance. Rude Buay whistles out and then throws a rock at Victor Crip. As soon as the drug lord turns around and faces Rude Buay, the agent caps him with several rounds while still lying on his stomach. He then gets up out of the fetal position and rummages through Victor Crip's jeep. Rude Buay discovers at least 30 pounds of Meth, two rifles, stacks of U.S. one hundred dollar bills, freebasing utensils, along with twenty kilos of uncut cocaine. Additionally, agent Rude Buay confiscates Crip's binoculars and his supped-up fully loaded Land Rover jeep. Using his elbow to steer the vehicle, the agent departs speedily down the hill.

21

While returning to the base of the hill, Rude Buay's phone rings. He fumbles to retrieve it from inside the pocket of his pullover jacket and does. It's Heidi Hudson. He immediately senses a sparkle in her voice. She is upbeat. Was she looking forward to once again connecting with her true partner in crime?

"Rude Buay, where the heck are you?"

She inquires.

"Nogales, Mexico,"

He responds.

"I will be joining you shortly, even if it costs me my J O B. Ortiz was not happy with me asking for the time off. He suspected I was going to be teaming up with you and didn't look so happy, " says Hudson.

"Very Interesting. Hit me up when you land." Says Rude Buay as he hangs up.

THE FOLLOWING MORNING, Heidi Hudson arrives in Nogales, Mexico, and meets the battered Rude Buay near his hotel across Independence Street. Noticing his swollen hands and, most noticeably, the fight inside of him not being realized brings tears to her eyes. After shedding some tears, she gets on the phone and connects with their other Jamaican allies.

IN MEXICO AND ITS BORDER TOWNS, the word spreads swiftly that a black man using a rifle shot up several tractor-trailers carrying Meth to be distrusted through the border tunnels. The cartel senses that it is Rude Buay but doubts that he could have escaped the hanging, much less the vehicular explosion. Alberto Gomez, Miles Tate, Denise Gomez, Shelly Hall, and the others are perplexed as it has been reported that the man sports a scorpion tattoo like the one displayed by Rude Buay. Also, upon learning about the death of Victor Crip, yet another mystery is created for them; they recently discovered Crip's corpse in the Nogales hills.

While the Dragons look for the mysterious Blackman, the Mexico police look for more evidence regarding the tunnel drug transporting operation. They not only tow away several vehicles from Independence Street but discover that these vehicles were equipped with a manhole on the floor to pick up drugs from suppliers through underground tunnels with manholes and deliver them to dealers ready to transport them across the U.S., Canada, the Caribbean, and China. Several arrests evolved.

The following day, city workers in Nogales embark upon sealing off those manholes and tunnels used as conduits for smugglers to transport drugs across the Mexican border into Arizona.

LATER THAT EVENING, Mildred, the Police Commissioner, and Banks, who have been searching tirelessly in Mexico for Rude Buay, arrive in the Mexican city of Nogales. They finally meet up with agents Heidi Hudson, Chelo, and Rude Buay in a small hotel suite and orchestrate a plan of attack to counteract the Dragon Drug Cartel further. At this meeting, which, in more ways than one, is like an ally reunion, Rude Buay talks about the harmful effects of Methamphetamine on the human brain and body. Some key points in the research delivered by Tamara bear weight in his speech, as well as how they would stop the Dragons by destroying their Mexican strongholds. The main objective is to decrease the number of drugs flowing out of Mexico to the U.S. and other countries as well. In the words of Rude Buay: "We will not only cripple, but we will freeze the trade." So, they divide and team up to conquer. Agent Heidi Hudson teams up with the veteran agent Walter Banks, Mildred Simms teams up with the Jamaican Police Commissioner Richard Baptiste, and Rude Buay teams up with Chelo.

Walter Banks and Heidi Hudson were paired up not too long ago in Jamaica, so their chemistry was tight. Mildred Simms and Richard Baptiste had also worked together when Rude Buay first fought against the

Dragons in Jamaica. They had also worked together for the Jamaican government in Port Antonio, so they were all in sync.

Rude Buay felt obligated to mentor Chelo and pass the baton to the man who risked his life to save him. Everyone except Chelo had been in this warfare before; he had never used a gun.

In three separate jeeps, all six officials pack up multiple guns and other weapons of mass destruction.

Immediately, they take on the streets of Nogales, Mexico.

22

With the death of the newly appointed Victor Crip, the Dragon Drug Cartel was now without a pivotal person to head up their drug smuggling operation at the Mexico/Nogales border. The word was out that agent Rude Buay could still be alive, except none of the Dragons had seen him. So, they turned down the rumor about his existence, feeling free to roam.
Alberto Gomez, their leader, was heavily taxed by the Dragon Cartel's global expansion, so he required a quality replacement in Mexico.

IT IS NOW 10:15 PM IN CHINA, precisely 15 minutes after the lockdown at the Shanghai Central Prison. All heads are accounted for except Salvador. The chemist and Drug Lord who worked previously for the Dragon Drug Cartel and was imprisoned less than three months ago is missing. He was initially arrested, charged, and sentenced after over ten thousand cans of milk packed with uncut cocaine were discovered inside a submarine down the Chinese river bound for the Caribbean. The estimated street value of the cargo was over $10M. Salvador was already serving a portion of that 10-year sentence.

Outside the prison gate and up the street, Salvador, in a warden uniform, boards a waiting taxi. The taxi takes off. About over an hour before prison lockdown and a few minutes after dinner, Salvador whisked away from the prison yard to the men's room. Earlier that day, after a phone conversation initiated by Alberto Gomez, Salvador accessed the warden's office and stole a uniform while carelessly sitting inside the warden's closet. He placed it inside a black plastic trash bag and stored it at the bottom of the men's restroom trash can.

Before lockdown and after dinner, Salvador changed into that uniform and boldly walked out of the prison. The guard on duty waved to Salvador as he exited.

Oblivious that he was not the warden whose name tag was prominently displayed on his jacket. Alberto Gomez had already arranged to have a taxi waiting for Salvador after lockdown. Salvador was whisked away to the airport. He met a woman who handed him a plane ticket, fake IDs, and a duffel bag there. Salvador went to the men's room, changed into civilian clothing, breezed through security, and boarded an aircraft heading to Mexico. The following day, he arrived in Nogales, Mexico.

Upon Salvador's arrival, Drug Czar and leader of the Dragon Drug Cartel, Alberto Gomez quickly appointed the chemist, better known as Sal, to head up the Nogales/Mexico border. The position that agent Rude Buay had turned down. Sal had been known for creating the Dragon X brand of cocaine in Colombia. This brand was the result of a glitch. One mixed with cyanide and responsible for killing several Jamaican kids almost a year ago. Sal was also the point person who assisted David Lee, the Chinese drug lord, in the packaging of cocaine wrapped in Ziploc bags and shipped in milk cartons. This narcotics shipment strategy caused the death of many, including little Leticia, the 3-year-old Jamaican girl.

As the man in charge of the Methamphetamine operation in Mexico, the Dragons had put in place not only a chemist but a hard-working individual in the person of Salvador. He was loyal to Alberto Gomez and dedicated to his cause: growing the cartel into a global operation. On several occasions, Alberto Gomez reminded Sal that we will not only expand across the five oceans but will also cause some of the most devastating recalls that the country (referring to the U.S.) has ever experienced. Salvador bought into that concept.

CHELO USED HIS LAPTOP, which was connected to his satellites and hidden cameras, which were recently set up in Nogales along the Mexican border and elsewhere. By doing so, he was able to eavesdrop on the Dragons.

The cartel also positioned itself in Vermont, close to the U.S./Canadian border. At that location, they used an old warehouse as a depot. The eighteen-wheelers would pull up, bound from Mexico, and then transfer their cargo inside waiting vans.

These were customized vans, usually manned by two or three people. They would load up their Meth supply onto the vans and head for the Canadian border. The border patrols on the Canadian side would do minimal checking of these vehicles operated by Canadians. So, these Meth smugglers got away scot-free. It was said that the ex-agent Miles Tate, a Miami native, had this drug smuggling operation locked down. Meth sales soared in Canada as a result of his involvement.

Grace McCloud has filled the void left by the deceased Frankie O'Neal, Johnny Too Bad, Amanda Kingsley, and Agnes Richards in Miami. This city, situated in south Florida, serves as a hub for the southern states and the Caribbean. Their shipments came through the Mexico/El Paso border on eighteen-wheelers. Products were unloaded and stored in a warehouse similar to the previously owned Milky Way. Marcus Ranks headed up the Tivoli Gardens/Port Antonio operations in Jamaica. Their shipments came through the Mexico/El Paso border on eighteen-wheelers via Miami and were sent out in small ships into Jamaica via Port Antonio and Ocho Rios. Ever since Rude Buay, and most recently his team, began concentrating on combating the trade of narcotics in Mexico, Ranks had some room to trade freely and became stellar at smuggling Meth along with other narcotics products into Jamaica. He was too clever for Jamaican law enforcement. In other words, he was slippery. A relative of Johnny Too Bad, Ranks had a vendetta not only against the U.S. but against Drug Enforcement Agencies as well.

OVERSEAS, IN CHINA, Sammy Chin tied the knot with the imprisoned widow of the deceased drug lord David Lee. With Lee's empire shattered and now in the rebuilding stage, his widow Chu Ling became a great fit for Sammy Chin. The only downfall was even though she was an adept drug dealer who unfortunately got busted. She had to operate from behind prison walls. The palladium on Chu Ling was very tight. Her main contribution to the trade was serving primarily as a referral source for Chin. Chu Ling was determined to be in the thick of things very soon, thus giving China that clout it once had when her previous husband, David Lee, was alive and ran the narcotics trade.

RUDE BUAY AND CHELO, followed in tow by Walter Banks and Heidi Hudson, accompanied by Mildred Simms and Richard Baptiste, pull up outside an abandoned warehouse in Mexico a few miles from Nogales, the neighboring town in Arizona. The agents are poised. They survey from their vehicle and gather satellite feed posted at the border.

23

While the agents waited undetected in their vehicles parked between the trees above the warehouse, several tractor-trailers pulled up and entered the warehouse. The agents waited for them to exit the building but never did. So, the agents moved in, ensuing an investigation and a possible drug sting. Upon arrival, the more than six eighteen-wheelers had all vanished. The loading docks and the back parking lot were empty. Rude Buay, familiar with disappearance tactics used by the Dragons, reflects on the disappearances of Johnny Too Bad and Frankie O'Neal at a Manor in Miami several months prior. So, the agent perceives and pursues a possible underground tunnel getaway.

Moments later, all six agents drive through a long, extended tunnel. In less than 15 minutes, they wind up in another warehouse, this time across the borderline into Nogales, Arizona. That fleet of eighteen-wheelers is still nowhere to be found, not even a trace. Rude Buay is also very mindful of the fact that the Dragon Drug Cartel had used this tunnel to transport narcotics from Mexico into the U.S. He had seen the underground tunnel that was built underneath that manor in Miami.

Moments later, Rude Buay gets on the phone with Michael Ortiz. Both men discuss the possible ways of freezing tunnel narcotics traffic to the U.S. Later that day, U.S. Border Patrols surround that same warehouse in Nogales, and with the aid of heavy-duty equipment, they put up roadblocks to stop further tunnel traffic into the U.S. Placing them one step ahead of the agents. As the news spreads, U.S. Border officials beef up border security to curtail any other tunneling from Mexico into the U.S.

THROUGH THE CALCULATED surveillance efforts of Chelo, Rude Buay learns that Salvador has arrived in Mexico and is filling the void left by the executed Victor Crip. So, he and the agents embark on a mission to find Salvador. Rude Buay and Chelo cover the Mexican side of the border, while Banks, Hudson, Simms, and Baptiste cover the town of Nogales, Arizona. With the disappearance of those eighteen-wheelers, they decided to beef up their security and investigation. Rude Buay and Chelo later return to Mexico through the same tunnel. On their way back, they meet with an eighteen-wheeler coming straight ahead at them as if pursuing a head-on collision. Rude Buay manages to shoot at the driver and blow out the front windscreen. The driver is untouched by that round. However, he tiers the truck on the right side of the tunnel while Rude Buay's jeep squeezes by on the left. Rude Buay's jeep comes to a stop. The driver of the eighteen-wheeler truck gets out and starts shooting at Rude Buay and Chelo. They retaliate with several rounds of their own. The cat-and-mouse duel continues for several minutes inside the dark, unlit tunnel. Finally, the driver takes off on foot through the tunnel, heading towards Mexico.

Chelo, excellent on foot, leads the way in the foot race, with Rude Buay following closely behind him. The driver shoots again at the two agents. This time, once again, he was only training his weapon. Rude Buay gets a shot off that sends the driver to the ground; another round finishes him off. After a search, the driver and his truck were searched, and over 100 kilos of uncut cocaine were discovered, in addition to large quantities of Methamphetamine and other narcotics inside the trailer. After calling in the Policia Rude Buay, Chelo leaves the scene to pursue more Dragons.

LATER THAT DAY, after receiving the news, Salvador consults with Alberto Gomez about the roadblocks placed by DEA inside the tunnel and impeding the flow of drugs to the U.S. along with the sting carried out on the now-deceased truck driver. Alberto Gomez not only wondered who was behind this operation but set out to capture them. At first, he thought it was the border patrols, but he knew he had been operating this

way for several months, and they had not caught on. So, he ruled them out.
He thought about the U.S. DEA. But he knew without the experienced agent Rude Buay in their camp, and they were playing major catch-up. Although he had heard that a black man had taken Victor Crip's life, in his mind, he knew that he had sent Rude Buay to the gallows. Additionally, to ensure the successful execution of his task, he had also backed up that expedition with a bomb attached to the truck carrying the agent to the gallows. So, he ruled out the Rude Buay comeback scenario. Could it have been Rude Buay's allies? Alberto Gomez knew they were not as efficient without the man he so severely wanted on his team. So, he sent Salvador on a rampage to bring in whoever it was that was raining on his Mexican global parade. Rude Buay had previously equipped Chelo with a semiautomatic gun but was concerned about the barefootedness of the man who had saved his life. Knowing how treacherous the search for the Dragons could become through the rugged hills of Nogales. So, he pulls up at a shoe store and steps inside to purchase a pair of comfortable shoes for his sidekick, Chelo. Planning to surprise Chelo later, he puts the moccasins in a shopping bag and returns to his jeep. To his surprise, the jeep is there, but Chelo and the laptop are missing.

24

When ex-agent Miles Tate learned that Chelo had been captured by the Dragons in Mexico, he traveled from Vermont, where he had been stationed, to participate in the interrogation. He had already passed on U.S. D.E.A. secrets to Alberto Gomez, leader of the Dragon Drug Cartel. This opportunity would make him look good in Alberto Gomez's eyes and give him a chance to get firsthand information from the man who had spied on the cartel from Colombia for many years. Tate was stoked!

Upon arriving in Mexico, Tate was met by Sal, the newly appointed Drug Lord to head up that enclave and also the man responsible for capturing Chelo. Alberto Gomez wanted to participate in the proceedings, so he flew from China to Mexico immediately. The interrogation was set for an office inside an abandoned warehouse in Nogales, Mexico. Chelo, who looked somewhat battered, was brought into the room that morning bound with ropes. Accompanied by two guards, they seat him on a chair in the middle of the room. Tied to the wooden chair, which permitted him no movement, or else the chair moved with him, Chelo sensed that his fate would be decided. He was unsure if they knew he was responsible for Rude Buay's escape. If they did, he envisioned not escaping and being either hung from the gallows or executed.

Alberto Gomez and Salvador looked on while Miles Tate began with the digging process.

"Good morning Chelo!"

"Morning," Responds Chelo.

"Where do you live, Chelo?" "Bogota, Colombia," Replies Chelo.

"What brings you to Mexico? You've been here for some time now."

"D.E.A. business,"

Reveals Chelo.

"Who is your affiliation?"

"The U.S. government,"

Chelo responds.

"So, you were brought in from Colombia to spy on the Dragon Drug Cartel?"

"I was brought here to work…"

Counters Chelo.

"Who brought you into Mexico?"

Interrupts Miles Tate.

"The D.E.A.,"

Says Chelo.

"Who…? Banks? Ortiz? Who do you report to?"

Asks Miles Tate.

"The D.E.A.,"

Answers Chelo.

"Is Rude Buay alive?"

"I don't know."

"You are such a liar. Which of those men I've just mentioned do you report to?"

Asks Miles Tate.

"None of them. I report to the headquarters,"

Says Chelo."

"Every spy is accountable to someone, even if that person is part of a group. So, who are you accountable to? Who are you protecting?"

"The D.E.A."

Tate punches Chelo in the stomach.

"Give me the truth, man! I don't need the D.E.A. bullshit. I have worked for the organization; you have to report to someone. Come on!"

That blow strikes Chelo hard. He coughs up blood as a result. Alberto Gomez looks at him as if to say: don't waste my time. I did not fly in from China to be lied to.

"Who was with you when you were captured?"

At this point, the Dragons are still unaware that Rude Buay has escaped death once again, is alive, and was with Chelo before being captured. "No one. Why don't you ask Sal? He is standing right across from you."

Responds Chelo very calmly.

"Where are the rest of your guys?"

Questions Tate.

"I am not my brother's keeper. I work for the Drug Enforcement Agency."

Responds Chelo.
"Where is your satellite located?"
Asks Tate.
"That's a D.E.A. business."
Responds Chelo.
That feels like a slap on the face to Miles Tate. He realizes that he is not going to get anything out of Chelo. Alberto Gomez and Salvador have the same opinions.
"How would you like to work for us?"
Interjects Alberto Gomez.
Chelo doesn't answer.
Alberto Gomez presents an attaché with crisp U.S. One Hundred Dollar Bills stacks.
Chelo looks them over.
"We'll pay you well. You sure know how to keep secrets."
Says Alberto Gomez.
"No, thank you."
Responds Chelo.
"Give him a day or two to think about it. In the meantime, prepare the gallows to hang his ...."
Says Alberto Gomez.
Tate ceases his questioning.
Salvador removes Chelo from the room, puts him in his pickup truck, and escorts him back to the tiny house where he is confined.

25

While Rude Buay drives through the neighborhood looking for the missing Chelo his phone rings. It's his boss, Ortiz, on the other end. Rude Buay looks at the number on the caller ID and delays answering the call. After several rings, he accepts the call.

"Bascombe, this is Ortiz. Would you like me to call you back?" Asks Michael Ortiz.

"We can talk now."

Says Rude Buay.

Ortiz feels it in his agent's voice.

"You don't sound too…"

"Chelo is missing. Possibly captured!"

Informs Rude Buay,

"You are kidding me. Without him, we are dead in the water. Was it the Dragons?"

"Most likely! They have not claimed responsibility yet, but…"

"Bascombe, I told you; you've gotten too deep. Without him, it's over. Your entire team of agents could be wiped out in an instant. If you don't know where they are, it's like walking through a minefield.

You need him to monitor those bastards, especially at the border."

"That I know very well,"

Responds Rude Buay.

"I'm aware that Hudson recently joined you. She could have told me what her objective was instead of saying she wanted some time off."

States Ortiz.

'Really? Boss, I am unsure what Hudson does ..." Says Rude Buay.

"My suggestion is that you tell your team you are packing up and return to Miami, where at least it's not so bad and we have more control, " says Ortiz.

"No thanks. I am not a quitter. There isn't a quitting cell in my makeup. I will fight them in the desert, and I will fight them in the mountains, I will fight them in the tunnels, I will fight them amongst the cactus, I will fight them at the border, I will fight them in the air, and on the water ... I will fight them everywhere. I am not giving in. All it takes for evil to prevail is a bunch of men with no backbone."

Declares Rude Buay.

"You are putting the lives of your teammates at risk, Bascombe. Maybe you should ask yourself the question. Why are we in Mexico? Additionally, what does the U.S. have to gain? They are our neighbors, not our friends. They bring us more harm than good. Why don't they sell it to their people? Their governmental views are opposed to ours. It is time to get out."

Says Ortiz.

"I hear you, boss. I am not going to quit so they can feel they have won. Plus, the man who saved my life from the gallows has probably been captured. And if there is even the remotest possibility that he is alive, then I've got a job to do, and that is to find him. Quitting is not an option. When the dream is strong enough, the facts don't count. I need your support. If I can't have it, that's okay, and I will fight this war alone till the end. I may lose some battles, but I will not lose this war."

States Rude Buay.

"This is not the Winston Churchill era, Bascombe. He had Britain behind him. What do you have? Plus, Chelo's understudy Bruce is very wet behind the ears."

Says Ortiz.

Rude Buay continues,

"Until one is committed, there is hesitancy, the chance to draw back, always ineffectiveness. Concerning all acts of initiative (or creation), there is only one truth, the ignorance of which kills many ideas and splendid plans, that the moment one definitely commits oneself, then Providence moves too.

All sorts of things occur to help one that would otherwise never have occurred. A whole stream of events issues from the decision, raising in one's favor all manner of incidents and meetings and material assistance, which no man would have believed would have come his way. Whatever you think you can do or

believe you can do, begin it. Action has magic, grace, and power in it.' So, said
Goethe,"
Quotes Rude Buay.
Ortiz removes the phone receiver from his ear and stares at it, thinking Rude Buay has got to be crazy. He is fighting a Mexican war as long as the river Nile. Not only is he shorthanded, but he's fighting with two injured hands.
"Hello,"
Says Rude Buay.
There is no answer coming from Ortiz on the other end of the phone. So Rude Buay hangs up on his back. After digesting the interlude between him and Ortiz, he reaches over to the front passenger seat. There sits the package with the pair of moccasins that he purchased for Chelo. He opens it and retrieves the shoe box. Rude Buay stares at the pair of moccasins.
"Requesting D.E.A. presence at an abandoned warehouse in Nogales just outside the Mexican border and across from Independence Street. Officer down! I repeat! One Border Patrol Officer down …!"
It is the voice of Bruce Chavez, Chelo's Mexican understudy.
Rude Buay makes a U-Turn in his jeep and heads speedily in that direction.

26

Rude Buay approaches the warehouse where the eighteen-wheelers were first seen. He had thought about using the tunnel but changed his mind and opted for the local street instead. In less than fifteen minutes, he's at the border with Nogales. Moments later, he pulls up at the warehouse that was once used as a clothing depot.

Flashing ambulance lights welcome him along with busy medics surrounding the corpse of a uniformed border patrol officer.

Immediately after Rude Buay arrives on the scene, Mildred Simms, Richard Baptiste, Walter Banks, and Heidi Hudson pull up. They jump out of their jeeps and join in the investigation. According to the eyewitness report of an elderly Mexican man:

Several cars were in line at the U.S. border crossing. Border patrol officers, after detaining several Mexican motorists, proceeded to search their vehicles. While rummaging through their cars, several teens arriving on foot from Nogales, Mexico, emerged at the border crossing. In a confrontation, they demanded the release of those arrested. These kids, armed to the max

carrying AK47s, opened fire on investigating border patrol officers as well as border workers.
When it all ended, not only were several border patrols killed, but the kids attempted to take over border operations there in Nogales.
It was right about then that agent Rude Buay arrived on the scene.
The pack's leader was a feisty Mexican kid of dwarf stature adorned in a scarf. Yells out:
"We are the young "Dragons," and we are in control."
Rude Buay, looking at him from a distance in his jeep, says to himself:
"A minor is in control; he's got to be kidding. He could still be wetting his bed."
But looking at the waving AK47 in the kid's hands and the army of kids rallying for his support, the agent realizes that this is serious business. Plus, there were no border patrols in sight except for those dead bodies lying around.
So Rude Buay decides to negotiate after summoning his backup of agents.
"Hey Kid! My name is agent Bascombe, D.E.A. You are indeed a tough kid. But whoever set you up to this is such a weakling, a coward. They should have done these acts themselves. You have no doubt so much potential and all your life ahead of you. Whoever set you up to this has nothing to live for…"
Interrupting the kid responds,

"Your name is not Bascombe, it's Rude Buay ... aka Rude Boy. We don't need a sermon because we are not in church and today isn't Sunday. Plus, I dislike Sunday school. You are the man with the scorpion tattoo and causing a lot of trouble at our borders. You think this is Jamaica…! You've killed Johnny Too Bad, David Lee, Ian Baynes, Axel James, Desmond Scott, Jose Mendez, and Ricardo Herrera. You are not going to do the same for me!

The kid shoots off a round at Rude Buay. It misses. "Look! Behind you, coming through those hills, are 10 eighteen-wheelers. We want their safe passage through this border, which has for too long been like an iron wall to us Mexicans. When we feel they are safe, we might be willing to discuss plan B. I won't miss the next time around."

"What's inside of those trucks?"

Asks Rude Buay.

"None of your business!"

"Kid. Ever since 9/11, any vehicle entering the U.S. has to be checked. If I allow your trucks, though, as an agent, I would not be doing my job and could cause harm to many Americans." The kid shoots at Rude Buay. Again, he misses. The agent dodges out of the two rounds. "That was just a warning. I want what I say, and I get what I want."

Says the kid.

"You are spoiled! What do your friends think? Are they in with you on this?"

Asks Rude Buay, who would not let up off his aimed rifle at the kid.
"We don't have to listen to you. Look around you. The trucks are coming."
Says the kid.
Rude Buay peripherally sees another group of kids forming a circle around him.
"The choice is yours! In a minute, over 30 bullets could be penetrating your body. Only one of mine… Do you want war, or do you want peace?"
Yells the kid.
"Okay. I will let the trucks through, but one at a time."
Says Rude Buay,
The kid radios,
"Come on through, only one by one!"
Before the trucks could descend across the border, two jeeps emerged, racing alongside them and raining tear gas onto the border compound. Rude Buay grabs his mask and protects himself. Many stray bullets scatter from wielding AK47s, the experienced agents in both jeeps are unscathed. Caught up in the tear gas deposit the kids fall to the ground. The eighteen-wheelers are stalled in their tracks. Mildred Simms, Richard Baptiste, Walter Banks, and Heidi Hudson emerge from their vehicles. Along with agent Rude Buay, they pounce on the gassed kids, confiscating their weapons. Moments later, not only is the border reopened and manned by replaced border patrols, who are flown in,

but 30 kids are arrested and detained along with ten tractor-trailer drivers.

After a search of the eighteen-wheelers, over 300,000 pounds of methamphetamine is seized along with 100,000 kilos of uncut cocaine.

27

After this seizure, it became official news that not only was agent Rude Buay alive but that his team of agents was conducting U.S. D.E.A. duties in Mexico at the U.S. border. Alberto Gomez now knew for sure that someone was covering Rude Buay when he was sent to the gallows, or the men trusted to hang him and set him free instead. So, he put out a countrywide search in Mexico to have Rude Buay once again captured so he could pull the trigger and take agent Rude Buay's life for good if he refused to team up. Rude Buay quickly learned of the Drug Czar's objective by signs placed on telephone poles. Hence, not only was he in pursuit of Rude Buay for the possible kill, but Rude Buay was also in pursuit of him and his entire team for Operation Clean Sweep. Not long after that, Bruce discovered Alberto Gomez's plot by tapping into a hotel phone line during his conference call with Salvador, Shelly Hall, Denise Gomez, Miles Tate, Marcus Ranks, Sammy Chin, and the remaining young Dragons. Bruce, tipped off by an informant at the hotel, was granted brief access to that Hotel's phone

communication system. The informant made his side money that way.
Rude Buay, meanwhile, knew that no matter the many "what ifs" that surrounded Chelo's possibility of being still alive, he had to try his best to search and rescue him out of the grasp of the Dragon Drug Cartel. Rude Buay now waits outside his car at a local multicolored pottery shop in Nogales. Bruce informed him that Alberto Gomez, Denise, and Shelly Hall frequented that block to shop and dine on the delicious local cuisine known to awaken one's taste buds.

ONCE AGAIN, Bruce Chavez's voice is transmitted through the D.E.A. radio circuit. "Requesting D.E.A. presence at a food warehouse in Campillo and Belto Juarez. Two agents down."
There was no information on precisely who the fallen agents were. So, Rude Buay takes off in that direction as do Banks and Heidi Hudson. Mildred Simms and Richard Baptiste also responded to the call. Three identical jeeps are now racing through Nogales in Sonora, Mexico. Rude Buay's jeep arrives at the scene, followed by Bank's jeep and then Mildred's. It's a bloody scene as two American agents lie on the street bathed in their blood and killed execution-style.
Rude Buay jumps out of his vehicle with his hands still bandaged. Walter Banks and Heidi Hudson, using latex gloves, gather information on the deceased agents by searching through their pockets and wallets.

"He is one of ours!"
Yells Hudson after viewing the first agent's ID. She views the second ID now handed to her by Walter Banks. Mildred Simms and Richard Baptiste yellow tape the area as they keep their eyes open for perpetrators.
Removing her gloves, Hudson says,
"Both U.S. agent's IDs are from New Mexico."
"What are they doing here by themselves? They should have known better than to be operating independently."
Says Rude Buay.
"What if Ortiz sent these men in to derail our progress? Heck, I wouldn't put it past him."
Says Hudson.
"Really?"
Asks Mildred.
"He is up for a promotion and needs people on his side."
Informs Rude Buay. "Anything he can do to rank up, huh?" Says Richard.
Rude Buay then calls in the Mexican Policia.
"Let's get out of here!"
Says Rude Buay.
As they enter their vehicles and depart, Rude Buay senses being followed. His instincts are right on target as bullets instantly ring out, raining on top of their cars.

BEFORE THE TWO AGENTS were gunned down.

Both agents showed up at the warehouse. The purpose was to strike a deal with Denise Gomez and Shelly Hall for the purchase of 200 pounds of methamphetamine. The two men claimed they were from Los Angeles, California, and could not acquire the product in the big city.

A drought had emerged in LA since those eighteen-wheelers were seized, loaded with narcotics, and bound for San Diego.

Conversely, those two agents from New Mexico were sent in by Michael Ortiz and Al Cortez. The latter was the head D.E.A. in New Mexico and wanted to help win support for Ortiz (to be known for) fighting the Dragons in Mexico. Both Special Agents were aware and concluded that Rude Buay and his team were taking the matter in Mexico into their own hands. More so, most Americans were now more tuned into what went on in Mexico and the drug trade because of the huge amounts of killings that ensued. They wanted to make sure their borders were intact, and protection beefed up against the Mexicans. In a nutshell, Ortiz's involvement was waking up, smelling the coffee, and looking for shoulders he could lean on. So, he contacted his ally, Cortez, in New Mexico.

Those two agents from New Mexico, posing as Drug Lords, were led to the van loaded with drugs. They then returned to their car to hand over the attaché case filled with cash and collect the van's keys from the drug dealers. They had planned on one agent driving the vehicle to LA while the other followed in their car bearing California tags. Denise Gomez and Shelly Hall became suspicious. They wasted no time and snuffed them out with multiple rounds. When Rude Buay and his team arrived, Shelly Hall and Denise Gomez were immediately interrupted as they attempted to reclaim possession of the 200 pounds of Meth aboard that van. Rude Buay and his team had passed the parked van and the car up the street not too far from where the two agents were gunned down.

They searched the van, and not only was it loaded with meth, but evidence indicated there could have been a chase of the two agents before they were shot and killed.

WITH THE DARK-COLORED JEEP pursuing Rude Buay and his agents, the street race continued from Campillo onto Avenue Alvaro Obregon. Gaining some advantage and way ahead, Rude Buay and his team pulled off the road and into a secluded rest stop. The pursuing jeep continued and passed the rest area along the Avenue quickly.

Moments later, the three agent vehicles merged onto the Avenue in pursuit of the dark-colored jeep and its unknown occupants.

28

The three jeeps continue along the Avenue, quickly catching up to Shelly Hall and Denise Gomez inside that vehicle. Inside the lead jeep is agent Rude Buay, followed by Walter Banks, and behind Banks is Mildred Simms. Meanwhile, Shelly Hall and Denise Gomez are still oblivious that these D.E.A. agents are following them. In their mindset, they have no idea who they are in pursuit of and are now their followers. Finally, it dawns on them that the agents took a detour. So, instead of continuing on the Avenue, they, too, take a detour through the hillside. They embark on a downgrade. As their vehicle makes its descent, Rude Buay, still in pursuit, spots it.

Rude Buay radios Banks' and Simms' vehicle.

"That car is about a mile away going through the hills. Step on it!"

Says Rude Buay.

"We are right on your tail, Rude Buay,"

Says Banks. "We are covering you, Banks," Says Mildred.

Richard Baptiste, the Commissioner, concurs. The three agent's vehicles are now gaining ground on Denise Gomez's and Shelly Hall's vehicles.

Shelly Hall looks in her rearview mirror and discovers they are being followed closely. How she wished the table had turned right about then. The winding, treacherous hills and valleys beckon along this now desolate two-lane highway. Shelly Hall speeds up, but right about that time, Rude Buay's jeep is speedily catching up to hers.

The agents prepare for an imminent faceoff with the two women. Rude Buay has one arm on the steering wheel and the other holding on to that rifle he has grown accustomed to.

The passenger window in his jeep is now rolled down as he places the barrel of his rifle on that door so it protrudes outside and points towards the vehicle ahead.

Banks' jeep is on Rude Buay's vehicle's tail. Heidi Hudson, sitting in the passenger seat, equips herself with her loaded semi-automatic. At this point, Hudson relives those taunting memories she suffered under the hands of oppression by Shelly Hall and Denise Gomez. Banks, looking across at Hudson, knows she is focused and ready for battle.

Inside Mildred Simms' vehicle, which tails Banks, is Baptiste, the Jamaican Police Commissioner. He is armed with a semi-automatic weapon. Mildred maintains command of the road and is armed with the same type of weapon. Baptiste could sense the tension but not the extent of Mildred's vendetta against the two femme Fatales. He rolls down the window and cues his gun in the same manner as Rude Buay's, as if by design.

At the same time, Shelly Hall's vehicle picks up speed. Her gun sits between her seat and the passenger seat. While occupying that passenger seat, Denise prepares for battle with her weapon in hand. The agent's vehicles also pick up the pace.

Rude Buay gets a few shots off. Unfortunately, nothing connects. Denise responds with a few of her own. Same result, Zilch, Nada, Nothing Connects!

Rude Buay's vehicle is now so close it's almost rearing Shelly Hall's. The road opens up, providing a shoulder. Rude Buay speeds up and takes it. He is poised to get a good shot off at Shelly Hall. Shelly Hall drives out of the shot, which sails into space. Shelly Hall's vehicle is now in full view to agents Banks and Hudson as Rude Buay tries to make up for that missed opportunity to shoot Shelly Hall. Heidi Hudson blasts several rounds at the two women. While Rude Buay and Shelly Hall jockey for position, Hudson tries passing on the other side and is almost at even keel with Denise's raised gun. Shelly Hall speeds up, oblivious that she has derailed Rude Buay's focused gun on her. Now she drives, leaving room on the left. Rude Buay tries positioning it parallel to her vehicle so he can get a great aim at Shelly Hall. Instead, Shelly Hall tries forcing his jeep into the gutter.

Hudson's round of bullets connects with the two rear tires on Shelly Hall's vehicle and punctures both tires. Shelly Hall's car is slowed as it wobbles. Hudson manages to get another round-off, which blows out the rear windscreen.

In the meantime, a shot from Hudson's gun strikes Denise Gomez. Rude Buay also gets a shot off, which hits Shelly Hall. Not only is Shelly Hall hit, but she also loses control of the vehicle. As a result, her vehicle nosedives over the steep embankment, rolling several times. It stops after crashing into a huge tree. The agents leave their cars and assess the damage from the roadway up above. From their vantage point, the two doors on this totaled vehicle are ajar. Mildred Simms and Heidi Hudson finish it off with several rounds, setting it ablaze. The agents depart in haste.

29

Rude Buay and his agents are combing the city of Nogales, Mexico, for any clues to finding Chelo.

"Requesting D.E.A. presence at the Nogales, Arizona border! Five border patrol officers are down. They are at the scene where two illegal trailers are trying to cross into the U.S. from Mexico. They could be loaded with narcotics." Bruce's voice echoes over the radios inside the three jeeps manned by the D.E.A. agents.

Bruce conducted his survey from the hills of Nogales, Mexico, in a small house overlooking the U.S.-Mexico border.

Rude Buay, Walter Banks, Heidi Hudson, Mildred Simms, and Richard Baptiste take off towards the crime scene. Upon arrival, they catch one of the drivers, who later revealed his name as Javier, searching through the pockets of one of the fallen border patrol officers. The other driver waited inside the cab of his eighteen-wheeler in anticipation of getting the go-ahead from Javier. The agent's presence halted that decision to drive his trailer across the U.S. border.

During their investigation, the agents discovered three border patrol vehicles parked on the street: Vehicles that probably served as impediments to the trailer's crossing into the U.S. Next to those means of transportation were three dead officers and two on the pavement outside the border compound.

Upon the arrival of the agents, Javier and the other driver did not surrender but fired several rounds at them. The agents before they could get a shot off, they heard gunshots from both the men:

"Click! Click!

Those were the sound coming from the two drug smuggler's guns. The two men try fleeing the scene back into Mexico but are caught by the agents and placed in handcuffs.

Rude Buay questions Javier about his involvement, sensing that he is the ring leader. Rude Buay asks him what he is looking for in the officer's pocket. Javier tells the agent he was looking for keys. He also tells the agent that he is from Nogales in Sedona, Mexico. He further discloses that he has two daughters, 10 and 11. Also, Javier says that his wife Nora was killed in a drive-by shooting several months prior, leaving him a widower. The other driver only reveals that his name is Jesus when asked by Rude Buay. Besides, he doesn't say very much. Rude Buay asks Javier for pictures of his two daughters. The smuggler has none to present, and neither does he have any photos of his deceased wife. Rude Buay asks him why he took the lives of the

Border Patrol Officers. Javier said bluntly: "They stood in our way. They block the street, asking what's inside the truck. I said none of your … business! They shoot … first. I had to defend." Rude Buay wants to believe him, but Javier doesn't look him in the eye.

Meanwhile, the accompanying D.E.A. agents discover large quantities of narcotics inside both trailers. Rude Buay asks the men why they were smuggling drugs into the U.S., to whom, and who they were working for. Javier tells Rude Buay they were paid to drive the trailers from Nogales to El Paso because of trouble at the El Paso border. In El Paso, they would transfer the trailers and drive back to Mexico. Javier discloses that the Dragon Drug Cartel hired them. When asked who they reported directly to in the organization, Javier informs them they reported directly to Salvador.

Rude Buay then questions Javier about Salvador's whereabouts. Javier says he couldn't know, and he didn't want to be any snitch, or else the Dragons would kill him by hanging him from a pole.

After pressuring Javier further to disclose Sal's whereabouts, Javier attains a comfort level with agent Rude Buay. So, Javier tells Rude Buay that Salvador stays at the Cactus Motel in Nogales. Rude Buay feels that he has gotten the info he wants. Before departing with the other DEA agents, additional border officers will show up at the border. They take Javier and Jesus into custody and charge them with murder and drug smuggling.

Rude Bauy says to his other agents, departing.
"Let's get … out of here!"

30

Upon arriving at the Cactus Motel, the huge cactus plants complement the signage. In mid-afternoon, the hotel parking lot is almost empty, and many guests are checking in and out.

Javier had lied so much when questioned by Rude Buay that he felt this could be nothing but a hoax. Even so, he went inside the motel lobby. Walking up to the counter, Rude Buay told the receptionist he was a U.S. D.E.A. and that he was looking for Salvador.

"He no here,"

The middle-aged woman says nervously. "Where is he now?" Asks Rude Buay.

"Nobody here right now. New people check in." Replies the woman.

Looking out at the almost empty parking lot, Rude Buay asks,

"Did he check out? I don't see his pickup truck. What color was it again?"

Rude Buay points his rifle towards the woman's head.

"Green!" Says the woman.

"Where's his room? The agent asks. "He left, señor." She responds.

"Is he coming back?"
Rude Buay asks,
"I don't know. No speak English!"
Rude Buay, get the message. She knows but would not divulge. So Rude Buay waits along with his agents. While they wait for Sal to show up, breaking news airs over a Jamaican TV station and is transmitted through to the agent's vehicles:
"Two Jamaican Police Officers were gunned down earlier this morning by drug dealers in Tivoli Gardens using weapons from the Fast & Furious program. It was said that police were informed about an alleged drug deal of Methamphetamine.
One source said: When police arrived on the scene, members of the Dragon Drug Cartel, aligned with Jamaican Drug Lord Marcus Ranks, stalked the two officers. Their arsenal instantly outmatched that of the police. The officers died suddenly.
Meanwhile, Methamphetamine in large quantities continues to pour into Tivoli Gardens, Port Antonio, and Kingston. It was also claimed that many teens who have used the drug in the past continue to suffer from the slowness of both their brain and body."
States the reporter.
Moments later, vehicles started pulling into the driveway sporadically. The guests continued to check-in. There is no sign of Salvador. The other agents looked at Rude Buay as if they weren't sure this motel raid was going to go down.

Finally, the green pickup pulls into the parking lot. Sal appears in skinny jeans, a white shirt with rolled-up sleeves unbuttoned at the top, a straw hat, and black and white alligator boots. Sal prepares to enter his room on the hotel's ground level.

Rude Buay steps out of his jeep armed with a gun in hand. He is covered by Walter Banks, Heidi Hudson, Mildred Simms, and Richard Baptiste. As soon as Sal turns the key inside the door lock and pushes it open, Rude Buay, in pursuit, yells out:

"Don't move Sal, U.S. Drug Enforcement Agents!"

Sal is alerted and tries closing the door on them. Instead, Sal abruptly aborts his entry to make his getaway. Rude Buay pushes him inside using the barrel portion of his rifle before Sal can get a shot off.

Sal's room is now filled with DEA agents. The atmosphere looks like an extended stay by its occupant, Sal, instead of a weekend getaway. The odor says he's been staying there for a while; his BO and the room have blended.

Sal remains crouched on the floor with the agent's guns pointed at him. Rude Buay moves past Sal's Meth lab, which is set up inside a cubicle. He couldn't help but notice the test tubes inside this well-structured laboratory. Additionally, he hears a moaning in the other room. He investigates.

Rude Buay is drawn to a man tied up on a chair with his back turned. Rude Buay pushes the chair around with his feet. Surprisingly enough, it is Chelo, tied up on that chair with multiple nylon ropes. Additionally, Chelo's right thumb and index fingers are bandaged and bloodied, indicating that some of his fingernails have already been removed. Rude Buay reminisces about the nail removal process he underwent at the hands of the dragons. He glances at his hands still bandaged. Even so, he senses difficulty untying the nylon ropes. So, he summons Heidi Hudson:

Hudson darts into the room. She pulls out a switchblade from inside her boots under her jeans. She cuts the ropes that bind Chelo. The battered Chelo gets up from the chair, somewhat lazy and discombobulated. Hudson helps him out to the living room.

"Let's move it!"

Commands Rude Buay.

They get ready to leave. Salvador is still face down on the floor. He tries to get up in retaliation. Even so, he notices three guns are pointed at him. His shirt is now unbuttoned. Visible on his body are multiple second-degree burns. Rude Buay senses that their origin comes as a result of Sal's involvement in Methamphetamine preparation. Rude Buay asks Salvador, "Where is Alberto Gomez?" Sal doesn't reply. "Sal, where is your boss Alberto Gomez?" Once again, Sal doesn't respond.

Rude Buay shoots Sal in his right leg.

Still, Sal does not inform Rude Buay regarding his boss' whereabouts. So, he shoots Sal again, this time in the other leg.

In pain, Sal responds.

"Jamaica!"

Rude Buay pumps two more rounds inside Sal's body, putting him out of misery. The agents depart from the motel room.

While the agents went to Salvador's room, the woman attendant at the front desk called some of Sal's contacts, alerting them that D.E.A. agents were after Sal and had headed over to his motel room. As the agents arrive at the front parking lot of the Cactus Motel, they are greeted by a group of armed men. The men of Mexican descent are in a huddle waving machetes and cutlasses toward the D.E.A. agents. One of the men says to the pack's leader:

"Let's chop them … up."

Rude Buay hears and proceeds towards them with his rifle in hand.

"Let's chop Rude Buay up to pieces."

Echoes the leader of the pack,

"I will take them on solo."

Says Rude Buay to his agents.

"You are crazy, mon! You don't know who you are dealing with."

Says Banks to Rude Buay.

"I wouldn't stop him if he thinks he can avoid getting chopped up by these Mexicans."

Says Baptiste.

"Get them, Rude Buay!"

Says Heidi and Mildred in touché fashion.

"That's okay. Their asses are mine."

Rude Buay thinks about taking them on with some sweeping rounds, but at the same time, the pack leader, Julio, holding on to an extended seamed cutlass, invitingly signals Rude Buay into a duel. Rude Buay never passes up a challenge, and he was not about to pass this one up. So, he advances towards Julio in confrontation. Julio separates himself from the rest of the crowd for leverage. He sucks Rude Buay into the duel.

To the amazement of the other D.E.A. agents, Rude Buay takes on Julio one on one with his rifle in hand. They begin sparring with each other. Julio's posse is now transformed into spectators and the other agents. All onlookers were now transfixed as the saber was swung at Rude Buay on many occasions. Rude Buay threw a few flying kicks at Julio for a while, none of which connected.

Finally, a kick from Rude Buay catches Julio in his stomach area. Julio tries to catch his breath. His cutlass soars and hits the pavement "CLING! CLANG!" as the kick from Rude Buay catches him unexpectedly. Rude Buay tosses his rifle in the direction of the agents and goes at Julio barehanded.

Julio ingeniously recovers his cutlass and swings at Rude Buay. Mildred and Hudson tremble like a leaf. Unfortunately, the swing from Julio misses Rude Buay. Julio swings at him again. Mildred has her finger on the trigger this time, ready to blast Julio.
Rude Buay does a 360 and plants a flying kick in Julio's neck area. Julio spins around and falls to the ground in pain. Julio struggles to get up and falls back to the ground. He clenches tightly to his neck. Julio's posse comes charging at Rude Buay with cutlasses and machetes. Rude Buay retrieves his rifle and blasts the entire lot of Julio's posse. Rude Buay and the DEA agents re-board their vehicles and depart immediately. Meanwhile, the woman attendant at the reception office takes stock of the bloodbath from behind the hotel lobby blinds.

31

The next morning, the agents arrive in Montego Bay, Jamaica, on the heels of Dr. Tamara Ross, who has just reported for duty at the Port Antonio General Hospital. Dr. Ross was immediately put in charge of over a dozen patients, primarily teens, suffering from Methamphetamine overdose. After exiting the airport terminal, the agents were met and greeted by a Distinguished Gentleman. He is dressed in white clothing and also sports a well-manicured beard.

"Mr. Rude Buay, it's good to see you again. If you survived the Villa, Tivoli Gardens, Shanghai, and Nogales, you could survive this. However, I must inform you that the man you will come up against, Marcus Ranks, is more dangerous than Axel James, Frankie O'Neal, Ian Baynes, Ricardo Herrera, and Johnny Too Bad. His skills outmatch theirs. Plus, he could very shortly be joined by Alberto Gomez. Here are the keys and directions. It is filled with gas. It has only been driven once. Your toys from the Fast & Furious program are in the trunk. You are going to need them." "Thanks, but I love my rifle. I've grown accustomed to it. Plus…"

Says Rude Buay.

The other agents look on at the exchange between the two men.

"Agent Rude Buay, you must match your firepower to the new weapons used by the Dragon Drug Cartel, or you and your team will be outmatched by Marcus Ranks in Kingston. It would help if you conquered your comfort zone. This is the age of the fast and furious. Your country needs you."

The Distinguished Gentleman mounts his white horse and departs. Rude Buay and his agents board the extended SUV and head speedily for Kingston.

The following morning, the agents arrived in Kingston. Walter Banks questions if they should divide to conquer. Rude Buay, on the other hand, feels that unity is strength. He feels like they are about to bring in Marcus Ranks. With him leading the quest, accompanied by Banks, Simms, Baptiste, Hudson, and Chelo, Rude Buay feels whoever they came up against had no chance.

As they drive through the busy streets of Kingston, a youth no more than seventeen crosses the street amid the traffic. Not only do many motorists, including Rude Buay, apply brakes, but they also honk their horns. The retard does not heed any warning. Luckily, he escapes being run over. He crosses the street and joins a weed-smoking huddle across the street. Hudson shakes her head in dismay in the rear of the SUV.

Later, they pull up at The Cave. This hole-in-the-wall was first on the list received from the Distinguished Gentleman. It was known as a possible hangout spot for Marcus Ranks.

The SUV pulls up and parks in front of The Cave. Rude Buay sees a youth leaving the spot.

"Hey, youth man! You saw Marcus Ranks lately?"

Asks Rude Buay.

"I don't talk to no police."

Says the youth.

"What you have against us?"

Asks Hudson.

"Nothing, I mind my own business. He just left an hour ago. Try the shooting range."

Rude Buay sticks a hundred-dollar bill inside the youth's hand. They take off hurriedly through Kingston.

32

The agents pull up in front of the shooting range nestled in a backlot of a slum in Kingston. They quickly exit the SUV. Rude Buay, Banks, and Hudson barge in while the others cover. Inside, a group of shooters hone their skills. They were later identified as Marcus Ranks' posse. These shooters are all hitting their targets, as they are all going for the shooting target's head.

Rude Buay, Walter Banks, and Heidi Hudson all signed up as guests to investigate the possibility.

Unfortunately, when the D.E.A. agents were finished, fitted, and set to begin their shooting workout, the posse had already returned their weapons and exited the back parking lot. The agents return the following day. Except for this time, they show up an hour earlier. Rude Buay, Walter Banks, and Heidi Hudson are now involved in their shooting exercise. They are accompanied by Chelo, who is undergoing an intense training session directed by agent Rude Buay. Chelo, very early on, is on target, hitting the bullseye. His shots land in the head and stomach regions successively. The agents applaud his efforts, especially Walter Banks, who has an extended version.

Marcus Ranks still doesn't show up. The agents return the gear and head out. On their way to the parking lot, Marcus Rank's posse barges in. When they exit their cars this time, Rude Buay approaches them with his drawn F & F gun. "Hold it right there! Drug Enforcement Agents!" Announces Rude Buay.

Before the posse of four men and two women could arm themselves, they find themselves surrounded by all six D.E.A. agents armed with F and F program weapons.

The other agents cover while Rude Buay, Banks, and Hudson search their vehicles. The agents discover inside the trunks several pounds of Meth and kilos of cocaine. Baptiste accommodates several pairs of handcuffs retrieved from inside the rear of the SUV. Moments later, the posse sits on the sidewalk in handcuffs and is questioned by Rude Buay. The agent continues:

"I understand you are affiliated with the 'Wanted Marcus Ranks.' Not only that but you were also caught in possession of illegal drugs as well as illegal firearms. Crimes like these could keep you in a Jamaican prison for a serious time. However, You can reduce those times substantially if you choose to cooperate by leading us to Marcus Ranks."

One of the women says,

"We don't know any Marcus Ranks!"

"Yes, you do, Megan Holt."

Says the Commissioner, looking at her straight on. The Commissioner continues after Megan Holt looks away:

"Our records indicate that you provided Officer Bascombe, with a constant supply of Methamphetamine. That drug not only caused the death of his daughter Glenda but also caused the officer to take his own life. That supply was traced to Meth prepared by the Dragons and sold in Jamaica by you, along with Marcus Ranks as the middleman."

"How much time will this deal be knocked off?"

Asks the other woman.

All eyes are now on Rude Buay.

The woman continues,

"Because ..."

"Shut up bitch ..."

Says the pack leader, a midget adorned in a black, gold, and green tam, covering up his dreadlocks hairstyle.

The Commissioner remarks,

"We will be willing to negotiate on your behalf."

"Look for the ship, Marc I. He docks at the pier at night."

The rest of the posse looks at Megan Holt as if she were crazy to rattle on their boss. Once again, the leader of that pack addresses,

"What makes you think these PIGS are going to help you get your time reduced?"

In the interim, the Commissioner calls in the Jamaican Police. They have just arrived on the scene. They quickly take the six members of Marcus Ranks' posse into custody.

33

The agents swarm the dock at Kingston later that night in search of Marcus Ranks. This stakeout results in Marcus Ranks's once again non-show.

The following morning, agent Rude Buay received a text message from Bruce, still stationed in Mexico, stating that the Dragons were meeting in South Beach, Miami. According to the text message, the attendees at that meeting are supposed to be Alberto Gomez, Miles Tate, Grace McCloud, Sammy Chin, and Marcus Ranks. So, the agents later boarded a plane bound for Miami.

IN SOUTH BEACH, MIAMI: On a busy evening, Hip-Hop and Rap music reverberates from sidewalk bars, restaurants, and nightclubs. Some even entertain with House music and R&B from underneath their tents. Hot women, some of them attired in tight jeans, others in miniskirts, and some in cheeky shorts, parade the streets during the early evening hours. The men salivate, casting multiple double-takes.

Drug dealers and buyers conduct business managing to avoid Law Enforcement Officers, using their two-way radio feature on their cell phones to alert each other of danger zones. Street after street is crowded with pedestrians. The vibe is like that of a Memorial Day weekend in South Beach. Buses even avoid making stops along some of those pedestrian-crowded streets. The sidewalks are roped off and barricaded, thus allowing a steady, easy flow of pedestrians.

The nearby restaurants, bars, stores, and clubs are buzzing with activity. Never before has South Beach drawn such a crowd except on a Memorial Day weekend. Miami police walk the beat as a routine. The drug pushers and buyers cleverly escape their surveillance as narcotics trade hands.

Meanwhile, in a South Beach hotel suite, a meeting is held: five members of the Dragon Drug Cartel convene to save the depleting Dragon Drug Cartel. Some of the topics being discussed are:

1) Eliminating Rude Buay and his agents to allow free trade between Mexico and the rest of the world if he does not agree to sign onto the team. 2) Adding new members to the cartel. 3) Sabotaging the efforts of competing cartels in Mexico like the Sinaloa Cartel. Alberto Gomez chairs the meeting. Additionally, he displays pictures on a TV monitor:

1. Several closed and out-of-business Nogales local banks.

2. Mexican drug smugglers were reverting to making pottery and other handcraft products.

3. Border patrols surveying the drug tunnel operations between Mexico and Arizona.

4. The discontinued drug activity at many abandoned warehouses in Mexico.

5. Pictures of Rude Buay's duel with Julio as taken from the woman at the hotel's POV.

6. Pictures of Sal's corpse.

7. Pictures of Victor Crip's corpse.

8. Arizona government workers were sealing up the manholes at the parking meters on Independence Street.

9. Eighteen-wheelers carry drugs across the U.S. border seized by border patrols.

10. The overturned car once occupied by Denise Gomez and Shelly Hall

At this point, Alberto Gomez turns off the monitor. He has seen enough. He is not the only one who is frustrated; the other members of his team are, too.
He articulates,
"Guys, we need to act now to recapture those D.E.A. agents and hold our cartel together. Let's not forget we are The Dragons. We Rule! I will not let another Mexican cartel thrive on what we have put in place for so many years."
"How soon will a new Chemist be reinstated…?"

Asks Miles Tate.
"Same question."
Interrupts Marcus Ranks.
"We have many orders to fill New England and neighboring cities." Says Miles Tate.
"Miami is going to be dry after this weekend. Plus, I can't keep my Cuban customers waiting much longer. Their patience is running thin."
Says Grace McCloud.
Before Sammy Chin can speak, Grace follows up by saying:
"It is the first time we have ever had a supply shortage here in Miami. Pushers have doubled their prices for both Meth and Cocaine. We are in no position to compete with members of neither the Sunshine Cartel nor the Sinaloa … in this marketplace."
"If anyone has an extra supply of Meth, let me know. I will have to smuggle it into China myself. Shipping it would take too long. Chu Ling's clients are waiting. Don't want to piss them off."
Says Sammy Chin,
"I have found a new Chemist; His name is Chico Rubio. The first mixes could be a little harsh until he gets seasoned. We'll have to market our product anyway."
Says Alberto Gomez.
"What about possible recalls?"
Asks Sammy Chin.
"No recalls. I don't like that dirty word."

Says Alberto Gomez.
"That's a hard pill for Jamaicans to swallow."
Says Marcus Ranks.
He is not clearly understood. So, he clarifies.
"Could we buy from another source until Chico Rubio gets a hang of this?"
"I would not endorse buying from the Sunshine or Sinaloa Cartel. They are part of what got us in this glut. If they had not tried sending so many eighteen-wheelers loaded with the product across the U.S. border, we would not be in the glut we are in. Never rush the Americans. They get you all the time. Slow and steady wins the race. This meeting is adjourned. If anyone runs into Rude Buay, I have my gun loaded with bullets initialed RB."
Alberto Gomez exits and boards a waiting limousine. The others board individual taxis as they leave the South Beach hotel.

34

Rude Buay, Chelo, Banks, Heidi Hudson, Mildred Simms, and Richard Baptiste embark upon South Beach with a vengeance. Once again, they pair up for battle with the Dragon Drug Cartel. Agent Rude Buay reunites with Chelo in the first car. Walter Banks and Heidi Hudson are in the second car, and Mildred Simms and Richard Baptiste are in the third.

The agent convoy moves through the streets of South Beach in a surveillance style. With many of the main boulevards blocked off with barricaded sidewalks, the agents take a detour using the open side streets. They pull up at the hotel where the Dragons had just wrapped their meeting. After parking their vehicles, they barge inside armed to the maximum. A hotel employee who is also an inside informant directs them to the executive suite. Rude Buay knocks on the door, but no one answers. Using his gun, he blows out the lock. They enter. A few pens and scrap paper residues are evidence that a meeting was held in session. The delegation, on the other hand, is absent. The agents depart to the outside, re-board their vehicles, and head off through the streets of South Beach. The streets, although only accessible to minimal vehicular traffic, have become more traffic-laden than when the agents arrived on the strip. The gridlock traffic creates a bottleneck for South Beach's exiting traffic. The agents are now caught up in that going-nowhere, very slowly, dilemma.

Rude Buay, as if equipped with the eyes of a hawk, spots the getaway SUV with Miles Tate in the driver's seat. He alerts his other agents via radio and pursues Miles Tate. Rude Buay's vehicle weaves in and out of traffic as he tries to catch up with Tate's. His other agents follow suit in tow.

Meanwhile, inside Tate's SUV, Tate, using his side mirrors, sees the aggressively pursuant. Rude Buay's vehicle has now passed several cars and aligned itself three cars ahead, making it the fourth car behind Tate's. Tate notices not only the pursuing Rude Buay but also the other two cars accompanying Rude Buay. In an instant, that vehicle careens around those three cars using the shoulder of the street and is now precisely behind Tate's SUV.

The pressure is now building on Tate's end as the beach exit is the only exit from Beach Street. The buses transporting passengers to and from South Beach have all clogged up the boulevards. Not only that, he knows that Rude Buay wants his head on a platter for deflecting and being a snitch. He also notices Chelo accompanying the agent and occupying the front seat. Two men who should have been dead are following him along with four other survivors.

Tate reaches for his gun and opts to exit on the street leading towards the beach. The agents are right up behind him, tailgating. Tate's vehicle is slowed by the sand on the beach, but more so, the vehicles of the agents in pursuit. The sedans finally split from the convoy and formed a periphery around the SUV.

Tate jumps out and fires off a few rounds at the agents before making his plunge into the water. Not only do his rounds miss their target, but Rude Buay is also only a few feet away in pursuit. Tate tries to swim away into the deep, but Rude Buay is about to corner him. The agent yells at Tate as he tries to dive:

"Tate, there isn't anywhere to run to. I told you if you ever became a snitch we would go fishing. Even so, you are too big a bait for Jack Fish. Plus, they only thrive in the Caribbean, not in Miami. The sharks would be happy though. They are always drawn to human blood."

Tate tries to get a kick aimed at Rude Buay. He misses. They have now squared off waist-deep in the water. Rude Buay throws a left jab and a right uppercut. Tate is hit by the jab to his face, but as he ducks in, the uppercut escapes him.

Rude Buay throws him a right jab, which lands in his mouth, causing him to spit out blood as a result. Banks, standing on the beach with the other agents, yells:

"Let me shoot the bastard. No need to get saturated with his blood! Nothing but a … traitor!" The water rises as they are drawn in more profound by the tide. Rude Buay pushes Tate under and refuses to let up. Tate begins kicking for his existence. Yet, Rude Buay does not let him up. Tate drinks until he can drink no more. Rude Buay releases him to his death and returns to the beach. Before Tate's body submerges, Chelo fires a round at the ex-agent. It connects to his head. Tate goes under.

As they get ready to re-board, he gets a call from D.E.A. headquarters requesting his presence at the Miami harbor. The call concerns a ship alleged to be loaded with narcotics. Without a chance to change from the wet clothing, Rude Buay and his agents rush to the Miami port, accompanied by sirens and flashing lights.

35

The agents pull up in their BMWs at Miami Harbor. They notice the harbor saturated with multiple ships. Using binoculars, they try to determine the target ships carrying out the narcotics transfer. Rude Buay zooms out and locates their targets. He alerts the other agents. The agents quickly board a speedboat heading in that direction. The speedboat takes off, navigating through the crowded port, leaving an extended trail of white water behind it.

As they are nearing the ship that made the transfer, that ship raises its anchor and takes off. The other boat, named *Marc 1*, is about to do the same. Banks, at the helm of their speedboat, pulls up in front of the *Marc 1's* bow. The man lifting the anchor alerts the rest of the crew. Bullets from Marc 1 begin to rain onto DEA, the agent's speedboat. The agents manage to dodge out of those bullets. Before Richard Baptiste, now in command of the ship, abandons it, he attaches a rope to Marc 1 using a lasso.

Rude Buay and Walter Banks have already jumped aboard the suspected Marc I. Two men aboard the *Marc 1* see the agents approaching and training their weapons on them. Seeing the agent's F & F's weapons, the two men have their backs up against the wall. Another armed man approaches from the hull. Rude Buay yells out:

"D.E.A.! Hands on your heads."

The three men comply with the agent's request.

"Where is Marcus Ranks?"

Asks Rude Buay.

"He is not here."

Says the last man to exit the ship's hull dressed in a dreadlocks hairstyle.

"Where is he?"

Asks Rude Buay.

"No idea."

Says the man.

"You are under arrest for drug smuggling." Says Rude Buay.

Banks, Hudson, and Baptiste put handcuffs on the three men while Rude Buay and Chelo descend inside the hull. Rude Buay and Chelo discover several bags of marijuana, over 500 pounds of methamphetamine, and about 300 kilos of cocaine, in addition to an assortment of weapons and U.S. currency. On the outside, the Marc 1 lifeboat's engine starts up. Helming it is Marcus Ranks, who had previously emerged from under some tarp on the other side of the Marc 1. He is about to make his getaway. Rude Buay sees Ranks inside the hull trying to make his getaway through the porthole. Rude Buay takes off with Chelo. Passing through the deck, Banks joins them. The three agents board the speedboat in pursuit of Marcus Ranks.

Meanwhile, Michael Ortiz is standing on the bridge overlooking the harbor and watching the unfolding events through a pair of binoculars. Rude Buay, Banks, and Chelo continue to pursue Marcus Ranks at full speed.

Ranks see them rapidly approaching and fire off a few quick rounds, tragically catching nothing but air. Banks is at the helm of the speed boat. Chelo is now on the phone with Ortiz, talking about their next plan of attack on the Dragons. Rude Buay gets a good aim at Ranks and blasts him. Marcus Ranks is hit in the chest. He falls over into the lifeboat. His boat continues and crashes into a pillar upholding the bridge. The agents return to the *Marc 1* and wrap up their narcotics seizure. They depart in the speedboat as Miami police, now on the scene, arrest the three drug smugglers and confiscate the seizure of narcotics.

36

The agents pull up in front of the club Dynasty dressed to the nines. Even so, Chelo is the only one who is not part of the group. They pull up outside and enter flashing their badges. Inside the club, it's a party as usual. The agents mingle. The vibe on the inside puts South Beach in the evening, on a whole other level. Go Go Dancers dance from inside huge glass cases. Hot babes saunter throughout the club. Surfer-type males interact with these Hotties. Some are fortunate to get a number. On the other hand, the more passive men wait at the bar to make their approach. The agents survey and have a few drinks.

RICHARD BAPTISTE'S WIFE Christine calls. Richard answers.

"When are you coming home, Richard? I miss you!" He tells her that the Miami situation has become very demanding. He also reminded her that he would be home on time for her birthday in two weeks.

After ending the conversation, Christine looks at the calendar hanging over the fridge, then plops down on the couch and continues playing her game of Solitaire while enjoying a glass of Merlot.

AT THE CLUB, Mildred approaches Richard and signals him to the dance floor. The DJ had just put on a dancehall tune, which the DJ mixed with a Soca beat. Mildred goes wild, putting Richard under severe pressure to keep up with her on the dance floor. She is now center stage with Richard. The other agents cheer them on, as does the heavily gathering party crowd. The band gets ready to set up for their musical performance. Rude Buay signals the time to leave. They head towards the backstage.

Behind the curtain is the new look. Chelo is dressed in a sharp business suit, tailored shirt, and smashing tie. On his feet, he wears the pair of moccasins that Rude Buay repurchased him in Mexico on the day he was captured by Salvador. It is a spit shine. This wardrobe upgrade gives him the look of a Cuban businessman, enhanced with a hat and a cigar. Grace McCloud walks through the back exit door. The femme fatale is carrying a duffel bag in her hand. Back there, Chelo waits for solo but with a certain degree of confidence. McCloud presents the bag to Chelo. He opens it and inspects its contents. He is satisfied. Chelo hands over the attaché case to McCloud. To her, it is the right amount of cash for the 15 pounds of Methamphetamine and the 5 kilos of cocaine. The case is closed quickly, and McCloud walks towards the exit door and into the parking lot. Chelo picks up the bag of narcotics heading towards the stage. Before

McCloud could get to the door, Rude Buay, Walter, Heidi, Mildred, and Richard had her cornered.

"Hold it right there McCloud! D.E.A., nobody moves!"

Chelo stays put to accommodate. The four agents pass him by and hold McCloud at gunpoint. McCloud calls them bluff and heads through the door, quickly dodging rounds of bullets before boarding the waiting limousine.

They pursue and shoot up trying to get away limousine. McCloud, showing resilience, opens the moon roof and fires off several rounds at the agents. The agents run out of bullets in their semi-automatic weapons as a result of the onslaught on the limo. McCloud is hit but continues to shoot back at the agents.

Chelo speedily wheels out an open trunk filled with F & F's from underneath the table. Rude Buay, Walter, Heidi, Mildred, and Richard once again return fire on McCloud and her limo driver, this time from state-of-the-art weapons. The limo gets demolished with McCloud and the chauffeur inside. The agents depart while the patrons rush to the back parking lot.

37

As the agents leave the club, they merge with the boulevard traffic. Rude Buay's phone rings. It's a familiar number, as revealed by his caller ID. On the other end is his boss, Michael Ortiz. Rude Buay, did you get them?" Agent Ortiz asks.

"Yes. I did!"

Says Rude Buay. "Both of them?"

Asks his boss.

"Yep!"

Says Rude Buay,

"McCloud and Chin?"

Asks Ortiz.

"Chin wasn't there."

Says Rude Buay.

"He followed McCloud to make the drop for Chelo and then he went to fill up at the gas station."

"Really? What is he driving?"

Asks Rude Buay.

"A Cadillac Escalade, ivory in color. Do not let him get away, Rude Buay,"

Says Ortiz.

Rude Buay is gamed.

The agents speed up.

Moments later, Rude Buay notices the Escalade speedily moving toward the club. He and his team make a U-Turn and follow that vehicle. As they close in on it, he recognizes Sammy Chin under the driver's seat. The blue lights on his dash begin to flash and revolve. The other agents follow suit as he is now tailgating Chin's vehicle. Chin would not let up. An intense chase ensues. Chin seems to be about to make a getaway on the open roads. He continues to pursue Chin with his agents following in tow. The chase continues through the back streets of South Beach. Rude Buay is now close enough to the Escalade and gets a shot off at Chin. The bullet hits the front left fender of the vehicle. Chin begins to fight back with several rounds. Rude Buay and his agent begin to shoot up the Escalade with an onslaught of bullets. Chin is hit. As a result, the SUV slams into a retaining wall. Rude Buay searches the SUV and discovers at least 50 pounds of Methamphetamine inside a duffel bag.

Rude Buay goes through Chin's wallet and discovers two hotel room keys and a check-in receipt billed to Gomez's credit card.

38

Rude Buay, mindful that Alberto Gomez is still at large where there is smoke. So, he heads for the South Beach Casa Nora Hotel. It isn't long after departing the scene that his phone rings. Once again, it's his boss. "We are down to the last man. They say he's invincible. Whatever you do, I want him alive. This is like your Holy Grail." "Let me call you back," Says Rude Buay.
Rude Buay ponders the statement. In his mind, he knows Alberto Gomez's life has been spared many times at his own hands. He knows what he has lived through at the hands of the most notorious Drug Czar ever to run a cartel, Gomez. Chelo, sitting in the passenger seat, senses Rude Buay's confusion.
Rude Buay calls back Ortiz.
"Sorry, boss, no can do. When I catch Alberto Gomez, I am going to kill him. Whether that pleases you or not, this man has been a menace to society. He has caused many innocent kids to die by his actions. It's like asking me to spare a thousand Osamas. Do you know what we are in for if he continues to breathe any longer?"
On the other end of the phone, Ortiz is not giving up and persists in his demands to Rude Buay. "Just bring

him in, Agent Bascombe." "I am sorry you must come and get him yourself if you want him under those conditions." Rude Buay puts Ortiz on speakerphone. He radios the rest of his agents:

"When we catch up to Albert Gomez, no matter the condition, let me have him. I want to be the one to drill his skull."

Rude Buay hangs up the call with his boss and pulls up outside the hotel. He speaks to the manager sitting behind the desk, a middle-aged woman of Cuban descent. The woman focuses more on Chelo than on Rude Buay. "I am looking for Alberto Gomez," says Rude Buay, disclosing his badge.

"No."

Responds the woman nervously.

"That's okay. There is no need to be afraid of him. Gomez can't harm you."

Says Chelo.

"You all have got to be crazy,"

responds the woman.

"We are not. We need to talk to him,"

Says Rude Buay.

He reaches inside his pocket, pulls out a money clip, and peels off 5 one hundred dollar bills. The woman's eyes light up.

"I'm on the Executive floor on the 23rd floor, but I forgot he has tight security. Do you want your money back?"

"That's okay; keep it, "

says Rude Buay.

He hurriedly leaves his car and picks up his Fast and Furious ammunition; Chelo also arms himself. The other agents are also armed and ready. The MOD is alarmed as Baptiste is stationed in the parking lot, Mildred is in the lobby, Hudson heads for the elevator, and Chelo takes the stairwell. Banks take the stairs to the 23rd floor, covering Rude Buay. Upon arriving, Rude Buay and Banks see the two guards pacing the 23rd floor. Rude Buay pops one, while Banks pops the other.

Rude Buay knocks on the door to Gomez's suite. There is no answer. Although they can hear the TV playing, no one answers the door. Rude Buay kicks in the door. Freebasing utensils and Alberto Gomez's F & F gun are used on the table in the room. Rude Buay grabs the weapon and charges in with both his and Gomez's. Alberto Gomez dashes out of the bathroom wearing a white bathrobe. He launches his gun on the table. Rude Buay shows it to him while balancing his on the other hand.

"Those guards just lost their jobs."

Rude Buay senses that Gomez is trying to make small talk so he can arm himself or buy time. Gomez looks peripherally for a substitute weapon. At this point, even a table knife would do in Gomez's mind. It's just some defense, but there is none.

"I don't think you have the balls to shoot me, Rude Buay."

"How about a fingernail every day for the next ten days?"

Asks Rude Buay.

Banks edges closer.

"Or how about both your eyes right now?"

"FYI, I am here to torture you before the vultures have you for their delight."

Says Rude Buay.

"So, you are into Moses' law."

Banks is animated and ready to end Gomez's life.

" An eye for an eye or a tooth for a tooth? I thought you were all about the Messiah. Who said, Forgive and it shall be forgiven you."

Continues Gomez.

"There is nothing to talk about. Let's shoot the bastard!"

Says Walter Banks,

Rude Buay shoots Gomez in the right leg with his gun and blows it off. The residue of that round leaves a massive hole in the wall.

"I am trying to be like the Messiah. It's a tough job. He walked on water, didn't he? Then, he turned water into wine. He even healed the sick. He also made the lame man walk."

Says Rude Buay.

"Shoot the sucker; don't let him break you down,"

Says Banks.

Rude Buay shoots Gomez in the other leg, this time with the Drug Czars' gun. Gomez is now on the floor, both legs severed from the knees down. He is undergoing tremendous pain.

"Jesus also knelt and prayed, didn't he?"

Says Rude Buay.

Alberto Gomez is groaning and in pain.

Rude Buay looks at Gomez's two jumping legs while the Czar suffers.

"Cuff him, Banks!"

Banks lays his weapon on the table and places handcuffs on the bleeding Alberto Gomez. Rude Buay takes out his cell phone and dials his boss, Ortiz.

"We've got him. He is now yours. FYI, he is going to need a pair of crutches." "Great job! I'll get some to him soon."

Says Ortiz.

Rude Buay and Banks exit the room, team up with the other agents in the parking lot, and drive to D.E.A. Headquarters.

About The AUTHOR

John Alan Andrews hails from the islands of SVG in the Caribbean. He began his acting career in New York. In 1996, he took his craft to Hollywood. He appeared in multiple TV Ad campaigns and films, including John Q, starring Denzel Washington. Andrews later found his niche—writing coupled with filmmaking—and not only starred in but produced and directed some of his work, which won multiple awards in Hollywood.

With over 80 books in his multi-genre catalog, including ***Rude Buay, which he starred in and directed as a proof of Concept - poised for an upcoming production, Andrews is currently drafting The PIPS a Mediterranean Private Investigative*** TV series. He has also co-authored multiple titles, including MACOS II, with his sons, Jonathan Andrews, and ***Jefferri Andrews***.

His latest books, Atomic Steps and Make Every Thought Pay You A Profit, are favorites among business leaders, and his twisted NYC Connivers legal thriller series appeals to both women and men ages 16 -85. The Pips Series (Body in a Suitcase). Also, Samuel A. Andrews—***Legacy*** *(A Biography).* His work can be found at **ALIPNET.COM** or **ALIPNET TV**, his recently launched OTT Streaming Platform.

John Alan Andrews states:
"Some people create, while others compete. Creating is where the rubber meets the road. A dream worth having is one worth fighting for because freedom is not free; it carries a massive price tag."

See Imdb: http://www.imdb.com/title/tt0854677/.

RUDE BUAY SERIES

RUDE BUAY SERIES

RUDE BUAY SERIES

RUDE BUAY SERIES

RUDE BUAY SERIES

RUDE BUAY SERIES

RUDE BUAY SERIES

RUDE BUAY SERIES

RUDE BUAY SERIES

RUDE BUAY SERIES

RUDE BUAY SERIES

RUDE BUAY SERIES

RUDE BUAY SERIES

RUDE BUAY SERIES

RUDE BUAY SERIES

RUDE BUAY SERIES

RUDE BUAY SERIES

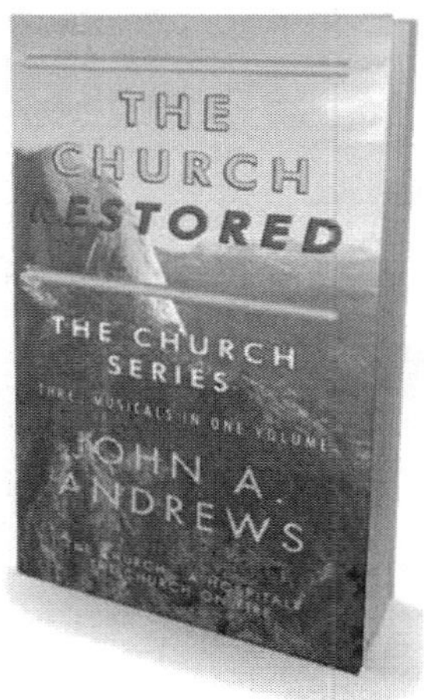

COMING
SOON

RUDE BUAY SERIES

RUDE BUAY SERIES

ALIPNET
ORIGINAL

Made in the USA
Columbia, SC
18 January 2025

62de9aed-1d29-4a3d-8bda-51631b178860R01

king's vow

ELLA KADE

KING'S VOW by Ella Kade

ISBN-13: 978-1-950044-34-4 (Ebook Edition)

Edited by: The Polished Author

Proofreading by: The Polished Author, Amira El Alam

Photographer: Xram Ragde

Cover Model: Bruno

Manufactured in the United States of America.

king's vow

We met in darkness.

Fate brought us back together and almost as quickly ripped us apart.

The world we lived in thrived on greed and deception.

Two dark souls converged and aligned in an eruption of vengeance and hatred.

Death almost ended us, and now nothing could break us. Or so we thought. What will happen when our world tries to tear us apart at every turn?

King's Vow is the intriguing first book in the Guerrera Syndicate series. If you like strong heroines, alpha males, and dark romance, then you'll love Ella Kade's mafia/drug cartel romance.

Buy King's Vow to immerse yourself in the dark world of the Guerrera's today!

CHAPTER ONE

arely

A GRIN TUGGED at my lips as I heard footsteps behind me. I didn't look back, but I heard plenty. Whoever was behind me thought they were light on their feet, but they were wrong. Each time I stopped at a traffic light, he slowed down and hid in the shadows where I couldn't see him unless I was trying to seek him out. No, I was going to let him think he was some 007 bullshit.

Instead of doing what most would do when they thought someone was following them, I slowed my pace. I wanted to get caught and see what would happen. Maybe, however, whoever it was wouldn't work up their nerve, and I'd make it to my destination before they got to me, or maybe just maybe, I'd have a little fun tonight.

I pulled out my phone, looking down at it, acting like I didn't know my surroundings one hundred percent perfectly. It wasn't smart for a woman to be out by herself at night in Stonewall and not have her faculties about her. It was a good thing I wasn't like most women.

The footsteps behind me quickened. It was difficult not to react as excitement built in the pit of my stomach and quickly filled my veins. I was a live wire ready to attack given the opportunity.

The footsteps came closer, and I heard the shift of fabric before I felt the slight bump. Not bad, but not good enough. I might not have noticed if he hadn't been following me for three blocks. Whoever he was, he had picked the wrong mark, and I was ready to show him how wrong he was.

In a blink of an eye, I grabbed the arm as he passed by and pulled it behind his back. He wasn't expecting my move and let out a shocked gasp before he rounded on me with his eyes wide.

I took him in. He was much taller than my five-foot-eight frame. He had to be at least six foot two or three. With his hood up, I couldn't make out much, only that he had a few days' worth of growth on his chiseled jaw and had the softest looking lips I'd ever seen on a man.

Rearing back, I pushed him in the chest with as much force as I could muster. He stumbled back a few steps and held both of his hands up in surrender.

"It's not going to be that easy," I laughed darkly as I stepped into his space. Keeping my hands on his chest, I pushed him into the alleyway in case there was anyone looking. He didn't put up a fight as I backed him up to the brick wall of one of the buildings. "Didn't your mother ever teach you not to steal from women?"

"I think she must have missed that lesson." His voice shocked me. It was deep and soothing, with a full New York accent. "Didn't your mother ever tell you to be scared of strangers in the dark?"

I yanked the hood of his sweatshirt down to get a better look at him. I wanted to see the face of the person who dared to steal from me. It caught me short at how striking he was even in the dim light. Dark, hooded eyes and dark hair cut short on the sides and lighter on the top with some curl.

I pulled out my knife and pressed the blade to his throat. He inhaled deeply but made no move to break away. Why did that turn me on? "She must have forgotten that one before she died giving birth to my brothers."

"What are you planning to do to me?" He said

barely above a whisper. With each word he spoke, his Adam's apple moved against the blade of my knife.

I tilted my head to the side. "I haven't decided yet." If he knew who I was, I was sure he wouldn't have picked me for his mark. "Why should I let you live?"

He let out a little slip of a laugh before my knife nicked his skin, and then he went still. I wasn't sure if he was even still breathing with how rigid his body went.

"You shouldn't underestimate me. I have no qualms about ending you right here, right now. You may think you can overpower me, but you can't, so don't even try. If you do, you might end up with more blood spilled."

One of his hands went for the knife. Again, thinking he was quicker than me and underestimating my speed, I dug the tip of the knife into his neck and watched as a streak of red trailed down and disappeared into his shirt.

"Fuck, lady, you're crazy."

He hadn't seen anything yet.

Leaning up, I licked the line of blood and moaned. The taste of copper and the salt of his skin had me panting. Pushing down the neckline of his shirt, I spied a small drop at his sternum and ran my tongue over the divot.

Dropping my knife, my hands went to the buckle of

his belt and quickly had his belt and his pants undone. Sinking my hand into his briefs, I gripped his cock and squeezed hard. He was so fucking hard for me. My lady boner was just as equally hard for him.

"What are you doing?" He muttered on a groan.

"Taking what I want just as you did to me." Pushing his jeans and underwear down past his ass, I squeezed once more before I let go, then I removed my panties and threw them down next to my knife. "Pick me up," I demanded.

He only hesitated for a moment before his large hands skimmed up my thighs and under my skirt. Gripping my ass, he pulled me in closer and then lifted me up. My legs instantly went around his waist, and my pussy started to grind down on his rigid length.

"Fucking hell, you're so hot and wet."

Violence turned me on. Big time. And so did he, even if he did try to steal from me.

Lining myself up, I sank down on his length, letting the feeling of being full and stretched more than I ever had before wash over me. With a dick this big, he didn't need to steal. Women would throw money at his feet to fuck him. Hell, even to his dick. For a second, I was sad I couldn't see it in the dark alleyway, and I'd never have a chance to marvel at its magnificence.

Unable to hold back any longer, I fucked him.

Taking my pleasure. My fingernails dug into his shoulders as I nipped at his jaw and along his neck. The tips of his fingers dug into the flesh of my ass, and I knew tomorrow there would be bruises. They would be the only evidence of our encounter, and soon they'd fade away.

With each rise up, I slammed down on his length, swirling my hips. I tightened my legs around him, digging the heels of my boots into his ass. I hoped I left my mark on him as well, so he'd remember me after tonight. Hell, I knew he would remember me for the rest of his days. This thief with the magical cock would never look at another mark the same way again.

He started to thrust up from under me, jerking his hips erratically. Pulling back my head, I stared down at him, tempted to bite and suck on his soft lips, but that was far too intimate. No, he would only get my pussy.

His big dark eyes looked up at me with wonder and lust while his brows pulled together.

"Stop thinking so hard. We both want this, and after tonight, we'll never see each other again."

Stilling inside of me, he closed his eyes and let out a deep groan. I could feel the pulse of his cock before he unloaded deep inside of me. If this fucker had an STD, I would hunt him down and murder him.

One hand left my ass, and with one sweep of his

thumb against my clit, I detonated. Stars filled my vision. My walls clamped down hard around his cock, never wanting the pleasure to stop. Burying my face in his neck, I bit down to stifle the scream that was building as wave after wave of ecstasy shook me to my core.

Once I came down, I sat there for a moment with my eyes closed. Damn, that was hot. Tonight would play a starring role in my future fantasies.

I tapped his bicep, and he slowly let me down until my feet were on the ground. I wanted to ask his name, but it was better off I didn't. I'd probably try to track him down if I knew.

Picking up my panties and knife, I shoved them into my purse. I wanted to relish in the feel of his cum sliding down my legs as I finished walking back to my car.

Mr. Thief, with the magnificent cock, stood there watching me. His dick was still hanging out, and even soft and in the dark, it looked spectacular.

Snapping out of his stupor, he chuckled and started to right himself. "I have to say this is a first."

"It's probably best you don't make it a habit until you learn to be quieter on your feet."

"I wasn't talking about that." He shook his head as he took me in. My breasts were still heaving. My heart galloped in my chest as I stood on the other side of the alley watching him. "That too, but I was talking about being accosted by a woman and her having her way with me."

"Well, don't worry. You'll never meet another woman like me," I called as I walked away.

CHAPTER TWO

bash

HEADING out of the science building, I had my eyes on my phone when someone crying out caught my attention. Looking up, I spied two guys from my English class punching and kicking some lanky little dude who didn't have a chance in hell at fighting back.

Not cool.

I'd heard them in class before, and they were straight-up assholes who were always shit-talking and laughing about beating up some guy or fucking some girl. Dropping my bag on the ground, I strode forward with my fist cocked back, ready to rumble.

I clocked the sandy-haired one in the jaw, making him tumble back, and then slammed his head on the hard concert behind him. Next, I grabbed the other by the back of his shirt and threw him off. He didn't even notice his friend had stopped joining him in all the fun they were having. His blue eyes widened as I gripped him by the collar of his shirt, and my fist came down.

Sandy hair was sputtering and trying to get to his feet as I hit his friend again and again. "Wow, man," he coughed and grabbed for my arm. He was easy enough to shake off, landing on his ass. "What the hell, man? We've never done anything to you," he shouted from where he was sprawled out on the ground.

I dropped his friend and rounded on him. "Are you telling me he did something to you?" I pointed to where the guy they were beating up was still laid out on the ground and curled up in a fetal position.

"He looked at my girlfriend," he said petulantly.

"Which girlfriend is that? I hear you constantly talking about fucking different girls all the time in class. Is one more special than the other?" I looked up at the quickly darkening sky and laughed. A storm was rolling in. Soon it would darken the sky to match my mood.

"What the fuck, Darren?" A girl from the crowd shouted. I turned to see a tiny blonde come running toward who I guess was named Darren. She stood in front of him with her eyes narrowed, and then, just as quickly as she came, the blonde reared back her foot and kicked him in the balls before running off with tears threatening to spill down her cheeks.

Darren cradled his balls as he rolled around on the ground, moaning. I turned toward the other guy, and he was out cold—something I hadn't even realized.

Moving to the kid they were beating up, I helped him off the ground and made sure he was steady.

"Thanks. You didn't have to do that," he mumbled from his cracked and swollen mouth.

I didn't, but I wanted to punch someone, and those two assholes were good targets. Plus, they needed to pick on someone their own size.

I looked him up and down. He was short and so damn skinny even that guy's girlfriend could beat him up. "You need to grow a pair before someone else tries to beat you up. At least start hitting the gym and bulking up."

"I…" his mouth hung open as he stared at me.

"I won't be around to save your ass next time." I tapped him with my shoulder and stalked off through the crowd that had gathered. What a bunch of fucking losers.

I made my way through a shortcut that was barely lit by the darkening sky as I headed to my bike. Soon it would be too cold, and I'd have to put her up for the winter and would miss taking her out on the open road during the winter months. The sight of two guys loitering around by my bike in the parking lot had me immediately on edge. No one messed with my bike and lived.

I kept my helmet in my backpack. If they both came at me at the same time, I could swing my backpack and clock one of them with my helmet. It would be unexpected and give me a chance to take the other guy.

"Can I help you?" I asked as I slowly walked up to them and my bike. My eyes scanned them and surveyed my ride to make sure they hadn't done anything to her.

They were both the same height as me and a little less bulky, but I knew they could lay me out if they wanted to. Their dark eyes glinted as an overhead light came on.

"We saw what you did back there," the thinner of the two said. He had on all black with a pair of aviators clipped over the collar of his t-shirt.

"Just doing my civic duty for the day." They didn't know I didn't give one shit about that kid. If they weren't careful, I might take them on as well.

The other cocked a brow as he took a slow drag from his cigarette. "Oh, the little guy was a good cover. I like what you did there. No one would be the wiser that you stole his wallet right after you saved him from getting his ass kicked even more by those two fools."

How the hell did these two see that? I hadn't

noticed them when I was out there, and I noticed everything.

"Don't worry." He took a drag and slowly let it out. "We don't care. In fact, we thought you'd be perfect for helping us out if you want to make some extra money."

I could always use extra money. I was living in a piece of shit apartment that was cold as hell last winter, and school was eating up every penny I had.

"Ah, look at his eyes light up, and he doesn't even know what it is yet," the other one laughed.

"As long as it's not gay porn, I don't care." I sat my backpack down on the ground by my legs and crossed my arms over my chest. "What will I have to do?"

"What's wrong with gay porn?" They both said at the same time.

Were they boyfriends?

"Nothing, but I'm not interested in guys, so there's no way in hell I'm going to be fucking some guy for money."

"I've heard that before and then…" the thinner one shrugged with a smirk.

"I'll never be that desperate. No offense if you two are boyfriends or whatever."

They turned to look at each other and then started to laugh hysterically. I wasn't sure what was so funny, but whatever. Maybe they were just fucking with me and wanted me in on some threesome.

"You just made my day." The one who was smoking on a wheezy laugh. "We're brothers, and before you say anything," he held his hand up. "We don't fuck. There's no incest happening in this family."

Well, that was good to know. I didn't have an innocent mind, but it sure as hell didn't go there.

"Good to know." I lifted a brow at them. "What is your way of making money?"

They looked at each other and had a silent conversation, and then finally nodded. When they turned back to me, they had matching smirks on their faces. It was then I could see the resemblance.

"Meet us tomorrow at four o'clock at the skate park," the skinny one said.

"Do I at least get to know your names before I meet you tomorrow?"

They both shrugged at the same time, one their left shoulder and the other their right. It was weird.

"I'm Alejandro," the skinny one said. "But you can call me Ale."

Throwing down his cigarette and then stepping on it with his heel, the other one smirked. "I'm Armando."

"I'm Bash."

Matching smirks lit up their faces. "We know." I

wanted to ask them how they knew but didn't get the chance before they walked off. I had a feeling those two were trouble, and we were going to have a lot of fun.

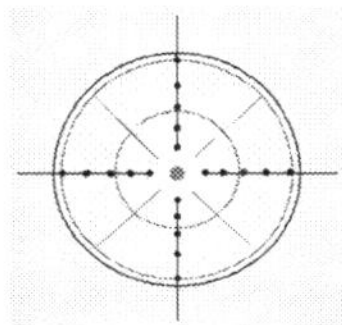

I'd been dragging ass all day. I wasn't sure what it was, but I couldn't sleep last night. It didn't help that I'd run out of coffee and hadn't been to the store yet to buy more. There was no way in hell I was hitting up the local Starbucks on campus and paying five dollars for a fucking coffee. I'd rather be tired than waste my money.

Parking my bike in the parking lot, I scanned for the brothers but didn't see them. If they stood me up, I would kill them the next time I saw them.

Getting off my bike, I placed my helmet on the seat and walked out into the open park. My hands clenched at my sides as I looked around. There were plenty of people here on their skateboards, but not the brothers. Just as I was about to turn around and head back to my bike, I spotted them. There were far off to the side with their backs turned, making it hard to recognize them. One of them shook hands with someone, and then the other person walked off, shoving his hands in his pockets.

Moving around the outside of the crowd, I made my way toward the brothers but slowed my pace and observed as someone else stepped up to them. They said a few words. Alejandro slipped his hand into the pocket of his jeans and then shook hands with the guy before the interaction was over. I had a pretty good idea of what was going on here.

As if they could hear me walking, they turned as one and landed their dark eyes on me. I wasn't sure how they heard me. I was stealthy, and no one ever heard me as I approached them—no one except for that smoke show that took me by surprise in the alley. Damn, that was hot. What I wouldn't give to see her in a dark alley and have her push me up against the rough brick to have her way with me again.

There was nothing sexier than a woman who knew what she wanted.

I dug the blunt tips of my fingernails into the palm of my hand as I tried to ward myself from thoughts of that night. I didn't want to roll up on these guys with a hard-on trying to bust through my zipper. Taking a deep breath, I focused my mind on the task at hand: these two dudes and how I could make my money so I wasn't scraping by for the next couple of years.

"We weren't sure if you were going to make it," Armando said, his eyes lit up with mischief.

Was this a test? I crossed my arms over my chest as I locked down my face. I knew they wouldn't be able to read anything on my face as I spoke. They didn't need to know how desperate I was to get out of my circumstances. "Like I said before, I'm pretty much down for anything, so hit me with what you've got."

"We don't trust easily, but we saw something in you that makes us think you'll be good for the job."

I had no idea what they possibly could have seen that would make them think they could trust me. We met twenty-four hours ago, and I sure as shit didn't trust them.

"There's been an uptick in sales here at the skate park, and we're normally at school. We need someone who can take this spot." Alejandro said so matter-of-factly like they weren't selling drugs to the skaters here.

I turned to look at the crowd of people enjoying the sun and skating. It wouldn't last. Once it got cold in a couple of months, they'd be inside, and I'd be without money again.

"Starting off, we'll pay you a thousand a week. If you move more product than we think you will, we'll give you a bump." Armando shrugged like a thousand dollars was chump change to him, and it probably was.

I took them in again. I didn't know shit about designer clothes or brands, but everything they had on looked expensive. Their tennis shoes were at least a couple of hundred bucks. They could definitely afford a thousand a week, if not more.

"And what happens if I get caught?"

Alejandro's eyes narrowed into slits. "Then you don't know us."

"Never even heard of us," Armando supplied.

Got it. I was on my own.

"When do you want me to start?"

Armando's brows rose. "Have you ever sold blow before?"

"Can't say that I have, but I'm not going to try to sell it. They'll come to me if they want it."

"Exactly," they said at the same time, with identical smiles. "I think you'll do just fine. Make sure to bring a skateboard so that you look like you're part of the crowd."

I looked them up and down. They so didn't look like the skaters here. I didn't have the baggy clothes they wore, nor did I have a skateboard. Was this a test? I'd steal one of these punks' boards if I had to.

Armando looked behind me and chuckled. "We'll have a board waiting for you when you get out of class tomorrow." He handed me a piece of paper. "Once the park clears out tomorrow, meet us at this address to give us the money, and we'll give you more product."

Sounded easy. Too easy.

If this was a setup, I'd kill them when I had a chance.

Alejandro patted me on the shoulder. "Don't worry. We won't fuck you over unless you fuck us over."

I wanted to ask why me, but I didn't really care. I'd be their best seller for as long as I lasted. By this time next week, I'd be living a whole different life.

CHAPTER THREE

arely

1 Month Later

A SOFT KNOCK at my door has me looking up from my computer screen. Looking across the room, I noticed the time. It was almost midnight. I stretched my arms over my head as I called out. "Come in."

Ale and Army stepped into my office. They were laughing like they always did when they were together. They had at least a thousand inside jokes that only they understood.

"Jefa," they said at the same time.

I nodded to them and waited until they sat across from me. "Boys, how are things?"

"Good," Ale answered.

Army looked to his twin and rolled his eyes. "Better than ever with the new guy."

"That's what I like to hear. Where are you going to put him once it's winter?"

"We're not sure yet. Maybe at school," Army answered.

"When you figure it out, let me know. Not that I don't enjoy you two coming to visit me, but it's late, and I want to get home. What did you come to speak to me about?"

Army pulled out a cigarette but quickly put it away. He knew I didn't allow smoking in my office, and he also knew I didn't like his smoking. Our father had been dying of lung cancer when he met his end, and I didn't want the same fate for my baby brother.

"Why don't we walk you out and tell you what we're thinking?" Ale stood and headed for the door.

"I like that idea." I closed my laptop and put it inside my messenger bag, along with a few other papers I would need tomorrow. "Are you both coming home, or are you staying at the dorm tonight?" The night was still young for them. As much as I didn't want to think about it, my brothers were attractive and young. The fact that they were here instead of off fucking someone said they were serious about whatever it was that brought them to me.

Army held his arm out for me to take as we walked to the door. "Where's Santi?"

"He's taking care of a matter."

"He should be here with you when you're out this late at night," Army tried to argue.

I couldn't help but laugh. These boys thought I was helpless. If only they'd witnessed the attempted mugging a month ago, they wouldn't think I was so weak.

"It's his job to protect you," Ale argued.

"And what are you doing now? Are you going to let something happen to me?"

"Of course not, but what would you have done if we weren't here?"

"I would have walked out by myself like the capable woman I am. If I thought I was in any danger, I wouldn't have sent Santiago off." I gave Army's arm a little squeeze, letting him know I appreciated his concern, but none was needed. "You're wearing on my patience. Now tell me what brought you here."

Ale turned and stopped in the narrow hall. He leaned casually against the wall. "The new guy, Bash, we want to submit him for the Scorpio Society."

That brought me up short. The society wasn't easy to get into. You had to pass a test, and each test was different. It would test you in ways you never thought possible, and if you passed, you were part of a secret society that would ensure your place in the world. My father was the first in our family to be inducted. Every member of our family was a part of it, and each year a member could submit someone they thought would be valuable to the society.

I pushed Ale to keep moving. "You think he'll pass?"

"We wouldn't suggest him otherwise," Army answered for his brother.

"If he passes, he can't be a street corner dealer, you know?"

"We know," they said in unison.

"I want to meet him first. Let me get a read on him, and then if he passes the test, we'll discuss where he'll be the most useful. If the test doesn't work out, will he be missed?"

There was always the possibility you might not live through the test. Of course, he wouldn't know that. Not until it was too late.

"When we first met Bash, he was living in a shit hole apartment, but he's since moved into a nicer place. He never talks about family or friends. He's got no one."

I wanted to stop walking, but my need to get home overrode the urge. "Do you talk to him about your family?"

I could feel Army's penetrating gaze on me. He was five inches taller than me, and I hadn't worn heels today. Still, I didn't look up. "We're not stupid, jefa. He only knows about us and only surface-level shit."

"Good. Bring him by the house tomorrow afternoon." We stepped out of the hall and into the back portion of the church. Taking a moment, we each did the sign of the cross before leaving out the back way that only we used.

Silently, we walked to my car. Ale opened the door for me and waited. Leaning up, I kissed Army's cheek and then moved to Ale. I gave him a kiss too before I got inside my car and turned it on. "Go enjoy the rest of your night."

Ale leaned inside and smirked. "You should have more fun in your life, Arely."

"That's not easy to do when you're running the biggest syndicate on the eastern seaboard." Who had time for fun when there was money to be made and hundreds of people to watch over?

"Still, you should find someone who makes it worth the time away from ruling the world."

Oh, to be so young and naïve. If only it was that easy.

I blew them a kiss. "I'll see you tomorrow."

They both saluted me and walked off into the shadows before I drove off.

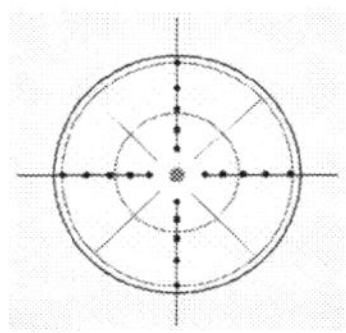

I WAS FINISHING up my late lunch when my phone pinged with an alert, letting me know Alejandro and Armando were here with their guest.

Ale was the first in the kitchen. He greeted me with a kiss on the cheek and then went to the fridge for something to eat. It was almost impossible to keep the fridge stocked with five men living in the house. Luckily for me, they didn't like most of the food I ate, so they left it alone. Santi, on the other hand, was constantly complaining about how someone had eaten something of his.

Army was laughing when he stepped into the kitchen. There was a deep, sexy chuckle that followed that I knew didn't belong to my brother, and it had me curious about their new friend. I wasn't prepared for who walked in with Army. Even though it had been dark, I would have been able to identify the man who tried to mug me anywhere. Immediately, I was on edge. Was he here to fuck with us? What were the odds he'd try to steal my purse, and then my brothers would find him?

"Jefa, this is Bash. He's the one we've been telling you about," Army introduced him.

Maybe I should have asked to see a picture of him before they brought him, but never in my wildest dreams did I think it would be *him.*

Bash stopped dead in his tracks as he took me in. Yeah, he remembered me too. It was an encounter I would never forget, and I bet he wouldn't either.

I stood from my seat at the table and moved to stand in front of it. I squared my shoulders as I took him in. He had on all black, and his hair had grown out a little more on top. The sides were cropped close and a dark brown, while the top was turning shaggy and a light to medium brown. His light brown eyes were laser-focused on me. Damn, they were a gorgeous color. They drew me in without me wanting them to. The skateboard he was holding in his left hand dropped to the floor, snapping me out of my perusal.

"What's your full name?" I demanded. I was going to have Santi do a background check on him immediately.

"Sebastian King," he answered without hesitation. The deep timbre of his voice sent a tingle down my spine. Why was he having this effect on me?

"Leave me alone with him," I ordered.

Ale and Army didn't hesitate to do what I asked of them. Ale looked back at me with his brows pulled together before they disappeared out of the kitchen, leaving Sebastian and me alone.

Sitting on the edge of the table, I crossed my arms over my chest. It didn't escape my notice how Sebastian's nostrils flared as his eyes were drawn to my full breasts that were pushed up with the movement. "Did you know who I was when you tried to rob me?"

"I don't know who you are now except Alejandro and Armando's sister. Did you send them for me? Have they been playing me?"

I threw my head back and laughed. "They have no idea we've met before today."

A sexy smirk spread across his chiseled face. "Are you going to tell them?"

"I don't share who I fuck with my brothers. If you want to inform them, go right on ahead." He'd be lucky they didn't kick his ass when they found out. "My brothers say you're good. Are you done trying to steal from poor defenseless ladies?"

Sebastian moved further into the kitchen, leaving

only a few feet of space between us. "I would say you were far from defenseless."

True, but he didn't know that when he tried to rip me off.

Pushing away from the table, I walked toward Sebastian. There may have been a little extra sway in my step. I couldn't help it. There was something about him that called to me. If my brothers weren't waiting for us, I'd climb him like I did in the alleyway and have my way with him. Running the tip of my black fingernail along his jaw, I put on my best don't fuck with me smile. "If you're going to work for us, there are some ground rules, and the first one is you don't steal from women."

"Is this because I tried with you?"

Stopping the perusal of his face, I dug my fingernail into the cleft of his chin. "Unless you're given orders, leave women alone. It's plain and simple. I don't care who you go after as long as they're male and not in my family."

Dipping his head down, making my nail dig further into his chin, Sebastian smiled like he wasn't phased in the least. "I knew you were one badass motherfucker that night, but I had no idea just how much." His left hand ran up from my hip to my ribs and then rubbed his thumb over the swell of my breast. This boy was cocky, and if he had been any other man, I would have chopped off his hand for daring to touch me without permission. "You run all of this?"

My back stiffened. "I do. Do you have a problem with a woman in charge?"

"Oh, mami, you should know by my performance the other night I have zero problems with a woman taking charge. In fact, I wouldn't mind running into you again. Maybe we can replay our night in the alley."

"Do you fuck many people in alleys?" I snapped. I went the next day to get tested, which, luckily for him, came back negative.

His thumb brushed over my oversensitive nipple as he smirked down at me. "I can say you're my one and only. How about you? Do you regularly fuck men who try to attack you?"

"I can say you're my first as well." I pulled out of his hold and pushed by him. "We should find Ale and Army before they wonder if I've killed you and fed you to the pigs."

"Do you really have pigs here?"

Looking over my shoulder, I looked him up and down, more than liking what I saw. He moved like a jungle cat and had the aura of a man in charge. Even with that presence about him, I somehow knew he wouldn't fuck us over. "I wouldn't do anything to find out."

We found Army and Ale outside arguing by the pool. The second they saw me, they froze and waited for a sign on whether I thought Sebastian would be a good fit for the society. I didn't know anything about Sebastian aside from what they'd told me, and while I'd hate it if, by some chance, he didn't pass, I thought he'd make an excellent addition to the society.

I gave them a nod, showing my stance on the matter—one Sebastian didn't have any knowledge of.

Santi appeared in the doorway with Pablo next to him. From the firm set to their mouths, I knew whatever they had to say wasn't going to be good.

"Hermana, we've got a problem," Santi grumbled, his eyes darting toward Sebastian. He wasn't sure whether to say more in present company.

"We've got a problem with one of the trucks," Pablo added.

My job was never done.

"It was nice to meet you finally, Sebastian."

"Call me Bash," he offered. I liked calling him by his full first name when everyone else didn't.

My gaze went to my brothers, who were back to arguing. "I expect to see you at Sunday dinner."

"Of course." They moved in sync toward me and kissed me on my cheeks. "Sunday."

They motioned for Sebastian to follow after them.

Being his own man, Sebastian took my hand in his and brushed his lips against the skin below my knuckles, sending a jolt of electricity straight to my clit. He looked up at me with his long eyelashes fanning out over his cheeks, and those light brown eyes told me he knew exactly what his touch was doing to me. "I hope to see you again soon."

I wouldn't mind seeing him either, but I didn't utter those words aloud. Instead, I gave him a tight-lipped smile before I took my hand back. Then I sauntered into the house, following behind Santi and Pablo, readying myself to put out another fire.

CHAPTER FOUR

bash

FOR THE LAST WEEK, I couldn't get her out of my head. She was in my every thought, and I didn't even know her damn name. It was a slow day at the skate park since it was getting colder, so I decided today would be perfect for dropping by to see her.

Twenty minutes later, I pulled up on my bike to the gates that surrounded the house. A big burly guy stepped out of the shadows before I had a chance to even hit the intercom.

"Do you have an appointment?" He asked in a heavy Spanish accent.

I was sure he knew I didn't. He probably knew of every appointment that occurred.

"I don't, but I want to see the boss. Tell her Ba…

Sebastian is here to see her." Once she knew I was here, she'd let me through.

The big guy took two steps back, hit a button on the earpiece I now saw he was wearing, and spoke quietly. This was some next-level shit here. My eyes darted around to what I could see with the ten-foot-high stone security wall. There were cameras and bound to be more security guards on the premises. It wasn't until then that I grasped the full extent of who she, Alejandro, and Armando were. They weren't a small-time operation. They were the top dogs, and somehow, they saw something in me and brought me in.

Two seconds later, he stepped back up to me and my bike. His brows were pulled tight, and he looked pissed. I had a feeling he didn't like my unannounced arrival.

I'd barely pulled up to the house before a man who had to be Ale and Army's brother came out. He was tall with dark hair and the same dark eyes they all shared. He looked like one I saw the other day when I was here. If I thought the security guard was unhappy to see me, this guy was pissed. His steps were fast as he rounded up on me and pulled a gun to hold to my temple out of nowhere.

"What gave you the dumb fucking idea you could just show up here out of the blue?" He growled out.

"Santi," she said in a bored tone. "Leave him be. He doesn't know the rules."

"Well, maybe someone needs to teach him." A nasty smirk grew on his face. "I'll happily take him out back and make sure he knows good and well what we expect out of this little bitch boy."

Bitch boy?

I reared up on him, using the two inches of height I had over him to look down at this asshole. "You might want to think twice about calling me a little bitch boy."

"Let me shoot him, A. He's a dime a dozen."

"He's already been tapped to take the test." Her voice grew closer until she had her hand on his shoulder and pushed him away. I got my first look at her in the sunlight. The sun glinted off her black hair, almost making it look dark blue. Her big brown eyes narrowed as she looked at her brother. Her plush lips were ruby red. What I wouldn't give to have them around my cock, leaving red streaks that I knew I wouldn't want to wash off for days. "Leave him. He'll either be in soon or no more."

What the hell did that mean? What test? No one told me about a test. If I didn't pass, I wouldn't work for them any longer?

This Santi fellow looked me up and down, and he found me wanting. He thought I was useless, and I didn't blame him. I was tricked out to look like a loser stoner skater boy. Little did he know I was far from the boy I looked *and* I'd fucked his sister in a seedy alleyway.

Or maybe he did know, and that's why he hated me.

"Come," she gripped me by the wrist and started to pull me away from her brother. I followed and looked over my shoulder at him with a big shit-eating grin before I mouthed, fuck you. "Stop antagonizing him. He will shoot you and won't think twice about it."

How the hell did she know what I was doing? Probably the same way she knew I was behind her the night I tried for her purse.

My eyes were trained on her tight as fuck ass encased in a pair of those tight legging, yoga pant things that had my mouth watering. "So, I guess you don't get many unexpected visitors here."

"Unexpected visitors don't get warm greetings. Ever. Normally they end up dead." She said it so matter-of-factly that I was shocked she was admitting to killing people.

"What's your name?" I needed a name to put with that ass and gorgeous face.

"Is that what you came here to ask?" She looked over her shoulder at me, her red lips curled up at the ends.

"Is there something wrong with knowing your name? Is it a secret, and if I learn it, I'll have to be killed?"

She rolled her eyes and then turned back around, pulling me further into the house. There was a loud slam and then the sound of glass breaking. I heard her sigh before she spoke. "You shouldn't have antagonized him. If you live, it's going to take forever for him to like you."

What was this talk about me dying?

Instead of asking that important question, another one came out. "Does that mean you like me?"

"If I didn't like you, you'd be splattered out on the driveway right now. Like I said, we don't take kindly to unanticipated guests."

Good to know. I guess I wouldn't be dropping by unannounced anymore. Not if I wanted to keep my head.

She pulled me into a sleek office done in all black leather with gold accents and dropped my wrist. She moved to sit on the edge of her desk and lifted a brow. "Why are you here, Sebastian?"

Did I tell her the truth?

Moving until there were only inches between us, I lifted a strand of her black hair and wrapped it around my finger. "I can't stop thinking about that night in the alley. Tell me you're the same."

"You came here to get your ego stroked?" She threw her head back and cackled. "This is the wrong place for that."

So, I was seeing.

I looked at the pristine desk she was sitting on and pushed forward until the tent in my pants pressed to her front. "Have you ever fucked anyone on this desk?"

Tilting back her head, her dark eyes turned black as she licked her ruby red lips. "Ah, now I see why you really came. You want a taste of what you had back in the alley. Haven't you ever heard it's not smart to mix business with pleasure?"

"That's for people who are afraid of what they're feeling. We aren't those people." I cupped the side of her neck and looked down to find her chest was rising rapidly. "Do I scare you?"

"Not in the least." She tried to shake her head, but my hold was unrelenting. "If anyone should be afraid here, it's you."

"Tell me your name," I demanded.

"And if I do, what do I get?" She widened her legs,

giving me the perfect opportunity to step between them.

"Anything you want." My fingers dipped into the yoga pants to find her bare wet heat greeting me. "I need a name to moan when I come. Don't deny me." Gripping the sides of her pants, I pulled them down her toned legs and threw them across the room.

Dropping to my knees, I came face to face with her sweet pussy. It was already glistening and smelled so damn divine. Leaning forward, I swiped my tongue through her folds and moaned. "Tell me your name."

Her fingers tangled in my hair and pushed my head back down, not answering me. Giving her what she wanted, I feasted on her cunt. I sucked on her lips, fucked her with my tongue and fingers until she was a quivering mess. All the while, my dick was hard as stone in my pants, begging for release.

Gripping her by the hips, I angled her, laving her with my tongue in slow strokes, swirling the tip of my tongue around her hood and sucking on her swollen clit. When she was close to the edge, I pulled back and stared up at her.

"What are you doing?" She tried to push her pussy into my face, but I had a firm grip on her hips. I wasn't giving her what she wanted until I got what I came for. When she figured out I wasn't going to continue to fuck her with my tongue, she huffed and ran her hand down her stomach and over her slick center.

Grabbing her hand in mine, I shook my head. "I'm not letting you come until you tell me your name."

"You know I could just kill you for holding back on me," she growled like a kitten.

"But you won't because you like the way I fuck you, and this is only the appetizer."

She looked up at the ceiling, her chest heaving, and muttered a few words in Spanish. I had no idea what they were since I didn't speak Spanish, but I was seeing it might come in useful with this family. She blew out a loud breath through her nose and looked back down at me. "Don't make me regret this."

I waited on bated breath. What if she had a horrible name she was embarrassed about? I'd have to pretend it was a great name and then eat the fuck out of her.

"Arely," she huffed.

It wasn't a name I'd heard before, but damn, did it suit her. It was as unique as the woman with her legs spread for me.

Slipping my tongue into her slick heat, I fucked her as I rubbed my thumb in slow circles on her clit. "You taste fucking amazing, Arely," I moaned against her core and felt her shiver.

Her small hands pressed into the back of my head, letting me know she wanted more. Coating my finger with her juices, I pushed through the tight ring of her asshole until she relaxed and let me in. I couldn't wait to stick my dick where my fingers were, but that would have to wait. First, I needed inside her pussy, and then I'd take her ass.

One of her hands moved to my shoulder, where she dug her fingernails into my flesh. Her hips rocked up, chasing her release as she moaned and writhed underneath me. Damn, she was so fucking hot. I lapped at her, and when I felt her walls start to quake around my fingers, I took her bud into my mouth, sucking hard.

Arely let out a shout that rang through the room as she clenched her legs around my head and fell apart. I kept licking as I watched her back arch as another wave of pleasure shot through her. When I finally dragged every ounce of ecstasy out of her, I stood and licked my lips.

"You're astounding when you come," I told her as I pressed the heel of my hand against my raging hard-on.

Arely's eyes fluttered open, and she smiled at me. It was almost innocent, not her usual smirk or one that held malice in it.

"I want to roll you over and fuck you from behind."

"What are you waiting for? Stick that big cock of yours in me and show me what I've been missing."

She didn't have to tell me twice. I had all of my clothes off faster than she could turn over.

I slid inside with no resistance. She was so hot, tight, and slick. After listening to Arely moan for the last ten minutes, and how fucking perfect she felt, I wasn't sure how long I'd last.

She reared back and ground herself on my cock. "Don't go easy on me."

Pulling back until only my tip was inside, I slammed back inside. I fucked her hard, loving the sounds coming out of her mouth and the way she asked for more. With each hard thrust, she ground back on me, taking me even deeper. The sounds of our hips slapping together was so fucking hot.

"I need you to come," I said hoarsely. I was so damn close, but I needed to feel her walls milk my cock before I let go.

"I'm close," she panted. "I n—"

Before she could say anything, I snaked my right hand around her side and started to rub fast circles over her clit. Arely bucked up into me as her walls started to squeeze my cock like a vice. If I wasn't before, I was now utterly addicted to her pussy.

Slamming into her one last time, I gripped her hair and pulled her back to my front as I unloaded into her. I bit down on her shoulder and moaned her name.

Picking her up, I carried Arely over to the leather couch that sat in front of a row of windows. Her office looked out onto a lake with bright green grass leading down to the bank, even as the leaves were starting to change.

Sitting down, I placed her in my lap and stared out into the expanse of her estate while I ran my hands over her bare legs and ass. We were quiet for a long time. I had no idea what she was thinking, but I was thinking about how I'd put up with her brother threatening to kill me if I got to fuck her like this.

After a few minutes, I felt a warm liquid run down my leg and onto the couch. I swiped to see what the hell it could have been, only for the substance to come back white. It was then I remembered I hadn't fucked her with a condom.

I shifted to wrap my arms around her and cleared my throat. "Not to kill the afterglow of the moment, but we didn't use protection."

Pushing up, Arely stood and tapped my cheek. "You don't have anything to worry about. My father had me sterilized when I was fourteen, afraid that I'd be raped and get pregnant." Without another word, she turned and moved toward a door on the left of the room and slipped inside.

I blinked, shocked, wanting to pull her back against me.

What kind of world had I condemned myself to?

CHAPTER FIVE

arely

THERE WAS a soft tap on my door before Santi walked inside my sanctuary. He took one look at me and halted in his steps.

"Where the fuck is Pablo?" I growled out as I looked at the spreadsheet. The numbers were chaos, and I had no idea what was wrong with them. That's why I had Pablo. He was my left-hand man. He handled the numbers, but he'd been MIA all fucking day. Santi was my right-hand man. He was my bodyguard and my best friend.

"He's doing work for the society today. I thought he told you." He eyed me up and down before he sat across from me.

"*He* didn't tell me shit, and I'm sitting here looking

at this fucking spreadsheet, *his* spreadsheet, and can't make any sense of it. Something's off, but I don't know what."

This was what I got for not handling it myself and doing it the way I wanted, but there was only so much time in the day, and I couldn't do everything.

Santi got up and came around my desk to look at the spreadsheet and then threw his hands up in the air. "I have no fucking clue what I'm looking at. It gives me a headache just trying to figure it out."

I felt the same way.

Closing my laptop, I swiveled my chair to look at my best friend. "Do you know when Ale and Army's friend has his test?"

He cocked his head and then shook it. "You know I don't. Why the interest?"

"He's making us money, and if he ends up dead, we'll have to find someone to replace him. There's only so much the twins can do while actually attending college."

Santi rolled his eyes and moved to sit back in the seat he'd vacated. "Yes, they might have to stop partying and fucking all the time."

There was a bite in Santi's words that had me wondering if he was jealous of them. We never had the chance to go to college. Instead, we were thrust headfirst into our roles when our father died, and before that, we did whatever our father instructed us to do.

"Don't look at me like that. I don't give a shit what they do, but you baby them too much. Hell, they probably don't even do their own homework and pay some chick or some nerd so they can make good grades."

Santi was probably right. If the twins could find a way out of doing their work, they would. It was safe to assume they hadn't done their own homework in years.

Leaning forward with his elbows on his knees, Santi raised one lone brow. "Are you ready to get out of here? I have plans for tonight that I'd rather not have to cancel."

Letting out a frustrated sigh, I opened my laptop back up. "You go on ahead. I have some more work I need to do, but I'd hate for you to miss out on your date."

"It's not a date," he shot back so fast I knew it was exactly that.

"You know you're free to have a love life. Don't let me or work stop you."

"The same thing goes for you. All you do is work.

You're either here or at the house with only family around. You should get out and do something with Bree or go to a book club or something."

I threw my head back and laughed. "Oh my god, can you imagine me at a book club? First, I don't want to read their boring-ass books, and second… just no. Eventually, I'll find my thing, and until then, I'm happy with you by my side."

"Now you're making me feel bad for leaving you here. Do you want me to send one of the guards here to watch over you and escort you to your car?"

"I'm perfectly capable on my own. No one knows about this place, and if they try to take me on the road, I'll sideswipe them."

"Damn, sis, you're hardcore," he laughed, but he knew it was true.

Dismissing him with a shoo of my hand, I settled into my chair, preparing for a long night. "Go and have fun for me."

He stood and came around to kiss me on the cheek. "Text me when you're leaving and when you get home, so I know you're good."

"I will. Now get out of here."

I watched as he left and got back to work. It was two hours later when I was finally done and ready to go home. My eyes were bleary from looking at my computer screen for so long as I texted Santi that I was leaving and slipped out into the cool night. Pulling my hood over my head, I hunkered down in my jacket as the cold air hit my skin. The heel of my boot got stuck in a crack of one of the cobblestones, irritating the fuck out of me. I bent down to dislodge my heel when I heard someone coming up behind me.

I whirled around to see Sebastian coming at me with a knife in his hand.

"What the fuck?" I gasped as I fell on my ass and started to rip off my boot.

The second Sebastian saw me, he ran to my side, and bent down to help.

I pushed him away and stood with only one boot on. "What are you doing here?"

"Some test. What are you doing here?" He looked around the area as if he was looking for someone else.

"It doesn't matter why I'm here. What's your test?" I hissed as I took an uneven step back.

"There was supposed to be someone coming out of the church with a hood on. When I saw the person, I was supposed to kill whoever it was. That's some fucked up test. Did you do this?"

"I didn't have to kill anyone, but yes, I took the

test." I looked over my shoulder at the church, knowing I was the only person here, and I was most likely the target since I always put my hood up when I wore my coat. "I think you were sent to kill me."

Sebastian's knife fell to the ground, and a second later, a shot rang out.

CHAPTER SIX

bash

THROWING MYSELF OVER ARELY, I tried to look over my shoulder to see where the threat was but couldn't see anything. This damn church's security was shit. There was one lone light at the side exit Arely came out of. Whoever sent me to kill her knew I wouldn't be seen, and neither would they.

My arms tightened around her thin frame and hugged her to me even more. Leaning in, I spoke so only she could hear me. "Are you okay?" I waited for a long moment, and when Arely didn't answer, I knew something was wrong. She couldn't be in shock. Hell, the woman attacked me when I tried to rob her. She was calm when I told her I was sent to kill someone.

Her.

Pulling back, I laid her on the ground and turned her over. There was a big red spot that was growing by the second, sweeping through the white material on her abdomen. Her usually sparkling eyes were closed, and her body was lifeless on the cold, wet ground.

"Arely," I rushed out as I put one hand over the blood and pressed down. Using my other hand, I placed two fingers at the pulse point on her neck and prayed to a God I didn't believe in for her to be alive. She had a pulse, but it was weak.

What the fuck do I do now?

Her warm blood coated my hand as I tried to stop the bleeding, snapping me out of my freak out. I needed to call an ambulance before whoever ordered this hit was successful and then killed me as well.

Pulling out my phone with a shaking hand, I unlocked it and quickly dialed 911.

"911, what's your emergency?" A male voice answered.

"My…" Fuck, what was Arely to me? I couldn't say boss, and she wasn't my friend. There was no category for us. "My girlfriend's been shot. We're at a church." For a brief second, my mind seized as I tried to remember the address that had been in the envelope I'd received only two hours ago. It was amazing how much your life could change in such a short period of time.

I rattled off the address and hung up. Sitting down on the ground, I ripped my off hoodie, pulled Arely into my arms, and pressed the sweatshirt to her wound, all the while trying to keep an eye on our dark surroundings. What if whoever shot her was still out there?

As I put more pressure on the wound, she moaned in pain. Even though the sound was agonizing to hear, I was just happy to know she was still alive.

"Arely, stay with me. I called an ambulance, and it should be here soon. Don't give up on me," I demanded.

Even in the dark, I could see she was pale, probably from all the blood loss. Her big brown eyes fluttered open, and I swear my heart nearly stopped as I watched a lone tear streak down her cheek.

"It's going to be okay." I tried to reassure her. "Help will be here any second."

I think she tried to nod her head, but she wasn't quite successful. Instead, it only listed over to the side until her face was flush with my naked chest.

"Seb…" her words stopped as her eyes slowly started to close once more.

"No, no, no." I shook her in my arms until, with heavy lids, she eventually opened her eyes enough to look at me. "You are not dying on me. This is not how our story is going to end."

Her mouth opened and closed a few times before she managed to get out one word. "Danger."

My gaze tracked up to scan our surrounding area. "I know. I'm keeping a lookout." There was a noise to our right, but it was so dark I couldn't see anything. Arely's tiny, cold fingertips skated along my neck, making me look down.

"Don't let them get me," she said shakily.

"I promise you I will never let anything happen to you. Not now. Not ever," I vowed. I'd never meant anything more in my life. I knew from that moment on I would give my life for Arely without thinking twice about it.

In the distance, the sound of sirens started to fill the otherwise quiet night. I crushed Arely to me, only for her body to feel lifeless in my arms.

"Arely," I shook her, watching as her arm fell to the side and her hand slapped the ground. Laying her back on the ground, I tried to feel for her pulse, only for nothing to be there.

My heart skipped a beat as I moved my fingers around, desperate to be wrong.

I had no idea what I was doing as I placed my

hands over her chest and started to pump. I wasn't sure if I was even doing it right. My only knowledge was from movies and television shows. Dipping down, I blew two puffs of air into her mouth and started to go back to pumping her chest when I was gripped by the shoulder.

The night had gone deathly silent once I started my attempt at CPR, my heavy breaths the only sound as I tried to bring Arely back. I hadn't heard the ambulance pull up or anyone get out. My sole concentration was on the beautiful but lifeless woman laid out in front of me.

"We'll take it from here, sir," one of the EMTs said. I had no idea which one. I could only sit there and watch as they worked on Arely for a minute before loading her up on the stretcher and placing her in the ambulance. They asked me questions, but I didn't remember what they were or if I even answered them. All I remembered was sitting beside her holding her hand, when the monitors started to shriek, and one of the EMTs shouted, "Flatline!"

I sat in a daze as I watched the EMT work on Arely. Sticking in an IV and pushing medicine as I gripped her hand even harder, wishing I could give all of my strength to her—except life didn't work that way.

They worked on her until we got to the hospital, only for her to be whisked away and I never saw her again.

End of part of anthology.

Want more of King's Vow with Arely and Bash? Pre-order the full novel now. Coming this November.

CHAPTER SEVEN

arely

WHY DID EVERYTHING HURT?

I tried to open my eyes to no avail.

Why was there water dripping on my hand?

I tried to pull my hand away, only for it to be grabbed up and pressed against something prickly. My fingers jerked. I knew they did.

"Arely," came from Santi's strained voice. "Open your eyes for me. Please," he begged.

Where was I, how did I get here, and why did Santi sound devastated?

Flashes of leaving the sanctuary and finding Sebastian outside with a knife in his hand flitted through my consciousness. Then the pain, being in Sebastian's arms and him vowing to always keep me safe, and then nothing. I couldn't remember anything after that.

Where was Sebastian?

Was he okay?

Did he get shot?

"Arely, come back to us," Santi demanded in a quiet whisper.

I was trying. I really was. It was so hard to break free from the fog that pulled my limbs down into the thick muck and made my eyelids feel like they were caked in concrete.

"I felt her hand twitch. I know she's going to open her eyes any minute now." Santi's voice cracked as it filled with desperation.

"I think you're imagining things," Pablo said from a distance. "She's been unconscious for three days now."

Three days?

I struggled to open my eyes and my mouth to speak to them. I needed to get up and tell Santi I was fine.

"I saw her finger move," Army said from my other side. "We really need to get her out of here before whoever tried to kill her tries again."

He was right. If someone in the society wanted me dead, I wasn't safe unless I was at home.

"There are two guards posted just outside, and the

four of us in here. She safe for the time being," Santi argued.

I knew nothing bad could ever happen to me with my brothers by my side.

"How can you say that? I mean, where the hell were you, Santi? You're her bodyguard, and for some reason, you weren't there with her. Maybe you want her dead so you can take over."

My hand was dropped, and there was a scuffle and bang. If I could have rolled my eyes at them, I would have. I would have yelled at them as well if my mouth was working. They were fighting when they should have been trying to figure out who wanted me dead.

I kept shouting in my head for them to stop until, eventually, the word passed my lips. It wasn't a yell. It was barely more than a scratchy whisper coming up my dry, abused throat.

"Holy shit, Arely," Santi croaked. My eyes cracked open just in time to see him skid across the cheap linoleum floor of the hospital room. Wrapping his arms around me, he hugged me, burying his face in my neck. "Don't ever do that to me again. I thought we were going to lose you."

Everyone crowded around my bed, touching some part of me, and it made me truly grateful for my family and their love. I couldn't imagine being in their shoes.

If any of them had been shot, I would have been so fucking worried and then burned the world down to find out who did it and end them with a slow and torturous death.

Turning his head, Santi whispered into my shoulder. "You took twenty years off my life."

I rested the side of my head against his. "I know. I'm sorry. When can I get out of here?" Every word that came out of my mouth felt like I was swallowing glass. It must have sounded like it since Santi stood and moved to pour me a glass of water.

Ale laughed. "Of course, you'd want to know when you can get out. You've been awake for all of five seconds, and you're ready to book. You died, Arely. Fucking died. If it weren't for Bash doing CPR on you, we'd be having your funeral right now."

I took a few long swallows of the water I was given and let it soothe the burn that trailed down my throat. Only then did I speak again. It didn't hurt quite as much this time around when I spoke. "Where's Sebastian?"

All of a sudden, no one would look at me. I tried to sit up to catch their eyes until a shooting pain rocked me from the inside out. I clutched my side and clenched my teeth together to prevent from screaming.

"Fuck, A. What are you doing? You're going to rip

your stitches." Army pushed me down and kept a hand on my shoulder to keep me from sitting up. It wouldn't be hard. As much as I hated to admit it at that moment, I was weak.

Reaching up to grip Armando's hand, I dug my fingernails into the back of it, letting him know I meant business. "I'm trying to get an answer out of one of you fuckers. Where the fuck is Sebastian?" I growled out.

"In the basement. We weren't sure if you'd want to talk to him before we ended him or not."

"What the fuck?" I shouted. "Why would he be in the basement? You just said he saved my life."

"He could be lying," Pablo spoke up from the end of the bed. "We can't take any chances with your safety."

"It wasn't Sebastian who shot me. While I don't know who did, I know it wasn't him. He was right by my side when we heard the shot. You need to let him go."

"I don't think that's wise. What if he had an accomplice, and being next to you is his alibi?" Pablo tried again.

"I'm the one in charge here, so what I say goes, and I am telling you right here and now that Sebastian had nothing to do with it. The second he saw it was me he was supposed to kill, he dropped his knife." I didn't remember much, but I did remember he was upset and held me close to his body. No one did that to the person they were trying to kill.

Santiago's head was giving a slight shake when he spoke. "Who the fuck did you piss off enough in the society that they want you dead?"

"No one. You know I don't have time for their shit. It would make more sense if it were someone wanting to take us out to take over our business."

"Isn't that the truth. We've been lucky so far," Ale muttered.

"You can't leave her alone ever again," Army said to Santi. "If you have something you have to do, either you call one of us or use one of the compound guards."

"Maybe we should hire more. Santi isn't enough if there's a whole brigade coming after her." Ale's face contorted as he looked down at me. "Really, A, you're lucky they were able to bring you back."

I knew I was lucky, and I might not be again if I was by myself the next time it happened—because it would happen again, especially if the society wanted me dead. I needed to figure out who was behind the attempt on my life and wipe them from the picture.

Pablo patted my foot and started for the door. "I'm going to get the doctor, so he can check you out and give you some sort of an idea of when you can break out of here."

The second he was gone, I turned to my other brothers. "When I get out of here, Sebastian better be at his house safe and sound. If not, heads are going to roll."

Santi lifted his hands in the air and took a step back. "Alright, it wasn't my idea to begin with. It was Pablo's."

"Right now, I don't care whose idea it was." I tried to sit up higher in the bed, but it hurt too damn much. Alejandro handed me a remote attached to the bed that would help. "Sebastian doesn't deserve to be locked up for saving me."

Sitting down in one of the chairs lined up by my bed, Armando nodded. "I agree, but we wanted to be sure on the off chance. Seriously, you have no idea how scared we all were. We thought we were going to lose you."

"Enough talk about me dying. I'm here now, and that's all that matters. I need one of you to go back to the house and get me a change of clothes and my toothbrush." My mouth had a horrid taste in it that the water I kept sipping on wasn't washing away.

"We'll go," Ale said with a bittersweet smile crossing his face. "We'll also let Bash out."

"Thank you. If you've been here while I was unconscious, who's been working?"

"Does your brain ever turn off?" Army chuckled.

"It's a twenty-five/eight job." They all scrunched their brows together as they stared at me. "Meaning it never ends. I need twenty-five hours in a day and eight days a week to get everything done."

Santi reached out and cupped my leg with his palm. "I can take on more. Or Pablo. No one even knows what he does with all of his time."

"Just thinking about all the work that I'm behind on is making me itch, so I just might take you up on that."

"You can't keep going like you have. If you hadn't been working so late—"

"Let's not start making this a habit," I interrupted him. "I know I should have gone home when Santi left, and I didn't. That's on me, but let's not forget someone made killing me Sebastian's test. It wouldn't have happened otherwise."

"I'm going to string whoever did this to you up by their balls and then flay his skin off inch by inch. And only then will the true torture begin," Santi growled out.

At the same time, Pablo and a gray-haired man, who I assumed was my doctor, walked in. His steps faltered as his light blue eyes widened in horror as

Pablo clapped his hand on the doctor's shoulder. He cleared his throat and made his way over to my bedside.

"Good to see you awake, Ms. Guerrera. Your brother informed me that you'd like to go home, but first I need to check you over, and then we can speak about your discharge."

If he knew what was good for him, he'd release me the minute he was done. Otherwise, I would make his life and everyone else's here as miserable as possible.

CHAPTER EIGHT

bash

I GROUND my teeth together as I heard a noise coming my way. I was in a motherfucking dungeon in Arely's basement. I'd been stuck sitting in a chair for… I don't know how long. All I knew was it had been multiple days. No food or bathroom breaks were the thanks I got for saving their sister. At least they'd left me a few bottles of water to drink.

The door swung open, and the one brother I didn't really know stepped inside. I think his name was Pablo. He sniffed the air as his face morphed into an ugly smirk.

"You're fucking disgusting," he snarled out as he took in the water bottles scattered on the floor.

"Would you have preferred I piss myself?" I raised a brow, taunting him.

Ale and Army barged into the room and pushed Pablo to the side. "Holy hell, Pablo. What were you thinking? He's not a motherfucking prisoner. Give me the key," Ale demanded as he came to my side and picked up my cuffed arm. Kneeling down, he looked me in the eye. I wasn't sure whose eyes were filled with more fire, his or mine. "I had no fucking clue. I've been at my sister's bedside this entire time."

"How is she?" I croaked out. I'd drank the last of my water hours ago. I wasn't sure what they had piping into this room, but whatever it was made my throat dry as fuck.

"She's awake and her usual self, although she's a little slower." He nodded to himself. "It might be a good thing, though. Arely needs to slow down." There was a long pregnant pause as he stared down Pablo with an outstretched hand. Pablo threw him the key and stormed out of the room. Ale quickly uncuffed my hand and then the leg shackled to a thick steel ring in the floor before he stood up and crossed his arms over his chest. "She was pissed as hell when she learned you were here." He sniffed and wrinkled his nose. "You should get cleaned up and go see her before she tears down the house."

"Follow me," Army called from the door. "I'll take you to one of the bedrooms where you can shower, and I'll find you some fresh clothes for you to change into."

I didn't care as long as I got to see Arely. I'd been thrown into this room with no explanation, but I knew that if she died, I died. They'd kill me even though I was the one who tried to protect her and performed CPR on her until the ambulance arrived. Still, they didn't care, and if I were in their shoes, I probably wouldn't either. I was sure they were rocked to their core, knowing someone tried to take out their sister.

I had planned to take the quickest shower known to man, but once the hot water started to fall over my body, I realized I was frozen down to my bones. Even under the hot spray, my body was shaking. After I thoroughly washed from head to toe twice, I stepped out into the opulent bathroom and dried off. True to Army's word, there was a pair of black sweats set out on the counter. I quickly changed into them and started to head out the door when Arely's other brother, Santiago, stopped me. His jaw tensed as he looked me over and then started to walk away. "This way," he informed me in a monotone voice.

I had a feeling Santiago didn't like me, not that I cared. They could all go fuck themselves if they thought I was going to take locking me away for days lying down.

Santiago stopped in front of a door close to Arely's office. "No matter what she says, she needs her rest."

I wasn't sure how I became the villain in this scenario. Ale and Army had approached me and then set me up for the fucking test. I was the one who didn't kill their sister and saved her instead.

Shouldering by him, I opened the door and stepped into the room. It was massive. My entire apartment could have fit inside Arely's bedroom twice over. The entire room was done in black, gold, and gray, with a few pops of red. There was a sitting area in front of large windows that looked out onto the lake and a massive fireplace that was roaring. The room was warm, making my hyper-alert body start to feel sluggish. Arely laid in a bed that had to be custom made because it was bigger than anything I'd ever seen before. Why did such a small person need such a large bed?

Propped up by a mountain of gold pillows in the middle of the bed, Arely looked tiny with her thick blankets pulled up to her chest. Her skin was so pale and drawn. As if she could feel me thinking about her, Arely's eyes slowly drifted open, and a hint of a smile tipped her lips.

"It took you long enough," she said hoarsely.

I crossed the room to stand beside her and took her

cold hand in mine. "I didn't mean to keep you waiting." How was she so cold with the fire and blankets? "How are you feeling?"

"Better now that I'm home." With her free hand, Arely tapped the space beside her. "Come sit."

My head was already shaking before I spoke. "I should let you rest."

"I'll rest just fine with you beside me. You look as tired as I feel, and if you're here with me, I know my brothers aren't harassing you or locking you up."

"Are you saying you want me to sleep… here?" This was not what I expected when I walked inside. I thought I'd get interrogated by her about what happened that night.

While I wasn't sure it was a good idea to stay, my body had other plans. I moved around the side of the bed and laid down next to Arely.

"If you don't want to, you can leave, but it would give me peace of mind." Her mouth opened, but she didn't continue to speak. She only looked me over.

"There's more to it, isn't there." It wasn't a question. I knew there was more she wasn't telling me.

She gave a little nod of her head before she turned on her side. It was a slow process, and I could tell that she was in pain, but I also knew she didn't want my help or to comment on it. Once Arely was curled up on her side, I pulled the thick comforter over her shoulders and waited. "You failed your test, and you might be in danger."

"I can protect myself, Arely. You don't need to worry about me." Was she worried one of her brothers would try to take me out? I didn't think Alejandro and Armando would do anything, but I wouldn't put it past the other two.

She tried to smile at me, but she wasn't very successful. Her eyes kept drooping as she spoke. "All the same, it would still make me feel better if you stay here until we figure out who was behind my assassination attempt."

"What about you? Are you safe? Someone out there wants you dead. Are they going to keep trying until they succeed?"

"They're not going to succeed, but yes, I do believe this won't be the only attempt." Her eyes fluttered closed, and little puffs of breath came out of her dry, cracked lips.

A fierce need to protect Arely came over me, and I would at all costs. If she wanted me by her side, then by her side, I would be. No one was going to stop me—especially not her brothers.

I was sure that not many people get to see Arely

vulnerable like this. "I promise I won't let anyone hurt you. I failed you once, but it won't happen again."

Lifting my hand, I caressed her cheek and pushed a lock of hair behind her ear before I settled in under the blankets with her and let the warmth drag me under.

CHAPTER NINE

arely

WE WERE HAVING a meeting in my bedroom because all the men in the Guerrera Family thought I was too weak to sit at my desk or on a lame-ass couch. I was the second oldest, but I was being treated like a baby, which was annoying. Even as a child, I wasn't treated this way.

Pablo glared at Sebastian from the other side of my bed. "Why is he still here?"

I narrowed my eyes at my brother. It had been three days since I'd been home, and they were handling me with kid gloves. "Because I asked him to stay, and that's all you need to know. Why don't you stop giving him a hard time and update me on where we are with who ordered my hit?"

"You think *they're* talking? No, they're acting just as

stupefied by this as we are," Santi growled out. "If it were anyone else, I'd be taking them downstairs one by one and getting answers out of them. But instead, *they're* saying that wasn't the test they assigned."

"And you believe them?" Pablo scoffed. "Let me handle the issue. You need to be hiring more security, anyway."

Sebastian crossed his arms over his chest in the corner of the room. "If Santiago can't be by Arely's side, then I'll be there."

"And you think we trust her life in your hands? You've got to be kidding," Pablo laughed darkly. "While these two hoodlums may think they know you, you're an outsider, and we don't trust—"

"You think you can trust someone you hire to do the job?" Sebastian interrupted him. "Hire all the people you want, but I vowed to Arely that I would protect her, and I don't go back on my word." He glanced at me and then back to where Pablo and Santiago were sitting at the bottom of my bed. "If her life is in danger, she shouldn't be driving herself. You need at least a two-car caravan with multiple guards when going places."

I sat up higher in my bed and gritted my teeth at the pain to not show them how much I was still affected. Sebastian raised a brow at me to say I wasn't fooling him, or maybe it was to see if I'd fight back at his suggestion. I did want to fight back, but he was right. As much as I wish I could, I couldn't take on multiple people at the same time. Neither could Santi nor Sebastian.

"I'm afraid he's right. They've already sent two people after me and failed. They won't make the same mistake again. Next time it could be an army, and we need to be prepared. I want everyone safeguarded. Don't go anywhere without your guns, and I want everyone here to have at least one person assigned to them at all times. It's not just me that they could be after. If they get to you, they know I'll do everything within my power to get you back."

"Fuck," Army sighed out. "We've had it too easy, but Bash is right. We can't be complicit anymore. We're going to up our game and make ourselves invincible."

We thought we were untouchable for too long, but it was clear some changes needed to be made. Hell, even my best friend Bree didn't travel alone, and she always had at least two guards with her. Her father made sure Bree was protected at all times, even while in the house.

Looking over to Santi, I knew this was eating at him. He felt as if he'd failed me, but in all actuality, I had failed them all. I thought I was invincible and nothing was ever going to hurt me when that couldn't be further from the truth. I was just as vulnerable as the next person when faced with a gun. "Maybe we should do something like the Zees do. If Bree can handle her security, I can suck it up."

"This isn't something that's going to be short-term. This is indefinite. Are you really saying you'll be fine with having guards around you all the time?"

"I don't want them in my bedroom, office, or in the sanctuary with me. They can stay outside the door, but no further unless needed." This was an order. I couldn't let my almost dying change my life entirely.

Santi moved slowly up the bed to sit beside me and put his arm around me. "Why are you being so agreeable?"

"Because as much as I hate it, we should have implemented this a long time ago." I didn't want what happened to me to happen to any of them.

"And you're okay with letting this gringo stay by your side when you don't even know him?" He said gringo like it was a bad word, and I wondered if Santi didn't like Sebastian because he knew something had happened between us.

"The man made a promise, and I believe him." I looked at my brothers' shocked faces and tried to put them at ease. "You weren't there that night, but the second Sebastian saw it was me, he put the knife down. He threw his body over mine when we heard the shot and took off his shirt to press against my wound. We were utterly alone, and if he wanted to, Sebastian could have killed me in a heartbeat. Instead, he vowed never to let anything happen to me. Whether you like it or not, Sebastian is here to stay."

Sebastian stepped forward. "Just like that night, I will promise to the rest of you that I will lay down my life for Arely."

Tilting his head to the side, Ale asked. "Why? You owe us no loyalty."

With only a few feet between him and the bed, Sebastian's gaze landed on mine. "It's hard to explain, and I don't think you'd understand unless you've been in the same situation."

There was no way to explain the crazy connection that started in the alley. If it had been anyone else, I would have shanked them and left them for dead, but instead, I had my wicked way with him without a second thought.

Santi rushed up from the bed, nearly knocking me over in his haste. He crowded Sebastian, his eyes on fire as he spoke. "If you cross us, we won't just take you down to the basement to sit for a few days. This time, you won't be leaving. I'll make sure your last days on

Earth are filled with more agony than you could ever imagine."

Looking at me over Santi's shoulder, Sebastian's light brown eyes glowed with an untold emotion. "If I fail, I fully give you permission to end my life."

CHAPTER TEN

bash

"WHAT ABOUT THAT ONE?" Army nudged me in the side as he tilted his head to some random girl he thought I might be interested in. I didn't even bother to look. I wasn't here to hook up. Little did they know, I was getting plenty of action behind the door of their sister's bedroom for the last month.

I took a sip of my beer before I spoke. "Why don't you stop worrying about me and find yourself a girl?"

"I want to make sure you're happy, so you'll keep protecting my sister. Seriously, you've been by her side every night for a month straight. How are you not dying to get laid? I swear if I go more than a couple of days, I feel like I'm going to explode. I'm surprised you're not sputtering out cum because you're so backed up."

Ale and I looked at each other, and the second our eyes locked, we died laughing. I'd never heard anything more ridiculous in my life.

As I started to come down, it was on the tip of my tongue to say I had been, but both Ale and Army were packing, and so were the two guards that were a couple of tables away. If they got pissed, they could easily order for me to be taken care of. It was their money paying the salaries of their new security force, not mine.

"You don't know what I do when I'm not at the compound," I laughed. I'd only spent a handful of nights at my apartment since Arely came home, and those were the only nights I'd been alone.

Ale was still laughing silently from his side of the table as Army spoke. "I swear I haven't seen you leave by yourself since my sister came home from the hospital."

I wasn't sure how Arely's family would feel if they knew I was fucking her on the regular, but I wasn't going to be the one to spill our secret. At least not without talking to her about it. Instead, I deflected. "Why don't you go find someone to hook up with before we start to see cum leaking out of your ears? I think it's already clogged up your brain."

"Fuck you." Army punched me in the arm before

walking off to the bar and flagging down a bartender.

I turned my attention to Ale, who had a wide grin on his face. "It's hard to get to my brother, but you did. He'll be looking for a way to get you back until he outdoes you twofold, so you better watch out," he chuckled.

I looked forward to Army trying.

Taking a long pull of my beer, I set it down and asked Ale, "Are you not looking for a hookup?"

"There's probably only one other gay guy in this bar, and he's with a bunch of girls." He scrunched up his nose. "It's not really my scene."

"Why'd you let Army pick this place then?"

He lifted one shoulder before he finished off his beer. "Unlike my brother, I won't explode if I don't have sex every other day."

If I didn't get to sink into Arely's tight heat every night, I felt like I was going to lose my mind. Not that I was going to share that with him. Tonight was one of those nights I'd be without her, but I had no excuse to go back to the house with them.

It wasn't like we were exclusive. I mean, we were in the sense that we weren't fucking anyone else, but it hadn't been discussed. We didn't talk much with words—only our bodies.

Ale cocked his head to the side and examined me

for a long moment. I let him see whatever he wanted to see. I had nothing to hide. I was loyal to the Guerrera family. They took me in and changed my life when I'd been struggling. It wouldn't be something I'd ever forget. "I know something's going on with you, and it's only a matter of time until I figure it out."

I smirked and signaled for the waitress. "I've got nothing to hide from you."

"If you're not looking for anyone to hook up with, we can leave soon." Ale nodded toward the bar and shook his head. "He's already found his mark for the night."

Army strode toward us with his arm slung around the waist of a tiny woman compared to his hulking frame. His smirk grew with every step he made. "I'm going to head out. You want to give this loser a ride home?" He nodded toward me.

On instinct, I was up in his face with my teeth bared. I may have been a lot of things in my life, but I was never a loser. If I had to kick his ass to prove it, I would.

Ale pushed between us, facing me, his hands on my chest, applying pressure. "Back the fuck down. You don't want to do this."

"The fuck I don't. Just because I don't want to dip my dick into some diseased skank, he's calling me a loser. You're the fucking loser if you can't control your dick," I shouted, spitting in Army's face.

"Hey," the girl cried out. "I'm not a skank."

"Oh, so just diseased then. Good luck with that one, dude." I laughed darkly. My gaze went to Ale. "I'm out."

Turning around, I pulled out my phone and ordered myself an Uber. I'd been letting Army drive me since I'd stored my bike for the winter. Now that I was making decent money, I really needed to get myself something else to drive.

I'd barely stepped through the door of my apartment when my phone lit up with a call from Arely. She was already talking by the time I hit accept. "What the fuck happened tonight with my brothers?"

I was still fuming. Before speaking, I went into the kitchen, pulled out a bottle of tequila, and poured myself a shot. When that wasn't enough, I did two more. I could hear Arely getting more pissed off by the second. I shouldn't have answered, but I had to. What if she was in trouble?

Walking back into the living room, I threw myself down on the couch and closed my eyes, letting the tequila relax me. "Your brother called me a loser for not fucking some rando tonight, is what."

Arely was so quiet I had to pull the phone away

from my ear to see if she'd hung up. After seeing she was still on the line, I put my phone on speaker, set it down on my chest, and waited. It probably wasn't smart of me to push up on Army, but I couldn't help it. No one, not even someone who wouldn't blink twice at killing me, was going to get away with putting me down.

"Did you want to fuck someone else?" were Arely's first words after the long silence.

"No, I wanted to punch your fucking brother in the face," I growled out and slammed my fist into the cushions of my leather couch.

"You want to hit him because he wanted you to have sex?"

What the fuck?

"Did you set this up? If you want me out of your bed, all you have to do is say so." Picking my phone back up, I stared at her name on my screen. "If Santiago needs to do something, you can call me. If not, I'll see you sometime next week." Hanging up, I turned off my phone, knowing if I didn't, it would keep ringing until I threw my phone across the room and broke it.

Heaving myself up, I grabbed the bottle of tequila from the kitchen as I moved down the hall to my bedroom to drink myself to sleep.

CHAPTER ELEVEN

arely

SLAMMING MY LAPTOP CLOSED, I growled out a frustrated sigh. Tipping my head back against the headrest, I looked up at the ceiling.

"You look like you're about reacy to climb the walls," Santi called as he walked into the room. I knew there was a smirk on his face, and if I saw it, I'd want to hit it.

"I need to get out of the house and back to the sanctuary."

"Anything you can do there, you can do here. It's obvious someone else knows about your office at the church, and it isn't safe."

Ducking my chin, I leveled Santi with narrowed eyes. "Even with my ten-man entourage?"

Santiago leaned against the wall with his arms

crossed over his chest. "It's four, and I thought you were fine with more security?"

"Just because I acknowledged that it's necessary doesn't mean I like it." Nor had I liked the fact that Sebastian hadn't been by the house except once in the last week. If it didn't tip off my brothers about what was going on between us, I would show up at his apartment and demand he fuck me. He was acting like… a child.

"There's another reason for why you're so damn bitchy lately. Is your period late or something?"

My body turned to ice as my insides caught on fire. With my jaw clenched, I did my best to eviscerate my brother. "You need to leave right now before I cut your balls off."

Santi's face turned white as a sheet. He knew I meant business. "Arely," he said softly. "I didn't—"

"I don't want to hear it. You're done for the day. Call Sebastian and get him in here now. Tell him I want to roll out within the hour," I ordered as I stormed out of my office and into my connected bedroom. Maybe it wasn't the smartest to have them so close together. It seemed I was always working. Well, today, I was taking the day off and getting away from my family, who had constantly been hovering since I got home from the hospital.

"What are you going to do?"

"What I'm going to do doesn't concern you. Just let security know we'll be rolling out in an hour."

With a plan formulating, I hopped into the shower and scrubbed and shaved every inch of my body. I was going to show Sebastian everything he'd been missing the last week by looking the hottest he'd ever seen. I put on my sexiest lingerie, tight black jeans, and a low-cut black shirt that would make any man drool. I put on a coat of mascara, my signature red lipstick, and pulled my long, black hair into a high ponytail. Before I set off out the door, I slipped on my sexiest and highest-heeled black boots. I looked just like I felt, a badass bitch, and no one was going to fuck with me today.

The second I stepped out of my bedroom, Santi was waiting for me in the hall. He walked along with me, talking and trying to apologize. "You know it helps keep you safe if the security team knows where you're going."

Without looking at him, I finally responded. "They will know where I'm going. I'm just not telling you." However, it wouldn't be difficult for him to find out where we were going once we were en route unless I forbade the team from telling him. The thought brought a smile to my otherwise stoic face.

What Santi said was a low blow and I wasn't

going to forgive him that easily. It wasn't like he had no idea what our father had done to me. Santi was the one who helped pick me off the floor after I was brought home and was lying in a pool of my own blood.

"Stop worrying about where I'm going and figure out how someone found out about the sanctuary."

"The only way someone found out about the sanctuary is if someone betrayed you." Pablo's dark eyes glistened with malice as he spoke. "Don't you find it convenient Santi had something to do that night and left you alone? What was so important? Has he told you where he was?"

Pablo's words echoed in my head like a soundtrack. Santiago was my best friend, but I knew he was hiding something from me. Still, I couldn't believe my own brother would betray me.

Santi quickened his steps until he was ahead of me and then stopped, blocking my way. "Is something going on with you and Bash?"

There was no way in hell I was going to answer him when he was hiding something from me. "Is there something going on with you that *I* should know about?"

There was only the slight widening of his eyes before he shut down. If he didn't think I saw it, something more was going on with Santi. We could read each other easily after being each other's sidekicks for most of our lives.

Pausing at the front door, I grabbed my purse. "Is Sebastian here?"

"He's outside with the rest of the team waiting for you." Stepping forward, Santi wrapped his arms around me and pulled me into a hug. I stayed stiff. I wasn't going to give in. Not today. Santi knew better than anyone how much it hurt that my choice was taken away from me. I wasn't even sure if I'd ever want kids, but now there was no possible way. While I was the head of the family, it was only my brothers who could grow our family.

I pulled out of his hold and opened the door. Looking over my shoulder, I found Santi staring back at me with sad eyes. "Don't wait up."

Sebastian was leaning on one of the two SUVs that sat out front. The moment I stepped outside, he straightened and tried to look unaffected, but he wasn't fooling me. By the time I was in the back seat and buckled up, he was trying and failing to hide his massive erection in his jeans.

"Where to, Boss?" A guy who was bigger than Lou Ferrigno said in his deep timbre of a voice. I couldn't remember his name and instead called him Hulk.

"The city." I didn't care where we went, but it

would take at least an hour to get there. I was tired of Stonewall and needed to get away. "Once we get closer, I'll let you know what I'm planning."

Hulk nodded and started to drive away. I heard him relay the information to someone else who was likely in the SUV trailing behind us.

I wasn't sure what I wanted to do except to have a good meal and be surrounded by hundreds of strangers. I'd been so isolated, and all I wanted was to feel normal. Plus, after what Santi said and knowing he was hiding something from me, I couldn't look at his face another minute.

Sebastian leaned forward, resting the side of his face against the headrest in front of him, getting my attention. "Is everything okay?"

I shifted in my seat and tapped my long, black fingernails on my thigh. "Oh, have you decided to start talking to me again?"

His jaw ticked before he leaned back and gritted out. "What's there to talk about? You didn't need me. Was I supposed to stand around your house waiting to see if you might need me and forget about the rest of my responsibilities?"

Yes, in fact, that was exactly what he was supposed to do, but I wasn't going to tell him that.

"Is this about money? Do you need more?"

Unclipping his belt, Sebastian slid into my space until our foreheads were touching. His nostrils flared as he looked down at me. "I work for my money. I am not a prostitute."

Throwing my head back, I let out an unamused laugh. My lips brushed his on the way, and all I wanted to do was kiss his mouth raw, but there was no way that was going to happen with a car full of guards. "I'm not going to pay you to fuck me. You should be compensated for guarding me when Santi isn't. You asked for the role. Did you think it was a volunteer position where you'd make no money?"

"I didn't do it to make more money," he gritted out quietly.

"Then why?"

"Because I want you safe." His gaze locked with mine, and I knew he was telling me the truth. I could feel it radiating between us. "But if you'd rather have one of the new guys and keep me on the streets, I'll deal."

Reaching out between us, I hooked my pinky with his. "I only want you. Now enjoy the trip."

We kept quiet for the rest of the drive as we looked at the scenery out of our respective windows. Still, it didn't stop Sebastian from rubbing his thumb over the top of my hand and the pulse point at my wrist.

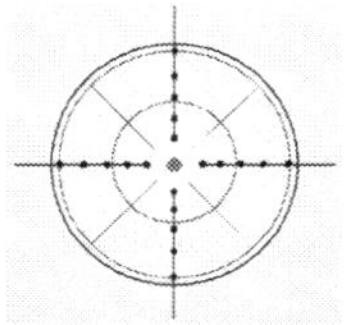

SEBASTIAN LOOKED AROUND THE TINY, dimly lit restaurant with red and white checkered cloth-covered tables scattered throughout the place. "Why here?"

"Because sometimes a girl just needs to eat her weight in carbs, and Italian is always good for that. Are you implying that just because I'm Latina, I can't eat Italian?"

Sebastian sat back in his chair and took a sip of his water. "I didn't say that, but this doesn't seem like your kind of joint."

"When I come to the city, I want the best, and this is the best damn Italian in New York City. It's run by this old Italian couple who opened this place forty years ago. What about you? What's your favorite food?"

He shrugged and looked down at the menu. "My family didn't have much money for food growing up, so I ate mac and cheese, ramen, and chicken nuggets." He looked around the room and then back at me again. "Do you think it's safe here?"

It was sweet that he was worried. "Do you think someone is going to try to take me out in the city with hundreds of people around?"

"I'm sure if a rival saw the opportunity, they'd take it. In all actuality, I'm surprised this was the first time anyone's tried to take you out."

He wasn't wrong; it was surprising. I guess I'd been lucky the last three years.

"You act like I've been running the family business since I was born. I took over after my father was killed three years ago." Even to my own ears, it sounded stupid that up until this moment, I'd had such a lack of security.

"Oh, I can see baby Arely kicking ass and taking names while running…" he tilted his head side to side as if he was afraid to say the word.

"You can say cartel," I laughed.

His light brown eyes flared. "Don't you worry?" He nodded around the room.

"You act like I shouted when I merely said the word. No one is listening to us. We wouldn't be here otherwise."

He nodded. "Do you want to tell me why we're really here in the city?"

"Because I was tired of feeling like I'm on lockdown in my own house. My brothers won't stop hovering, and they're driving me crazy."

"You know, they did almost lose you. You died at least once. It was scary for them. You might technically be their boss," he said it like it was a question, to which I nodded. "You're still their sister, and they love you."

I knew he was right, but it sure as hell didn't feel like it after what Santi said to me earlier.

Finishing the rest of the wine in my glass, I signaled for the waiter. "Let's not talk about my family. It will only put me in a bad mood, and that's the reason why we're here to begin with. Why don't you tell me what you're going to school for?"

"Really?" He chuckled, lacing his fingers together and placing them over his taut stomach. We should have gone to a hotel and fucked until we couldn't move anymore and then ordered room service, but I wanted a sense of normalcy. I should have known it wouldn't work. All I wanted to do was see Sebastian naked and thrusting inside of me with his mouth parted in a sexy 'O'.

I waited until my wine glass was full, and the waiter was several feet away before I spoke. "I figure small talk while eating should be safe."

In all actuality, what little I knew about Sebastian, it shocked me he was going to school. He was stealing to survive before he met up with Ale and Army.

His light brown eyes bore into mine. "And what are we going to do once we leave here?"

Tapping my fingernail on the rim of my wineglass,

I took in his broad chest and bulging biceps and licked my lips. I knew what was underneath, and I wanted it. It had been too long. "I wouldn't be opposed to finding a nice hotel to stay at for the night."

Sebastian leaned forward, putting his elbows on the table, and clasping his hands underneath his chin. "Is that so your brothers don't find out?"

While the words had never been spoken, it was understood that my brothers weren't to find out about us having sex. I was sure they had their suspicions—not that I cared.

"I don't care if they do." And I didn't. Especially not now. Nothing good came when the people you were supposed to trust the most were keeping secrets from you. "If you want, I can text them right now and tell them we'll be staying in the city overnight so you can fuck my brains out."

Sebastian's lips twitched. "That's not necessary."

"But?" There was more. I knew it.

"Then maybe Armando won't be trying to get me to fuck every chick that crosses our paths."

"You didn't think to say you're fucking someone already?" I liked that he was already so loyal to our family. It wasn't common for us to let outsiders in, but I knew I had made the right choice with Sebastian. I even kept my best friend at arm's length to a certain extent. Our lives were dangerous enough without having to worry about those we surrounded ourselves with. That's why Bree was perfect. Her father supplied the pharmaceutical portion of our business. She wasn't involved with her family business, but she knew about it and ours.

CHAPTER TWELVE

bash

WE SAT at a table that could seat ten. Arely was at the head of the table with her brother, Pablo, at the other end. I was on Arely's right with Santiago on her left. A petite Asian woman named Bree sat to his Santi's right. Ale sat beside Bree with Army to his left, and next to him was his girlfriend, the one he met the other night.

"When was the last time we all sat down for Sunday dinner together?" Ale asked his twin.

Army looked at his girl and shrugged. "It's been months."

"We should do it more often," Santiago suggested.

"Every Sunday from now on, we'll sit here, catch up, and have a brief meeting about business," Arely announced. "If you bring someone to dinner, they can hang out in the library or something during our meeting."

Her message was loud and clear. Devi, Army's newest girlfriend, wasn't going to be in the room for the meeting. I wasn't even sure if I was invited or not. I guess I'd find out.

There were head nods from everyone except the twins. Santi looked to Bree with knitted brows while Pablo stared at his sister from the other end of the table.

Two people dressed in all black started to bring in platter after platter of food. There were enchiladas, elote, chilaquiles, tamales, and a heaping bowl of guacamole with two large bowls of homemade chips.

Each platter was passed around as we piled all the amazing-smelling food onto our plates. Once I had filled my plate, I leaned over to Arely and spoke. "Is this normal?"

"For Sunday dinner, yes. Next time it will be something else, or we can vote on what cuisine we want."

We all started to dig into all the amazing food. There were multiple rounds of groans and moans.

I had just taken a long drag of my beer when Santi set down his silverware and cleared his throat. "Alright, are you ever going to tell us what's going on between the two of you?" I nearly spit out my beer when I saw his eyes were on Arely and me.

"What's there to say?" She shrugged like it was no big deal. "Sebastian and I are fucking. If you don't like it, keep your mouth shut since I've never said a single word about anyone you all were fucking."

Ale sat up taller in his seat and turned to look at his sister. "How long has this been going on?"

"Since before I met you and Army." He started to open his mouth but closed it as I kept speaking. "When I met the two of you, I had no idea you were her brothers."

Pablo leaned forward with a snarl on his upper lip. "How the hell did the two of you meet? I don't see Arely hanging around the university looking for a hookup."

Arely threw her head back and laughed. It didn't escape my notice when her hand went to where she'd been shot. "Do you think I'm so desperate that I'd be looking to hook up with college students?"

"I don't know. All you do is work, so it's possible." Santi laughed before he jumped and then yelled. "Why the fuck did you kick me? You've got those murder boots on," he pouted.

"Because you're an asshole, and if you say something like that again, I'm going to impale your shin with my heel," Arely growled. Her eyes were like lasers as she looked at everyone else at the table, willing one of them to speak up.

"You've got no complaints from me. I think Bash is cool." Army's eyes widened. "Unless you expect me to call him Papi or some shit like that. That's where I draw the line."

Now it was my turn to laugh.

One day we'd have to tell him he has to start calling me dad just to get a reaction out of him. It would be hilarious.

"I sure as fuck am not calling this pendejo anything," Pablo growled. "You shouldn't get used to him, though. He didn't pass his test," he arched a brow.

Santi stood and placed his hands on the table as he leaned toward Pablo at the other end of the table. I wasn't sure what the deal was between Pablo and the rest of them, but there was something. He was always angry. "The society isn't claiming they tried to kill Arely. If Bash suddenly ends up dead, it will only prove that they tried to kill one of their own. And then, we'll kill them."

Pablo chuckled as he shook his head. "You can't kill everyone in the society." His eyes flicked to mine. "If that wasn't indeed your test, expect another one soon. And this time, you better pass."

"Or what, they kill me?" I wasn't sure if it was all talk or not, but I wasn't going to let some fuckers kill me because I didn't pass a test.

Santiago's mouth turned down as he looked me over. "It can be deadly not to pass, but I wouldn't worry about it. Especially not now when it's been made to look like you were supposed to kill a member. Your next test will probably be easy."

"What if I don't want any part in this? Do I get a say?"

"Don't worry about it." Arely's hand gripped my knee under the table. "Like Santi said, I'm sure they'll go easy on you next time. Now that everyone's done eating, Bree, could you show Devi to the library or out back while we have our meeting?" Bree nodded and stood. "We shouldn't be long, and then you're all free to stay or go do whatever you want." Arely pushed back her chair and stood. "Let's go to my office." Her eyes followed her friend and Army's girlfriend out of the room. "Just in case."

I trailed behind and watched as Arely led the way to her office, which was right beside her bedroom. She really did work too much. Pablo and Santi quietly argued the entire way while Ale and Army were joking with one another. At first, I wasn't sure if I was supposed to be a part of this meeting, so I was shocked when I saw Arely standing inside the door to her office waiting for me. Did she trust me enough to let me in on whatever was going to be said? Once I was through the door, she closed it and went to sit behind her desk. Everyone was quiet as we all looked at one another, waiting for someone to speak or for something to happen.

"I need updates. This is how it's going to be from now on. Every Sunday, you're going to inform me of what's going on in your area. I don't want to be bothered by it during the week unless there's an emergency."

Everyone nodded their heads in agreement.

"As you know, things have slowed down at the skate park and not because Bash isn't there as much. The crowd has dried up, and now we're hitting up as many parties as we can to sell," Ale informed the room.

"Now that Bash is your fuck buddy and your bodyguard, will he be selling anymore?" Army threw out into the room.

"That's up to Sebastian what he wants to do and how busy Santi is. While we're on the topic of people we're fucking, let's talk about Devi." Arely leaned forward with her hands clasped out in front of her. Her dark brown eyes drilled into her brother's.

"What about her?" Armando started to pace back

and forth in front of her desk. "Are you going to tell me she's not good enough for me?"

"I think she's the wrong girl for you, but we're going to use her to our advantage," Arely smirked. The smile was evil, and it immediately caught my attention. Something wasn't right.

Her words caught Armando off guard, causing him to stop abruptly and turn to his sister. "What the hell are you talking about?"

"Your little girlfriend isn't who she says she is. She's playing you, Army."

"You're lying," he yelled, looking to everyone in the room for support.

"Unfortunately, I'm not. I had Santi do a background check, and it wasn't until yesterday that he finally struck gold." She looked at Santi and nodded.

"She was too clean, man. Not that a college student should have a rap sheet a mile long or anything, but there was hardly anything on her anywhere, even her social media. So, I did some more digging because it was too nicely wrapped up in a pretty little package for me, and that's when I finally struck gold. She's not a college student at all. She's been playing you this entire time. Didn't you think it was odd she was so understanding of everything?"

"I don't share jack shit with her, so there's nothing

to be understanding about. I don't even sell when she's around." Army hung his head and then shook it. "If she's not in college, then what is she?"

"D… E… A…" Arely said, slowly letting it sink in.

They couldn't be serious. How did she let Devi, or whatever her name was, into her house, knowing who she was?

"You're wrong," Army spat, but I could see in his eyes that there was a spark of knowledge there.

Santi picked up a folder off the desk and threw it to Army. "See for yourself."

Army caught it and sank into a chair as he looked over the pages. He sunk lower and lower with each page turned until his eyes came up to meet Arely's. "I had no idea."

"I know you didn't. I want you to work her. Get her to trust you, but don't share anything with her that will come back to hurt us. When she leaves you, I want her followed to see where she goes and who she's informing." Army nodded woodenly. "Bug her. Do whatever you have to do, so we know what they know. We aren't flying under the radar anymore."

"Fuck," Ale and Army growled at the same time.

Knowing she did a background check on Devi made me wonder if she had one done on me as well. It didn't matter since I didn't have anything to hide. She knew I grew up with no money and did whatever I had to do to survive. Arely knew that about me from day one.

"If no one has anything else to share, let's go and enjoy the rest of the night." Arely stood behind her desk, looking commanding as she looked over everyone in the room.

Arely being in charge of both a drug cartel and her family was hot as hell. All I wanted to do was pull her into the next room and fuck her senseless.

I waited until the room cleared to prowl toward her. Picking Arely up, she instantly wrapped her legs around my waist as I bent and took her mouth in a searing kiss.

She pulled away, her breath heavy with want. "Do business meetings turn you on?"

"You turn me on. Being all commanding and in charge has my dick so hard for you right now. I need to fuck you," I growled. Opening the door that led to her bedroom, I pressed her up against the door. Gripping her shirt on each side, I pulled, ripping it down the center. I didn't have time to remove clothes. I wanted my face buried in her succulent tits.

My hands moved under her skirt, and when I found her pussy covered, I ripped the fabric and plunged two fingers deep inside of her. "From now on, I don't want you wearing underwear. I want to be able to slip inside of you whenever I want."

Pulling my fingers out, she whimpered but quickly recovered. Her hands went straight to the button on my jeans. She had my dick out and was running her slick pussy over it in no time. Wrapping her arms around my neck, Arely lowered herself until my dick was fully sheathed by her tight, hot pussy. I groaned, pulling back and then slammed back into her already quaking core. Arely rode my dick like her life depended on it. Her mouth was frantic on mine. Our teeth clashed together, and I tasted blood. It only seemed to spur Arely on. Our tongues dueled, sliding against the other. Probing, tasting, and fucking each other's mouths. Even as she came apart, she kept up her pace. Riding me hard and grinding down as her pussy walls strangled my dick. I wouldn't last much longer. Coating my thumb with her juices, I slipped it into her ass, wanting her to come once more. We came at the same time, moaning into each other's mouths. I pressed her further into the door, pinning her there as I worked the last of our orgasms out of us.

I loved that she wasn't soft when I fucked her. There was nothing soft about Arely. She was pure fire, and I couldn't get enough of her, even knowing one day I'd be burned.

CHAPTER THIRTEEN

arely

THREE ORGASMS LATER, I breathed heavily into Sebastian's neck. His arms were still clasped around me as our heart rates slowly started to return to back to normal when my bedroom door flew open.

"Oh shit," Santi shielded his eyes and turned around to face the door. "If you two could stop fucking for a minute, we have an emergency."

Sebastian's arms slipped down my back and pulled my silk sheets up until I was covered. Only then did he slip out from under me to glare at my brother for his intrusion. "Have you ever heard of knocking?"

"We have more important things to discuss than manners in my own home," Santi growled as he paced around my room.

Turning, I held the sheet to my chest. "This is *my*

home—something you would all do well to remember. If you give me a few minutes to get dressed, I'll meet you in my office. Is this something everyone should be in attendance for?"

"Everyone is assembled in your office waiting for you. I texted you over an hour ago." His jaw ticked as he opened the door that led to my office. "Multiple times. You were too busy to respond, I guess."

"Very busy indeed." I could hear the smirk in Sebastian's tone. I wasn't sure what their problem was, but they needed to get over it. Neither of them was going anywhere anytime soon, and if they made me choose, they wouldn't like the consequences.

"Just hurry up. Don't make a detour on your way to your office," Santi grumbled before he slipped out of the room.

Climbing out of bed, I headed straight for the shower. I wasn't going to sit across from my brothers with Sebastian's cum dripping out of me. I was a little classier than that—not much, but some. I stepped under the cold water and didn't wait for it to warm up. Whatever was going on had to be important; otherwise, Santi would never have barged into my room.

Sebastian stepped inside, only for me to push him out. "What the hell, Arely? Are you really not going to let me rinse off?"

I ran my soapy hands over my body and removed the overhead sprayer. "You are not coming in here with me. If you do, it will probably take us another hour to see what they want, and I really don't feel like having another one of my brothers seeing me naked." Cleaning between my legs, I nearly came when the warm water came into contact with my clit. It was so damn sensitive, and it would only take a moment for me to come. Too bad I didn't have time for that.

Sebastian continued to stand there with his arms crossed over his chest. The move made his biceps and pecs flex in the most delicious way. He watched as my body shuddered before I put the sprayer back. "Have you ever gotten yourself off with your shower attachment?"

Turning off the water, I wrapped a warm, white towel around me before I stepped out and headed to my closet. "Many times. Do you have a problem with that?"

"No, more power to you. I was just thinking about how hot you would be getting yourself off. Maybe later we can take a shower together since I'm still dirty, and you can show me." The deep, husky tone of his voice had me wanting to drop my towel and get back under the shower spray. When Sebastian was around, I could never get enough. It was safe to say I was addicted to his dick and all the orgasms he gave me daily. It didn't help that he had the body of a bronzed god and knew how to use it. Sebastian King was my kryptonite.

Pulling out the first set of underwear I came across, I tried my hardest not to look at his naked form. "Right now, we need to focus on whatever the emergency is. In fact, you need to get dressed now unless you plan to walk in naked."

"Fine," he grumbled as he left the closet. Sebastian was digging into the bag he brought when he showed up last night. I wasn't sure what he was looking for because there wasn't room in it to have more than a few items, and they were all scattered on my bed. At least he had pulled on a pair of jeans. He'd left the top button unbuttoned, and for some unknown reason, it was damn hot. I wanted to pull his zipper down with my teeth and take his thick cock into my mouth.

"You shouldn't look at me like that," he said, bringing me out of my musing. "It's already hard enough to contain myself around you with you eye fucking me across the room."

"Let's go." I walked to the door that connected my office to my bedroom and opened it. Sebastian was right behind me, pulling a t-shirt over his head.

All eyes were on us as we stepped into my office,

except for Santi. Maybe he'd think twice about not knocking after today.

"It's about fucking time," Army huffed. "I was getting ready to meet up with Devi when this pendejo messaged us all for an emergency." Army signaled to Santi.

"How's it going with her?" I asked as I sat behind my desk. "Have you learned anything yet?"

"So far, she hasn't met up with anyone or planted any bugs. I'm keeping a close eye on her, though."

"Good, keep it up. We can't let the DEA learn anything about us." I looked at Santi with raised brows. "What's the emergency?"

"We've had a few ODs in the last couple of weeks, and I did some digging. I had a batch of our last shipment tested, and there's fentanyl in our coke. Anyone want to tell me how that happened? It's bad enough the DEA is on us, but if more people OD on our shit, they are going to be crawling up our asses. We can't have that."

I shifted to look at Pablo. "Is there any way we can trace who it came from?"

"Maybe we need to make a trip down to Colombia and remind them who they're fucking with?" Santi suggested.

Pablo steepled his fingers in front of his face and

nodded. A dark look crossed his face. "We can make a vacation out of it. It's been too long since we've been there. I think it's time we remind them who they're working for and what will happen if they fuck us over."

It would be nice, but I wasn't sure it was the right move. "Are we sure it's on their end and not here?" It didn't make sense the cooks in Colombia could get their hands on fentanyl.

"The twins can stay here and work with their guys. Your boyfriend too, if it will make you feel better," Pablo smirked, knowing I'd hate the idea of leaving them behind.

"Make the arrangements for us all to go as soon as possible. I don't want any more deaths associated with our drugs. While they may be risking their lives doing coke, they are not prepared for fentanyl."

"I'll get on it right away." Pablo looked to Santi. "How many guards are you planning on bringing with us?"

Santi chewed on the inside of his cheek for a moment before his eyes lit up. "One for each of us. I think if we have more, it will draw too much attention with the transport."

I agreed. We needed to stay as compact as possible on the streets we'd be traveling. Having two guys for each of us would cause a scene.

I looked around the room. "Is there anything else?"

"Yeah, how long until he's living here?" Ale asked with a chuckle.

"What?" I laughed, looking toward Sebastian.

"Yeah, he's always here," Army added.

"He's protecting me when Santi's not."

"And fucking your brains out every other second," Army chuckled and flipped Sebastian off. "I don't mind if he's living here. You asked if there was anything else, and we wanted to know."

"It's good to know some of you approve, but that's between Sebastian and me. If that's all, I have some work to do if we're going to be headed to Colombia soon."

One by one, they each came to kiss me on the cheek before they left the room. Sebastian was the last, and he lingered by the door. "You don't have to come if you don't want to. I understand if you don't want to miss your classes."

"You think I give a shit about class?" He shook his head as he came toward me. "I want to be there to protect you. Colombia is not a safe country to be in."

I sat back in my chair. "Is that all it is? You want to protect me?"

He sat on the edge of my desk and took one of my hands in his. "I like you, Arely. You should know that by now. If something were to happen to you and I wasn't there, I'm not sure how I'd live with myself."

"You shouldn't put that stress on yourself. I knowingly put myself in this danger from the start." Griping his hand, I looked into his troubled eyes. "You had no idea what you were getting involved in when you started this. I won't hold you to my protection."

"Damn it, Arely, I can't help it. I'm as drawn to protecting you as I am fucking you. Don't try to stop me."

I nodded, understanding.

There was something about Sebastian that drew me to him. It didn't matter if I wanted it or not. I knew his life would be better off without me in it, and yet I couldn't push him away. Instead, I brought him closer with each passing day.

"Come with me." I stood and walked into my bedroom and straight to my closet. I opened a drawer in my dresser that sat in the middle and left it open for him to look inside.

I watched as he fingered the contents inside before he looked at me over the dresser. "Why is there a gun in here?"

"It's for you. If you are to help guard me, you need a gun on you at all times, and you can fill up that drawer with your belongings. If you're going to be here as often as you have been, then you shouldn't have to live out of that tiny bag."

Pulling his hand out of the drawer like it bit him, Sebastian walked around the dresser like a lion on the hunt, and I was his prey. He could be the king of my jungle any time. "Are you asking me to move in with you?"

"No," I stepped closer to him. I would never step back when he was near. "This is me saying you can leave some things here to make your life easier. That is all."

Reaching up, one fingertip traced my jaw. His thumb pressed into my bottom lip as his eyes searched mine. "It feels like more than that."

I bit the tip of his thumb and then ran my tongue over it. "It's for the selfish reason of being able to keep you in my bed longer." Shifting closer, I unzipped his jeans and slipped my hand inside to find his cock already stiffening. I ran my palm up and down his growing length. "What do you say we take that shower now?"

His normally light eyes darkened as he pushed his jeans down his legs and stepped out of them. His long, thick cock slapped against his abs and bobbed as he moved. He pulled his t-shirt over his head and let it drop to the floor. I followed suit, removing my clothes as I walked through my bedroom and into the bathroom. I couldn't take my eyes off Sebastian as his muscles flexed while turning on the shower. He stood underneath the cold spray, and I watched entranced as trails of water sluiced down his perfect body. I wanted to lick each and every drop.

Stepping forward, he held his hand out to me. "Am I going to have to come out there and get you?"

"As much as I'd love for you to chase me, I'd much rather get wet and dirty with you now." Unclasping my bra, I slid the straps down my arms and let the garment fall to the floor at my feet. Taking Sebastian's hand, I let him pull me under the now warm spray and melded my body to his. His lips brushed against my shoulder and moved up the side of my neck to my waiting mouth. The second our mouths connected, it was like a shot of lightning stuck us both. My hands skated down his torso to his treasure trail that led to the promised land. His cock rested against my stomach as his hands cupped my ass and brought us flesh to flesh.

His hands kneaded the globes of my ass as I kissed every inch of him I could. "Fuck, you've got the best damn ass I've ever seen. Not today, but soon, I'm going to claim that sweet ass of yours."

Wrapping my leg around his hip, I guided his cock between my legs and started to rock. "Yes," I moaned.

"I love how hungry your pussy is for my dick. Turn around," Sebastian ordered at the same time he gripped my shoulders and brought my back to his front. One of his large hands cupped and massaged my breasts, while the other slowly trailed down from my sternum all the way to where I wanted him most. Two fingers dipped inside of me, pumping twice before pulling out.

"More," I moaned.

Raking his stubble up my neck, he stopped at the shell of my ear. His voice was gravelly as he spoke. "So much more. Grab the sprayer and show me what you do to yourself with it."

I did as he wanted and took the sprayer off the wall and turned the dial until the water was coming out like a jet. The feel of his hard body against my back already had me on edge. I was so worked up it wouldn't take much for the water to set me off.

Widening my stance, I lowered the showerhead until the warm water blasted between my legs and came into contact with my clit. My body jolted at the pleasure. My other hand curved around Sebastian's hip and gripped his ass.

"I won't last long," I shuddered as I moved the sprayer back and forth.

He pushed me forward until my front was pressed

up against the cool tiles. The dueling sensations of the tiles and the warmth of the water and Sebastian at my back had my body overloaded. I needed more.

As if he could read my mind, I felt his cock nudge at my entrance only seconds before he thrust his hips and was fully inside. I let out a long moan. My pussy quivered and stretched at the fullness he always provided. Using the sprayer, I hit us where we were connected, and it set Sebastian off.

A low growl unfurled from deep in his chest as he pulled back and slammed into me time after time. My free hand moved to claw at the walls trying to find purchase. He felt too good inside of me. Each thrust brought me closer and closer to the promised land.

His rough hand gripped my hip and angled me in a way that only made me feel him deeper. Pulling the water from where we were joined, I hit my clit and nearly came on the spot.

"Whatever you're doing, keep doing it," he panted in my ear. "The way your pussy just clenched around my cock was nothing short of spectacular. I want to feel you grip me like a vice and never let go until you've milked me of every last drop of cum."

Turning my head and angling it up, I pressed my lips to his, opening up when his tongue probed inside. I gripped his neck with my free hand and let him fuck my mouth the same way he was fucking my pussy.

When we were like this, there was no outside world. There was only him and me. Our bodies moved together in tandem like they were made for each other, making me wish for our joining to never end.

Tingles slowly spread from the nape of my neck down to my toes while at the same time lighting a fire inside of me. I pressed the water closer to my nub, knowing it would set me off while Sebastian continued to crash into me from behind. And just like that, the world stopped. I arched into him, and he ate the scream that came out of my mouth. My entire body quaked as I rode higher and higher, clenching around his cock, never wanting to let it go. I could happily die with Sebastian inside of me, claiming me the way that he was. It was freeing and addictive.

Pulling me back from the wall, he took the sprayer and brought it straight to my highly sensitized clit, and held it there. His other arm bound around me like he was holding me together while he continued to piston inside of me. It was all too much. When I didn't think it could get much better, my pleasure intensified. Breaking apart, I let out a soundless cry, and my body exploded like a supernova. My eyes were open but unseeing as white, hot pleasure coursed through my body.

I felt it when the water dropped away from my center. My body instantly sagged against his. If it wasn't for his strong grip on me, I had no doubt I would have been a puddle on my shower floor. My head lolled back in time to see Sebastian's mouth part in the sexiest 'O' face I'd ever seen. The feel of his hot cum releasing inside of me had my walls constricting around him once again. My pussy was greedy for every last drop. I wanted it all.

We stood there for a long moment. I wasn't sure how long. My body shook with aftershocks while Sebastian held me tight to his body, and he breathed heavily into the top of my head. I wondered if he was as spent as I was.

Eventually, he picked me up in his arms. I nuzzled into his neck, wrapping my arms around him. I was so close to falling asleep that I barely felt it as he wrapped me in a towel. I only knew we were walking when I felt the cool air hit my overheated skin. A second later, I was being wrapped in blankets with Sebastian at my back.

I turned, resting my cheek on his chest and molding my front to his. I wanted every inch of us that we could to be touching. With his arms around me, he pulled me closer. My leg went between his as I slowly started to fade away.

This was perfect, but I knew it wouldn't stay that way. I knew in that moment I would fight heaven and hell to keep what we had. It may have just been the beginning, but it was everything, and I wouldn't let him go.

CHAPTER FOURTEEN

bash

WHILE I KNEW ARELY and her family had money, I had no idea they had private plane kind of money. The inside was all white and gold, making you feel like you were ensconced in luxury. The plush leather seats were soft and molded perfectly to your body. If I could live on this plane, I would.

I sat by the window, looking out at the world below me. I'd never flown before, nor had I left the country, and today I was doing both in style.

Arely, Santiago, and Pablo were in the back having a meeting while Ale and Army sat on a couch playing a video game and fighting about who was cheating. The rest of the seats were filled by the guards that were brought for our protection.

When I woke up this morning, a passport sat on the

bedside table with a note to pack and be ready in an hour. I wasn't sure how they got me a passport so fast. It was only five days since they decided to make the trip, but I wasn't going to question it. Two hours later, we were boarding their plane.

"Enjoying the view?" came Arely's honeyed voice as she sat down beside me.

"I've never flown before," I muttered as I continued to look out the window.

She ran one lone fingernail from my hand up my arm and circled back down. "You should have said something, and I wouldn't have left you to your own devices during takeoff. I'm guessing since no one said anything, you didn't mind the takeoff."

I caught her hand in mine as I shifted to look at her. "I was fine. The reason for never flying wasn't because I thought I would freak out. It was merely the fact that I never had any money or any place to go."

She gave me a small, almost innocent smile. Except there was nothing innocent about Arely. She was a hardcore badass. She probably came out of the womb that way. "I know it might seem like I've always lived like this, but I haven't—only the twins. When I was young, we were poor. My two brothers and I lived in a one-bedroom apartment with our parents. I don't remember much since I was so young, but I remember my father working night and day to provide for us. He started at the bottom and worked his way up to being the boss." She blinked, coming back into focus, and looked at me. "I'm not naïve. I'm sure he killed people to get where he was. That's the price you pay for living in this world."

Arely was right. I would never have guessed at any point in her life she'd been poor. Maybe she could appreciate where I came from.

"Be prepared for a culture shock and be on your toes. Some of the places we're going are violent. That's the only way of life they know."

Why was she telling me this?

"You haven't had any training, but I want you to remain vigilant. Keep your eyes peeled for anything. If you think something is wrong or going down, tell someone. Anyone in our group."

"I won't let you down," I vowed.

She leaned forward, her eyes locked with mine. "I know you won't." Sitting back in her seat, Arely closed her eyes and relaxed.

"How did your meeting go?"

She kept her eyes closed as she spoke in a low, unaffected tone. "One of the worst parts about working with family is the fighting. We fight about *everything*.

Each of us thinks we're right and doesn't want to back down."

"So, it went how you expected it to go." I looked back out the window and to the water below.

"It did." This time, she sounded exhausted.

"Why don't you get some sleep before we land," I suggested.

"Good idea."

I thought she was going to lean her chair back like I'd seen some of the guards do, but instead, Arely curled up on her side and rested her head against my arm. It felt like only a matter of seconds before she relaxed against me and her breaths slowed. One of the stewardesses came by with a blanket and placed it over Arely. She snuggled in closer and let out a contented sigh.

I was lost in the heat emanating off her body and her soft breaths when Ale spoke, breaking me out of my trancelike state. My brows furrowed as I tried to make out what he'd said. "She looks good on you. I've never seen her happier or more relaxed than when she's with you."

"But if you hurt her, we'll kill you, and you know that isn't an idle threat. We. Will. Kill. You," Army said like he was talking about the weather, not my demise.

If Arely hadn't been using me for a pillow, I

would've gotten up and in their faces. Almost as if she could feel me tensing, her arm wrapped around my middle.

"I don't plan on hurting her," I clipped out. I had no idea where this was going with Arely or my place in their world, but I knew it wasn't going to be as easy as it had been. "But let's get one thing straight. You won't be taking me down if something does happen."

"Oh, listen to the big words from the *big* man. He thinks just because he's sleeping with the boss, he's calling the shots." Army laughed bitterly.

"Shut up, all of you," Arely spoke in a deadly calm voice I hadn't heard from her before. It seemed her brothers had, though. They shut their mouths and looked the other way. The entire time, she kept her eyes closed and looked as if she was sleeping against my arm.

Leaning close, I spoke quietly for only her to hear. "Arely, I—"

This time, one eye peeked open, and the fire burning in that one eye had me hard in a nanosecond. "Don't."

I only wanted to tell her I wasn't going to take their shit because they were her brothers. I wouldn't take it from anyone. Not even her, but now I had other ideas.

Taking the hand from around my waist, I ran it

down my abs and to the growing bulge in my pants. "Does this plane have a bedroom in the back?"

"It does, but we are not going to use it," she said simply.

Even at her denial, my dick didn't listen. He grew harder as I cupped her hand over the straining fabric.

One corner of my mouth tipped up before she spoke. "If you want, you can head back and jack yourself off in the bathroom."

"No help from you? That doesn't sound nearly as fun." I wasn't ruled by my dick, but I was twenty years old. Even with all the sex we'd been having, I was always down for more.

"Fun times are over for now. You'll have to wait until—"

"I have no problem waiting for you." I removed her hand, placed it on my stomach, and covered it with my own.

"Good. Why don't you get some rest? You're going to need it. We're going to be very busy the next few days, and I need you in tip-top shape."

Arely was right. I couldn't protect her if I was dragging. Wrapping my arm around her, I leaned my seat back. With the seat molded to my body and Arely's body heat at my side, it didn't take long for me to start to doze off.

It felt like a matter of minutes when my eyes popped open, and our plane was descending. I wasn't going to lie. I was excited to visit another country, even if it was one that was as dangerous as Colombia. I wasn't under the impression we wouldn't run into trouble. I knew it would happen. I just didn't know how or when.

Looking to my right, Arely was sitting upright and talking to Santi. The second his eyes landed on mine, he clapped her on the shoulder and walked to the back of the plane.

"He doesn't like me," I stated. Hell, it felt like the twins were starting to not like me. Maybe it was because I wasn't under their control any longer.

Pulling her hair to the side, she ran her fingers through her long tresses. "He doesn't like many people outside of our family. Plus, he's afraid we're getting too close, and I'm going to get hurt."

"I don't plan to hurt you."

"I know that. If I thought that was your plan, you wouldn't be here or in my bed. We're getting close, and feelings are bound to develop." Her brown eyes bore into mine as if willing me to spill my deepest, darkest secrets.

Did her words mean she had feelings for me?

Before I could ask, we touched down with a slight

jerk of the plane. The second we stopped, everyone was up and out of their seats. The guards headed off the plane, where they immediately went to three black Suburbans sitting on the tarmac. They scanned every inch of each vehicle before Javier stepped back onto the plane.

"All clear. We'll get the luggage, and then we'll head to the hotel. It will be the same protocol as when we were in New York. You will all wait in your vehicle until we check each room." He nodded once and then slipped back off the plane.

"So that's where you went," Ale laughed.

"If you wanted to know so badly, you could have asked me. I have nothing to hide."

Army's face scrunched up. "None of us have anything to hide from each other. That's what makes our family work."

"Someone is hiding something," Arely whispered to herself. I wasn't sure if I was meant to hear what she said or not. Was she telling me to be on the lookout even with her own family because someone couldn't be trusted? I wanted to ask her about it, but it would have to wait until we were alone. If she suspected something, why would she bring whoever it was along? Was it so they wouldn't know Arely was questioning a member of her family?

Taking up my place behind Arely, I watched each member on the plane. If Arely didn't trust them, neither would I.

Now I had to be more vigilant than ever in keeping her safe with this new knowledge.

CHAPTER FIFTEEN

arely

AT FIRST, when Sebastian insisted on being my bodyguard, I placated him. Santi was all I needed, or so I thought, but as I watched him keep a constant vigil on the streets around us, I knew he wouldn't let anything happen to me.

I could tell he was shocked by the conditions of the area we traveled through. While many parts of Colombia were beautiful, there were double as many that were dirty, poor, and violent.

That was my world.

We left our gorgeous hotel with the best views to traverse through the poorest parts of Medellín, then out into the country to visit one of our labs. They had no idea we were coming. Well, that wasn't true. I was sure word was out that we were in the country, causing great panic.

Leaning over, Sebastian spoke so quietly, I could barely hear him over everyone else talking. "Do you really think they'll admit to putting fentanyl in the product?"

My body gravitated toward the heat he was emanating. I simply couldn't help myself. Putting my hand on his golden, bronzed arm, I locked eyes with him. "Not if they want to live, but they need to know we're onto them."

He leaned closer this time. So close, I could feel his breath across my neck with each word he spoke. I closed my eyes, remembering the same feeling when I woke up this morning with Sebastian curled around me—his body was always protecting mine, even in our sleep. "And what if it wasn't them?"

If it wasn't, I would find out who it was and end them. It didn't matter who it was.

"Word will get out, and whoever it is *will* be scared. I will not let anyone destroy me and my family."

Sebastian nodded and then looked over my shoulder. I knew who was watching us. Santi was always watching. My best friend was slipping away.

"What's his problem?"

Running the tips of my nails along his arm, I shifted closer to him in the backseat of the SUV. "They're not used to seeing me with anyone. It's going to take them a while to get used to the idea."

His eyes grew dark, liking the idea.

"I keep my sex life out of my home for the most part. I don't let just anyone in."

And yet I'd let Sebastian in without a second thought.

A shot rang out. It was close. All eyes turned to the windows as we canvased the area looking for where it might have come from.

"Shit," Santi yelled from the front passenger seat. "Behind."

An explosion sent a shock wave through our vehicle. My ears rang as I turned to see what Santi had seen. Behind us, the second Suburban with our extra guards sat on fire in the middle of the street.

"Ve," Santi shouted.

"Dónde?" Our driver shouted back with a quiver in his voice.

"I don't know, just lose them and take us somewhere safe," Santi hissed.

"Somewhere they won't be expecting us," Sebastian shot out.

"What about other car?" The driver asked as he took a sharp left.

"They'll find their own way." Santi turned in his seat, looking out the back. "Más rápido."

Gunshots rang out into the sticky air. I could hear them hitting our SUV and silently prayed we would make it out of here.

Sebastian pushed me down and practically laid on top of me as the tires of our SUV screeched. I felt the driver accelerate as he tried to break away.

I could feel my phone buzzing in my pocket, but there was no way for me to answer it. I was frozen in fear as shot after shot rang out and pelted our SUV.

"Be prepared to shoot," Santi yelled. I could hear the panic in his voice. Something I hadn't heard in... forever. Santi was always calm, cool, and collected. We both were, but in that moment, I was scared. I didn't want to die.

The next few minutes were a series of turns that threw Sebastian and me from one side of the SUV to the other. I'd lost track of how many times we turned.

"I think we lost them." Santi's voice sounded both far away and close.

I tried to sit up, wanting to see for myself that we were safe, but Sebastian wouldn't let me up. He grunted when I elbowed him in the stomach but held fast.

"Stay down, Arely," he gritted out.

"It's over." I tried to push up using all my strength, but I was no match for Sebastian or his weight.

"Let's play this safe. I'll get off you, but you need to stay down just in case."

The second his weight started to shift, I pushed up and twisted to look out the back. We were in the middle of nowhere on some one-lane road speeding past green fields. My body instantly started to shake, the shock starting to wear off.

Sebastian grabbed me by the side of the neck and pushed me down until my head was resting in his lap. Closing my eyes, I let him hold me down this time and wrapped my hand around his thigh. Being connected to him helped ease the growing dread that started to slither in my stomach.

If we didn't play this right, I was going to die, and quite possibly my brothers as well.

"Hey, asshole, this isn't the time for my sister to be giving you a blow job," Santi growled.

My eyes sprung open, and my hand shot out, punching Santi in the arm. "Shut the fuck up, and call the others to see if they're okay."

My body started to shake for a whole different reason.

What if they didn't make it?

Rotating toward Sebastian, I buried my face into his stomach. As much as I tried to hold back the wetness that started to build, I couldn't. Not with the possibility that Pablo, Ale, and Army might be dead.

Sebastian's hand cupped the back of my head and started to run his fingers through my hair slowly. He didn't tell me it was going to be okay, and I was thankful he didn't make any promises he couldn't keep.

"Arely," Santi said my name so quietly I was terrified to hear his next words. They could either break me or set me free of the terror building inside of me. "They're all fine. We're going to figure out a place to meet up where no one will be able to find us."

I nodded, not wanting to let him see me weak. He patted my hip, and then I heard him turn around. Santi and the driver spoke back and forth about options on where we could go for the night. The entire time, Sebastian ran his fingers through my hair. I wasn't sure how he knew what I needed, but the way his fingers played with my hair put me in a trancelike state. All I could do was feel his touch, making it seem as if there was no outside world beyond our little bubble.

Halfway between sleep and awake, I felt the car jerk

to a stop. Instantly, I was on alert. My body tensed, ready for anything that might come our way. Sitting up, I looked around, taking in my new surroundings. The sun was further west than I expected. How long had we been driving?

"We should get inside. The rest will be here in about twenty minutes. Keep your heads down and try to look inconspicuous."

I was pretty sure that was going to be next to impossible with the three of us and our two guards. Santi always stood out in a crowd; there were no two ways about it. At least I had dressed down, thinking we were going to be traipsing through the jungle.

The second I stepped out of the SUV, I wrapped myself around Sebastian like he was a lifeline. Even though Santi had said Pablo and the twins were safe, I wouldn't fully believe it until I saw them with my own two eyes.

The moment the door opened, music spilled out, causing me to look up to see where the hell we were. There wasn't a name on the establishment, making me hesitant. Would we really be safe here?

The room was filled with tables and booths, sultry music filling the air. Barely clothed women writhed on the laps of men while they smoked and drank.

The rest of our party walked through like we

weren't in some strip joint. I continued to follow Santi and the driver as they navigated through the maze of tables. I could feel the heat of the guards directly behind me. I was sure they wondered why they took this job now that half the team was dead.

I spotted a hallway that was lined with doors. I tried to keep my head down and not make any eye contact. I wanted to be forgettable. No one could find out that we were here. Luckily, it seemed as if the patrons had more important things to watch than our brigade of misfits.

I could feel Sebastian's body start to vibrate with tension the closer we got to the hallway. Halfway down the hallway, the driver opened a door and waited for us to pile in. It was only then that I started to wonder where we'd found this driver. Was he on our side? He could have easily led us into an ambush.

Taking in the room, I realized it was a bedroom. Was this where our driver lived?

Letting go of Sebastian, I stepped to the driver. We were the same height, but he had at least seventy-five pounds on me. "What is this place?"

He smiled kindly, like we hadn't just been in a shootout not that long ago. "No need to be worried. You're safe here. No one is going to be looking for you in Sonsón, let alone a whorehouse."

A whorehouse. That made sense.

"You stay here, and I'll wait out front for the rest. Once they arrive, I'll bring them back, and we can figure out where we're going from here."

Santi nodded to one of the guards, and he followed our driver out. If we lived through this, I was going to have to find out his name and make sure he got paid handsomely for all he'd done for us.

Sebastian moved to lean against the wall with his eyes trained on the door. "Shouldn't we keep the guards with us, just in case?"

Santi's eyes slanted Sebastian's way, and he let out a huff of air. "I don't want him out there by himself on the off chance he's not trustworthy. He could be calling in the calvary, and we wouldn't know it until it's too late."

Sebastian nodded with his eyes still zeroed in on the door. "Smart thinking."

"Yes, thank you." Santi rolled his eyes. "I've been doing this for longer than two weeks. I didn't get the job because I'm fucking the boss."

Sebastian took his eyes off the door for one brief second and glanced over to where Santi was sitting on the bed. "No, you got the job because you're her fucking brother."

"Enough," I hissed out. "There's a time and a place for this shit, and it certainly isn't now. We need to figure out if this was done by rivals, whoever tainted our shipment, or the society."

Leaning forward, Santi placed his elbows on his knees and rested his chin on his clasped hands. "Do you really think the society would do it here of all places?"

"Why not?" I held my arms out at my sides. "No one would suspect them."

"No one suspects them now. They weren't who tried to kill you."

"Someone sent the test to him," I nodded toward Sebastian. "It looked exactly like all our tests. If it wasn't the Scorpio Society as a whole, it was a member. How else would they have got Sebastian's test to him and made it look authentic?"

"I'm not saying I don't believe it wasn't someone in the society, but I think it was one person. Who have you pissed off?"

I let out a bark of laughter. "Who haven't I pissed off?"

"True," he smirked for a second, and then his face fell flat. "I think today is someone different. Who? I have no clue, but I don't think we should cut our trip short."

"And back down?" I shook my head I could feel my blood start to boil at the thought of anyone thinking we were weak. "No way in hell. That's not going to look good. We need to show we are a force not to be messed with."

"Then we need to hire more guards. An army to surround us, and until then, we need to lie low."

We were stupid to bring so few guards. We should have brought them all, but the logistics of getting them here seemed more difficult than it was worth. Now we were regretting that decision.

Easy wasn't the best way.

The door swung open to reveal Ale and Army, both trying to barrel through the door at the same time. The second they saw me, they came running through the small room and hugged me on each side.

"Thank God you're okay. When we saw that explosion…" Ale shuddered.

"We thought they got you, and then you were gone." Army held me tighter.

"Your driver was smart. No one will look for us here." Pablo eyed the room with disdain.

Yes, I didn't prefer to hide out in a room where there was no telling how many people had sex on a given day, but beggars couldn't be choosers. I was just happy we'd all made it out alive.

Pablo sat down next to Santi on the bed and hung his head. "What are we doing now?"

"I'm calling in the calvary—all the guys we have in New York and more from here. From now on, we're going to have an army behind us. I should have anticipated this. They probably saw we only had a few guards with us and decided now would be the perfect time to take us out."

Pablo's heavy brows furrowed. "Who?"

"I don't know." Santi shook his head. "It could be any number of people, but we should have come here strong. I can tell you now, we are going to leave here as a force no one wants to mess with. And once I figure out who the attempt was made by, they're going to wish they'd never even thought of trying to hurt us. I'm not just going to end their life. I'm going to first ruin their family and friends' lives, and then I'm going to torture them slowly. And then torture them some more."

Pablo clapped him on the shoulder. "First, you've got to figure out who did it. Now, what are we going to do in the meantime?"

"I have spoken to the owner of the establishment, and you are welcome to stay here for as long as you need. The men are welcome to sample the ladies too while you wait."

"Free whores?" Ale laughed. "What fun. Are we all to stay in this room or—"

"Unfortunately, this is the only open room unless you're with a girl," our driver said.

Ale looked at me and frowned. "I guess you're stuck with me then, hermana."

"I'm always happy to have you, Ale. You know that."

Pablo jumped up and clapped his hands. "I don't know about the rest of you, but I'm all for some free pussy." He looked to Army and Santi. "Are you going to join me?"

Santi was already shaking his head. "You go ahead and have your fun. I've got to get more men."

Army followed Pablo to the door. "Why not? My fake girlfriend isn't here to please me."

Pablo looked back to where Sebastian was standing. He'd barely taken his eyes off the door. I wasn't sure if he was hearing what they were saying or not. "What do you say, Bash? Are you coming?"

Sebastian's only answer was to narrow his eyes and cross his arms over his chest.

Pablo laughed, shaking his head as he ushered Army out the door.

"Try not to catch any diseases while you're here," I called out as they left the room.

The room was silent for several long minutes. We were frozen until Santi pulled out his phone and started to type.

Ale looked down at the bed with his entire face scrunched up before he perched himself on the edge of the mattress. "I seriously can't believe they are out there getting their dicks wet right now."

Santi looked up from his phone with one brow raised. "Are you seriously telling us that if there were any guys out there that you wouldn't be doing the same thing?"

"You act like I'll stick my dick into any asshole that will open for me," Ale scoffed and moved further away from Santi. "That's not how it works. I won't fuck any willing man."

Sebastian pushed off the wall, and with two strides, he was standing in front of me. Taking my hand in his, he pulled me over to the one chair in the room. It was a sickly yellow color that had seen better days with hardly any cushion left in the seat. He sat down with his legs spread wide and pulled me down onto his lap.

I went willingly. Snuggling into his side and trying to let go of all the rampant thoughts of earlier fade away. Tilting my head up, I found his light brown eyes focused solely on me. They were turbulent, but I didn't blame him. He probably wished he'd never gotten involved with my family. "What's this for?"

Dipping his head down, he spoke quietly for only me to hear. His lips brushed along the shell of my ear, making my body come alive. "Because I wanted to be able to feel you in my arms to make sure you're really here."

CHAPTER SIXTEEN

bash

SITTING in that tiny room for days while we were waiting for more people to arrive was torture. I was itching to find out who had tried to kill Arely once again. She'd mentioned after she was shot that it was the first attempt on her life, and now there'd been another. I was starting to wonder if maybe I was bad luck for her. If I wasn't around, would she be safer?

Santi had been on the phone non-stop to bring the rest of the guards from New York down here while simultaneously trying to find people he could trust here to keep us safe.

I knew little about how their organization worked, but I was learning. The more I knew, the easier it would be for me to protect Arely and the rest of her family. Nothing could happen to her brothers. The joy that spread across her face when she saw her brothers walk through the door told me she'd be devastated if any harm came to them.

"What's the plan once they arrive? Are we still going to the lab?" Army tapped his foot impatiently. I wasn't sure why he was so anxious. He'd been with one whore or another the entire time we'd been here. The rest of us, sans Pablo, had been stuck in this room the entire time. We didn't even leave to eat. Our food was brought to us, and we used the little bathroom that was attached for the rest of our needs.

We were all on edge and bored out of our minds. I couldn't wait to escape this place. I wanted to go back to the hotel and get some real sleep other than the little I'd gotten while sitting in the chair that was now mine and Arely's. She slept fitfully on my lap for short periods of time, but mostly she paced the room, making me, Ale, and Santi dizzy.

Santi sat his phone down, and an evil smirk crossed his face. "Oh, we're going, and we're going to make sure the word spreads that if anyone fucks with us even the most minute amount, we'll kill them all. We pay our people more than anyone else, and for that, they should be loyal."

Arely slipped off my lap and started to pace the room once again with her hands on her hips. "Hell fucking yeah, they should be. If they were working for anyone else, they'd be making at least half of what we fucking pay them. After that, we're going to check into another hotel. We'll send the guards to collect our things from the other hotel."

Reclining back on the bed, Ale put his hands behind his head. "Are you saying you don't want to spend any more time in this lovely abode?

Coming back to me, Arely sat down on my leg and faced the rest of the room. My arms were around her waist without thinking. Any chance we could get, we were touching each other. I wasn't sure of her motivation, but for me, it was to reassure me that she was alive and well. I'd nearly lost my mind when the bullets started to hit the SUV. We were trapped, and the only thing I could do was place my body on top of hers. With each passing day, our shock wore off and led to anger. We were ready to fight, and whoever got in our way should be scared. We weren't going to take prisoners. It was shoot first, ask questions later. If anyone got in our way or seemed like a threat, their lives would be ended. "While I appreciate that they've let us stay, I want to get the hell out of here and take a shower someplace where I won't come into contact with mold and a myriad of diseases."

And there was no way for me to be deep inside Arely when her brothers were less than ten feet away.

"It shouldn't be too much longer. Last I heard, they were an hour out, and that was forty-five minutes ago. I'd say pack your stuff up if we had anything with us." Santi flashed a smile before he typed something on his phone.

He hadn't left the room the entire time we'd been here. Neither had Arely nor Ale, but it made me wonder if he was here to protect her or for another reason.

Pulling her back to my front, I spoke softly in her ear. "What's wrong?"

She shook her head, and I understood she couldn't talk about it here.

Turning my head to get a better look at her, Arely rested her forehead against my jaw. "I'll tell you later when we're alone."

I nodded as my arms tightened around her.

Santi jumped up, and I could feel his excitement from across the room. We were all ready to get out of this shit hole and seek revenge for the others. It didn't matter that they were guards that I didn't know. They were a part of the organization, and I wouldn't let their lives be canceled out in vain.

"Let's go. We're going out the same way we came

in. Keep your heads down and go to the SUVs I tell you to." I'd barely made a face before he continued. "We're splitting up into more cars. If one car goes down, we all won't fall."

Pablo pushed into Santi and tried to look down on him, but they were the same height, so his intimidation tactic didn't work. "Just tell us our seating arrangements now, or are you afraid we'll fight you?"

"Fine, you're with Army," Santi squared off against his brother. "Bash is with Ale, and I'll be with Arely. Each SUV will have three guards with them, and we'll also have a caravan full of guards in front of and behind us. No one is going to touch us."

I didn't like the idea of not being with Arely, but I understood his tactic.

Santi looked around the room, daring someone to speak. "If you don't like it, then you can stay here because this is how it's going to go down. I'm doing this for everyone's safety."

"I don't like Sebastian not being with me, but I understand your reasoning, and if you think it's best, then I won't complain."

"You heard her. No complaining."

That wasn't what she said, but I wasn't going to argue. I wanted to get the hell out of there.

"Let's go," Santi clapped his hands.

We all stood at once. Taking Arely's hand in mine, I moved toward the door until Santi stopped us. "Say your goodbyes in here. I don't want us out in the open for too long."

Arely turned in my arms and glared at her brother for one second before she twisted back into me. Reaching her hand behind my neck, she pulled me down at the same time she pushed up on her toes. Our lips connected, and a gnawing feeling unleashed itself inside of me. Being apart from Arely was going to be gut-wrenching. I knew I wouldn't be able to take a full breath until she was back by my side.

It wasn't a passionate kiss. It was one of connection. I was surprised when Arely pulled away, and the torment in her eyes matched my own.

Pulling her front to mine, I pressed her cheek into my chest and rested my chin on top of her head. "If you need me, I'm just a phone call away."

"Oh, please, it's not like you're not going to see each other again." The incredulity in his tone let us know he thought we were being ridiculous. "I'll make you a deal. If you ride with me on the way, you can travel with Bash on the way back."

Arely nodded into my chest.

The overwhelming need to tell her I loved her pressed inside my chest. I didn't want the first time I said those words to be with all these people around. I wanted it to be private and only for her.

Even though we'd barely talked the last three days we'd spent holed up in this room, something had grown between us. It was unlike anything I'd ever felt before.

Pushing back, Arely gave me a half-smile. "Let's go." I walked ahead of them with Ale by my side.

"Did they bring guns for everyone?" I heard Arely ask from behind me.

"They brought a whole arsenal," Santi answered her. "What do you want?"

"Nothing big, just a handgun or two. I want to be able to protect myself if I need it." She let out a sigh loud enough for me to hear. "I should have brought my own, but…"

"I know. I had no idea our trip would turn into this." Santi sounded sad and resigned. "I guess we should be thankful we've had as much peace as we have since Father was killed. I've been consulting with others about security. By the time we get back home, no one is going to be able to touch us."

"I hope you're right. I feel like people are coming at us from all sides." Arely's voice shook as she said the last part. I looked over my shoulder at her, but she was looking at the floor as she walked. "We can't let them think they can take us down."

"We won't let them. I promise. Today we have an army with us. Literally. Nothing is going to happen to you."

"I don't want anything to happen to any one of us. I love each and every one of you, and if one of these cowardly assholes took you out, it would wreck me."

"We feel the same way about you. When we get back home, we should go over all the logistics of everything I've set up."

"Yes, we certainly need to talk." The hardness in her voice had me wondering if Santi was what she said we'd talk about later.

I was momentarily blinded when Pablo and Armando opened the door and stepped out into the bright sun. Slipping my sunglasses on, I looked back at Arely one final time before we were separated. With a firm nod, she let me know she was going to be okay.

I watched as she got in the SUV behind us and then as we drove away. Santi wasn't wrong about the army. Behind Arely's SUV was an army truck with a canvas top, the back full of men.

"My sister has you so fucking whipped it's funny. I didn't think you'd be the type," Ale chuckled. He was leaned back in his seat with his eyes closed, acting like someone hadn't tried to kill us just days ago.

Sitting back in my seat, I scanned the area as we

flew through the little town. "She's a special woman. Would you prefer that I cared nothing for her and treated her like shit?"

Peeking one eye open, he took me in and then closed his eye again. "I'm not saying that. While some of the others have a problem with whatever you two have going on, I like seeing my sister happy."

"Life and death situations bring people together. After the other day, I… can't explain it." I wasn't sure her brother needed to know all the ways I felt for his sister. If he knew, he'd probably want to kill me himself.

"I've seen how close you two have become and how you didn't want to be separated. Maybe this short time apart will help you realize what your feelings are."

"I don't need time apart to know how I feel. The only thing I want is to keep her safe." It took everything in me not to look back at her vehicle. "I can't do that from here."

"It might not be the way you want, but if someone comes up, you can shoot at them."

But I couldn't lay my life over hers.

The driver and guard in the front passenger seat spoke rapidly in Spanish, making me once again wish I knew what they were saying.

"Do you speak Spanish?"

"Not much. Why?" I bit out.

Ale smirked. "Because you looked clueless as to what they're saying. You know, you really should learn."

Up until now, I hadn't seen it as a problem. While the Guerrera family spoke in Spanish on occasion, they mainly spoke English, but here, almost every conversation was in Spanish—which was to be expected.

I knew the basics, and that was it. Rapid-fire talking like what was going on in the front seat, I had no idea what was being said. Maybe I should enroll in some Spanish classes at the university next semester.

An hour of complete silence later, the driver spoke. Ale sat up and stretched. "We're almost there."

"Thanks." I looked down at my phone to see no new messages. I wanted to turn around to check to see if Arely was still behind us, but I kept looking forward, flipping my phone on my knee.

"She's fine, you know. She's stronger than all of us combined. If it weren't for her, we'd probably all be living on the streets or worse."

I knew if it weren't for Arely, I wouldn't have been able to move out of my shitty apartment into one that actually had heat in the winter.

"I know not everyone feels this way, or at least they don't want to admit it, but you coming along has been good for her. All she's done for the last few years is work and take care of us. She wouldn't let us do anything for her, but now she's happy when you're around. Or at least when she's not getting shot at."

It felt good to know that Arely let me take care of her when she wouldn't let the others.

The SUV came to a slow roll before stopping on a tree-lined gravel road.

"From here, we walk," Ale announced.

I'd never thought about where this drug lab would be until now, but being out in the middle of nowhere made sense. The only question was how we'd find it.

Stepping out of the SUV, I stretched my legs and watched as Arely and Santi got out of their car. All the men in the trucks lined up along the road. Santi barked out orders, or at least what I thought were orders, since I had no idea what he was saying.

Army and Pablo were fighting until Arely marched up to them and smacked them both in the arms. "You're not helping the cause. Now get your shit together, or you can stay here while we head into the jungle."

Army stood up straight while Pablo slouched against the SUV. Arely circled her finger in the air and started to the tree line.

"Fucking hell, Arely, you can't just go without us," Santi shouted as he ran after her.

I took off after her as well. What was she thinking leaving like that? It wasn't hard to catch up to her, even with her brisk pace.

Santi reached out and put his hand on her shoulder. "Arely, slow down and let everyone catch up. We need you to be safe."

She twirled around with her eyes narrowed. "You don't need to tell me. That's what I heard the entire drive here. When have I done anything unsafe?"

Santi turned back around the way we came with a clenched jaw.

I bit my tongue to keep from saying she'd been unsafe only seconds before. "I don't want to fight with you." I closed my eyes and turned back to the way we'd come. There were footsteps and shouting, but I knew they were from our people, not enemies.

"We're not fighting. I want to get to this damn lab, get some answers, and then get the hell out of here. Is that so hard to understand?"

It wasn't, but it still didn't explain why she ran ahead.

"Do you know your way to the lab?"

"No, but I wasn't going to listen to Santi direct people for half an hour. The ego trip he's on is going to his head." She huffed, crossing her arms over her ample chest.

Wrapping my arm around her shoulders, we stood and waited. I didn't think her brother was on an ego trip. He was trying to keep us all safe. Something had happened on the way here, and she was lashing out, which was so unlike Arely.

A minute later, her brothers and the army they brought with them broke through the trees. I thought there would be yelling, but there was none—just two pissed-off siblings. Santi and our driver from the other day walked past and down a barely discernible path. We got in line and followed behind a group of men in army fatigues who were also carrying guns.

Slipping my arm from around her shoulders, I gripped Arely's hand in mine. I could feel her vibrating, but I didn't know if it was from the ride here, the outcome at the lab, or someone trying to kill her. Or maybe it was all three combined.

We walked for almost forty-five minutes before we stepped into a clearing. There were two long hut-like structures with at least two dozen people working underneath them. The second they saw us, they froze. Terrified eyes stared back at us.

Arely broke away to stand front and center. It was only now I noticed the gun she had slipped into the back of her pants at some point. She spoke in rapid-fire

Spanish, and the workers grew wearier and wearier with each word.

I wished I knew what she was saying. All I knew was that my dick was taking notice, and he liked it. Arely was always hot and assertive, but this was a whole other level. I couldn't wait to get to a hotel and fuck her brains out.

Arely was growling her words now. I assumed no one had admitted to fucking with their product, but then one guy stepped forward and dropped to his knees. He was pleading with her. I really wish I knew what the hell they were saying.

Arely lifted her hand, motioning for the man to rise and come forward. He did so hesitantly as her voice rose. She wasn't shouting. No, Arely was in total control as she spoke. After a few moments, she nodded and then followed the man who'd stepped forward under one of the huts.

I couldn't stay back any longer. I followed her and watched as he showed her around. The working conditions were unfavorable. If the people in the United States could see how hard these people work and how hot and dirty their environment is, maybe they'd complain a little less about their sad jobs.

From what I could gather, one hut was where they made the paste from the leaves, and the other was where they transformed the paste into the actual cocaine. I seriously doubted they had any fentanyl hidden here. It wasn't made here in Colombia, and I doubted they could afford to buy it. Everyone was dressed in dirty clothes that looked as if they'd been worn hard for at least a decade, with holes and tears in them.

Santi stood at the end of one of the huts with his arms crossed over his chest and his eyes drilling into Arely. "Are you ready?"

She nodded, looking around once again. "It's time to go."

We headed back the same way we came, only this time, there was about a foot of space between Arely and me. The trip back didn't seem to take quite as long as the way there. Everyone was quiet except for a few low words spoken here and there.

The second Arely's feet hit the gravel road, she turned and spoke to the army that formed two lines. This time, she didn't sound pissed.

Ale brushed past me, laughing. "You really need to learn Spanish if you're going to stick around."

Arely's head swung around. She looked me up and down, and I swore I could see the disappointment in her eyes that I didn't speak Spanish.

"Let's go," she ordered—her first words in English in over two hours.

"Arely," Santi called to her, but she only held up her hand as she walked toward the SUV she was in earlier.

I slid in beside Arely, watching as everyone loaded up. It wasn't until we started to move that I spoke. "What happened between you and Santi?"

"Brother and sister shit. Nothing you need to worry about," she bit out.

"I'm not worried. If you want to talk about it… you can." I wasn't much for expressing my feelings, and neither was Arely. It was probably one of the reasons why we worked well together. Still, it seemed like it was something more. I knew she and Santi were close, but with each passing day, it seemed as if they were drifting farther and farther away. Something I didn't understand.

"I'm fine. I just want to get to the hotel where I can take a nice, long, hot shower and eat some good food. And then to get out of this country."

Moving closer, I brushed her hair aside and gave her a little nibble on her earlobe. "I can't wait to be alone with you, so I can be deep inside of you and feel you come all over my dick."

Her whole body shuddered, telling me Arely felt the same.

CHAPTER SEVENTEEN

arely

IT FELT like it had been ages since I last hung out with my best friend. We were in the theater room with a blanket covering both our legs, each with our own popcorn bowls on our laps and drinks at our sides. It was just like being at a movie theater, except you didn't have to listen to other people eating or hear them talking or snoring through a movie.

We hadn't picked a movie yet. Instead, Bree and I were catching up on everything that had transpired since the last time we could really talk. The Sunday dinner she attended didn't count.

"I feel like I've hardly seen you since…" she looked down at my stomach where I'd been shot. "And now you've got yourself a boyfriend."

I looked down too, and it was as if I could see

through my clothes. I saw the pink, puckered scar that still twinged every once in a while when I moved a certain way. Everything changed after I got shot.

"I'm sorry. I should have called you back after you left all those voicemails. I was so preoccupied with who shot me that I let a lot of things slide to the wayside."

"You don't need to tell me you're sorry. I can't imagine what you've been going through. Plus, if I know your brothers, they probably wouldn't let you out of their sight."

She wasn't wrong there.

"Only when Sebastian was around would they let me breathe. They hovered over me every second of every day. At one point, I was hoping for a complication just to go back into the hospital, so I could get away from them," I laughed. There was no way I was going back to the hospital, but there were many times I just wanted to be left alone with my thoughts.

"Speaking of Sebastian. He seemed… I guess the word I would use is intense. Which isn't a shocker since he's involved with you," she laughed, and I joined along with her. "But he didn't seem that way with you."

"I don't mind his intensity. It pays off in the bedroom, if you know I mean." I rolled my lips to try and contain my smile, but it was no use. My mouth curved up in a big smile.

Bree clutched her hands to her chest. "I want that."

"Why don't you have it? You're a smoking hot Chinese bombshell. You walk by, and guys jizz in their pants, so what's the problem?" I wasn't lying. Bree was one of the hottest women I'd ever seen. She could easily be a supermodel if she weren't so shy. Her shyness and the fact that she didn't know she was absolutely beautiful only created more allure.

"You think my father will let me date just anyone? They have to go through the inquisition and then some before he'll even grant them one date with me. He scares everyone off before we even have a chance."

Even though her dad was a tiny man, he was scary as shit. He had cold, dead eyes for everyone except Bree.

"Well, I guess we just need to find a guy who can pass the test. Not only with your dad, but with me, too." Bree looked down at the floor and bit her lip. "Unless you already have someone you like."

"Even if I do, he won't be deemed worthy by my father." She looked back up at me and tried to give me a smile, but it was so forced it looked like she was in pain. "Let's get back to you and Sebastian. He looks… younger. How old is he?"

"Oh, he's young, alright. He's definitely not who I would have pictured myself with, but I really like spending time with him even if he is only a sophomore in college."

"A sophomore?" Her brown eyes widened.

"I know. Who would have thought that at thirty, I'd be a cougar?"

"Certainly not me. I thought you might just marry your job and say to hell with men."

"Oh, hell no. I like sex way too much to give up men. Especially Sebastian. He makes me come unlike any other man ever has, and his stamina is otherworldly."

Bree lifted a brow. "Does he have a brother? Maybe I can get a taste knowing my father would never let me date someone so young."

"Unfortunately, he doesn't, but who's to say he didn't have a hot older brother?" I conjured up what I thought Sebastian would look like in ten or twenty years, but I couldn't without seeing what his dad looked like. All I knew was he'd be hot.

Bree started to laugh and fan me with her hand. "You've got it so bad."

"You would be too if he snuck into your bed and had his wicked way with you." I sighed. I couldn't help it after thinking of the way he'd left me feeling boneless while sprawled out on my bed this morning. The man had talent—one I wasn't willing to give up anytime soon.

Bree blushed, and it brought me back to the present. I couldn't help but wonder who it was Bree had a crush on. She was a quiet person but also so damn strong. I knew if she wasn't ready to reveal who she liked, she wouldn't.

Grabbing her hand in mine, I gave it a slight squeeze. "We need to do this more often. I missed you, and you know you are always invited to Sunday dinner."

"Maybe I'll stay tonight then. It's better than eating dinner with my family. I'm not sure why my father requires us all to eat together if we can't speak during dinner. Eating dinner with you is always so lively."

That was a good way to put it. My brothers were always entertaining. I couldn't remember the last time I'd eaten dinner at Bree's. It felt like everyone was just sitting around watching you eat, waiting for someone to speak when they knew it would never happen.

"Of course, you can stay. I'm not done with you yet. We haven't even watched our movie or eaten our popcorn."

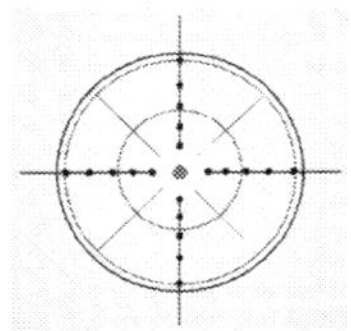

Standing at my bedroom window, instead of seeing the lake behind my house, all I saw were guards walking the perimeter with guns on their backs. This was my life now. It wasn't quiet, and I couldn't leave at a moment's notice. I had a whole brigade of men who went everywhere I did. Good luck to anyone who tried to take me out now.

I was shocked to find Pablo standing just inside my door when I stepped into my bedroom from my office. "I didn't expect to see you here. Is everything okay?"

Stepping forward, he moved to my side and placed my hand in the crook of his elbow. This wasn't the norm for us. "Perfectly fine. I thought I'd walk you down since Santi is talking with Bree, and Bash isn't here yet."

I cocked my head in his direction to find my oldest brother with a slight curve of his lips. "Do you have a girlfriend I don't know about?" I asked, wondering if this was why he was acting the way he was.

For the briefest of seconds, he paused but then kept going. "How did you know?"

"You seem happier." It was the only explanation. "You know, if you want, you can invite her to dinner."

"I know, but it's new yet. I don't want the lot of you to scare her off. When the time is right, I'll introduce her to all of you."

"Do you really think we would scare her?" I laughed. It would be fun to try and chase off Army's fake little girlfriend, but I knew the task wasn't easy since this was her job. I wasn't sure how he kept her in his company, knowing who she was.

Pablo lifted a brow. "Hell, yes, you would. Why do you think I keep my love life away from this house?"

He wasn't wrong. Our dynamic could be a lot to take in. Still, I hated the thought that he felt like he couldn't share that part of his life with us.

"If you ask, we'll try to behave."

"Don't worry about it." He smiled. "When the time is right, you'll meet her. I was surprised to find Bash wasn't back yet."

Today was the first day Sebastian had left my side since we'd gotten back from Colombia last week. He was practically living here. When I told him he could leave a few things here, I should have just asked him to move in. It wasn't like he would be bringing his furniture with him.

"Where did he go off to?"

"I didn't ask." I didn't feel the need, and if I wanted to, I could call him if I needed him, which I didn't.

We reached the bottom of the stairs. Pablo patted my hand wrapped around his arm. "Do you trust him one hundred percent?"

"Yes. I have no doubts about him." Stepping away, I looked him up and down, trying to understand why he had asked. "How can you? He's saved me and put his body before mine to keep me safe."

"I don't know. It could all be fake. With each step, he's worming his way into our family and business, and the closer he gets, the more bad shit happens. What if he's working for someone to take us all out?"

"While you have reason to be paranoid, it isn't Sebastian. He didn't send himself the test to kill me. He's not a part of the society yet. You weren't there all the times he's saved me."

"You almost died when you were shot. I don't call that good saving. Just… be careful. He might not be who he says he is." He held up his hands as I narrowed my eyes at him. I didn't understand why this was coming up now. "Don't get me wrong. I like the guy. I do, but now isn't the time to let down your guard."

"Santi did his background check on Sebastian. If there was anything to find, he would have."

"Right, Santiago, who left you at the church

unattended? He was your one bodyguard. Why would he leave you unprotected? Has it ever occurred to you that he's the only one who knew where you were?"

Yes, it had, but I wasn't going to tell him that. I didn't like where this conversation was going.

"Have you asked these questions to Santi?" I turned and headed in the direction of the dining room. "If not, you can bring them up at our meeting after dinner."

"Maybe I will." He quirked a brow, challenging me.

Before I could throw a comeback at him, Sebastian came through the door, clutching his side. The clothes he left in earlier were dirty and torn.

Running over, I wrapped my arm around his waist as he started to list to the side. "What the hell happened?"

"Some asshole stabbed me when I was leaving my apartment." He winced when his side came into contact with mine.

As he spoke the words, I felt the cold wetness on his side. My eyes scanned to find where he'd been injured.

"And you came here, why?" Pablo sneered.

Looking up from trying to find the wound, I found Pablo looking at us with disgust. "What the fuck is wrong with you? Go get the others," I barked out.

Slowly, I moved Sebastian over into the sitting room and down onto one of the couches.

Sitting down beside him, I lifted his shirt to find a stab wound to the right side of his ribs that was sluggishly pouring out blood. "Don't worry. We'll get you patched up. Santi knows someone who can help. Believe it or not, but this isn't a regular thing around here."

Our eyes met, and he frowned. "Was it wrong of me to come here? What if I led them right where they want to be?"

"No, you did the right thing. If this is retaliation for the Guerrera Syndicate, they might have tried to finish the job at the hospital."

Leaning forward, he pressed his forehead to mine. I was surprised he was so calm and subdued. "I'm just glad it wasn't you this time."

"I'm sorry this happened because of me. I tried to give you an out before it was too late." But now everyone knew Sebastian was a part of us and if they knew that, they probably surmised he was special to me. The worst possible position to be in.

"Arely, I'll be fine." Slowly, he brought his warm palm up to cup the side of my face. He stared at me for a long minute as if he was looking into my soul. "I'd gladly get stabbed a thousand times over to prevent you an ounce of pain."

A loud throat clearing broke us apart before Santi spoke. "Alright, if you two lovebirds could break apart, I'd like to take a look at the wound."

Reluctantly, I stood to give him the room he needed, even though I didn't want to leave Sebastian's side. Needing to be close to him, I rounded the back of the couch and placed my hands on Sebastian's shoulders.

"While I could staple this up, I'm going to call the doctor to make sure no organs were hit, or it isn't more serious."

"More serious than an organ being hit?" Sebastian laughed weakly.

Santi stood from inspecting the wound, his eyes landing on me. "How about we take him to the guest room down here until the doctor arrives?"

"Fine, help me get him up." I wanted Sebastian in my bedroom, but I wasn't going to put him through going up the stairs for my wants. Being downstairs would be easier for everyone involved, and I really didn't want the doctor to know where my bedroom was either. With each passing day, I learned not to trust many people.

How had it gotten to the point where I wasn't sure

if I could trust my brother and very best friend in the whole world but could trust Sebastian, who was only twenty years old, and I'd only known him for a few short months? Was I being naïve and letting my feelings blind me? I didn't think so. My gut was always right, and it told me I could trust Sebastian. It also told me that he was true to me and only me with all of the evidence that was starting to stack up against Santi.

Even if that was the case, I had to watch out for someone out there who wasn't on our side.

Santi and Ale helped Sebastian to the only guest room we had on the first floor. He didn't protest until they tried to help him lie down.

"I've got it," he pushed them away. "I'm not a total invalid, and I don't think I'm going to die anytime soon."

"Fine, bro, I was just trying to help." Ale stepped back. "If you need me, I'm just a call away. What should we do about dinner? Everyone's been waiting—"

"Go on with dinner. There won't be a meeting tonight." I waved them away.

"Arely, you don't have to do that for me. I'm fine by myself until the doctor gets here." He winced as he went to lie down, and that was all I needed to stay. Not that I planned on leaving him, anyway.

"I'm staying, and that's final." I moved to sit on the bed beside him. "You guys go eat and let Bree know I'll call her later."

"Like Ale said, we're just a call away. I'll be back once the doctor gets here. It wasn't life or death, so it may be a while."

"For what I pay that man, he should be chartering a helicopter to get here as fast as he can, but whatever. Leave us until he gets here," I ordered.

I kept my eyes on my brothers until the bedroom door was shut, and I heard them walk away. I moved closer to Sebastian, lifting his shirt to see if the bleeding had slowed down. It hadn't. It was flowing more than when I looked at it before. It was probably from Sebastian moving around.

"I'll be right back," I said, looking over my shoulder as I went to the en suite bathroom and ripped the hand towel from where it hung on the wall. "I should have done this sooner, but I think I was in shock." I climbed back onto the bed and pressed the towel to where he was bleeding.

He closed his eyes and looked strangely peaceful for someone who'd just been stabbed.

"Does it hurt?"

"Like a bitch, but I can handle it. I'm sure it's

nothing compared to being shot." His left eye popped open and fixed on me.

"You have no idea who it was who stabbed you?"

"None. I haven't seen him before." He closed his eye and reached for my hand at the same time. "It might not be related to you. I mean, not directly. It could be I sold him drugs at one point and thought he could kill me and steal the drugs and money."

"Did he rob you?"

"Fuck no. I fought back. He's probably more injured than me after I slammed my fist into his face a few times. I doubt he'll be coming back for more."

"I don't want to risk the chance. You have enough of your stuff here. You'll stay. I can send a few guards to your house to gather the rest of your belongings." Blood started to seep through the towel, making me press harder.

Turning his head, Sebastian opened both eyes and looked at me. His light brown eyes held pain in them, but something else I couldn't recognize. "Is that your way of asking me to move in?"

"No, this is me telling you you're moving in. I'm not going to risk you getting hurt again." I brushed a strand of hair off his forehead and ran my fingers over his brows and cheekbones.

"If you want me to stay, you need to talk to me. You

said you were going to tell me what's going on with you and Santi in Colombia, but you haven't said a word to me."

My whole body deflated. "Because I don't like to think about the possibility that he might have betrayed me."

"What?" His brows puckered. "How could you think that?"

"It's not just me. Pablo even suggested it might be Santiago before you got here." I took in a deep breath and held it for as long as I could. When I exhaled, I was only filled with sadness. "He's the only one who knew where I was, and he left me there for a hookup, which he shouldn't have done as my head of security."

His face relaxed as he asked. "What's at that church?"

"That's where I used to do most of my work. Who's going to suspect that a drug ring is being run in the secret bowels of a church?"

"Not many," he frowned and paused. "You're right, but don't all of your brothers know of the church?"

"They do, but it's not their job to protect me." I leaned my head back against the headboard and let out a defeated sigh. "The only person who knew I'd be there that late was Santi. Even though I don't want to believe it, all indications are pointing straight at him."

"I can't believe it either. Pablo, yes, but not Santi. Hell, I can't imagine Ale or Army turning their backs on you."

"Neither can I," I faced toward the bedroom door and thought of my family, who were eating dinner as we spoke. "But it's looking as if someone did. The question is who."

"Are you going to fire me now?"

His question was so far off-topic and out of the blue. I swung my gaze back to look at him. "What are you talking about?"

"I got stabbed, and I wasn't even protecting you when it happened. All I did was walk out of my apartment building," he laughed bitterly.

Sliding down on the bed, I cupped the side of his face. The scruff on his jaw prickled underneath my fingertips. "I'm not firing you unless you feel like you're no longer up for the job."

His gaze never wavered as he spoke. "I never want to leave you. I'll fight for you until my last breath."

Leaning forward until my mouth was close enough to brush against his, I spoke from the heart. Each word breathed life into what was happening between us as my lips grazed his. "Good. I don't want you to ever let me go."

Pressing forward, Sebastian removed any space that

was left between us. Our mouths locked together, tongues dancing and caressing in a sensual dance. I moaned into his mouth as I tangled my fingers in his hair to deepen the kiss.

A loud knock broke us apart, and a second later, Santi and the doctor stepped into the room.

Doctor Phillipstein was in his late sixties with white hair and wrinkles that showed he'd lived a good life. He was tall and wiry and moved with grace not many had as they aged.

"Alright, young man, let's see the damage and get you patched up." The doctor lifted up the towel and inspected the wound. "Why don't the two of you leave us, and I'll come get you when we're done?"

I looked at Sebastian to see if he wanted me here, but he nodded, letting me know he was fine.

With Sebastian being treated, it was now time to do something I never thought I'd have to do.

CHAPTER EIGHTEEN

arely

STEPPING out of the guest becroom, I made a right. "Where's everyone else?"

Santi came into step with me as we walked down the hall and out into the backyard by the pool. It was already dark, but the area was lit with lights and the glow from the pool. "Finishing dinner. Why? Did you want me to get them?"

"No, I want to talk to you and only you, my best friend." I rounded on him. "I need answers, and I need them now before anyone else gets hurt."

He stepped back and then moved to sit down on one of the outdoor couches. "I don't know who hurt Bash. Not yet, anyway."

"You still haven't figured out who tried to kill me or all of us." I stood in front of him, not willing to get comfortable. This wasn't that type of conversation. "The one thing I can't put my finger on is how whoever sent Sebastian to kill me knew I'd be at the church. Only our family knows about it."

"Anyone could follow you, Arely. It wouldn't have been hard. I'm not saying they would know the base of our operations were there. They could think you're highly religious and going there to pray or confess."

"Okay, I'll give you that, but whoever it was would also have to know about the Scorpio Society and be able to get their hands on the parchment they write out the tests on."

"You don't think I know that," he shouted. "Every time I think about it, I get sick to my stomach knowing I left you there unprotected. And now, now," he raised his voice even louder. "You've got your boyfriend watching out for you."

"Shouldn't any good boyfriend or girlfriend watch out for you?" I raised my brows, waiting for his response.

"Yes, but they normally aren't protecting them from harm and death on a daily basis. You replaced me with *him*. How do you think it makes me feel?"

"And how do you think it makes me feel that my own brother and best friend might have tried to kill me?"

Santi's eyes widened into saucers as he stared up at me. His face was slack-jawed in utter shock. "You seriously think it was me?"

"My heart doesn't want to believe it, but all clues lead back to you, and it's not only me who thinks so."

He jumped up and started to pace in front of the couch. "Oh, your boyfriend who tried to kill you is blaming me," he scoffed.

"Actually, he doesn't. And he didn't try to kill me. There's a difference between being sent to do the deed and attempting it. Once he saw it was me, he dropped his knife."

Stopping in front of me, he crossed his arms over his chest and widened his stance. "Oh, the same knife that stabbed him today?"

"Do you really believe he stabbed himself?" I laughed darkly, not believing his accusation in the slightest.

"You believe I could put a hit on you?"

"Santi," I sighed and moved toward him. Gripping his biceps, I looked into his dark, troubled eyes. "I don't want to, but what would you have me believe when all signs point in your direction?"

He spread his arms wide and looked down at me with devastation written across his stricken face.

"Believe that as your brother and best friend, I would never do anything to harm you."

"You can't deny that you're hiding something from me." I shook his arms where I held him. "Tell me what it is, and I'll forget about the other."

"I can't do that. It's not only my secret to tell," he shook his head. Sadness swirled in the depths of his eyes as he implored me to believe him. "You know in your heart it's not me. If anything, I'm being framed. What better way to get to you than to eliminate the people who are protecting you? Set it up to look like it's me, and then kill off your boyfriend."

What he said made sense, but how could I believe anything else without proof?

"Why would I want to kill you and build an army to protect you? It doesn't make sense. Trust your gut, Arely. I love you more than anyone else on this planet, and to know that you think I might hurt you wounds me deeply. It feels like I'm the one who was stabbed." Tears swelled in his eyes, and I did the only thing I could. I pulled my brother into my arms and hugged him as tightly as I possibly could.

"I love you, Santi, but I don't like that you're hiding something from me. You and I don't keep secrets from each other."

"I know," he choked out. "It won't hurt you but

someone else if I tell this secret. Trust me to know I'm doing what's best for all of us," he spoke into the crown of my head.

I nodded, knowing all I could do was trust my gut in this moment. It was too difficult to bear the thought of my brother betraying me.

Pulling out of his embrace, I smiled sadly. When had we gotten this way?

"Are you keeping this from me because you hate Sebastian?"

"I don't hate him. In fact, I like that he's made you happy. For so long, you only lived for work. While we all appreciate the world you've built for us, making our business more profitable than Father ever did, you've taken too much of it on your shoulders. We are all here to help you. Don't you think Ale and Army would be more useful than working on the streets?"

"Of course I do, but I want them to go to school—something we didn't have the opportunity to do—and enjoy it. What if they don't want to be a part of this life? I want them to have options."

Santi's mouth cracked into a smile. "They're not going anywhere, but I'm sure their business knowledge will help us in the future. They'll be able to make our legitimate businesses more profitable. The point is to enjoy your life and put more on our shoulders. You can start small, but we all want to help you more."

He was right. It was time to make it more of a family operation than an Arely one. I had taken on the brunt of the work for too long.

"I will." I looked back to the house, wondering if the doctor was done with Sebastian yet. "Since we're not having a meeting, any news on the fake girlfriend?"

"No, she's keeping her head down, and from what I know, isn't pushing when Army keeps her in the dark about what he's doing. This would be the best time to have him stop selling and do something else that can't be traced back to him while she's on our tail. We have to make sure she doesn't learn anything."

"This is why I keep you around. You have all the good ideas." I hugged him one more time before I looked back at the house once again.

"Get back to Sebastian. I know it's killing you to be away from him. Do you…" he stopped and then shook his head.

"Do I, what? Ask me, Santi. Anything."

"Do you love him?" He quietly asked as if the question pained him. I didn't understand why it was so hard for him to ask such a simple question.

"I think I do, but I haven't said it to him or anything."

"Why not? You're certainly not shy and always go after what you want."

No, I wasn't. I knew that when I went back in there and saw Sebastian again, I would tell him how I felt. And maybe, just maybe, he'd feel the same.

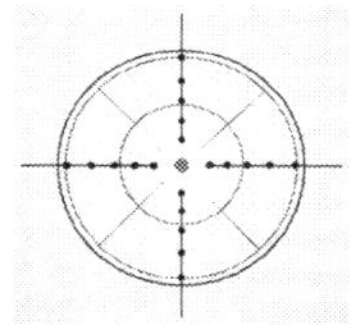

STEPPING INSIDE THE GUEST BEDROOM, I found Sebastian sprawled out on the bed with a bandage over his wound.

"Why do you look scared? I'm fine." He gave me a tip of his lips. "The doctor said I'll be as good as new in a couple of weeks as long as I don't tear the stitches out."

"We'll have to keep you in bed to make sure that doesn't happen." I moved toward the side of the bed he was lying on before sitting down.

"If you're anywhere near me in that bed, it's a surefire way for me to rip at least a couple."

I patted his chest just above his heart. "I'll try to be gentle with you, then. I'd hate to be the cause for your recovery time to be extended."

"I wouldn't mind," he smiled drowsily. It wasn't until then I noticed how tired he looked.

"How are you feeling? Did the doctor give you some drugs?"

"The best fucking drugs. I can't feel a thing." He wrapped his arm around my waist and pulled me close to him. "I'm tired, though."

"I bet. How about you get some sleep, and when you wake up, we'll eat some of the dinner we missed?"

"Shit, I'm sorry, I fucked up dinner. Did you at least have your meeting?" His eyes drooped and then popped back open.

"No meeting, but I did talk to Santi while the doctor was in here with you."

"That must have been a long talk. I think the doctor was in here for at least an hour, and then I took a nap." There was a long blink, and then his eyes landed on mine.

"It wasn't that long at all. I think it's the drugs." Tracing my fingers over his forehead, brows, and then his eyes, I held them there for a moment before I ran my fingers through the strands of his hair, trying to lull him to sleep.

Once I knew he was asleep, I slowly got up and left the room. I had no idea how long he'd sleep, but I figured it would be at least an hour or two.

I moved through my quiet house, surprised by the silence but happy for it nonetheless after the day I'd had. I slipped out into the backyard, knowing I'd find at least one guard who could help me. I was almost to the lake before I felt a presence behind me. They weren't supposed to interrupt me unless I was in danger.

Spinning on my heels, I turned to find a man standing in the dark. I couldn't make out who it was, but I knew it was one of my guys. Santi and Javier had hired so many men I had no idea what their names were.

"I need you to round up a team to head to Sebastian's house and pack up all of his personal items. Leave the furniture and don't make a mess out of his place. Once you have everything here, I want you to put it in the hall outside of my bedroom. Do not step inside my room under any circumstances. Do you understand?"

"Yes, Ms. Guerrera," he bowed his head. "I'll get on it right away." He turned and disappeared into the night just as quickly as he appeared.

Even though it was too cold to sit outside without a jacket or a blanket, I made my way down to the dock. I sat at the end with my feet hanging off, looking out at the dark water before me. It was peaceful here and was one of the reasons I bought the house. That and the fact there were enough rooms for everyone and more. I liked keeping my family close, and having them all under one roof was one way we stayed that way.

Boots hitting the wooden planks alerted me to someone coming up from behind me before he spoke. "I thought I'd find you here," Ale said as he sat down beside me. "How's Bash?"

"Sleeping peacefully. Dr. Phillipstein gave him the good shit. I sent some of the guards to get the rest of his things. He's going to stay here from now on."

"Arely," he chuckled. "Bash was already living here. The only difference was he didn't have all of his things here. Don't wait for everyone's approval. Do what makes you happy, even if that is Bash." He laughed harder at his own joke.

"I don't care what anyone else thinks. If they have a problem, tough shit. I'm not going to let Sebastian get hurt because of us again." Looking out into the darkness, I watched as each attack played out before my eyes. It was too much and happening far too often. "If someone hurts one of us, we end whoever it was slowly and painfully."

"I agree. When you first brought on all the guards, I thought it might have been an overreaction, but now… shit, it's like we need a posse with each of us wherever we go to protect our backs."

"Maybe we lie low for a while and let the street guys do the selling. We need to change up how we do everything. Once we have a new plan in place, we emerge stronger than ever and let them know they can't touch us. If they try, they die."

Out of the corner of my eye, I saw him nodding. "While I don't like hiding, I do think we need a new structure for how we do things. We need to make sure everyone is on the same page."

"We'll have a meeting tomorrow, but let the others know I don't want anyone leaving until after we all talk." I started to stand. Ale stood first and held his hand out to me. I took it, letting him help me to my feet before I gave him a short hug. "I'll see you tomorrow."

"Get some rest."

I wasn't sure how easy that was going to be.

We walked back to the house in silence. Everything was so easy with Ale. He was the strong, silent type who never spoke unless it was important. Well, unless he was with Army, then he was relaxed and carefree. I wanted him to be that way all the time. I knew it was hard for him to be gay in the world we lived in. He knew our family would support him no matter who he chose to spend his life with.

Before heading up to see if Sebastian's things had been delivered, I peeked in to find him still passed out in the exact same position I left him. Only for a moment did I think about joining before I closed the door and made my way upstairs to my bedroom. Along the wall, I found a pile of clothes still on their hangers and a large duffle bag packed to the brim, along with Sebastian's backpack. I felt my mouth turn down as I realized this was all of Sebastian's personal belongings. He barely had anything to his name. Maybe I should have gone to his apartment to see how he lived and to understand him better.

Back and forth, I went about unpacking his belongings to mingle with my own. I thought I might have to make room and get rid of a few things or put them in another closet. Instead, after all of his clothes were hung up in the space I'd designated for him, it still looked sparse. Even the drawers on his side of the bathroom barely had anything in them.

This was something I could rectify.

Grabbing my laptop out of my office, I headed back down to the guest room to find Sebastian still sleeping. I was starting to get hungry now that the adrenaline from earlier had worn off. However, I had promised Sebastian we would eat together. Crawling up on the bed beside him, I sat with my laptop and pulled up a few websites where I usually shopped for my brothers. An hour later, and almost a thousand dollars spent on clothes, Sebastian started to stir.

Turning on his side toward me, he wrapped his hand around my forearm and gave me a sleepy smile. "Have you been here the entire time?"

"I couldn't just sit here and listen to your snore the entire time."

The corner of his mouth tipped up. "I don't snore."

"How would you know? You're sleeping," I chuckled.

Sebastian moved closer to me, snuggling into my side. He was quite affectionate when he was sleepy and drugged. "I've never had anyone complain before."

He must have still been seriously drugged if he thought I wanted to hear about all the women who hadn't complained. Snapping my laptop closed, I slid off the bed and started for the door. "Now that you're awake, I'm going to get something to eat. You're welcome to join me if you'd like."

He was still where I left him, with his brows knitted together. "I'd like to take a quick shower and clean up, if that's alright with you?"

"You don't have to ask my permission. This is your house too."

I barely had the door open when he spoke again. "I

thought that was a dream. Do you really want me here?"

"Your things are already hanging in my closet upstairs. Come join me when you're done." I slipped out the door and made my way to the kitchen. Maybe I should've put his things in one of the guest bedrooms, but no, I wasn't going to play games. Just because he said something stupid, I wasn't going to throw him out of my bed.

We had voted for Italian tonight. I put the lasagna in the oven and went about making some new garlic bread to eat with it. Pulling out the salad, I set it on the island. There had been more, so much more, but my brothers had eaten it all. I swear they didn't eat all week in preparation for Sunday night dinner—which I knew wasn't true because most of the time, they stayed here, and there was always food. The only ones who didn't live here full-time were the twins, which gave them the full college experience.

"It smells good. I'm sorry we missed it the first time around." Sebastian ambled into the room and sat at the island across from me. His hair was still damp. He'd changed into a pair of gray sweatpants and a bright white t-shirt that stretched across his chest.

"I don't think you intended to get stabbed, so it's quite alright. The lasagna should only be another few minutes. Do you want to start with a salad?" I started to plate myself some when he reached across the space and took my hand.

I met his turbulent brown eyes and set down the serving tongs. "You didn't have to move my things here or hang them up. I'm perfectly capable of doing those things for myself."

"Perhaps, but we're on lockdown until we have a meeting tomorrow to figure out a new structure. You should have had protection with you." His jaw ticked, but I continued. "If you didn't want to take your guy, you should have at least had a gun on you."

"I didn't think I needed it since you weren't with me, but now I see the error in my ways." He looked down at his side.

"I gave you an out before."

"And I didn't take it. I'm never going to take it." His usual light brown eyes darkened as he stared at me.

"It's too late to get out unless you want to relocate. You're in, and everyone knows about you."

"How?"

"Do you not realize people are surveilling us to find kinks in our armor when we're out? You've been seen by my side too many times. You're associated with me, either as my guard, and the quickest way to get to me is to take you out, or as my lover and hopefully my weakness."

His throat bobbed before he spoke. His hand gripping mine tighter. "I don't want to be your weakness."

"Too late. Each and every one of you is my weakness. I would go through Hell to get any of you back."

Before I could say more or read his expression, the timer on the oven went off, signaling the lasagna was done. Stepping back, I pulled it out and set it on the counter beside the garlic bread. I put a serving on each of our plates and stood across from Sebastian as I ate. He may not have been hungry since he was drugged, but I was hungry before he showed up bleeding. Once the adrenaline of the night wore off, I became tired and ravenous. I was halfway through my meal when he cleared his throat. I looked up from my plate to find him standing and coming around to stand in front of me.

"Do you not like the food?"

"The food is fine," he muttered as he wrapped his arms around my middle and pressed me tight into his body.

I chanced a glance over to see he'd barely touched his dinner. "What's wrong?"

"Nothing's wrong. I just wanted to feel you in my arms." He dipped down a brushed a minty kiss on my lips.

Wrapping my arms around his torso, I buried my face in his chest and breathed him in. "I like being in your arms."

"I've been wanting to tell you something since we were in Colombia, but I've been holding back, waiting for the right time."

I could hear his heart start to beat faster and faster with each passing second. Pulling back, I looked up at him to find Sebastian's face pale. Was he going to end us?

He knew too much, and if he wanted entirely out of our lives, there was only one way to do that, and I really didn't want to have to end his life.

"The time we spent together in Colombia, even though we didn't have a moment alone, made me realize my feelings for you."

That he had none? No, that couldn't be right unless he wanted to get his rocks off a few more times before he ended things.

"Who would have ever thought that me trying to steal your purse would bring us to this moment?" He chuckled nervously. "I sure didn't, but I've never been happier to get caught." He rubbed his thumb over my bottom lip and pressed against the flesh. "I love you, Arely, and with each passing day, it's been harder and harder to keep those words inside. I needed you to know how I feel about you. It's okay if you don't feel the same way."

And here I was thinking about how I'd hate to kill him.

Cupping the sides of his face with both of my hands, I pulled him down until his forehead met mine. "How could you think I don't feel the same? I never thought I'd find someone I wanted to keep forever, but I have. You're it for me, Sebastian King."

Gripping my hips, he pulled me tighter against his body, letting me feel his hard length against my thigh. His eyes lit up, and I knew I was in for the most delicious night of my life. "What do you say we ditch the food down here, and I eat you upstairs?

CHAPTER NINETEEN

bash

SITTING IN THE SUV, I watched as one of our dealers flipped through his money and then pocketed a sizable portion in one pocket and stuffed the other down his pants. I guess he thought we wouldn't deep dive into his underwear to look for the money he was stealing.

Stepping out of the car, I walked silently, not letting him know I was coming until the last minute. He didn't hear me until it was too late, and my forearm was wrapped around his neck, applying pressure. He struggled, but I didn't let him go. Instead, I nodded toward the car. It pulled up in front of us, and the back popped open. I threw the dealer into the back and tied his arms and legs together before hopping into the backseat. Twisting around, I sneered at him.

"Did you really think we wouldn't figure out you've been stealing from us for the last month?"

"I had to. My girl just had a baby, and those things are expensive as hell," he shouted back like he was in the right.

"That still doesn't give you the right. What's your girl going to do now when you don't come back?"

"No, you wouldn't do that." He paled. "You can't. I have valuable information about who's been trying to take out the Guerrera's. I pr—promise to tell you everything I know if you let me live."

"Unfortunately, that's not for me to decide. I hope for your sake that you're telling the truth because if not, you're going to wish I'd killed you now."

I turned around and watched the scenery go by as we made our way back to the estate. It didn't take us long to pull up outside the house. Grabbing the dealer by his bound hands, I shuffled him inside the house, down the first flight of stairs to the basement, and then down to the dungeon. I hadn't seen anyone else brought here since I'd been locked away in it, but it still smelled like blood and piss—a combination that would set off anyone's gag reflex. Along the way, I passed Pablo, who looked on with curiosity.

"Who do you got there?"

"A dealer who's been stealing. He says he has

important information to give up. I'm going to lock him up and then get everyone before interrogating him."

Pablo gripped the guy's arm. "I'll take him while you get the others."

"Are you sure? I can do both." It was rare that Pablo spoke to me, so I was shocked he offered to help me. He was part of the business side, not the muscle.

"Yeah, Arely is up in her office with Santi."

The dealer tried to jerk away from Pablo with no success. I elbowed him in the ribs, causing him to groan and clutch at his side. He looked up at me with terrified eyes. I wasn't sure what had changed since being in the car. He knew if he lied to us or his information was shit, he was forfeiting his life.

"Thanks." I turned on my heel and took the stairs three at a time until I reached the floor with Arely's office. The door was closed as per usual. I knocked lightly on the door before I opened it. Arely sat behind her desk with a scowl on her face.

I moved to stand beside her desk. "I have someone downstairs that says he knows who's been trying to take you out."

They both jumped up at the same time. "Where did you find him?" She asked.

"I told you I was close to figuring out who was stealing from you. I caught him in the act. When I threw him in the back of the car, he begged for his life."

"And you think he's being truthful?" Santi raised a brow at me and gave me a look that said I was naïve.

"I'm not sure, but I wanted to make sure we at least tried to get the information out of him."

"Good job. Even if he doesn't know, we have to make him an example."

I knew that. However, I wasn't sure if they'd expect me to kill the guy or not.

We hit the bottom floor and found Pablo walking out of the one of the rooms with blood all over his face and shirt.

"What the hell happened to you?" Santi asked, looking his brother over.

"He tried to escape, and I had to shoot him." Pablo brushed by us like it was any other day and not that he just informed us he'd killed the one lead we'd had in months.

Santi stalked toward the cell. He peered inside, and when he looked back at his sister, he shook his head.

Arely flew up the stairs after Pablo.

How could that guy have tried to get away? His hands and feet were bound, and who cared if he tried to run? He wasn't a threat with his hands behind his back.

Stepping into the room, I found the dealer in a pool of his own blood. He wasn't tied up anymore, but I didn't understand why Pablo would have untied him.

"Help me get him out to the pig stye," Santi demanded.

Grabbing the guy's legs, I lifted at the same time as Santi. "The what?"

"Pigs. They're great at making evidence… disappear," he smirked.

I guess when they mentioned pigs all those months ago, they weren't lying.

We climbed the stairs, Santi holding the dealer's upper body as he traversed backward while I held his legs.

"I don't understand why he tried to escape. If he had good intel, he might have been let go."

"Fight or flight instinct. When he saw where we were putting him, rational thought left him." He raised his head to look at me. "It's happened before."

I wasn't sure what that said about me that I let them hold me down here for days without thinking of trying to escape.

"You know, you surprised us when you didn't fight."

"I knew I was innocent," I shot back. Mostly my thoughts had been on Arely and if she would make it.

Beyond that, I hardly thought of anything else when I was held. "Just like you."

His jaw hardened. "It's fucked up. Someone is trying to frame me. I would…" his throat bobbed as he stared down at me. "I would never hurt Arely, let alone attempt to kill her. This whole thing is fucked up. We've never been under siege like this before."

"Everyone wants what you have. I guess you should be flattered." I chuckled darkly.

"If I'd had all of our security set up like it is now after our father was killed, none of this would have happened. We were all too young and dumb to realize what we were getting into at the time. It doesn't help, but I thought being a part of the Scorpio Society brought us a level of protection that obviously is not there."

One of the guards opened the door for us, and we stepped out into the cool night air.

"You know now, and that's all that matters." I looked around, wondering where these pigs were as I followed Santi into the garage.

"Let's put him in there," he nodded toward a side-by-side. "We'll drive back." Putting the body on an attached trailer, we got into the utility vehicle, and Santi drove off into the dark. "I guess Arely didn't share the location of our pets."

"No, she didn't." Not that I cared.

"She's not used to opening up to others outside her family. It might take her some time to… learn."

I wasn't going to tell Santi that his sister told me more than he knew. He obviously knew she'd told me about her suspicions about him.

After a few minutes, we pulled up to a barn that I'd never seen before. You couldn't even see it from the house. It made me wonder just how much land they owned. Once the motor cut off, I could hear the squeal of pigs. I'd never been around pigs before, so I was unsure what to expect. I stood back in surprise when three large pigs ran over to Santi for him to pet them.

"Are they usually so… affectionate?" I wasn't sure that was the right word to describe them, but they did want attention and some rubs.

He nodded toward the side-by-side, and I followed him. "I think I'm the only person who comes out here to visit them except for the groundskeeper. He tends to the area and feeds them."

"And what? We just throw this to them, and they…"

"Eat the body," Santi finished for me. "It's not something you want to stick around for. First, help me strip him."

You'd think it was easy to strip a dead guy, but that

was far from the truth. His body was stiff, making it difficult to remove each item. After trying unsuccessfully to get his leg out of his jeans, I pulled out my knife.

"Ah, I was wondering how long it would take you." He was grinning down at me as I hunched over the body and cut the clothes away. "You're smart for a young guy."

"Does my age bother you?" I grunted as I rolled the body to the side to pull the clothes out from under him.

"It's never been your age. It's you." He shook his head when I narrowed my eyes at him. "It could have been anyone. I'm not used to having to share Arely with anyone but my family, and even then, I was top priority."

"And you feel that now you aren't? I can attest that your sister loves you very much." I didn't want to betray Arely, but I felt if I spoke to what I could, it might help their relationship. I could do that for her even if I didn't give a shit about her brother. "You need to spend more time with your sister, not less. Remind her of the love you share and how much she means to you."

"Oh, and I'm supposed to do that while you're glued to my sister?" He sneered, his face twisted up in rage.

"I'm happy to give you alone time with her." Why couldn't he spend time with her while I was at school? I wasn't sure. The twins and I were back in class with our own army surrounding us in the shadows of the university.

"I'm not sure she wants to spend time with only me. Her trust in me is shaky at best."

"And you think distancing yourself is helping matters? It's not. Ask her to lunch one day while I'm gone to class. Do something except let more time and space separate you."

He huffed. "You know my sister well, it seems." He clapped his hands together. "Enough of this talk. Help me carry him over to the pen."

I guess our talk was over. I helped Santi pick up and throw the body over the side of the pen and watched in horror and fascination as the pigs ran to the body and started in on their job. The sounds of flesh ripping and teeth scraping against bones wasn't a sound I would soon forget.

If things between Arely and I didn't work out for some reason, I wondered if I would be dragged out here for the pigs to eat?

CHAPTER TWENTY

bash

I COULD FEEL ARELY'S eyes on me as she watched me dress. She wasn't happy that the day after someone claimed they had information that would help us, the Scorpio Society decided it was finally time to give me my test.

"Ale and Army could follow behind to make sure—"

"You know they can't do that. I have to go alone in case anyone is watching." I turned to look at her standing at the mouth of the closet. "If I don't pass, will I really die?"

"Not necessarily, but let's not take that chance. You're going to pass whatever test it is they have for you, and then you're going to come home to me. Are we clear?"

It was hot that she was so worried about me.

"I'll send you a text the second I'm finished." I hadn't even read what it was they wanted me to do yet. All I'd done was inform Arely that I'd received my second test and I'd be back later. As soon as I saw it sitting on the driver's side seat in the SUV once I got out of school, I probably should have gotten it over with, but I also knew I couldn't get rid of the guards who kept to the shadows wherever I went. Instead, I went home and told Arely to call off the men, so I could finally be a part of the society that had sealed our fate together.

"Fine, but you see Santi before you go and get an arsenal before you leave. I won't have you taking any chances."

Crossing the room, I enveloped her face with my hands and kissed her raw. Her body crashed into mine as her arms wound around my waist, pulling me closer as if she could defy physics and make us into one being. We broke away, panting, breathing in each other's air. I rested my forehead to hers as I spoke. "I would never do anything to purposefully leave you. I'll be back before you know it."

"I'm going to hold you to it." Her fingers traced the contours of my face, her eyes following after them before she nodded and took a step back.

I thought she'd follow me out of the room, but Arely stood where I left her, her eyes distant when I looked back at her before slipping out into the hallway and down the stairs to where Santi's office was.

The door was open like it always was. Still, I rapped on the door frame before I stepped inside. Santi's eyes shot up to meet mine. "Is everything okay?"

"As far as I know. I've got to get outfitted. I'm…" I pulled the parchment out of my pocket and waved it in the air, the wax seal gleaming in the light.

"Say nothing further. I'll make sure you're fully prepared for whatever comes your way. Although, I'm surprised you haven't opened it up yet."

"It's killing me not to, but I needed to do this, and I didn't want anyone trying to talk me out of whatever it is I have to do."

"You'll do perfectly. I am sure they won't ask you to kill anyone, so it should be plenty simple. Although whatever it is will be for their gain, make no mistake about that. It will most definitely be something illegal."

"I have no problem with that."

"If you did, you wouldn't be here." Santi stood and strode over to the wall. He pushed on one of the books until the wall opened up to a secret passage.

"Are there more of those through the house?"

"Wouldn't you like to know?" he chuckled. "Ask my

sister when you get back. Now let's outfit you with as many weapons as we can without it being obvious you're armed."

"Do you think they'll be watching me?" Like they did the night I was sent for Arely.

Santi's eyes flicked to mine. "I can't say, but I wouldn't put it past them. Just be careful. Their tests are always dangerous because they want you to prove your worth. You'll do fine. Maybe not before you met us, but now…" he smirked as if he was responsible for me being able to defend myself.

Pulling open a drawer, Santi picked out two knives and set them on the counter in the middle of the armory before he went to the wall and studied the guns. "Which are you most comfortable with?"

"I have the 9 mil I always carry." I looked at the wall filled with guns. They were mostly handguns, but there were some rifles and semi-automatics—not that I'd be needing them. "Do you have a holster where I could put one at my ankle?"

"Smart thinking, kid. Now I see what my sister sees in you," he chuckled as he went back to the counter and pulled out a Smith and Wesson 380 in a holster. "It's not forbidden to be armed, and I'm sure they're expecting it after your previous test, but it's best to have them hidden away. You'll do just fine."

Slipping the holster on, I tucked my jeans over it and put one of the knives in my sock on the other leg, and pocketed the other. Looking down, I couldn't see any noticeable bulges.

Santi looked me over before he closed the drawer and left the room. "Put your phone in the pocket with the knife. It will hide it better."

It occurred to me that this might be a trap to get to Arely once again. "Are you going to be extra vigilant about security while I'm gone?"

"No doubt. They won't be hitting us unaware. Don't worry about us. You focus on your task at hand."

I wasn't sure if it was possible not to worry about Arely when I was gone. When I was at school, my mind was always drifting to thoughts of her and her safety, even though I knew she always had a team of people to protect her.

Always being on guard was something I was used to, but worrying about someone else's welfare was entirely new to me.

Waiting until I was outside of the compound, I pulled the test out of my pocket and read what I was tasked with doing for the first time.

2410 South Hickman

Get the footage in the basement dating for the last year. Drop it off in the trashcan on the corner of Stein and Lubbock by midnight.

Simple enough. It was almost as if they knew of my pickpocket ways before I fell in with the Guerreras. Stealing was in my wheelhouse. Killing people who were not trying to kill the ones I care about or myself was not. I could do this with my eyes closed. I would have liked to scope the place out before I went in, but I didn't have that luxury.

Turning on my bike, I soared down the road that led into Stonewall, letting the wind clear my mind of everything else I had to accomplish tonight.

Rolling to a stop at the address given to me, I eyed the Mexican restaurant. What footage could they possibly have here that would be damning?

Whatever, I didn't care. I was going to complete my mission, drop it off at the location they wanted, and get the hell home to my woman.

After parking a block away, I walked the perimeter twice to get the lay of the land. There wasn't a door that led directly to the basement, so that meant I had to go through the restaurant, which wasn't ideal, but I'd manage. I was lucky I had my tools so I could pick the lock. I didn't think breaking and entering a restaurant would be part of my test. I didn't spot a security system, which wasn't too smart on their part. Still, I kept my eyes open because if there was footage to be had, there were most likely cameras somewhere. At least in the basement.

Pulling my mask over my face, I walked to the back of the restaurant and quickly let myself inside the kitchen area. With my flashlight in hand, I went in search of a door that would lead downstairs. When I didn't find it, I headed into the seating area. The door wasn't easy to find. It wasn't meant for everyone to use, but I found it with two heavy-duty locks on it that were harder to pick than the previous one. Picking locks wasn't something I regularly did, so it took me some time. All the while, I had a time clock ticking down in my head. The footage I was supposed to get needed to get out of my hands by midnight at the latest. Otherwise, I was out.

I was sure Arely and the rest of the Guerrera family wouldn't care if I didn't pass the test, but the fact that no one could reassure me I wouldn't die if I didn't pass wasn't reassuring. If I lived, I didn't want Arely to have to keep part of her life hidden from me. This society they belonged to was a secret for a reason, and I already knew too much, which meant I'd probably be killed if I didn't pass.

Going downstairs, I was shocked to find a large room that was bare except for a couple of platforms with poles running through them. Definitely not what I was expecting. The closer I looked, I noticed booths lining one wall. Were there performances here? Was I sent on a task to keep an indiscretion out of the eyes of someone's wife? If so, this was the easiest fucking test ever.

I scoured the bottom floor looking for a door to a surveillance room but soon realized I wouldn't be able to see it with a blind eye after only finding a room filled with furniture. I set about knocking and pushing on the walls for a secret room where the footage might be hidden.

If I could have pulled my hair out by the root, I would have. Frustration was mounting as I tapped every inch of the last wall when I heard it. The sound was hollow. Fucking finally. I looked to see if there was anything that would trigger an opening but saw nothing but a plain black wall. Maybe I'd watched too many movies to expect something so obvious as a book to pull out or a sconce. I went about pushing where I thought the seam might be and was close to slamming my body into the wall when it finally gave in and slowly hissed open.

Now I just had to figure out where the last year of this place was. I was sure it wouldn't be neatly on one tape. That would be too easy. I wanted to pull out my phone and check the time, but I knew I'd already spent too much time searching, and seeing the little amount of time I had left would only make me reckless. I needed to keep my head in the game and get this shit done.

The room was small. It barely fit a desk inside with a chair. The wall with the desk pushed up against it was filled with monitors that were turned off. I hit the keyboard to bring the computer to life to find it needed a password. Each monitor mocked me to attempt to get inside. There was no way I was going to figure my way in when I had no idea who even owned the place. Instead, I focused on trying to find physical copies. Opening and closing drawers, I found a zipped binder full of DVDs. Each one had a month and year printed on them. This was too easy. Each disk was put in order by month and year, dating back three years. I was sure no one would notice the disks were missing until the next month when the next disk was added to the collection.

Was each disk a month's worth of surveillance?

It didn't matter to me what was on them as long as I didn't get caught. After pulling out all twelve disks, I looked for anything I could put them in. There was no way the pockets of my jeans or leather jacket would hold them all without them falling out. In the corner by the desk, I found a trash can that was empty of everything but a trash bag. Removing the bag, I placed the discs inside and tied the end.

Putting the binder back where I found it, I made sure it looked as if I hadn't been in the room. Walking back out into the large barren room, I wondered what went on here. I quickly shook my head, knowing I had no time to dwell on the matter. I needed to get out of here and drop these discs off. The only problem was I couldn't lock the door that led down. As soon as someone noticed the door was unlocked, they'd be hyper-alert an intruder had been in their midst. It didn't matter to me. By then, I'd be long gone.

It didn't take me long to get back to my bike, which I'd parked down the block. While I didn't see any cameras on the outside of the restaurant, I wouldn't be surprised if there were some. The security might seem lax, but I had a feeling it was all for show. They'd know the figure who walked by more than once was likely the one who broke in, but there was no way in hell anyone would know it was me except for the one who sent me here in the first place.

Rolling my mask up to the top of my head, I took in my first breath of fresh air in what felt like hours. After a couple of deep inhales, I pulled on my helmet and set off to the corner of Lubbock and Stein. I was so ready to get back to Arely and into our bed. I was always horny as fuck after a successful job and now was no different.

I still wasn't used to calling her house ours. I didn't even move my things in. I woke up after being stabbed, and all my clothes were hanging in her closet. I didn't fight her on it, though. It wasn't like I wanted to spend time away from Arely.

Five minutes later, I was driving away from the trash can where I was instructed to drop off the information and headed back to the Guerrera compound to fuck my woman.

And just like that, I was part of a society that might have planned to kill the love of my life. I vowed there and then that I would do everything in my power to find out who was behind sending me to murder Arely.

CHAPTER TWENTY-CNE

arely

"YOU OWN THIS PLACE?" Sebastian said from my right side as we stepped inside the restaurant.

"Yes, we do. We have to have some legal businesses. Otherwise, the government would be all over us," I quietly said as we passed a table.

"Makes sense."

Out of the corner of my eye, I watched him take in the surrounding room. I wondered what he was thinking after the other night.

"This is nice and smells damn good." He placed his hand over his stomach and smiled. "It's making me hungry."

It had been far too long since we'd last been here. Maybe we should start having our family dinners here and our meetings downstairs. The only way we could do that was if Army's fake little girlfriend wasn't in attendance.

We walked past a mural of the desert and into the room that was set up for us. The tablecloth was white with multi-colored dishes set in front of each chair. Wine and water glasses sat to the right of each plate with a big, colorful flower centerpiece in the middle of the table.

"If there's anything else you need, Ms. Guerrera, please let us know," the hostess said before she scurried out of the room.

Sebastian chuckled next to me.

"She usually has to deal with Pablo," I said as an explanation, which was enough.

"And there's a whole other level?"

"Down below. It only happens once a month. If the authorities came in, we don't want them to find anything."

"Why have it here at all?"

He was right, and he had no idea what happened downstairs once a month. We should have it in a separate location altogether, but no one wanted to travel miles out of town for their debauchery. After all that transpired in the last few months, I need to have Pablo start looking for another location for us to buy under a dummy company.

"We should change it." I sat down in my seat at the head of the table. "I've been too busy with other things and haven't been here in so long the entire thing hadn't crossed my mind." I smiled over at him as he sat in the seat beside me. "Thanks for looking out for us."

"Always." He bent down to kiss me but was interrupted when the door flew open, and Santi stepped inside.

Santi had a mischievous grin on his face as he looked over at us. "Oh, tonight is going to be a good night, Sebastian boy. You have no idea what we have in store for you."

Sebastian's eyes flicked back and forth between us before finally settling on me. "Why the surprise?"

"Because I want to see it through the eyes of someone who's never experienced it before."

Santi chuckled as he sat in his seat on the other side of me. "It will be priceless."

Leaning back into Sebastian, I laughed. "Are you nervous?"

"Never." He answered instantly, and I knew he meant it. I had a feeling he'd only been nervous when I was shot by the way he talked.

Santi looked to the door and back to me. "Where are the twins?"

"Your guess is as good as mine. They should be

here by now." Dread started to pit in my stomach. "Do you think they're okay?"

"Yeah, it's probably just Ale not wanting to go downstairs," Santi replied, looking over his shoulder at the door.

"Text them and see where they are," I ordered.

"I already did." He looked down at his phone and then back up to me. "The dots are jumping, so give them a minute. Ale is responding back."

My heart rate slowed, knowing Ale was okay. I knew if he was responding, then Army was safe as well.

"They're on their way. It took Army an hour to get rid of the 'girlfriend,'" he said with air quotes before laughing. "She may be DEA, but she's way too innocent to see what's going on downstairs."

Sebastian huffed and rolled his eyes. "Now you guys are just fucking with me."

Leaning over, I whispered against his ear, making sure my lips brushed against the shell of his ear. "I guess you'll just have to wait and find out."

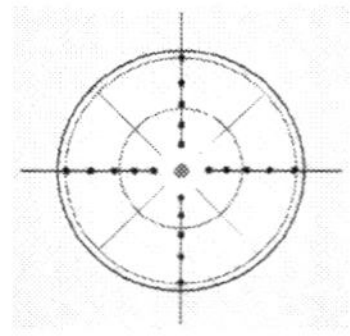

Sitting through dinner with my family was difficult when all I wanted to do was get downstairs. Everyone but me, Sebastian, and Santi left to do their own thing once dinner was over.

I couldn't keep my eyes off Sebastian as we took the stairs down to the party. I wanted to see his reaction once he saw what was going down. This was our monthly playtime with the Scorpio Society. I was sure there were other times between our parties they got together, but I had no interest in going to them unless it was required.

The second we hit the landing, I watched as his eyes widened for a brief second and then shot at me. "This happens every month?"

I nodded and turned to the room. It was full of people sitting on various couches and chairs. Two gorgeous and naked women danced on platforms with poles. For the most part, people were talking in their quiet circles, but in the back of the room, in the dark corners of booths, I knew what was transpiring there even if I couldn't see it.

"What do you think?"

"I think I'm going to like the Scorpio Society," he absentmindedly said as he scanned the room.

"Yes, it has its incentives." I curled around his arm and looked up at him with raised brows. "What do you say we go find ourselves a place to sit and have a drink while we watch the show?"

His eyes lit with intrigue as he moved through the room and scanned his surroundings. Once he found a chair that sat back away from the others, he pulled me down on his lap. "Arely," his voice trembled.

I twisted to look at him and saw the worry wash over his face before it was gone. "What is it?"

"My test."

Ah. For a brief second, I thought he wouldn't mention it, but I had no reason not to believe in Sebastian. He was loyal down to the marrow of his bones.

"What about it?" Gripping his hand, I traced his fingers with the tips of my own.

"They sent me to steal something. Discs. What was on them, I have no idea, but..." he swallowed, his throat clicking with the attempt, and looked back out to the room. "They sent me here. Down here. I had no idea you owned the place."

"Of course, you didn't. How could you? You'd never been here before." If he'd known it was our business, would he have still stolen the discs?

His face grew solemn as he flipped his hand over and clutched mine. "Have a damned you?"

"How so? There would be nothing on those tapes

to incriminate me except that it's in my place of business." My lips twitched. "How do you think you got in so easily? Do you think we have such shit security here that we'd let anyone break in and steal from us?"

"Knowing this is yours, no, but at the time, I had no idea. Now that I see what happens here, I can see why someone wouldn't want what they did for anyone to see."

"Oh, I can assure you no one sees what's on those discs, but they are even stupider than I thought if they think that was the only copy. Everything goes into the cloud. When we get home, we'll scour the meetings to figure out what they want to be hidden forever." I turned back around to look at the room while I tried to see if anyone was looking at us, giving away any hints as to who it might have been.

"Do you partake in the activities when you're here?" He breathed into my ear.

Was he wondering if I was on the video or any video? "I've been known to join in a time or two, but rest assured, nothing was caught on video. Do you want to join in the festivities?"

I felt him grow hard underneath me. His arms wrapped around my waist, pulling me even closer.

Wrapping his fist in my hair, he pulled my head back until I could see him out of the corner of my eye.

"I'm not sharing you with a single soul. Not now. Not ever."

"What about watching and maybe a little lap dance?" I circled my hips and ground down on his erection. "I want to show every one of these assholes the Guerrera queen has herself a king."

"Fuck, I like the sound of that." His hips bucked up and pressed his hard length into my core. His grip loosened on my hair, making it so I could move a little easier. I wanted to see his face, but listening to the way his breath quickened and his grip on my waist tightened was enough for now. There would be other times when I could see his face, even though this would be the first.

"Do you like to watch? Are you a voyeur, my queen?" He asked, panting.

"There's no harm in watching a little live entertainment. If you want, we can move closer. They won't mind. In fact, I think they like it." I arched my back and swiveled my hips.

"I'm not sure how long I'm going to be able to sit here with you grinding on my dick before I have to fuck you."

Arching my head back, I flicked his ear with my tongue. "You know, I wouldn't be opposed to moving someplace darker and riding your cock. Why do you think I wore this skirt tonight?"

"I don't think there could be a more perfect woman than you." He stood with me in his arms and sat me down. "Let's go have a look around." His hand skated down my back and cupped my ass before giving me a slap.

I laughed and laced our fingers together before I guided him toward a large bed where three couples were giving everyone a show. It was a tangled mess of one woman on her hands and knees while a man fucked her from behind, and she gave another man a blow job. Simultaneously, he had another woman on his face as he ate her out. While this scene was playing out, a man and woman roved their hands over and licked every inch of the four other bodies.

We stopped in front of the group of writhing bodies. Sebastian pulled me in front of him with one arm around draped over my collarbone, and the other pressed into my stomach. I felt his hot breath before I heard him. "When's the last time you participated in one of these?"

My body shook silently. "I've never been front and center. Having all of these assholes watch while I take my pleasure is not on my list. But if you must know, it's been at least a decade. Before you even knew what a hard-on was."

"Good," he pulled me tighter. "I guess I won't have to kill anyone then."

"I think you should keep talk of killing anyone in the society quiet. Everyone is a badass in their own right, and most have zero qualms in killing if they need to."

The sound of his throat clicking as he swallowed had me turning my head to look up at him. His face was a mask of indifference as he spoke. "I'm not sure if I'm ever going to be okay with them until I know with one hundred percent certainty that they had nothing to do with trying to kill you."

Pushing out of his grasp, my hand caught on his wrist and pulled him along, and I didn't stop until we were far enough away where no one could hear us. The second I was sure no one would overhear us, I spun around and narrowed my eyes at him. "Do you think I've given up on who tried to kill me? I know someone in the society had some sort of hand in trying to take me down. Trust me. When I find out who it was, I'm going to kill them after slowly torturing every last secret they hold. I will not give up, but I'm also not going to let them think I'm still looking into them. They gave you the easiest test known to the society, trying to placate me and the rest of my family, but they should know we will never forget."

"I shouldn't have said anything, but the thought of any one of these men touching you makes me want to burn down the world." Cupping my face with both of his hands, his eyes bored into mine. "And the thought that any one of these people tried to kill you has me wanting to bring on the apocalypse to make them feel exactly how I'd feel if anything ever happened to you."

Pushing up on my toes, I crashed my mouth into his as I pushed him further into the shadows and down onto the seat of one of the booths. My hands roamed over the planes of his chest, through his shirt, up the sides of his neck, and tangled my fingers into his hair as I swept my tongue along his.

Sebastian moaned into my mouth as his hands slipped underneath my skirt and cupped my bare ass. "Fuck, who knew me wanting to kill the world would be such a turn-on for you?" He chuckled as we broke apart and panted.

"I find it more than hot. The fact that you'd go to the ends of the world for me tells me more about how you feel about me than three simple words." I scrambled to undo his belt and pull his thick length out of his pants. The feel of velvet-covered steel filled my palm. I didn't waste any time as I placed his cock at my entrance and slowly started to sink down until I was fully seated. The way he stretched and filled me had me closing my eyes as I tried to soak in every ounce of pleasure and remember this moment.

"You're so fucking hot riding my dick and taking what you want," he groaned, cupping my breasts through my shirt.

I thought he'd watch the show behind us, but Sebastian never took his eyes off me. Bunching my skirt up in the front, he watched where we were connected, and, as impossible as it was, I felt him grow harder. The heat in his eyes burned bright, spurring me on. I rode him harder, slamming down on his length. Sebastian's hands moved to my hips and angled me in a way that had him rubbing against my g-spot with each stroke.

Pushing up my shirt until it was around my neck, he pushed down the cups of my bra until my breasts sprung free. His lips latched onto one nipple while the other plucked at the other. My core clenched around him as a wave of euphoria started to sweep over me.

"King," I gasped out as shudder after shudder wracked my body.

Letting go of my breast with a pop, he looked up at me, letting me see deep down into his soul.

"My Queen." Pushing his hips up, he stilled underneath me as I felt him pulse and swell deep inside of me. Groaning into the side of my neck, his fingers dug into the flesh at my hips as he held me still and unloaded inside of me. I knew I'd have bruises later, but I didn't care. I wanted something to help me remember tonight, even if only for a little while.

epilogue

Santi

MY SISTER and her boyfriend were so disgustingly in love it was annoying. They'd shown up tonight with matching crown tattoos on their ring fingers. I wasn't sure if that made them married or what. When I asked, they didn't answer. They only smiled at each other before they sat down at the table.

"Oh, good," Arely stood with a big smile on her face. "I wasn't sure if you'd make it or not."

Turning in my seat, I steeled my jaw as I saw Bree gliding toward the table with a sweet smile on her face.

"You know I never turn down an invitation to dinner." She hugged my sister and then sat down in the seat beside mine. "Hi, Santi," she said in the softest of murmurs.

"Bree." I tipped my chin in her direction and then stared off over Bash's shoulder, trying to focus on anything but the woman sitting next to me. The heat from her small body lapped at me in waves.

"Will the others be joining us?" Bree's voice was so sweet it nearly gave me a toothache.

"If they want to live, they will." Arely flashed a smile as if she was kidding. I mean, she wouldn't kill our brothers, but she would punish them if they didn't show up. That is unless they had a very good reason.

"Army's girlfriend." She could barely keep the sneer out of her tone as she said the word. "She likes to be difficult and make them late for *everything*. They need to start lying to her about the time so they can get here at the appropriate time."

I knew if Devi weren't an undercover agent, Arely would have demanded Army get rid of her. No, she wanted the girl to see we were a normal family and report back that nothing underhanded happened. Army was going crazy with his new role of being mentored by Pablo. He was to learn so he could take some of the weight off Pablo's shoulders, just as Ale and I were doing for Arely. It wasn't easy for her to give up control, but she wanted to spend more time with Bash and less time worrying about how shipments were doing and ways to expand our legitimate business to hide our other.

"Maybe they should just tell her how much you dislike people not being punctual. Surely the threat of you being angry with her would be enough to make her prompt," Bree giggled.

"Perhaps you're right. I will make my distaste for her lack of manners known once they show up. While we wait, why don't you tell me about the date you went on the other night? Was it a love match?" Arely laughed as if she knew it wasn't, but my heart was stuck in my throat. Bree went out on a date, and this was the first time I'd heard about it.

Bree stiffened next to me, and I could hear her swallowing down her nerves. "You know I have no interest in the men my father sets me up with. Eventually, he'll give up and realize I'm never going to get married," she said softly.

"Unless you find yourself in an arranged marriage. I see that happening before he ever thinks of you as unworthy of marriage."

I didn't know Bree's father personally, only professionally, but what Arely said had merit. I couldn't see Mr. Zee ever thinking his daughter was undesirable.

"I will never marry into a loveless marriage, and if my father ever tried to force me, I'd kill myself before letting it get that far."

"Bree," Arely gasped. "Don't say that."

"You don't know how some Chinese men treat their wives." She closed her eyes, hung her head, and shook it sadly. "Especially in arranged marriages. I will not be some concubine or servant just so my father can proudly say I'm married."

"No, I don't, but still, I won't let you kill yourself. I won't let your father marry you off either, but you've got to put yourself out there. Especially if he's pushing you." There was a pregnant pause before she asked. "What about the guy you like?"

Bree's head shot up and looked at me. "I never said—"

"In unspoken words, you did. I know you like someone, but you won't say who. Why not? Is he a horrible man I wouldn't approve of? Because really, I wouldn't care if it was the devil himself as long as he treated you well."

"I haven't… we haven't. It's not like that. He barely

knows I exist, let alone want to date and marry me." Bree blushed. Her shaky hand reached for her drink, only to knock it over.

I stood quickly and dashed out of the room to grab a few towels. I was back and drying up her water while I tried to process what Bree had said. I wanted to shout. I knew she existed. I would date her, marry her, and give her as many babies as she wanted, but all I could do was sit silently. I knew her father would never approve of me.

"Why don't you fake date someone to get his attention? If he sees you dating someone else and thinks you might be off the market, I bet he'll come running because I know there's no way in hell if you like this guy, he doesn't know you exist."

Bree rolled her eyes at my sister. "Just because you're happy doesn't mean that's a possibility for the rest of the world. I've accepted my fate."

"What about Santi? He could take you out on a few dates. Hell, maybe we could even go on a double date. You wouldn't mind, would you, Santi?"

All eyes were on me as I tried to swallow. Arely had no idea what she'd just suggested. I wasn't sure who this mysterious man was that Bree liked, but I was going to make her forget all about him. By the end of this faking dating arrangement, Bree Zee would only have eyes for me.

"I'm always happy to help out a friend," I smiled tightly. I didn't want to come across as too eager and let anyone figure out what I had in store for my sister's best friend. Bree Zee would soon be mine.

Did you enjoy KING'S VOW If so, please consider leaving a review on Goodreads, Amazon, or BookBub. Reviews mean the world to authors especially to authors who are starting out. You can help get your favorite books into the hands of new readers.

I'd appreciate your help in spreading the word and it will only take a moment to leave a quick review. It can be as short or as long as you like. Your review could be the deciding factor or whether or not someone else buys my book.

To stay up to date on all my releases subscribe to my newsletter.

https://view.flodesk.com/pages/6104ad460475fa3dd9f250b0

acknowledgments

My family- your support means so much. Thank you for all of your encouragement and giving me the time to do what makes me happy.

Thank you **Bex** for making my story into a book.

Thank you **Casey** and **April** for inviting into this world and all of your support.

To all my **author friends**, you know who you are. Thank you for accepting me and making me feel welcome in this amazing community.

To **Wildfire Marketing Solutions and Catherine**, thank you for all your knowledge and for helping me make Away Game a success!

Lovers thank you for always being there.

To each and every **reader**, **reviewer**, and **blogger** - I would be nowhere without you. Thank you for taking a chance on an unknown author.

about ella

Ella Kade is a forbidden and dark romance writer who enjoys writing captivating characters with sinful intent.

Read Ella to get immersed into her words where she ruins lives and slowly puts them back together.

https://view.flodesk.com/pages/
6104ad460475fa3dd9f250b0

also by ella kade

Made in the USA
Middletown, DE
03 December 2022